FORSAKEN FATE

A Progression Fantasy Epic

Aaron Covington

ISBN: 979-8-89694-791-2 - Ebook
ISBN: 979-8-89694-792-9 - Paperback
ISBN: 979-8-89694-793-6 - Hardcover

Printed in the United States of America

BEFORE THE JOURNEY

FREE Prequel and Deep Lore of *Forsaken Fate*

Want to know what really happened before Saulice was born? Discover the hidden truths in the **exclusive prequel story** and lore files, only available to readers like you.

What You'll Get:

-The secret betrayal that sparked the Thousand Year War

-An illustrated breakdown of the Ten Titans and their fount affinities

-The prequel: *The Brand Before the Storm*

Claim your free content now:

https://subscribepage.io/pJkARs

DEDICATION

To every kid someone branded before they even
had a chance to begin. To the ones handed names
they never earned, and labels that never fit.

Those who stood outside the door, unseen, unheard-
still burning with something no one recognized.

The rejected. The underestimated. The
ones who kept going, anyway.

Failure does not define you.

You were never a curse.

There is more to your story than they could see.

You were always destined to be reborn and
rise beyond your 'Forsaken fate'.

PROLOGUE

Nine-year-old Saulice crouched behind the last pillar of the Trial's Gauntlet, mud clinging to his knees like fingers refusing to let go. His breath came sharp and shallow, puffing into morning mist that lingered over the village field.

Blood trickled from his left palm where the rope bridge had splintered. He pressed it against his tunic, to hide the bleeding. It wasn't pain that marked the weak, but hesitation.

The last stretch waited ahead: three narrow beams over a pit of churned earth. He'd been close to beating someone, Baren, a soft-footed fisher's son who tripped on the second rope climb. But when Saulice stumbled on the landing plank, the chance slipped. Baren rung the final chime.

Alderman Corfrick, perched on the judge's dais, folded his hands behind his back.

Saulice stared down at the wood grain beneath his boots. The air carried a chill, but his neck burned.

He rose.

The first beam flexed beneath his weight, groaning softly. He held his arms out to keep balance, knees slightly bent, jaw tight. A hush fell over the field as he took one step, then another. The mud below waited like a promise.

Halfway across, the wind kicked again.

He teetered, drawing gasps from the onlookers. One man cursed.

Saulice dropped lower, nearly to his knees. His hands flared out wide for balance. He didn't think about the mud below. Didn't think about Corfrick. He thought of her.

His mother's voice was gone. But the warmth in her laugh still flickered in his memory. His world had turned upside down the night before. Nevertheless, the Trial waited. Unchanged. Unforgiving.

He closed his eyes and imagined her voice, steady and familiar.

You're brave, Saulice. That's all it takes.

He clenched his jaw tighter, adjusted his footing, and continued forward.

By the time his foot hit the final platform, he was shaking. It was not fear, but the silent scream coiled in his chest. He slammed his palm against the end bell. It rang with a hollow, almost mocking tone, echoing off the nearby rooftops.

No applause followed. No voices broke the silence of judgement.

He stood at the edge of the rotunda, apart from the others. One child after another stepped forward to test their fount. Elder Judic had named it the Fount Affinity Test, Hamlen's second rite, sacred in tradition but simple in form. They brought those who completed the Gauntlet here. Two shards were on a platform veiled in ivy and mist, and they used only those. A flickering ruby for Fire, and an emerald whose pulse echoed deep with the rhythm of Earth.

Children queued in a quiet line. Parents and siblings hovered close. The space buzzed with muted hope.

But Saulice stood apart, drenched from the Trial and soaked through to the bone, his tunic clinging in streaks of mud. His hands had stiffened from the cold, but he didn't warm them. He watched, still as stone, the throb in his wounded palm keeping time with each name called.

But he wasn't alone.

He scanned the edge of the crowd, searching for a familiar face. Far off, near the shade of a leaning sycamore, his uncle Dedric lingered. He folded his arms across his chest, his face drawn tight. His eyes locked on the rotunda as if willing it to vanish. He didn't move, didn't call out, but he was there.

Will stood third in line.

When his name was called, he approached the dais with clean boots and a pressed tunic. His posture was upright, chin lifted, shoulders back with the ease of someone who had never once doubted where he belonged. He placed his hand on the ruby first.

It flashed red.

A solid wave of light curled beneath his fingers, steady and bold. Saulice saw Corfrick's shoulders stiffen, the clasp of his hands growing tighter behind his back. Pride flickered in his expression, so brief most would miss it, but Saulice caught it all the same.

Will touched the emerald next. Nothing. It remained dim.

Elder Judic gave a single nod and bound a plain leather bracer around Will's wrist.

The crowd clapped.

Corfrick didn't. But the corner of his mouth twitched upward, just barely.

"Fire," he said, as if declaring it to the air itself.

Will turned from the altar with a grin.

The line shortened.

Mira stepped forward, face bright as she passed her mother's open hands. Baren came next, nerves obvious but soothed when the emerald pulsed faintly beneath his touch. Even Harlett, the smallest of them all, who had sobbed his way through the Gauntlet, left the dais with green light trailing across his knuckles.

Each walked away changed.

Marked.

And then there was one.

Saulice stood alone.

Elder Judic raised his voice, calm but echoing. "Saulice Sawyer."

He stepped forward, legs aching. His skin stung, but he kept his jaw firm.

Let it work, he thought. *Let something answer. I made it this far. I didn't fall. I didn't quit. Shaddai, if You're still watching... I'm ready.*

He touched the bandage at his collarbone. The wound was still warm beneath. The fire hadn't taken him, not completely. But it had taken her. His mother. The sound of her voice. The place he once called home.

All of it felt distant now, like echoes behind a door he could no longer open.

The crowd started talking again, murmurs wrapped around his name.

"That's the boy from the fire."

"His mother passed, didn't she?"

He closed his eyes, just for a breath.

I'll speak with action. I'll show them.

The ruby and emerald shimmered faintly beneath his shadow, their light subtle but alive, like breath beneath glass. They pulsed at different rhythms, one steady and low, the other flickering like it might vanish if watched too long.

The shards responded with faint light once more, just enough to catch along the hem of his sleeve.

Judic motioned toward the altar. "Lay a hand on each. Ruby first."

He hadn't looked at the ruby. Not since stepping onto the platform. He didn't want to. Couldn't. He could not forget the smoke filling his lungs and turning his breath into knives, nor the flames crawling the walls the night before as if they knew his name.

If the fount gave him a Fire affinity, what would that mean? Would it mean the flames had started because of him? That his fear wasn't a memory, but proof?

His heart sagged, and he turned slowly toward the ruby, accepting whatever fate Shaddai chose for him.

It pulsed like a heartbeat. Eager. Alive.

His hand hovered, suspended in the charged air above it. Already, he could feel the heat. Not imagined. Real. His fingers trembled. Sweat ran the creases of his palm. He didn't want this. His entire being cried out against reaching, especially after the fire and the night that almost consumed him.

But his hand moved anyway.

It ignited with a sound like bone splitting stone, the ruby cracking as pieces flared apart. Then came the hiss, not of flame but of something older, coiled in the silence that followed. Something that had waited to be woken.

The force of the explosion hurled Saulice from the altar, flinging him across the square. He hit the ground in a cloud of dust and ash. The impact stole his breath; the world ringing.

Smoke curled from the sundered shard.

The crowd gasped. Elder Judic froze. Even Corfrick, silent and unmoving, blinked.

Dedric stepped forward; fists clenched at his sides.

Saulice stirred, breath shallow. The emerald sat untouched on the altar, steady and cold.

He crawled forward, hand outstretched. The pain from the ruby still roared beneath his skin, but it no longer mattered.

His fingers brushed the stone… and nothing happened.

He waited. Hoped.

"Please," he whispered.

The emerald stayed still.

Elder Judic stepped forward.

"That is enough."

And Saulice, blinking through the blur, whispered the only thing he could think.

"It should've been the emerald."

He couldn't hear.

Sound had vanished, stolen by the explosion still ringing in his bones. All he could feel was dust beneath his cheek and the throb in his chest from where he'd landed.

For a moment, Saulice didn't move or breathe.

The pain returned, all at once, sharp and absolute. His shoulders throbbed from the fall. His palm burned, raw and blistered where the ruby had shattered. Each breath sent a dull ache rippling through his skull.

He tried to rise.

A groan escaped as the world tilted. He propped himself up on his elbows, arms trembling. Voices blurred, floating in from the edges, some shouting, some hushed. The rotunda swam with motion.

Figures had gathered. Elder Judic crouched near the altar, inspecting the fractured ruby like it had broken a sacred promise. Children stared from behind the rope, some shrinking back, others whispering.

At the edge of the crowd, Dedric stood frozen, caught between stepping forward and staying still, fists clenched at his sides, jaw locked. Corfrick didn't move.

Saulice rose to reach for the emerald.

"No," Dedric muttered, disbelief cracking his voice.

Judic straightened, tone flat. "He did not manifest an affinity. He completed the Gauntlet. But the shards rejected him."

"They didn't reject—" Dedric began, but Judic's gaze cut across him, and whatever passed between them silenced the rest. Not fury. Not scorn. Something heavier. Understanding forged long before today.

Saulice still felt the ruby's heat lingering like ghost fire across his skin, its hum buried beneath the roar in his ears. But no affinity answered. No bracer. No light. Only silence.

"You must kneel," Judic said.

He didn't move.

The crowd pressed in. Mira clutched her mother's arm. Will watched, unreadable.

Finally, Saulice lowered himself to the stone.

The air thinned.

An official stepped off the podium, returning seconds later with an iron-bound box. They lifted a brand from within it, its sigil glowing faintly red.

Saulice stayed still. He didn't flinch. He was too tired to flee, too hollow to speak. The officials approached without cruelty, their faces blank. There was no anger in them. Just law.

Judic said nothing. Corfrick watched. Dedric turned away.

His heart pounded. Not with panic, but with quiet shame.

I passed the Gauntlet. I made it further than they thought I would. And still… this.

They raised the brand.

He closed his eyes.

And it pressed into his skin.

His back arched, but he didn't scream. Saulice wouldn't give them that. Something broke inside him, a last thread of hope, torn loose and drifting into ash.

When it was done, Saulice stood alone.

Branded and burned.

A quiet breath escaped him.

He could still feel the emerald's retreat, the ruby's violence, the silence of the crowd.

His hand throbbed where the mark had been scorched across the back of his hand. The symbol was simple, circular, and cruel: a diagonal slash through flame-wrapped scales.

Forsaken, not unworthy, but irredeemable.

The wind had returned.

It coiled low through the square like it knew the show was over. The crowd thinned as children were led away. Parents whispered false comforts in their ears.

Saulice stood in silence.

The scorched skin pulsed with every heartbeat. The brand itched beneath the crusting burn, but he didn't touch it. He couldn't.

Dedric hadn't come to him yet. He was still frozen by the tree, still watching from a distance like the damage might unmake itself if ignored.

The ruby shard lay in two fractured halves. Its light had faded. Whatever power it once held had bled out in the explosion.

Saulice's stomach twisted.

A whisper curled at the edge of his thoughts.

A pressure.

Like someone watching him from the inside out.

Jaw clenched, he turned away. He couldn't shake the image of the ruby splitting, of the force that slammed him to the ground. Not rage or fury.

Judgment.

And yet… something had answered. Hadn't it?

He wandered toward the edge of the square, shoes dragging through broken earth. The pain in his wrist had dulled to a constant throb. His breath fogged in the cold.

"Wait," came a voice from behind.

Saulice didn't stop, but his steps slowed.

Dedric caught up in three long strides and placed a hand gently on his shoulder.

"I didn't know it'd go like that," he said, voice low. "I thought…"

"Thought what? That I'd light it? That I'd get a pretty bracer like Mira?"

"No," Dedric said. "I thought maybe you'd finally be seen."

Saulice blinked.

And then laughed. Once.

A bitter sound.

"I was seen," he muttered. "And that was the problem."

The square behind them emptied to nothing but wind and broken footprints.

But Saulice couldn't stop replaying the moment the ruby split. Couldn't forget the pulse that ran through his bones.

Couldn't forget how, for a moment, he had touched something far larger than himself.

Something older.

And it had not welcomed him.

It had judged.

-ACT I-

THE FORSAKEN SOUL

CHAPTER 1

ASH AND ECHOES

Saulice trudged through the southern foothills of Hamlen, his dragging feet kicking up dust behind him. Even though he'd slept little — a common occurrence now, he somehow kept pace with the horseshoe-shaped cloud ahead.

He adjusted his leather bracer with a wince; the raw skin beneath flared like always. Five years, and the thing still hadn't broken in. They probably hadn't meant it to. It had no socket or stone, only worn leather, a bracer born of pity.

A pair of townsfolk passed him on the road. Their chatter faded. One of them tugged a child aside, hand tightening around the boy's shoulder. A mutter followed as they passed, low and bitter.

"Cursed one."

The word cut sharper for how quietly it was spoken.

They remembered. All of them did. The boy who shattered every shard they'd ever tested—ruby, emerald, lapis, all ten. Each one had splintered under his fingers with refusal, as if the fount itself recoiled from whatever he carried. Alderman Corfrick had called it judgment. The Trials had spoken. Hamlen had listened.

Saulice's calling was silence.

He tightened the strap in irritation. He'd never wield a ruby like the paladins in Dedric's stories. Never belong. Not really.

The word still clung to him like dust in his lungs.

Forsaken.

But at least he had work now. Dedric had convinced the postmaster to take him on, though Saulice still didn't know how. Fourteen, and while other boys recited ballads or chanted the Creeds of Shaddai, he carried satchels through back alleys.

No one paid to school a Forsaken. The Alderman had made that clear the day Saulice stood before the village elders with ten broken shards and nothing to show for it but dust on his palms.

Dedric taught him when he could. Letters by lantern light. Maps sketched in charcoal. The rest, Saulice learned from addresses inked in shaking hands and stamped with wax so old it peeled at the corners.

Talo, the postmaster, didn't ask questions. He kept to himself. Maybe that was why he gave Saulice a chance. Or maybe it was the half-rate discount Dedric offered for his work as a blacksmith. Either way, it was enough to sway the man's position.

With Shaddai's favor and a hundred copper colts, Saulice might even buy his apprenticeship before year's end. He clung to that number like a promise, not a future but a foothold.

He passed the field where the Trials had been held. Barley now rose in rows where dummies and blunted spears had once knocked him breathless. The dirt near the old Trial post had been salted once, he remembered, to "cleanse" the ground after he'd failed. Superstition, the elders had called it, though none of them stepped there again.

When Dedric was away, Saulice would take the practice blade from the hearth and slip outside, crouching in the barley rows where no one watched. He'd hold the sword just so, like the paladins in Dedric's stories, their feet grounded, shoulders square, wrists tilted toward the sky.

For a heartbeat, it felt real, like the world might answer back.

But then the leather would twist in his grip, too wide and too stiff, and the weight would pull wrong through his arm. And always, that empty bracer would hang there, silent.

Dedric caught him once.

He didn't raise his voice.

Just stared for a long moment.

"You planning to practice that where they can see you?"

He took the blade and walked away. That was the end of that.

Saulice shifted his satchel. The strap gnawed into his collarbone again, and he pulled it tighter. It slipped anyway. His boots had a hole near the toe. The bracer on his arm smelled faintly of mildew where it never quite dried.

But it was his.

Something, he reminded himself, was *still* better than nothing.

By noon, Saulice had delivered all but one letter. Most of today's stops had been in the northern district. There, across the quaint river crossing through Hamlen, guild members lived alongside the wealthy, behind their stone-walled courtyards and glass-paned windows. The roads were cleaner, and the cobblestones less worn.

The southern district was another matter. South of the river resided every man, woman, and child who toiled with their hands. And that made Saulice's job easier. People there didn't stare for quite as long. They put their energy into their crafts rather than debating the color of their tunics.

He pulled the final parcel from the satchel.

Elegant black ink curled across the leather casing.

Alderman Corfrick.

Saulice groaned and checked the satchel again, just in case. The package remained, the wax seal unbroken. His fingers tightened around it. That should have been the first letter, not the last.

He turned toward the lower fields. The sun pressed hot against his shoulders as the village thinned behind him.

Passing a wheat row, he absently plucked a few stalks and shoved them in his pocket, letting their weight settle.

A voice murmured ahead.

Saulice looked up.

A man in white robes stood beneath an aspen, face shadowed by leaves the color of burnished gold. Saulice squinted, raising a bandaged wrist to block the glare. The pressure of the old brand beneath flared with the motion.

"Master Talo?"

The figure looked up from a thick book. Thin white hair crowned his scalp like wisps of smoke.

"Good day, young Saulice," the postmaster said, lifting one hand in greeting. A glint of green flashed from the bracer on his wrist, emerald set in burnished bronze.

"Finished with the deliveries?"

"Almost," Saulice replied, swallowing hard. "Just one left, the Alderman's. I didn't see it until half an hour ago."

The postmaster raised a single brow.

"The Alderman?"

Saulice squirmed. "I must have buried it when I loaded the satchel. My apologies," he said with a quick bow. "I'll take full accountability."

Talo waved off the gesture. "He won't be happy. That'll be your problem."

Saulice nodded. "Might I ask what brings you to the fields today, postmaster?"

Talo shut his book, brushing dust from his robe. "Studying. Focusing my mind. Exercising my will."

Saulice blinked. "To what end?"

The old man chuckled. "One's skill in forging the fount fades if neglected. I come here to keep mine sharp, and occasionally, make it more powerful."

He stepped forward, planting his feet apart on the dry earth. "*Watch, Saulice.*"

The old man took a breath and raised both arms, slow and deliberate. His fingers trembled with focus. The emerald in his bracer pulsed with his breath. Threads of green light spidered out and across the bracer, fading into the grass like morning mist.

The wind stilled as a pressure gathered, subtle like the hush before a storm.

The ground rumbled.

Crack.

The earth split, and a boulder the size of a wagon wheel rose through the dust. Saulice stepped back, breath caught in his chest. The green light flickered across Talo's robe. For a moment, it felt like the world itself had turned toward him.

The stone pulsed in silence, and Saulice stared, wide-eyed. Not just at the power, but the certainty.

For a moment, the world fell still. Sacred.

The old man dropped his hands, and the boulder plummeted with a thunderous crash, bursting dust in clouds and showering Saulice in wheat and crushed grass.

Talo wiped his brow, grinning through the exhaustion. "Now," he said, catching his breath, "I can do that. It only took me two decades."

The envy came unbidden, curling deep in his ribs like a second heartbeat. He shrugged it off as best he could and bowed again to Talo.

"I was unaware that one could increase their forging ability." He hesitated. "Perhaps a stone would accept me if I trained my will, postmaster?"

Talo's smile faltered. "A good question. One I don't have a suitable answer for. All I know is you either have a fount core… or you don't. I'm sorry, lad."

"Of course," Saulice replied, disappointed at the implied response. "Well, I shouldn't keep the Alderman waiting. Thank you for the captivating lesson."

"Take care now," Talo laughed, dusting off his garments.

Moments later, a black split-railed fence came into view. The lawn beyond was trimmed with high hedges to hide the house from the road. The Alderman's home glinted with polish, each stone along the path fitted like a soldier in a line.

Saulice unbuckled his satchel. The parcel was still there, warm from the sun. He held it for a moment, brushing the wax seal.

He stepped onto the lane. Each footfall crunched louder than it should have. The timber porch loomed ahead. He hesitated.

He could lie. Say the rain came. Say he had slipped. He looked up. There was not a cloud in the sky. His grip tightened.

Three knocks.

Silence.

He waited. Counted five breaths.

The door cracked.

A pair of freckled eyes glared from the gap. Saulice fumbled, the parcel slipped, and the seal split beneath his thumb. Before he could recover, the door flew wide.

Alderman Corfrick filled the frame, blue tunic pressed, hair combed in thinning streaks across his scalp.

Saulice straightened.

His thin grey comb-over caught the wind, matching the blue tunic that marked him as the senior steward of Hamlen. The Alderman's glare was dark, weathered, and heavy as judgment.

"You arrive late," Corfrick rasped. "Do you think, as the Alderman, I can afford to wait on your schedule?"

Saulice bowed low. "Good evening, Alderman. I have a parcel for you. I didn't—"

"Excuses." Corfrick snatched the letter from his hands before he could finish.

His eyes landed on the broken seal.

His face darkened. "You opened this?"

"No!" Saulice blurted. "You startled me when you opened the door."

Corfrick's stare bore down on him, unblinking. His fingers worked the seal apart, unfolding the letter and pulling out something else.

A ruby fount shard.

Ruddy light glinted off its surface. Corfrick's lip twitched.

"You won't be breaking this one," he muttered. "Tell me, boy… when you look at your hand, what do you see?"

Saulice stiffened. "Sir?"

"Do you look at it and remember? Or do you *pretend* you are something else?"

Saulice's throat tightened. He clenched his fists behind his back until his knuckles ached.

"That quiet suits you. Forsaken boys should know when not to speak."

Heat surged in Saulice's chest. He opened his mouth, but his jaw locked tight. His breath snagged, shallow and fast. Not out of guilt, but from knowing it would not change a thing. His hands curled behind his back, nails pressing crescent moons into his palm.

The Alderman took a step closer.

"A fountless boy has no place in a world shaped by the divine. No shard. No bracer. You are a scar that refuses to heal."

"I—" Saulice's voice cracked. "I was only trying to deliver your parcel."

Corfrick scoffed before straightening. "You will report to the northern square at midday tomorrow. Independence Festival. Do not shame the village by being late."

The word *Festival* sank like a stone in Saulice's gut. Every year, the square became filled with banners, drummers, and children displaying their gifts before the town. A celebration of potential. A parade of futures he would never experience as they did.

Corfrick leaned in, eyes narrowed.

"But… you will stand to the side, of course. Would not want anyone thinking you were part of the display."

"Yes, sir," Saulice whispered, bowing deeper. He could feel Corfrick's eyes pressing into the back of his neck like a boot.

"Go. And remember my words."

Saulice turned. If he stayed longer, it would break him. His feet moved without thought, quick and clumsy down the gravel path, the satchel thumping hollowly against his hip. He did not dare look back.

Not until he reached the road.

There, just beyond the hedges, he stopped. He blinked harder than he needed to. Then again. And again, until the wind dried what he would not name. His breath came ragged.

He hated the way Corfrick looked at him. That they all did. Like he was a stain or a burden. Even at the market stalls, the brand spoke before he did. Coins left on the edge of tables. Eyes darting past him. Doors that closed a breath too soon.

The words echoed.

Your silence suits you.

A scar that refuses to heal.

His jaw clenched, throat burning with all the things he had not said and all the things he was afraid to say.

He was not nothing. He could not be. Not when his dreams still burned so loudly inside him.

Even if he had no bracer, he would find a way. He had to. It did not matter if the village saw him as a cursed child, Saulice would keep pressing forward.

The wind rose behind him, brushing wheat and cloak alike, like a whisper from the deep. He turned toward the village, squaring his shoulders.

They would stare. They would whisper. And still, he would walk into that festival tomorrow.

Someday… they would remember his name.

CHAPTER 2

THE AWAKENING

The sun hung low and sharp over Hamlen's northern district, casting long shadows and little mercy. Saulice staggered to a stop, sweat clinging to his brow as if even it refused to let go. He gasped for breath, adjusting the leather strap of his courier's pouch before it could bite deeper into his shoulder.

Of course, it was Carisa's house. He'd nearly forgotten the note Talo had left him, scribbled in smudged ink at the bottom of the dispatch board: *Deliver this parcel first... no delays.* Saulice had sorted his rounds before dashing off into the heat.

Now he stood there, panting, heat dripping off his skin, wondering if Talo's ink-stained notes were just another way to laugh at him. The postmaster had a talent for making every day feel like a test.

He lifted his sore hand and rapped his knuckles against the stained door.

It creaked open almost instantly.

A freckled face peered out, framed by auburn hair pulled into a tight bun. Her eyes, sharp, green, and lined with age, fixed on him like a fox spotting a wounded rabbit.

"Well?" she barked, already smirking. "The stoop's not your altar, boy."

Saulice stiffened. He'd caught his breath.

Her eyes flicked to the blank leather bracer on his wrist.

A grin twitched at the corner of her mouth. "Ah. You're him, aren't you? The Forsaken boy." Her tone dripped with amusement.

His cheeks burned. Not from shame, but restraint. Dedric's voice echoed in his head, *Let them talk. Words cost nothing, but replies could cost you everything.*

He kept his gaze low, tugging the strap of his courier's pouch tighter, fighting the tremble in his fingers as he sorted through ink-rolled parcels.

Before he could fully remove it, she snatched it clean from his hand.

"Hmph." She slipped it into the embroidered side pocket of her linen gown, then reached inside the house without looking.

"Give this to Talo." A small silk-tied pouch was shoved into his chest. "Today, not tomorrow. And make sure he knows who it's from."

Without another word, the door slammed shut.

He blinked once, twice. The door was shut, but the sting lingered. He stared at the door, then down at the stoop.

He knew he shouldn't, but he spat on it before turning away, swallowing the burn in his chest. Most days he could take the comments and just shake them off. But some mornings, like this one, every word dug a little deeper.

Saulice lingered at the edge of Boniven Bridge, leaning against the railing as a stream gurgled beneath. It always felt like his halfway point, the quiet between the shouting. North of the river, he was a stain on fine silk. South, they treated him like a poor person.

He watched the water swirl around river stones and bunches of wood from a beaver dam upstream. A memory uncoiled—his mother's laugh, clear as wind chimes. Then fire, the crack of timber, and Dedric's hand pulling him through smoke.

The memory slipped away as footsteps approached, just a mother and child crossing the bridge. The toddler grinned at Saulice, thumb in mouth.

Saulice rose to wave, but the mother caught sight of his brand and pulled the child close.

Saulice sighed and headed toward the village square.

The Independence Festival was already stirring, smoke and spice filling the air. When he reached the crowd, Saulice found a spot behind an empty cart and leaned against it, just in time to see Alderman Corfrick take the stage.

"From both sides of the Boniven River," his voice boomed, "our forefathers shed blood for Hamlen, and for Candur."

He paused, scanning the crowd with a practiced smile. "Of course, it has been decades since anyone from Hamlen has possessed a fount affinity strong enough to catch the attention of Brynswick. A pity," he added with a short laugh. "They say it is the place where the strongest fount forgers in the realm sharpen their gifts. Nonetheless, the King has need of his subjects."

Saulice had heard of Brynswick. A fabled Academy, spoken of in the same breath as the famed argonauts who'd saved Candur in the Thousand Year War. Such an Academy was far from the grasp of a Forsaken boy.

The Alderman's tone shifted. "A third of all boys who have not come of age will be required to serve four years in the King's Guard..."

Saulice's breath caught. His mind swirled with impossible hopes.

Me? Could I? Could I serve?

He wouldn't need a shard. Just fists. And a place to belong. Maybe... just maybe Shaddai hadn't cursed him after all.

The thought never bloomed.

A hand clamped on Saulice's shoulder, yanking him into a narrow alley.

He stumbled, spun, and came face to face with Will Corfrick, the Alderman's grandson. Saulice's breath caught.

"Well, well," Will sneered, voice oily with satisfaction. "Snooping from the shadows, Forsaken?"

He wasn't alone. Gerald and Henry flanked him, already grinning.

"Nay," Gerald said. "The dog's just behaving today. Finally learned how to sit."

Saulice's hands curled into fists, but he kept them down.

"Buzz off," he said low. "Corfrick told me to listen in."

Will scoffed. "Sure he did."

He lashed out, fist slamming into Saulice's gut. Air whooshed from Saulice's lungs and he stumbled back, gagging. Gerald and Henry were already on him, grabbing his arms and twisting them behind his back. He struggled, kicking, but the alley was narrow and quiet. No one came.

Will unclasped Saulice's courier's pouch and dumped it onto the ground. Parcels, crumpled notes, and Carisa's silk pouch scattered like grain.

Will's eyes locked on the pouch. "This yours?" he asked, snatching it.

"That's for Talo!" Saulice cried, straining against the grip pinning his arms. "Don't touch that."

Will ignored him, opening the pouch and revealing a red fount shard. It was no stone, such as Dedric and the elders carried in their bracers, but it still emanated slivers of power. Will gripped it, and the shard lit up, a fire-colored smile flashing across his face.

Saulice froze. His eyes locked on the shard. His back already felt the phantom sting.

"That's for Talo." His voice weakened.

Will's eyes narrowed as he circled Saulice. "So what?"

He clenched the shard, and sparks flew. They sizzled through the air and bit into Saulice's back. His tunic smoked. Pain tore across his skin.

Fire burned in his mind, followed by smoke. A woman's scream echoing inside a house, Dedric's hand pulling him free through a wall of flame.

Saulice clenched his jaw. He would not cry. Not in front of them.

"Still scared of a little fire?" Will hissed. "Going to curl up like after the Trial?"

They laughed.

His ribs tightened. Not just today, but every day, look, and whisper. Even the way people crossed the street, knowing he was the branded boy. The Forsaken child. No one held hope for him.

All because Shaddai *had* accursed him. And Hamlen never stopped reminding him of it.

A growl curled in his throat.

"Let me go," Saulice whispered. "Now."

Will leaned in, pressing a knee into Saulice's spine. "Or what?"

"You'll see."

He threw his head back, slamming it into Gerald's chin. Gerald spat blood and let go.

With a surge of strength he didn't know he had, Saulice twisted, elbowing Henry in the ribs while stomping down on his foot. The boy howled and stumbled back.

Will moved to grab him again, but Saulice was faster, rage leaking into every movement.

He tackled him, knocking him flat. Will shrieked as his head struck the cobbles.

Saulice climbed on top of him, fists flying, fueled by years of humiliation. He didn't see Will anymore. He saw every sneer, every door slammed in his face, every time a child was pulled away like he was a danger.

His fists blurred. His vision narrowed until only Will remained. He heard Gerald shouting, but the words made little sense.

Thunder cracked above.

Wind howled down the alley, and the sky darkened with unusual speed. Dust rose in a spiral around them, spinning toward Saulice.

Will raised his arms to shield his face. "What—what is this?!"

Saulice stood over him, chest heaving, fists trembling. The storm above roared to life, clouds churning, wind screaming through the alley like a living thing.

A sudden pressure built in the air.

As violent winds swept across the alley, Saulice glanced at the sky with bloodshot eyes. The clouds moved to blot out the sun. Peals of thunder silenced all. Henry and Gerald froze.

Goosebumps raced up Saulice's arms, but the cold wasn't fear. It was something older. Sharper.

He saw Will's smirk, and behind it—the faces of Hamlen. The old man who spat at his boots. The priest who turned away. Corfrick.

Something inside him cracked.

It flickered. Then it blazed.

He would not run again. Saulice would not be the one left shaking.

They would feel it. All of them. Every bruise and scream.

Saulice leapt, arms extended toward Will, focusing on the mocking faces reflected in his firelit eyes.

Before his hands found Will's neck, the sky flashed with golden light.

Lightning *surged*.

It didn't come from Saulice. It came from the heavens, merciless and golden. A blinding bolt cleaved through the clouds, shattering the earth behind him as though the world was cracking open.

The shockwave lifted Saulice from his feet.

And everything went black…

———————————

Saulice came to in fragments.

First, sound, as mist slid over pine needles with a sound too smooth, like breath on glass, too soft to trust. Then, pressure, as thick air folded in around him, like he had been sealed in a jar.

He opened his eyes, and nausea surged. The forest warped around him like a dream just past waking.

The trees stretched too high, gnarled and black at their roots, their trunks bleeding sap that shimmered faintly gold in the dim light. The mist didn't drift. It prowled, as if it had a task to complete.

Saulice staggered upright, nausea coiling in his gut. His breath curled in white tendrils, though the air pressed humid and close. No birds sang. No wind stirred. Only that mist, pulling toward something deeper in the woods, something vast and powerful.

He saw little choice but to follow.

Branches reached toward him as he pushed into the dense canopy. Roots snarled underfoot, each step feeling like trespass. He slowed the farther he went, his instincts screaming that he wasn't supposed to be here. This was a threshold.

He reached the clearing.

The cliff face rose like a dead god's spine—blackened and brutal, carved in old pain. Its surface was marked with claw scores and half-buried chains the width of oxen. They shimmered faintly, stretched taut across stone, anchored deep in the rock.

And bound to them was something giant.

Even seated, the figure dwarfed the clearing. His bare chest was laced with scars, his hair thick and matted, hanging like ropes at his waist. He sat still, as if asleep.

Saulice tripped on a twig, and the snap echoed.

Chains *groaned.*

The giant stirred. With a sound like mountains shifting, he rose, uncoiling one limb at a time. Muscles rippled beneath pale, rune-scored skin. Golden light sparked behind his hair as his eyes opened and locked onto Saulice.

A pressure slammed down over the clearing. Saulice stumbled backward, eyes wide, every part of him screaming to run.

"I should have crushed you," the giant declared, voice like a blade drawn over stone. It rose up in a frenzy, jerking its head in every direction before settling on Saulice.

"Crushed you in your father's arms," it added.

Saulice froze. His voice caught in his throat.

The giant took a step forward. The chains lit like brands and yanked him to a stop. He snarled, flexing against them, testing their strength.

Saulice fell to one knee, the air thick with static.

This wasn't a dream.

It wasn't just fear.

What filled him now was awe, sharp and staggering. And beneath it, terror rooted him in place.

The giant's golden eyes bored into him.

Saulice's lips barely moved. "Wh… who are you?"

The chained figure stilled. "They call me Lazarus," he said, his deep voice shaking dust from the trees. "The Titan of lightning and justice. Of judgement."

His eyes narrowed. "But now… I rot inside the bloodline of a coward."

Saulice's heart skipped. "My… my father?"

"You think I don't recognize the fount running through your pathetic veins?" Lazarus spat. "I felt him. I tasted his will the moment he forced mine into yours. He used you as a prison. A vessel to contain me, just like all the others."

"No. That couldn't be," Saulice whispered. His legs trembled, but he stood.

Lazarus paused mid-stride.

"You carry my seal, boy. You *are* a Harbinger. Like it or not, your breath is now my prison."

The mist swirled tighter around Saulice's feet, tugging at him like water rising. He stepped back, but the mist followed.

"Your years of ignorance have made you unready," Lazarus said, his voice rough with certainty. "Your body is weak. Your spirit, fraying. I can feel it; even your core buckles with every breath you draw."

He stepped forward until the chains flared and halted him with a hiss.

"You're already breaking."

The words landed heavier than any blow. Saulice's fists trembled.

"If all this is true, then why not just end it?" he asked, barely audible. "Why not find some way to get free of me and be done with it?"

Lazarus paused.

"Because once," he said slowly, "I gave my word I would not destroy another innocent to chase old wounds. I've kept that word… even when wronged as I have been."

His gaze flicked skyward. "Besides, there are debts yet unpaid. Lies buried in the mountain spines of Myre. I will have what I'm owed, whether in your body or in mine."

"Owed what by who?" Saulice asked. "Why would *my* father bind *you* within me?"

Lazarus jerked forward, and his voice dropped to a predatory growl. "You are not ready for that answer. Not yet."

But Saulice saw something in his eyes. A deep pain paired with recognition.

"Your father was a final lock on a prison already built, boy," Lazarus continued. "He was not the architect."

Saulice rubbed his hands together, doing his best to comprehend this seemingly mythical being's words. "Then who did this?"

Lazarus didn't answer but looked toward the cliff.

"There are names you cannot carry," he said.

Before Saulice could speak again, the mist surged, and the sky above cracked with light.

The forest spun away, taking the Titan and the cliffside with it.

And Saulice was gone, left with but a name.

Lazarus.

WHAT SHOULD HAVE SLEPT

When lightning split the sky above Hamlen, it did more than scorch the heavens.

It woke something.

Deep beneath the rotted marrow of the battle-torn Timfathen, a region long abandoned to rot and silence, a cave forgotten by map and memory shuddered. Water dripped in steady rhythm from stalactites high above, splashing onto moss-covered stone. Algae bloomed where sunlight had never reached, and insects skittered across a throne of cold, black rock.

They scurried over the brow of a statue. Only, it was no statue.

It was Baalo, Lady Veartaya's most loyal disciple and the second great terror of Myre. He sat entombed in silence, as he had for more than a hundred years. The stone that bound him pulsed like a heartbeat stirring. The ancient seal, forged by the five greatest argonauts of their age, had held. But not even their combined strength could destroy him, only delay the inevitable.

And now?

The power that sparked through the sky was no ordinary fount. It reeked of something older, something divine. Baalo's mind, buried in dreamless rage, stirred at the scent. Even in sleep, he knew that flavor. He remembered the pain it brought. He remembered the roar of a Titan.

The stone cracked faintly across his sealed lips.

Baalo's spirit, chained to the core of the earth, twitched. And remembered.

Something called to him.

Baalo's awareness bled outward like smoke through cracked stone. At first, he felt only the weight of a century of silence pressing down on him like a tomb.

But then it came. There was a flicker, a taste of something ancient. Then a jolt through the ley lines of the world. Not fount or the will of some foolish mage, but something older.

Lightning.

It threaded through the bones of the Timfathen like a whisper of judgment, burning through the darkness. Baalo didn't need to see the sky to know the truth.

Lazarus had stirred.

Even now, the Titan's scent lingered in the fount signature, clean and savage. Wrapped in judgement. His power was meant not to be wielded but endured.

Baalo's fingers twitched beneath their stone encasing.

Cracks traced across the rock that held his lips sealed. With effort, he stirred his spirit against the bindings. At first, like an ember beneath ash. Then he remembered.

The moment those fount-wielding argonauts had subdued him. Cowards, all of them. Five of the strongest in Candur's army had needed to act in tandem. Even then, they had not slain him, too incapable. So, they carved their prison from the roots of Myre and sank him into stillness.

But lightning disrupted stillness, as was its nature.

Baalo exhaled, the sound rasping like wind through shattered glass. The stone at his jaw split, flaking away like brittle scabs. He clenched the remnants of his inner core.

"You left me to rot," he whispered. "You feared the storm would return."

He had been told the seal would never fail. But he also knew Veartaya's prophecy: that lightning could not be caged forever.

Baalo's spirit trembled with the echo of his master's words. And somewhere, far beyond the Timfathen, a prophecy had sparked to life.

"Lazarus…" he hissed. "Titan of lightning. You again dwell within a Harbinger? How convenient for me."

He flexed his corrupted fount inwardly, grinding against the ancient runes laced into the stone. Dust spilled from his shoulders as the bonds pulsed. The bindings, once absolute, now flickered like lamps in a storm.

They feared Lazarus, Baalo knew. All of them. The four races. The other Titans. Even Veartaya had respected him.

But Baalo did not fear lightning. He craved it. It was the key to unsealing her chains, to waking the one who had commanded him to burn this world clean.

The seal groaned.

And Baalo smiled, thunder blooming behind his teeth.

Baalo closed his eyes—or would have, if the stone still coating his face had not sealed them shut. But his spirit did not need sight. He reached outward.

Fount surged through the ancient channels of his body like water forced through rusted pipes. After a hundred years of stillness, even this was dangerous. But he pushed past the searing heat building within him.

He *needed* to see.

He bent the fount through his core like a twisted lens, focusing on the storm's echo. The moment Lazarus had awakened. That strike, that detonation, had left a scar in the fount; a mark no human spell could make. He latched onto it.

In an instant, Baalo's spirit tore free of the cave.

He flew across stone and soil, over rivers and city walls. His essence jetted through ancient ley lines, chasing the pulse like a bloodhound to fresh spoor. The further he chased, the brighter it blazed.

Candur.

The small mountain range known as the Twin Peaks.

Then… a small remote village.

His spirit crashed to a stop above a scorched clearing ringed by a stunned crowd. The stink of smoke, sweat, and iron filled the air. And there, at the center of the crater, lay a boy. Blonde hair matted with ash. His tunic smoldered at the seams. Around him, three others, all older boys, covered in bruises and burns.

The smallest one wasn't breathing. Not at first.

Baalo's gaze narrowed. The fount clung to him, coiled deep within his chest like a living storm. His bracer was blank. But Baalo could feel the weight behind the boy's spirit. Immense. Ancient.

Familiar.

Then came the name, spat from the mouth of a tall man with clenched fists and a face twisted with disdain. His voice broke across the crowd, but Baalo heard it as though the man stood at his side.

"Saulice Sawyer."

Baalo recoiled.

Then he laughed. It was a soundless, venomous thing, gleeful in its silence.

A child. A boy no older than fourteen. And yet… he bore Lazarus.

The Titan of Lightning had chosen another host.

"Lazarus, you fool," Baalo whispered. "Still binding yourself to broken things."

He studied Saulice's face. The child was bruised and shaken, but he was alive. The storm's will still flickered behind his glazed eyes. Baalo immediately sorted his options.

The boy is nothing, but through him I can reach the Titan. And through the Titan, I can reawaken her.

Baalo etched every detail into memory: the shape of his jaw, the way he curled like something trying not to shatter. He memorized the boy's weakness.

And he began to plan as the vision faded.

Baalo's spirit slammed back into his body with a thud that echoed through the stone chamber. His eyes, still buried behind a rock mask, pulsed with fury.

So this was how fate played its hand.

Lazarus had returned, sealed inside a child.

And the boy's name was Saulice Sawyer.

The name tasted like ash in his mouth.

Baalo did not rage. He *brooded*.

Lightning crackled in the distance as if mocking him, and his frozen lips curled against the stone.

"They thought me forgotten, buried, and broken," he hissed. "But the storm remembers me."

The fount inside his core churned, ancient and undiluted, and he layered it inward, folding it repeatedly like tempered steel. His veins protested, and his stone shell groaned beneath the strain, but Baalo knew precisely what he was doing.

He had done it before, in war, in ritual, and in sacrifice, each time with the same deliberate control. He folded, pressed, and layered, holding the power until the moment came to release it.

With a thunderous crack, stone exploded outward, spraying shards across the cavern floor. Dust swirled in thick clouds as Baalo's form emerged—tall, gaunt, and pale as death, his skin etched with glowing veins of fount. His right arm came free first, his torso followed, and soon both legs crushed the shattered base of the throne beneath him.

He stood for the first time in a hundred years.

The chains that once held his essence twitched, sensing their failure. He stretched, and his muscles popped while his bones groaned like old timbers.

A low, guttural chuckle rumbled from his chest and shook moss loose from the ceiling.

"Lazarus," he whispered, "do you know what you've done?"

The boy would lead him to the Titan, and the Titan would lead him to *her*. Not yet by force, and not yet by chains, but the first stone had been placed on the board.

Baalo reached the deepest forge, where shadows thickened like tar. He pressed his palm to a sealed iron gate and whispered into the darkness beyond. The air stirred with the scent of blood and wet stone.

"Wake," he murmured. "Hunt."

Somewhere in the blackness, claws scraped stone and a low, rumbling growl swelled in answer. His fearsome companion, the Black Bellet, would find the boy, and through the boy, Baalo would grasp the Titan. And through the Titan Lazarus, Baalo would find Veartaya and release Veartaya from her slumber.

CHAPTER 3

THE STORM AND THE STRANGER

Saulice woke to the world spinning. His stomach churned like he had been flung in a hundred directions at once. Groaning, he blinked and found himself staring at two blurry figures shouting over him.

"All four? How does lightning strike four people at once, Dedric? That nonsensical boy did this. I don't know how the Forsaken did it, but I'm sure it was him!"

"A better question, Alderman," Dedric snapped, arms crossed, "is why these boys were bunched in an alley. I thought I made myself clear about your grandson. It's plain as day Will and the others jumped Saulice."

Even dazed, he caught the anger in his uncle's voice. Raw and ragged. So rare that it startled him. Corfrick's face matched, flushed red like he had been boiled in a stewpot.

"You dare blame Will for this chaos?" Corfrick pointed a trembling finger at Dedric's chest. "That twisted boy. Ever since that fire took his mother, he's been nothing but trouble. You should have left him in the ashes."

Saulice's stomach heaved. He clutched his sides and turned away, bile rising at the memory of fire and screaming. Of Dedric dragging him from charred beams. He didn't want to remember.

A thud cracked through the air. Groaning followed. Blinking up, Saulice saw Corfrick crumpled on the ground, and Dedric's fist clenched, hovering mid-air.

"Come, lad." Dedric scooped Saulice into his arms. His voice thickened with urgency. "We've done it now."

They fled through alleyways and narrow roads. Dedric moved faster than Saulice thought possible. Each step jostled his aching head and burning back.

"Slow down," Saulice moaned.

Before he could say more, a shadow passed overhead. A grey owl with wings spread wide and eyes locked on his. Watching.

"What is it?" Dedric asked between strides.

Saulice watched it fly off. "Nothing. Just my stomach."

He heaved over Boniven's Bridge, retching into the water below.

"I didn't mean for any of this to happen," he muttered.

Dedric hushed him, placing a finger to his lips. "We'll talk. Just rest now." His gaze darted from building to alley to passerby. "When we get home, pack your things."

Saulice blinked. "Why?"

"The Alderman thinks you tried to kill his grandson. Word's already spreading. Half the village thinks Shaddai is going to smite us because you're cursed."

Saulice's breath hitched. His fingers curled against Dedric's shoulder, knuckles whitening.

"They really think that?" he asked, but his voice was barely more than a scratch.

Dedric didn't answer.

He didn't need to.

"Then the Alderman got what he deserved."

Dedric gave a brief grin. "Didn't have a choice. I tried reasoning, but Will and the others weren't in good shape."

Saulice flinched at the memory of sparks flying. Fists swinging. That hunger. That power. It had been more than rage. It had been something darker.

It was primal.

He squeezed his eyes shut. "They had me pinned. But I broke free. I felt this rage, uncle. It was like something else inside me."

"When we found you, you were unconscious. All of you were. Whatever happened back there, it wasn't natural. That storm and those clouds. They came out of nowhere."

Saulice managed a weak chuckle. "I had some dream, like this out of body vision. There was a giant chained to a cliff. He called himself a Titan. I know it sounds stupid, but it felt so real!"

Dedric stumbled, and his arms tensed. "Did he say a name?"

"Lazarus, I think?" Saulice squirmed. "Said I reeked of the man who sealed him. He wasn't really making sense."

Dedric's steps faltered. "Shaddai help us."

He picked up the pace. Wind whipped around them. Behind them, Hamlen shrank.

Saulice bit his lip, closing his eyes. They had attacked him. Yet the Alderman blamed him for everything. It was infuriating.

He pressed his eyes shut, but the thoughts poured in anyway. The nobles who jeered. The elders who whispered. The boys who cornered him in that alley, laughing. Every insult he had buried scraped up like a reopened wound.

And now he was the danger? The mistake?

What was he supposed to do now? Hide and disappear into the hills?

His uncle's life was here. The forge. Their cottage. The steady stream of tools and armor that passed through his calloused hands. Dedric had given him everything—a roof, a name, a silence that never felt like absence. And now he was throwing it all into the fire.

For Saulice.

Why?

They passed the last row of leaning homes in Hamlen's southern stretch. The river curved beside them. Thick reeds and nettle lined its banks. Just beyond the roadside brush, Dedric shoved through a tangle of brambles. A forgotten gravel path lay buried beneath dead oak leaves.

Their thatch-roof cottage stood at the end. A crooked shape at the edge of the woods. Wild grass had grown waist-high around it. The windows fogged with dust. As a child, Saulice had hated the yard's tall grass. But now he saw it differently. It was a shield. It made thieves think twice.

But today, it wasn't enough.

When they rounded the last bend, Saulice froze. A woman in a blue and white cloak leaned casually on one of their drain barrels. Her arm was draped with an owl. The same one that had followed them. The bird's amber eyes stared directly at him.

Dedric stopped cold. His shoulders tensed.

"Mel?" he rasped, as if her name were ash on his tongue. "Hells. Is that you? What in Shaddai's name are you doing here?"

The woman rose, sweeping her sleeves past her elbows. A steel bracer glinted on her left forearm; a green emerald set deep in the band. She drew back her hood.

Saulice had never seen his uncle stiffen with fear. Never.

Dedric stared, silent and slack-jawed. As if waking from a trance, he lowered Saulice gently to the ground with a firm hand on his shoulder.

"Head to Sloan Hill," he whispered. "I'll bring what I can carry. Go now."

Saulice hesitated. "But—"

"Now, Saulice."

He nodded and stepped into a shaky hug, before turning and limping toward the hidden road. The image of Dedric, frozen in place, burned in his mind.

Whatever this woman's arrival meant, it was something heavy.

He didn't know who she was.

But his uncle did. And that was enough.

––––––––––

Dedric stood still; shoulders broad but bowed with restraint. His eyes locked on Melandra's as she stepped from the fog, her presence striking like wind from a sealed tomb. Familiar—but carved from something colder now.

"Is that the boy?" she asked. Her gaze flicked past him. "I saw the lightning strike, Dedric. Why are you hiding a Harbinger?"

Dedric didn't flinch. His jaw tightened, but his eyes stayed on hers. "My alliance to Furies Fist died with Mortare, Melandra. I am no soldier. Not anymore."

Melandra took a step closer. "That's good and fine, but I still am. And surely you must have considered the danger his life would pose *without* being properly trained."

Dedric's hand lowered toward the bracer beneath his sleeve. "He's just a child."

"He's a child with a Titan in his chest!"

"He didn't choose that burden."

"But he carries it." Her eyes narrowed. "And you're shielding him. Harbingers are traditionally trained from their birth. Do you know how dangerous this is?"

"I won't give him up," Dedric said. "Not to the Order. Not to you."

Melandra's face turned still. "Even if his presence endangers everyone in Candur? Every citizen in this backwater village?"

Dedric didn't blink. "He's the reason we still have a chance."

Melandra touched her steel bracer slowly. It emitted a glowing green light. The soil beneath Dedric's feet rumbled in warning.

"Then you've chosen your side."

His hands hovered near the weathered bracer beneath his sleeve, where an old opal fount stone pulsed with faint light, unused for over a decade.

Melandra didn't blink. She raised her right hand slowly, wrist twisting in a tight, elegant spiral. The earth beneath Dedric rumbled.

She exhaled one sharp breath and her fingers snapped upward in a motion so fluid it might have been part of a forgotten ritual.

The ground tore open and a dozen earthen pillars burst from the soil in a perfect arc, each one hammering upward with titanic force.

Dedric rolled forward, avoiding a pillar that would have broken his spine. He drew a hidden dagger mid-movement, but it was useless. A mere relic. He tossed it and gripped the opal within his bracer.

Wind answered him.

Air surged from every direction, wrapping around his limbs like invisible armor. Dedric rose with the gale, body lightened by the fount's power, every motion eased. It was an old stance and though rust had dulled his rhythm, the fount manifested.

Melandra answered in kind. Her fists slammed the ground in a practiced rhythm, each blow pulsing with the glow of her emerald bracer. A column burst to intercept him. When he leapt sideways, she twisted one hand sharply. The terrain shifted. Gravel curled upward into spines like a rising jaw.

Dedric swiped a hand. A sharp arc of wind disrupted her earth-forged creations. But even with the wind at his back, he was rusty. Slowed by years of neglect and missed training.

Melandra rolled. She planted her palms into the dirt and pressed into the earth.

A crater exploded beneath Dedric's feet.

The shockwave lifted him, spun him sideways, and slammed him into a tree trunk. He groaned, clutching his ribs, heart hammering.

"You never did play fair," he coughed.

"And you always underestimated me," she snapped.

Their battle continued. Friends once upon a time, now enemies, dancing through root and stone. Melandra summoned walls and spears. Dedric parted them with blades of wind. It was not graceful. It was not clean. It was thunder meeting avalanche, fury against restraint.

When Dedric's steps finally faltered, when the light of his pendant flickered from strain, Melandra closed the gap. Her foot swept under his stance, knocking him back.

He landed hard, gasping.

"Enough of this," she said, voice strained but steady. "You've proven your point."

Dedric gritted his teeth. Wind flickered around him like a dying storm. "I wasn't trying to win."

Her jaw twitched. "So why fight?"

He looked toward the distant hill where Saulice waited, hidden in memory and shadow. "Benedict is gone, and so is the boy's mother. He's got only me, Mel."

By the time he rose, she was sprinting. She descended with twin spears of stone.

He dodged one. The second grazed across his ribs.

He tore through the air into tall grass before going still.

Dedric lay still, every breath like fire. He wiped blood from his mouth with the back of his wrist. A smear remained across his chin. Melandra stood a few paces away, arms folded, her fount stone still glowing. Her owl watched in silence.

"I won't let you take him," he said again, though it sounded more like a plea than defiance.

"Dedric," she said quietly, "he's not safe here. You served the Fist for nearly two decades. What if there's another lightning blast? The next one *will* be worse. You and I both know it."

He closed his eyes. Saulice's face flashed behind his lids. Not the boy with the bracer and the bruises, but the boy who had cried himself to sleep for months after his mother died, never once knowing that

Dedric sat outside his door every night, just in case the grief was too much.

"He's not ready." Dedric forced himself straight up , despite the pain lancing through his ribs. "He still dreams of building stone walls and fighting for kings who'd never let him through their gates. He still flinches when someone yells too loud. He doesn't understand the world's true nature. The endless bloodshed and chaos."

Melandra's jaw tightened. "No one is ready, Dedric. Especially Harbingers. But waiting won't save him; it'll kill him. And others."

Melandra's hand slipped from his shoulder.

Without warning, she stepped back and raised her bracer.

The earth responded before Dedric could breathe. A curved spike of stone struck his side with a cracking thud. He hit the ground hard, lungs seized. The wind howled once, then vanished.

"Tell me where he is," she said. "Or I'll end this here."

Dedric's breath came ragged. "You'll have to kill me."

Her jaw clenched.

She held an earthen spear with a shaky grip. And then she twisted her hand—just enough to splinter the spear into dust. Her bracer dimmed, and she stepped back.

"Then you'll take me to him."

Dedric's pulse roared in his ears.

"No," he rasped.

"You have no choice," she said.

Dedric didn't answer.

She reached down and gripped his collar, fount still glowing, the ground shifting beneath them as if ready to obey her word.

"You will take me to him," she said. "Or I'll tear this forest apart until I find him myself."

Blood trickled from Dedric's mouth. He coughed, teeth clenched from pain. But he didn't resist. He couldn't stop her. Not like this.

Melandra's grip tightened. "Now."

He gave a single, shaking nod.

But as she hauled him to his feet, his lips moved. His words were quiet and low, almost lost in the rustle of the trees.

"Shaddai… shield him," he murmured, "from all of us."

CHAPTER 4

THE CHOICE

Saulice dangled his legs over the edge of Sloan Hill, his mother's grave beside him. The stone marker caught the last amber light of the sun while shadows stretched along toward the southern district of Hamlen. He buried his eyes in his knees, remembering her in life, and the day after her death, his Trial. It had not been that long ago, had it?

For five years, he had tried not to think of that night. The scars ran too deep for the world to see, and part of him feared the truth would come rushing back. This time though, he knew he was to blame. Will and the others might never wake again.

He clenched his jaw, accustomed to the hunger that gnawed his belly and the silence that came with being unwelcome. Wasn't it enough to be Forsaken? What was Shaddai trying to make of him?

He thought of his mother, of the faint impression of her voice that had become more dream than memory. He had never seen his father, only heard whispers of his disappearance shortly after Saulice's birth. Now, even the earth he had known seemed to turn against him.

Grabbing a fistful of dirt, he hurled it across the hill.

"Why me?" he shouted to the clouds.

Dropping to his hands and knees, just as his mother had once taught him to pray, he let his tears fall against the dry soil.

Only the wind replied, sweeping over him like a sigh, stirring the grass without offering comfort. He crumpled in on himself and sobbed, quiet, ragged breaths filling the air.

All he had ever wanted was a place to belong. Was that too much to ask? He longed for a friend and for just one day without shame. He wanted to wake one morning without dread. Somewhere in the world, there had to be more than this. More than the stares, the whispering, and the weight of being scorned.

And for the first time, even as he wept, Saulice wondered if he would ever find it.

Leaves crunched somewhere down the hill behind him. He froze, then ducked behind his mother's gravestone. Two tense voices drifted closer, one male, one female.

"I told you already," the woman said.

"As you keep reminding me," the man snapped. "It doesn't mean I have to like this." His voice echoed faintly against the stone markers. "Give me a moment with him… please."

Saulice pressed his forehead to the worn granite, his chest growing heavier by the second. He decided he would not come out until he knew for certain what they wanted.

He curled tighter into himself, guilt rippling through him. Will and the others—he had not meant to hurt them. Yet something had snapped, a blind rage that did not feel entirely his own.

The wind shifted, carrying the scent of burning torches and distant shouts. He flinched.

"Saulice," Dedric called. "Come out. We need to talk."

"The scary lady isn't going to hurt me?" Saulice called back from behind the stone.

He peeked out and met the woman's gaze. Her eyes were calm, but something steeled in them. Hair darker than Dedric's fell to her shoulders, framing skin like sunlit olive bark.

Her arms hung still at her sides, the posture of a soldier awaiting orders she did not believe in. She looked at him once, only once, but the glance held questions she did not speak aloud.

He could not tell if she saw him as a threat, an orphan, or a burden.

When he blinked, she was standing beside him.

"Argonauts don't harm citizens, especially those who have done nothing wrong," she said, her voice low but firm. "I'm here to help. There are men in those woods who would do far worse than hurt you."

Saulice stepped out, his fists clenched at his sides. He wanted to cry and yell, but instead he ran into Dedric's arms and gripped him hard.

"Uncle, I didn't mean to hurt them. I swear it."

Dedric hugged him back, tighter than he had in years.

"I know you didn't," he whispered, his jaw tight as his eyes flicked toward the treeline. "Listen… Melandra is an old acquaintance. You don't have to like her. Just do what she asks, for now. Do it for me."

Saulice turned to glare at her. "But she hurt you."

"No, she didn't," he joked.

Melandra scoffed as if the evidence was overwhelming.

"It's a little more complicated than that," Dedric said, a tired smile on his lips. "Melandra is here to help you."

"Help? What kind of help?"

"There's much I wish I could tell you, boy, but you aren't safe here anymore," Dedric said, watching the torchlight grow. "The Alderman won't stop until he's bled you for what happened today."

He bent lower, placing his hand on Saulice's shoulder. "And this is only the first time something like this will happen. I know you're confused, and this is a lot to take, but your life is not the same as everyone else's. Ever since your father disappeared, I have shielded you from the eyes of others, thinking I was keeping you safe. But Saulice… I was wrong."

Saulice swallowed hard. He already knew he could not stay. Hamlen had judged him from the day of his Trial, before it, even. His life here would never amount to more than a cautionary tale.

Saulice looked out over the southern rooftops. Hamlen was the only home he had ever known: the people, the fields, the blacksmith shop, Talo. It all blurred before him. He knew he would miss the smell of molten metal curling through the rafters of Dedric's forge, and the way the wheat stalks swayed like dancers in the spring wind. But what pressed like fire against his ribs was the knowledge that he had been hated here, judged, and left out.

Now he was something more than they feared, and he would go because if he stayed, he would rot.

"I'll go," he said, his voice low but sure. "I… I have to, don't I?"

Dedric's eyes glistened. He turned away quickly. "Do me proud, Saulice."

Dedric rose slowly and dusted his palms clean. Shadows from the tombstones stretched across the hilltop while bronze hues from the last fingers of sunlight curled behind the trees. With a heavy breath, he unslung the worn satchel from his back and pressed it into Saulice's hands.

"This is yours now," he said, meeting his eyes. "There's some coin, food, a spare tunic. A few other things you'll figure out when the time's right." He hesitated. "Let's just say… things I always hoped you'd never need."

He paused and swallowed hard. "You'll understand one day."

The satchel was heavier than Saulice expected. As he slung it over his shoulder, something inside shifted with a soft metallic clunk.

Melandra stepped closer, her hand light on Saulice's shoulder. "We have to move."

"Where are we going?" Saulice asked, clutching the bag's strap.

"To Axbridge," Dedric answered, his voice thick with restraint. "More specifically, to Brynswick Academy."

"What? That place is for fount forgers. Only the strongest in the realm are invited there." Saulice trailed off, stunned. "They'll never accept me."

Melandra met his doubt with firm eyes. "They'll accept you. And you're not going alone."

A sharp snap of twigs and the crunch of boots turned all three sets of eyes toward the break in the trees. Torchlight bobbed behind skeletal branches. It grew closer until three figures emerged at the edge of Sloan Hill.

The Alderman stormed forward, his face ruddy with rage. The flames cast sharp lines along his sunken cheeks, one sporting a bruise. Two guards flanked him, each in blue and gold surcoats marked with the sigil of Candur. The light of their torches shimmered across nearby gravestones, stretching eerie silhouettes up the surrounding mausoleum walls.

"Where is he?" Corfrick spat, his voice raw. "Where is that plague-ridden child?"

Saulice stiffened.

Shadows leapt across the graveyard, flickering as the torches drew closer. The long grass bowed with the sudden wind. Even the stone markers seemed to flinch at the fury in Corfrick's voice.

Dedric stepped in front of Saulice without a word. Melandra shifted beside them, her stance subtle but protective.

"What of him?" Dedric asked, deceptively calm.

"You know why I'm here, blacksmith." The Alderman's lip curled. "My grandson! My only grandson lies motionless—paralyzed, the healers say—and your boy still breathes."

"Will jumped him with two others," Dedric snapped. "You call *that* justice?"

Corfrick's nostrils flared, his eyes wild. "Justice? The boy's cursed, conjuring lightning through forbidden forging, no doubt. I have all the evidence I need to convict him now."

Dedric stepped forward, shoulders squared. "He was defending himself! You let it happen, encouraged it even."

The guards exchanged uncertain glances.

Corfrick bristled. "By the authority granted me by the High Council of Candur, I order that the Forsaken be taken into custody for questioning and judgment."

Saulice's blood ran cold.

"No," Dedric said.

"What did you say?"

"You're not taking him, Corfrick."

Corfrick lifted a hand to signal the guards forward. "Then you've made your choice."

Dedric exhaled. "So be it."

He drew himself up—not as a blacksmith, but as something older and harder. Melandra tensed beside him, and Saulice caught her exchanging a look with Dedric. Unspoken understanding passed between them.

The torches flickered violently in the wind. Shadows danced across Corfrick's face, elongating the rage twisting his features.

"Step aside," Corfrick warned. "I will not ask again."

"Should have stopped asking a long time ago," Dedric muttered. He looked back at Saulice. "Go."

Saulice's feet were frozen.

"Now!" Dedric said. "Take Melandra's hand and don't look back."

As Saulice turned, Dedric grabbed his bracer before sliding his palm through the air in a tight arc. A sharp gust tore through the torches, sending flames sputtering and shadows spinning. The air shifted behind them—loud enough to confuse pursuit, quiet enough to go unnoticed.

Melandra reached for him again. Her touch was firm, not forcing but steady. Saulice looked up at his uncle, tears welling in his eyes.

"I'll see you again?" he asked, his voice cracking.

"You will," Dedric said. "I promise... I'm proud of you, Saulice."

The words struck harder than any farewell. Saulice nodded, choking down his sobs, and turned to Melandra. She led him toward the far edge of the graveyard, where trees bent low over a narrow deer path. As they crossed the line between meadow and forest, Saulice cast one last glance over his shoulder.

The torchlight flared brighter behind the tombstones.

The clash came a moment later. Steel rang against stone and the wind howled as Dedric met the guards with everything he had left.

Saulice tried to stare ahead, avoiding a backward glance. He straightened his shoulders, wiped his face, and stepped into the trees. Torchlight glinted off her bracer as she cast one last glance behind them.

"Until we meet again, WindWalker," she yelled out, her voice fierce and strange with emotion.

Dedric did not reply, but twitched visibly as though the name had once meant something to him. His broad shoulders rose and fell as he took one last breath of the night air. He cracked his knuckles slowly and shifted his stance between the gravestones. The flickering torchlight drew sharp lines across his face.

Saulice's throat burned, but no more tears came. There was no turning back now.

He fixed the image of his uncle in his mind, unyielding and braced against the dark, before turning away. The forest waited, and somewhere beyond it, the rest of his life.

CHAPTER 5

THE FLIGHT FROM HAMLEN

Saulice shot upright with a gasp, heart thrashing against his ribs, the wagon's slow motion rocking beneath him as the wind bit through the open tarp. Sweat clung to his chest like a second skin. His limbs kicked instinctively, as if something had bound them.

"Stop—get out—"

His arms struck only canvas. The nightmare clung to him like smoke that refused to lift. Cold air slapped against his sweat-soaked skin, yet it did not fully wake him. The dream still coiled around his ribs like a living thing, thicker than fog and heavier than fear.

The chains had followed him. Heavy links dragged across stone slick with moisture. And always those eyes — twin storms above the mist, watching from without and watching from within.

Lazarus.

He mouthed the name as though it were a sentence already passed.

Ahead, Melandra sat in silence, reins gathered loosely in one hand. Her posture carried the same tension as her voice — controlled, waiting. The other hand hovered over a black tin kettle suspended above a basin of coals. Steam twisted into the wind. Her sleeve had slipped above her forearm, revealing the bracer fitted snug against her skin, steel dulled with wear and time, socketed at the center with a green stone that pulsed once, then again.

The light was not constant. It breathed.

"You've been staring at that long enough," she said, her gaze still fixed on the trees.

"I've never been so close to one before," Saulice murmured. "The way it moves, it's like it's alive."

"It's a fount stone," she replied. "It doesn't move. It just directs my fount."

"You mean you don't use it to control the earth?"

"I conceptualized it, yes. But the fount in my core is what enables me to perform the forging. The stone itself directs the fount from my core. It gives the power a focused direction."

The answer stirred something in him, not doubt exactly, but a need to understand. "So, it's like a conduit?"

Melandra's lips tightened. "Closer than most guess. The fount stone is a channel, not a source. It mirrors what already lives in you. But if your core is shallow, the stone will stay silent. And all cores are silent until they've been awakened. The Cadre at Brynswick will teach you all of this."

"My core?" His brow furrowed.

Now she turned, the firelight glinting in her eyes. "Your fount core," she said. "The part of you that can shape the fount- the spiritual flow Shaddai imbued in all living things, before these very lands existed. After you awaken the core, you must fill and expand it, increasing its capacity to hold the fount. You'll become a stronger fount forger. But without an awakened core, every stone in Myre is just ornament."

He shook his head. "No one ever taught me any of this."

She let out a small, bitter breath. "Of course they didn't. Forsaken children are meant to stay ignorant. And Hamlen isn't exactly one of Candur's most sought trade markets."

The word hit harder than he expected. He looked down at his wrist, the blank bracer pressing against his skin like an accusation.

"So even if I'd passed the Trial..."

"It wouldn't have mattered," she stated. "You'd only know as much as Hamlen could teach, which isn't much. The fount doesn't tolerate reckless desire, but disciplined control. Forging the fount is no easy task."

A howl pierced the forest behind them, thin and deliberate, too precise to be natural.

Melandra moved instantly, snapping the reins. The wagon jolted forward, wheels carving through frost-laced mud.

"They're closer now," Saulice murmured.

The wagon struck a shallow rut, bouncing hard. Saulice caught the rail for balance, his eyes drifting again to the emerald set in Melandra's bracer. The light was steady now. Not bright, but sure.

"You said the stone is basically a conduit, but aren't they weapons? The argonauts use them to fight for the King, don't they?"

"That is because peace requires strength," she said. "But strength without alignment is just noise."

"And alignment comes from the core?"

She nodded. "You don't *just* command the fount. You join it and match its rhythm to your own. That's when it listens."

Saulice hesitated. "And what if there's something *else* inside? Something someone didn't ask for that might be fighting against them?"

Melandra didn't answer.

And in the silence that followed, Saulice noticed the wind had gone still in the trees. Not absent. Waiting. Turning. Curling around him like a question only his breath could answer.

The trail narrowed until the wagon could no longer pass without risking the wooden axle cracking against exposed roots and rain-carved ruts that cut across the slope. Melandra pulled the mares to a halt and climbed down without a word.

Saulice followed.

"Foot trail picks up from here," she said, scanning the ridge ahead. "Too narrow for wheels. Too loud. They'll hear us before they see us if we continue with the wagon."

She unlatched Dedric's bag from the rear panel and tossed it to him. "Pack what you can carry. Leave the rest."

"You think they're that close?"

She gave a curt nod. "Close enough that a creaking wagon gives us away. The Alderman likely has men combing every inch of these woods so he can find you, and those men will have dogs. Only problem is that the next stretch of our trek is forest-choked. The wagon's sound will travel farther."

A moment later they were moving again, packs slung, feet muffled by a carpet of ash-laced needles. The mist thickened as they descended into a shallow glade, where the blackened trunks leaned like monuments to something old and forgotten. Ash dusted the ground in patches. Saulice thought it might have been sacred once, though now it smelled of dampness and endings.

Melandra stopped beside a crooked spruce and motioned toward a rotted log half-covered in moss. "Sit."

Saulice looked at her, confused. "Why *here?*"

"I need you focused," she said. "Not panicking. Not looking over your shoulder. So, now's your chance to ask whatever it is that's bugging you so bad."

He lowered himself, planting his hands on his knees. The log creaked but held. She crouched nearby, scanning the tree line.

"*Ask,*" she said, softer now. "Before we lose this breath."

He felt a cold dread, confident he wouldn't like the answer to his question. "Lazarus… he's not just a figment of my imagination, is he?"

"No. He's real. As real as the brand on your wrist. As real as the fount core you never learned to shape."

"I only heard stories," Saulice said. "Whispers. That the Titans, that he, destroyed realms. That no one could trust them."

Melandra's expression softened slightly. "Those are half-truths told to keep children from disobeying their parents. Shaddai forged the Titans before his ascension, ten in total. Each tied to an elemental truth. Shaddai purposed them to keep peace across Myre."

He looked down. "But the Thousand Year War…"

"The war came because Veartaya turned against creation. Her corruption spread like rot. The Titans intervened. Kings nor armies could beat Veartaya. It was the Titans, and their Harbingers that ended it."

"Harbingers?"

"Hosts. Mortal vessels that the Titans were sealed inside, like yourself."

Saulice traced the edge of his bracer. "But why me?"

"That's the question, isn't it?" she said. "Your uncle hid you for a reason. I've known Dedric for a long time, and he's no coward. So he wouldn't have left fighting for left Furies Fist unless it was warranted. Someone sealed Lazarus within you as a child, Saulice. And the list of suspects is short."

"Sealed?" Saulice echoed. "How is that even possible? And why would someone have done that to *me* of all people?"

She straightened slowly, brushing ash from her glove. "There are ways. Ancient ones. Taught only to those aligned with Shaddai's nature. It costs nearly everything. As to who, the last time your father was seen, was in Mortare just before Lazarus destroyed it."

The clearing fell silent again. The mist swirled low over the ground while the trees held their breath.

Saulice's voice dropped. "So, he's gone. My mother's dead. And… I'm just supposed to deal with it? Why do I have to suffer the consequences of *his* choice?"

Melandra's gaze eased. "Ah, I've seen that face and sat where you're sitting. But that's the mark of true maturity, child. Answering for everyone else's mistakes, on top of your own."

"You don't get it. Before the lightning strike… I didn't feel like myself. It was like I was watching myself burn from the inside."

Melandra's gaze sharpened. "Then it's started."

"What has?"

"The Titan's awakening. Lazarus isn't dozing anymore."

From the woods behind them came a rustle. Then barking, low and controlled.

Saulice crouched and then whispered. "If he's inside me, does that mean I can just forge *lightning* whenever I want?"

Melandra's tone lost any softness it had carried. "No, you dolt. It means you're a hair's width from losing control. You are his host, not his master. If you want command over that power, it won't come through rage. It comes through merit. That's why I'm taking you to Brynswick."

He clenched his hands. "I failed the Trial three times. I couldn't even make a shard glow. You're just wasting your time."

"You didn't *fail*," she said. "The shards shattered because they couldn't withstand what was already inside you."

His breath slowed, though it didn't ease the tension twisting through his gut.

"I don't like this," he muttered.

"You don't have to like it," Melandra said, already moving again. "But you do have to face it."

A horn sounded. Distant, but not far enough.

She turned to the trees, her voice low but certain. "Time to move. We're running out of quiet."

The trail bent downhill where frost had melted into slick mud, and the trees pressed tighter around them like watchers leaning in.

Melandra slowed near a crooked ridge, her boots angling sideways as she stepped through a cluster of roots. She glanced once toward the canopy, then signaled for silence, her fingers sweeping low across her side.

Saulice followed, his breath soft and his steps deliberate. The filtered gray light dulled the edges of everything. His eyes scanned for motion: branches swaying, faint steps, the suggestion of presence ahead. Two figures were coming toward them from around a bend.

A twig snapped under his boot.

Melandra's hand caught his shoulder instantly, pulling him low into the brush as her other hand hovered near the emerald bracer on her wrist.

Then a voice rang out, overloud, nervous, and entirely unthreatening.

"Oi! Don't throw nothin', yeah? We ain't tryin' to get skewered. Shaddai's name, we're just lost travelers, swear it."

A bald man stumbled into view, his vest torn, his satchel swinging like it had more weight than sense. He froze mid-step, eyes wide and hands raised.

"Friendly, yeah?" he said. "Name's Oreas. I'm a merchant. Mostly, that is. Bit off course as of late."

Melandra rose slowly, her posture still coiled. "That way isn't safe. We're being followed."

"Ain't we all," Oreas muttered. "Bad sorts found us three days back. Scared the beasts, cracked the cart axle, lost my best cheese wheel. Been hoofin' it through bramble and regret since."

Another figure stepped forward behind him, taller, cloaked, and entirely still.

He moved with eerie grace, a long frame wrapped in a flowing brown robe clasped at the shoulder with dull brass. Fine hair covered his arms and gathered beneath his collar, curling faintly at the edges. His face bore the features of a man, but stretched and softened, like a painting unfinished.

Wide, sea-green eyes scanned the tree line, glancing peripherally without urgency. He had carefully wrapped his dark hair in a single bun atop his head, like the crest of a priest or scholar, or something far older. The creature looked like a sloth made human in the image of silence.

Saulice stood, breath caught behind his ribs.

He had never seen a *fallet*. Not outside the half-rotted books in Dedric's study. Not beyond drawings shaded by the weight of myth. Yet this one moved like the trees had parted to let him through.

"I am Drezz," the figure said. "Of Fallenan."

Saulice stared. "You're real."

Drezz lifted his head. "As are you?"

"We're just passin' through," Oreas said quickly. "If we'd known you were in the neighborhood, we'd have brought tea."

Melandra kept her gaze fixed. "You said you got hired. By whom?"

"The court of Fallenan," Drezz replied. "My people no longer train in the fount. I was sent to relearn what we abandoned. Before it's too late."

Oreas gave a snort. "Which means I got stuck escorting a seventeen-year-old, made into a cook, translator, and the occasional beast wrangler. None of that was in my contract."

"Apologies. I've just never seen one of your kind before," Saulice said.

"We do not leave home lightly," Drezz answered. "And *rarely* by choice."

Melandra relaxed slightly. "Someone tracked you as well?"

"Relentlessly," Drezz said. "But we've shaken them. For now."

"Then let's not test that luck," Melandra said. "Stay near and we'll move together."

The group walked in silence for a while, mist curling around their feet as the trail narrowed to a shadow-choked corridor. Oreas trailed in the rear, muttering about thorns and knees and mornings that refused to be warm. Drezz stayed beside Saulice, each step placed with perfect balance.

"You carry weight," Drezz said eventually.

Saulice turned. "What kind of weight?"

"The kind that hums beneath your steps," Drezz said. "Like the roots are listening."

Saulice didn't respond. But his chest tightened in a way that felt like an acknowledgment.

Melandra stopped near a moss-covered stone and scanned the ridgeline. "We're close to the Twin Spires. We'll make for the pass."

Oreas dropped onto a crooked stump with a grunt. "Bless Shaddai's bones. My knees ain't forgiven me since last morning."

The mist swirled thickly between the branches.

Saulice listened.

Somewhere behind them, a dog barked once. Then again. The latter was fainter, but still too close for comfort.

"They're still on us," he said.

Melandra nodded once. "Then we don't slow."

CHAPTER 6

THE STONE REMEMBERS

Two narrow paths wove along the edge of the cliffs, one stacked above the other, both carved through ancient stone. Shards of shale jutted from the ridgeline, slick with dew and dusted in frost. Wind threaded through the Twin Spires with a restless howl, dragging clouds low across the sky.

Oreas groaned, pulling his foot from one of the trail's many ruts. "Shaddai must hate boots."

Saulice trudged a few paces behind, shoulders tight beneath Dedric's satchel. The chill bit deeper here, and the ache in his legs had not eased since they left Hamlen.

Melandra stood ahead on a ledge, her eyes never still. She had spoken little since dawn, but her pace left little room for conversation.

Drezz moved beside Saulice, small and sure-footed, his fur catching the wind. At times he paused to brush his pawed hands against lichen on a rock wall or glance toward a cloud bank, as though recording thoughts he never spoke aloud.

No one broke the silence for a long while.

Then Oreas cleared his throat and half-shouted, "Melandra, is there an actual trail, or are we just following your bad mood up the mountain?"

She did not turn.

"There's a safe pass east," she called back, ignoring the jibe. "But I am not trusting marked trails. Not after yesterday."

Saulice adjusted the satchel strap. His shoulder ached, and ash still clung to his boots. He scanned the skyline. Only rock stretched before them. There were no towers, no buildings, and no gates.

That should have eased him, but instead it unsettled him further. The stillness of the mountainside felt patient, almost knowing, as though the stone had witnessed worse than them and remained unmoved.

"You alright, boy?" Oreas asked, bumping Saulice with an elbow. "You look like a ghost borrowed your face."

"Just tired."

"Fair enough. The Spires might be short, but they will still chew through you if you do not respect the climb."

They crossed a narrow stretch where the path curved sharply inward, forcing single file. Drezz walked ahead of Saulice, quiet but steady.

Melandra led them without a word. Saulice had expected barked orders, commands, or warnings. Instead, she left no trail but the slight indentation of her boots, each step deliberate.

Sometimes she paused only to look at the stone. She was not searching for danger, but for memory.

He wondered if she had chosen this path because it kept her above the cities. Above the eyes. Above some guilt that followed her.

When the trail widened again, Melandra called a halt. Oreas dropped onto a stone with a sigh loud enough to echo.

"Go on without me," he wheezed. "I'll catch up when the trail's flat and the sky rains cheese."

Saulice found a perch of his own, knees pulled up, arms wrapped close. Drezz remained standing near the ledge, eyes on the cliffs.

"You alright?" Saulice asked.

"I'm thinking."

"About what?"

"The Trial." He said it flatly, as if speaking too loudly might give it more power than it deserved.

Saulice tilted his head. "You mean… your fount affinity test?"

Drezz nodded once. "I've read what little has survived of Fallenan's texts. But no scroll can prepare you for the feeling of being rejected. If no stone responds to me, I will be nothing but an empty symbol. A relic of hope returned to my people without a scrap to offer."

"You don't know that."

"No," Drezz admitted, "but I have never seen a fallet forge. Not in my lifetime. Not in my father's. What if our kind… lost it?"

His voice cracked, just enough for Saulice to hear the weight behind it.

"Monarch Farthum sent me to learn," Drezz said. "To reclaim what was forgotten. But what if there is nothing left to reclaim?"

Saulice looked down at his boots, at the caked dust, at the scuffed edge of Dedric's satchel.

"You ever heard of someone breaking a fount stone?" he asked.

Drezz turned, startled.

"I did," Saulice said. "Multiple times."

Drezz blinked.

"They said I had no affinity. That I was *Forsaken*."

"Yet here you are," Drezz said, tilting his head. "Perhaps we are both impostors. You, with a power no one understands. Me, with none I can prove. We make a fitting pair."

Saulice gave a dry laugh. "Is that your way of saying I'm alright?"

"I would sooner draft a treaty."

But the faint spark in Drezz'ss eyes said more than words.

They stood quietly for a moment. Saulice looked down at his wrist.

The bracer was heavier than it should have been. Worn at the seams, sweat-darkened, nicked by travel, but worse than the damage was the blank space at its center. No socket. No stone. Just emptiness.

He twisted the strap slightly and lifted his sleeve, exposing the *Forsaken* brand on his hand for a second.

"I've wanted to burn it a dozen times," Saulice admitted. "But I keep wearing it. I don't know why."

"Perhaps because you have made it your own. The bracer may have been meant to shame you," Drezz said. "But you have carried it through fire and fight. Every scar on it is part of your journey, not theirs."

He paused. "It does not say you are powerless. It says you are still here."

The words landed harder than they should have.

Saulice did not answer right away. But something in his chest eased. He nodded once.

The wind passed softly over them.

Melandra said nothing as she moved ahead, scanning the ledges with her usual cold precision. Oreas muttered something about setting up camp, then wandered off to find flat ground. No one else spoke.

By the time the fire was lit beneath the shallow overhang, the light had already faded. The camp settled quickly. One by one, the others turned in with blankets drawn close. Even Oreas, who had spent twenty minutes complaining about rocks and roots, now snored against the slope like he had done it a hundred times before.

But Saulice could not sleep.

He stayed by the fire, knees drawn up, Dedric's satchel beside him, staring into the flicker of orange heat. The flames cracked quietly beneath the stone shelf, throwing shadows across the rock face like breath that would not settle.

He could not settle his mind.

Not after the lightning.

Not after the brown-clad.

Not with the Twin Spires jutting into the night above him, silent and unshaken.

He shifted, restless, then started rummaging through his pack.

Behind him, Drezz stirred. The fallet's ears twitched before his eyes even opened.

Saulice did not speak.

Neither did Drezz.

He blinked slowly, adjusting to the glow. His frame stayed half-curled in the blanket, but after a moment he rose, movements careful and practiced. Ash slid from the folds of his cloak as he stepped closer.

Saulice watched, saying nothing. Drezz moved like someone used to shrinking his presence, trained to remain unnoticed.

"I did not intend to interrupt," Drezz said, voice calm, the syllables crisp as though shaped by a language that used fewer words but weighed each one more heavily.

"You didn't," Saulice replied. "Couldn't sleep anyway."

Drezz lowered into a crouch by the fire. He did not sit. His green eyes reflected the light in quiet ripples, unreadable and calm.

"The wind here carries too many voices," he murmured. "The stone remembers more than it should."

Saulice tilted his head. "That a Fallenan saying?"

"It is something my Falne used to say… my father."

The silence that followed did not stretch. It settled between them like something imbued with intention.

"You were awake because of the brown-clad?" Drezz asked.

"Not just that," Saulice said. "It's… everything. Since Hamlen."

"The village where you lived?"

He nodded. "I used to think it was the entire world. Now I know it was a dot on a map."

"Even dots matter," Drezz said. "They mark beginnings and ends."

The fire popped. Saulice shifted.

"And you?" he asked. "Why are you awake?"

Drezz was quiet for a long breath.

"I think perhaps I do not wish to sleep," he said. "When I dream, I see fires in the treetops. Ropes snapping. Wood splintering. Air reeking of smoke and blood."

Saulice's chest tightened.

"There was an attack before I left, on Leafhorn," Drezz said. "One of Fallenan's smaller settlements."

He did not elaborate. He did not need to. Saulice could see the memory behind his stillness, the way some pain did not need retelling to be understood.

"I'm sorry," Saulice offered.

Drezz inclined his head in acknowledgment. The silence returned, warmer now.

Saulice broke it again. "Your speech… it's different, not that it's bad. Just formal."

A faint smile touched Drezz'ss mouth. "The old tongue of Fallenan is rigid. I am still unlearning what does not serve me here."

They sat without speaking. The fire dipped lower. Saulice leaned forward on his knees, elbows resting atop them. Drezz remained still as stone.

"You know," Saulice said eventually, "when I first saw you, I thought maybe you were this forest myth. No human has seen a fallet in who knows how long… at least where I come from."

Drezz arched a brow. "A flattering one, I hope."

"Not exactly," Saulice admitted. "Dedric had this half-burned book full of drawings. Said that the fallet never left the north, and that few had met one."

"We are not so rare as myths," Drezz replied. "But Fallenan entertains few outsiders. And we do not leave."

"Why did you?"

Drezz exhaled slowly. "I… am the son of Monarch Farthum."

Saulice blinked, unsure if he heard correctly.

"I was sent to Brynswick not just to study," Drezz said, "but to recover what we abandoned. Centuries ago, the fourth and final sage of Fallenan banned fount forging. He claimed power made people proud, and pride the father of war. So he destroyed every record of fount forging we could access. Burned the books, the tombs, even erased history. After that, he shut the realm's gates."

He looked into the fire, blinking.

"But now rebels challenge my father. The brown-clad. They want the old ways, without wisdom. They wield fount weapons we no longer understand, nor do we know where they receive them."

"So… you're royalty?" Saulice asked.

"I am a symbol," Drezz said without pride. "A living name. Sent to reclaim what was lost before my homeland tears itself asunder."

The fire cracked and flared.

"I thought you were just some rich student," Saulice muttered. "Dragged along by that merchant."

"Oreas is unpolished," Drezz said. "But he is loyal. Brave."

"Still loud."

Drezz'ss ears twitched faintly. "Undeniably."

They were quiet a while longer.

"You've surprised me too," Drezz said at last.

Saulice leaned back, shocked. "How's that?"

"I expected signs of you breaking. But… you're still walking," Drezz said. "That matters."

The silence returned. Not heavy, just true.

Drezz extended his furred hand, clawed and steady.

Saulice shook it without pause.

Their hands parted quickly, but the space between them had changed. It was not the fount. It was not fate. It was something simpler.

Respect.

The fire had burned to embers, glowing low beneath charred logs. Neither of them moved.

Drezz eventually stirred the coals with a long stick, sending a final trail of sparks into the night air. Neither spoke again. They did not need to. The silence between them now felt different.

Saulice leaned back against the stone, eyes tracing the edge of the outcropping above them. Stars glittered beyond the Spires, sharp and quiet. For once, the world did not feel like it was watching him. Just listening.

He did not remember when sleep finally came. But when it did, it came without dreams.

Morning arrived, soft and grey.

Light spilled across the ridge in thin streaks, catching on damp stone and the silver edge of mountain mist. Their camp had already been broken by the time Saulice woke, though the last of the heat still clung to the rock where the fire had burned.

He pulled himself upright, blinked against the pale sky, and found Drezz already standing near the ledge, arms folded, cloak fluttering. Melandra paced a little farther ahead, scanning the path below.

Oreas was the only one who had moved little. He lay sprawled beneath a crooked pine, moaning dramatically as he rubbed his ankles.

"Don't bury me here if I die," he groaned. "Bury me somewhere flat. Or sandy. Somewhere that doesn't smell like rock sweat."

"You're not dying," Melandra said without looking at him.

"Feels like I am. My feet are writin' angry letters to my knees."

She ignored him again.

Oreas grunted louder, then shifted his gaze to the boys. "Well," he said, fishing a battered apple from his pack, "if we don't get eaten, stabbed, or frozen by dusk, we'll be near the foot of Axbridge tomorrow."

Drezz'ss ears flicked. "That close?"

Oreas nodded, chewing with one side of his mouth. "We'll hit the hill pass by late morning. After that, it's a winding drop and a gatehouse with guards who check for fleas."

"Fleas?" Saulice asked, still rubbing sleep from his eyes.

"Figure of speech," Oreas said. "Mostly."

Melandra stepped away from the ridgeline, snapped grit from her gloves. "Once we're in the city, we go straight to the Academy. No markets. No wandering."

"What about an escort?" Oreas asked.

Melandra stopped walking.

"You know… someone to help 'em settle in," he said, gesturing toward the boys. "The Academy's full of nobles and whispering tongues. These two'll need someone who knows the halls from the courtyards."

Her brow lifted, but she said nothing.

"I know someone," Oreas added, more softly now. "Bright girl. Doesn't take part in the usual backbiting. Keeps her head down. Good judgment. My daughter Rayne could help them well enough."

Melandra turned, eyes narrowing with recognition. "Rayne… she's yours?"

He nodded. "She's my daughter. Second year. We ain't as close as I'd like, but she's steady. She doesn't lie. Knows when to talk and when she shouldn't. Like her mum in that way."

Melandra's gaze lingered on him, just a fraction longer than necessary. A small shift, barely there, but enough to mark her surprise.

She turned fully now, considering. "I'll speak with Valos. If she agrees, she'll be assigned."

Oreas nodded once but said nothing more.

They set out again, the trail easier now and less cruel.

Saulice walked in silence, but the knot inside him had not loosened. Not really.

They had crossed a pass no map had prepared him for. Climbed through fear, shared stories by firelight. But now, the path turned not toward beasts or blades, but people.

Drezz walked beside him, eyes still watchful but calm. Oreas rambled softly to himself behind them. Melandra kept to the front, her pace unhurried now, but still purposeful.

Somewhere beyond the ridge, the first towers of Axbridge waited. Cold stone, proud walls, banners Saulice could not yet see.

He adjusted the satchel on his back and kept walking.

Toward the city. Toward judgment. Toward whatever shape the future might force him into.

CHAPTER 7

THE BLACK BELLET

Oreas' breath turned to white mist in the mountain air. "Ah, that is a sight worth seeing."

They had left camp before the sun cleared the peaks, pressed forward by Melandra's clipped commands and a sense that the world behind them was folding in. Just hours into their march, they crested one of the Twin Spires' ridgelines. They were not true mountains, but the slopes were steep and winding enough to leave Saulice's legs quaking.

He bent over, palms pressed against his knees as he gasped for air. "Can we rest for just a minute?"

"You will rest when we reach Axbridge," Melandra said without slowing or glancing back.

Saulice groaned but kept moving. His feet ached in rhythm with his breath. The slope finally broke into a gentle descent, and the pounding in his skull began to ease.

Melandra and Oreas led the group down the ridge trail, their voices drifting ahead in uneven cadence. Oreas asked endless questions about fount forging, argonaut rankings, and the color of enemy blood. Melandra ignored half of them, though Oreas continued undeterred.

Behind them, Saulice and Drezz walked in silence, at least for a time.

The morning mist peeled away as they descended into a forest of pale pines and twisted brush. Shadows clung to the spaces between trunks, the last hints of night slowly dissipating.

Saulice glanced sideways at the fallet. Drezz's ears twitched with every branch crack, his green eyes narrowing as they scanned the path.

"You alright?" Saulice asked, keeping his voice low.

"I do not know," Drezz admitted. "The trees are still, but the air feels wrong."

Saulice almost said Drezz was imagining it. Almost. But the hair on his arms had started rising too. He shifted his satchel and looked behind them, yet saw nothing but branches and scattered patches of sky.

Just three days ago, he had been a post bearer who only drew scolding when parcels were delivered late. Now he was a fugitive walking toward a city he had never seen, carrying a satchel of secrets, and following an argonaut who trusted none but her own shadows.

How had it all changed so quickly?

Melandra slowed ahead. She glanced over her shoulder. "Stay sharp. We are close to the lower tree line. This is where it grows tricky."

Saulice's boots sank into soft loam. The trail had become little more than a deer path tangled with roots and littered with old stones. He spotted claw marks on a nearby tree. They were old, but wide. Far too wide.

"Melandra," he whispered, pointing.

She followed his gaze and scowled. Without a word, she touched the emerald in her bracer. Her fingers slid across it in a slow, deliberate arc. A faint pulse answered her gesture. Her left hand twitched, not yet forging, but ready.

Drezz lowered his voice. "Should we draw weapons?"

"No," she muttered. "We stay quiet, and we move."

The air changed.

He could not explain it. A pressure settled around them, not from above but from every side, as if the forest itself had stopped breathing.

A hoot echoed overhead. Melandra's owl, Aurora, swept down beneath the canopy in a frantic spiral, screeching.

Saulice froze.

"Something's coming!" Melandra shouted. "Fast."

A roar tore through the canopy. It was deep, thunderous, and wrong. Not like a bear. Not like anything Saulice had ever heard.

His blood went cold.

Powerful wings beat overhead, shaking the trees as something flew faster than his eyes could follow. A hand grabbed him just in time.

The treetops split, and a black blur vaulted from the canopy. Its roar ripped bark and leaves. Wings too ragged to fly stretched wide, then folded like blades. The creature slammed into the trail ahead, stone cracking beneath its weight.

Melandra did not curse. She did not blink.

But her eyes widened. "Black bellet."

Oreas swore aloud and scrambled behind a pine trunk. "I thought those things were wiped out. I read it back in school. Sealed and buried after the Thousand Year War."

"Wrong," Melandra muttered. "This one is alive, and I have seen it before."

The beast crouched low. Its black scales shimmered like rain-soaked ash as muscles rippled beneath them. Four hooked claws spread from each foot, and jagged bones jutted from its back where its wings folded. Its maw parted with a rattling breath. A rusted collar with spikes on all sides hung loosely around its neck, covered in ancient symbols no longer legible.

Amber light pooled in its throat.

Everyone dropped to the forest floor.

Flame burst forward in a wide arc. A deep red blaze licked through the underbrush and trees just beyond them. The volley sucked the air from the world.

Saulice shielded his face with his arms. Heat slammed into him like a wall. Smoke curled through his thoughts, and suddenly the trail blurred. He heard wood cracking, screams behind the floorboards, and his mother's voice.

He was not in the forest anymore. He was back in the attic crawlspace, nine years old, heat rising like a tide.

The air burned. Saulice clenched his fists until his nails bit into his skin.

Melandra did not answer. She kneeled on the earth, forging spears from the ground six at a time, fighting with all her might to distract the beast. Her wrists flicked like a bowstring. With each motion, another volley of stone rose beneath the bellet.

Flick. Rise. Flick. Rise. Each spear slowed the creature, but none stopped it.

"Saulice!" Drezz called. "Get out of there!"

But Saulice did not. He could not.

The bellet's flames halted for a moment, then it inhaled again. Melandra braced herself as embers glowed between its teeth.

She would not have time to escape.

And Saulice knew it.

The flames had not left the bellet's maw yet, but in his mind, she was already burning. Smoke swallowed her face; her hair turned to ash.

Another fire would take from him. Another person gone. Just like his mother.

Something inside him snapped.

And he *ran*.

Boots tore through scorched dirt. His mind broke free from its cage of fear. He slammed into Melandra, knocking her out of the way just as the bellet released another blast.

The blast grazed his back. He yelped as heat bit through his cloak and his shoulder screamed with white, searing pain.

They rolled out of trajectory, Melandra landing hard beneath his elbow.

"What in the *Hells*, Saulice?!"

"I have already lost people to flames," he panted. "I will not stand there while it happens a second time."

She stared at him, and for once, she said nothing.

But the fight was not finished. The bellet stomped toward them.

Melandra rolled aside and raised her hands to forge a stone shield. It surged upward just in time to block a claw but was shattered on impact.

Oreas darted in and swung his second hatchet. It struck the beast's back unsuccessfully. The bellet roared and staggered, then swiped at him. Oreas twisted away, escaping by a hair's breadth.

Drezz lunged with his blade. The dagger sank shallow into the bellet's side, drawing a howl. The bellet turned on him, jaws parting as fire welled inside.

There was no time.

Saulice seized the nearest branch. It was charred, heavy, and still hot as hell.

Simultaneously, Melandra slammed her hands to the ground with a grunt, forging two massive stone swords.

Saulice charged. He did not call out or give a warning. He only leapt at the bellet's neck as fire brightened in its maw.

The beast turned too late.

He rammed the branch into its open mouth. Heat seared his hands, but he forced the wood into a patch of soft flesh in the back of its throat before jerking back and falling. Saulice's back struck the ground, and his vision flashed white.

Flames sprayed sideways as the bellet shrieked, jaws snapping on splintered wood.

Then came a rush of motion — Melandra.

With a brutish stroke, she drove her stone blade through its eye and deep into its brain.

The bellet spasmed once. Twice. Then it collapsed.

It was dead at last.

Saulice stayed on the ground, gasping for air. His blistered hand still clutched a splintered piece of wood.

The creature's corpse steamed. Smoke curled from its throat and ruined eye. The collar around its neck pulsed once, then cracked. Its runes flickered out.

Behind him, Drezz limped forward. His blade trembled in his grip.

"It's over… We killed it," he whispered.

"We did, didn't we?" Saulice replied, struggling to believe the words.

Melandra stood in silence by its corpse, as though analyzing.

Oreas peeked around a tree, his brow high and voice hushed. "I mean… she *definitely* killed it… right?"

Saulice stared at the creature. Its mouth still hung open, exposing ember coals glowing in its throat.

But its eyes, even when lifeless, felt wrong.

As if something had left them and slipped away.

He swallowed hard.

The forest burned in patches around them. Smoke and ember light danced across the spires.

Melandra stepped closer. Her voice was quiet. "You acted like a fool."

"I know," Saulice murmured. He forced himself to stand. "I have already watched someone burn. And I saw you. I saw the fire catch in your hair." His breath stuttered. "I could not let it happen again."

Something shifted in her posture. Her hands, still bloody, curled slightly at her sides.

"You are not ready for a fight like that!" She sighed in resignation, then glanced away. "But I suppose even fools sometimes show courage."

She turned into the trees, calling for Oreas to help stamp out the brush fire near the trail.

The scent of scorched pine and singed flesh clung to the clearing. Fires crackled on either side of the path.

Oreas stomped one out with the flat of his boot. "We are leaving, right? Tell me we are leaving."

"We are leaving," Melandra said. "Now."

Drezz limped as he walked. His tunic was scorched across one shoulder, but he steadied Saulice without being asked.

"You were brave," the fallet said.

"I was terrified."

"That is not the opposite of bravery."

Saulice did not answer. He was not sure he believed that yet.

The climb out of the ravine slowed them. Melandra scouted ahead while the others picked their way over a tangle of burnt limbs. The trees had thinned, the ground scarred by ash.

Not from the fire they had escaped. From something older. Buried deeper in the earth.

A reminder.

Oreas huffed behind them. "You ever seen one of those things up close?"

Drezz shook his head.

"Me neither," Oreas said. "Thought they were nightmares in bard songs. You ask me, anything that breathes fire and smiles ought to be extinct. Not good for the heart."

"It was strange," Saulice murmured. "Almost like it was aware."

Oreas grunted. "All beasts got eyes."

"No," Saulice said. He stopped and looked back through the trees. "Not like that. Its eyes moved as if something else was inside. Watching us the way a person would."

Melandra did not respond. But she glanced over her shoulder.

Silence held them for the next hour. Their pace slowed, every step heavy with fatigue. The trail bent and rose, carrying them toward higher ground until it leveled into a patch of broken earth. Burned ferns dotted the path like bruises.

"Here," Melandra said, pointing to a curved ridge. "We will make a new camp past that rise."

Saulice wanted to argue. They needed distance. What if there were more? What if this one had sent a signal?

But when he looked at her, he saw the lines beneath her eyes. The shallow cut across her neck. The way her arms hung lower at her sides.

She was spent. And *that* was saying something.

So were they.

As they crested the ridge, the last of the smoke faded behind them. The black bellet's body was gone from sight.

But not from memory.

Not from the stories that would come.

CHAPTER 8

AXBRIDGE

The city rose like a punishment.

Axbridge wasn't carved into the landscape. It was hammered into it. A wall of ash-grey stone loomed in the distance, smooth-faced and uninterrupted. It was as though it had swallowed the hills beneath it. Guard towers punched upward at intervals, each flying a blue and gold banner. The royal colors of Candur, catching the late morning wind like warnings.

"Move your feet, boy," Melandra muttered behind him.

He obeyed, half-tripping as he caught up. Drezz walked at his side in silence, his fur matted at the arms and legs, a scratch running across one thin ear. Yet his posture stayed upright, and his golden eyes flicked left and right with quiet precision.

"Are they watching us?" Saulice whispered as the walls loomed closer.

"They are," Drezz replied, calm as ever.

Ahead, the outer gate to Axbridge grew massive. The road funneled into a wide causeway that narrowed toward a gatehouse lined with soldiers. At least sixty travelers waited in a line that crawled forward, some slouched in wagons, others gripped papers or clutched their cargo. The entire scene buzzed with the low hum of complaints and creaking wheels.

"Wait'll they see our paperwork," Oreas muttered. "Might take half the day. Longer if they start asking about the furry and our burnt-boy."

Before Saulice could ask what he meant, Melandra strode off the path toward the checkpoint. A guard stepped to intercept her, but she halted, pivoted, and raised her left wrist high. The insignia slashed into her steel bracer caught the sun, a lion's head gleaming with authority. Saulice had never noticed it before.

The guard put a hand up to stop them. "Aye! You can't just cut the line. Get to the back before I have you whipped."

"I am Sentinel Melandra Valcere," she announced. "Might I remind you that members of Furies Fist are not subject to inspection. I have four companions under protection and demand immediate clearance per the Axbridge Accord. Now," she said, closing the distance between her and the rough-shaven man, "step aside and let us through."

The guard's demeanor shifted instantly, and he stepped aside.

There was no inspection. No questions.

The iron-barred gate groaned open.

"Let the argonaut pass," the guard barked, clearing the crowd.

The onlookers grumbled as Melandra cut through their line. Saulice caught the whispers as they passed.

"What's she pulling?"

"That boy's got no crest."

"Is that a fallet?"

Oreas offered an exaggerated wave. "Hope the stew's still warm by the time y'all get in."

Drezz ignored the stares. Saulice tried to, but it was harder with every step. Especially when he noticed a pair of younger guards staring at his bracer.

The blank leather looked meager beneath Axbridge's banners. No crest. No stone. Nothing but stitched loops and questions. For a moment, the gates did not feel like they were welcoming him at all.

Inside Axbridge, the sound did not echo so much as roll, a tide of clattering carts over cobblestone mingling with the click of hard-soled boots. The snap of fabric in the wind carried across the square, woven into a pulse that Saulice could feel in his chest.

The road was wider than any he had seen before. It split three ways beneath a massive stone canopy. Straight ahead, vendors stood behind weather-beaten stalls, hawking wares at passing crowds.

The air reeked of too many things at once: grilled meat, soap, oil, and iron. Yet unlike Hamlen's roughly split districts, here the chaos was ordered, structured into lanes and stalls, streets and distinct sectors. Clean enough to not feel filthy, but alive with tension. The whole city seemed like a beast holding its breath.

Saulice shuddered.

They passed beneath scaffolding stacked with crates and iron rods. Above, a boy about Saulice's age swung a hammer beside a thick-bearded man. Both were shirtless, sweating, and laughing as sparks leapt from their work.

For a fleeting moment, it reminded him of home.

But then the boy waved at someone below, caught the back of the man's hand, and reeled sideways. Saulice looked away before the scene could play further.

Drezz remained at his side in silence. His fur was matted, his eyes sharp. He studied everything—the slant of rooftops, the angles of alleyways, the spacing between guards. He was not paranoid. The fallet was simply prepared.

"They hurry so no one looks too close," Drezz murmured, his voice low. "Too many eyes."

Saulice followed his gaze and began noticing it as well. People glanced and whispered, eyes shifting while they talked, yet none lingered on any one thing. The movement felt constant, a restless current of assessment.

Especially when they looked at him. His cloak reeked of damp moss and old smoke. Every crease in the fabric held the memory of wet bark, scorched grass, and something faintly animal. Threadbare seams along his shoulders pulled tight whenever he moved, threatening to split with a single wrong bend. No part of him looked untouched by the wild.

They moved through what Melandra called the lower ring. It was not shaped like any ring Saulice had ever seen. More like a fractured hive of brick buildings and sloped roofs, piled in crooked stacks. Tattered awnings flapped between windows where small children stared with wide eyes.

Not all the eyes were cruel, but neither were they warm.

"Is this still the city?" Saulice asked.

Melandra did not slow. "The poorer end."

"So where are we going?"

"Up."

The road angled into a long sloping ramp flanked by decorative fencing. The stones beneath their feet were tighter laid, newer and free of grime. The crowd thinned as they climbed, and with each step the buildings grew taller and straighter.

Here, balconies bloomed with potted vines against painted glass that gleamed in the morning light. A woman passed them with her nose upturned and a dog smaller than Drezz'ss foot trotting in silk booties.

Another pair of city guards saluted Melandra as they went by. Their eyes lingered on Drezz'ss tail and on the dirt crusted along Saulice's shoulders. They said nothing. They did not need to.

"People fear what is never announced," Drezz said, brushing ash from his sleeve.

They passed through an arch marked with a crest Saulice could not read. The stone here was lighter and freshly washed compared to the grime-dark walls of the lower ring. Men and women moved briskly along the lanes in pressed coats, every iron bracer stamped, many inset with polished stones, gleaming in the late morning sun.

Saulice scanned them instinctively, searching for something familiar, something worn. He found nothing. No leather. Not one. No rough hide bands either. His own bracer, cracked and sweat-darkened, felt louder with every step, like some mistake clinging to his arm.

Gold and blue banners hung from ironwork poles. They snapped overhead like declarations as children in matching uniforms marched in lines behind a grey-robed instructor. The city was beautiful, and so much of it shone.

But the farther they went, the harder it became to breathe.

They stopped beneath a wide bridge of polished black iron and carved stone. A mural along its underside showed five argonauts standing in a half-circle, each with a different elemental stone glowing in their bracers.

Saulice stepped forward. Awe fluttered in his chest.

If only that could be me, he thought. *That's a path I'll never get to walk, let alone attempt.*

His gaze fell to his own bracer. Leather. Untouched. Silent.

The moment cracked.

"I have traveled to many cities in my time," Oreas said at Saulice's side. "Still don't know how I feel about 'em. Kinda prefer the country. Flat country."

Saulice blinked and turned. Oreas stood with hands on his hips, brow furrowed, and nose wrinkled as he gazed toward the bluff ahead.

From here, Brynswick Academy was fully visible, a triangular mass of grey spires. No flowers. No banners. Just a single black gate with guards posted like statues outside.

"Looks more like a prison than a school," Saulice said.

"Not far off," Oreas muttered, straightening. "Well, I suppose this is where I leave you all."

Saulice's chest tightened. "You're not coming with us?"

"I've got business I'm late attending before I can see my little lady." He grinned. "Besides, I'm allergic to places with clean walls and too many rules."

He clapped Drezz on the back, rough but warm. "You keep that nose high, little furry. These soft-tongued types might act like they've never seen a fallet, but that just means you're rarer than rubies."

Drezz bowed. "I am grateful for your guidance, and your company."

Oreas crouched to Saulice's height until their eyes met.

"And you… Don't let those walls fool you. Just because they let you in doesn't mean they've stopped weighing you. The ones who smile the most are often the ones writing your worth behind your back."

Saulice lowered his gaze. "Do you think I'll make it?"

Oreas tilted his head. "That depends."

"On what?"

His smile widened.

"On whether you can keep walking when you don't know where the path ends."

He rose, winked at Melandra, and disappeared down a narrow alley, whistling an off-key tune about goats and luck. She returned his wink with its opposite, lips flat and unreadable.

Drezz watched him vanish. "He was strange," he said.

Saulice nodded. "But kind."

They turned toward the Spine.

At the top, Brynswick loomed with icy walls waiting. The road narrowed as they climbed, sloping into a steep curve along the mountain bluff. Wind curled between the ridges, sharp and dry, and with each step the city behind them shrank.

Ahead stood a wide arch of slate and iron carved to last. Over the lintel, the words *Brynswick Academy of Argonauts* were etched so shallow they looked half-erased by time. Two guards stood motionless at the iron doors, breastplates lacquered in deep grey, spears resting slanted against the wall.

They did not move.

Melandra lifted her cloak, revealing her steel bracer with its lion head insignia. "Sentinel Melandra Valcere," she said, voice sharp. "Authorization under Fury's Fist. I am here for registry."

The guards offered no reply, but after a pause one stepped aside and pulled a hidden lever in the stone. The gate creaked open.

A cloaked figure emerged beyond. His robes were stiff as dried bark with hems starched by wind, and silver links draped across his chest in a semicircle that marked authority. His posture was straight-backed and severe, but without cruelty.

"Master Valos," Melandra said, halting before him.

"Sentinel Valcere," he replied. "Your arrival was expected sooner."

"We met resistance."

Valos's gaze moved from Saulice to Drezz. His expression did not shift, yet Saulice felt its weight. It was not malice, but the cold machinery of judgment. These were the eyes of a man who measured everything—risk, worth, consequence.

"Resistance," Valos said, tasting the word. "Your report to Furies Fist will clarify, I assume."

"In full. You'll have copies sent to your office before the week's end."

He did not press. Instead, he produced a stiff scroll from his robes and unrolled it with care.

"Provisional enrollment forms. For the boy. As for his acquaintance… that has yet to be decided."

Drezz stepped forward.

Valos's brow twitched. "The fallet presents a complication. Our records do not confirm any recent exchange with Fallenan governance."

"That is not unexpected," Drezz said politely. "Fallenan has not sent students here in over a century. But I assure you, I can pay."

Valos's gaze flitted across him once more. "*This* would be a slight irregularity."

"I am accustomed to being an irregularity," Drezz replied, bowing.

Valos made no comment, only nodded. He retrieved another scroll from his robes and leveled his eyes toward Saulice.

Saulice stood straighter.

But the man's gaze had already fallen to his blank bracer.

He paused, then chuckled. "Is there no fount affinity registered to the boy?"

"None," Melandra answered before Saulice could speak. "He has been issued a bracer for evaluation but has not received a stone."

"Has he manifested?" Valos asked.

"Not within my presence, but he has survived things no boy his size should have endured. A black bellet was only the latest."

Valos raised an eyebrow. "Interesting."

Saulice blinked. He wanted to explain, to tell Valos that Melandra had saved him, that the bellet nearly tore them apart. But Valos was already writing.

"Unconfirmed affinity. No shard. Your academ status will be determined following his Trial scoring."

"Wait," Saulice said, his voice rising. "That's already been done. I've taken my trial assessment."

Valos did not look up. "You took the realm-wide version, yes. But Brynswick has its own standards. Our examinations are more telling."

His pen scraped as he scrawled notes on a clipboard. "He will be placed under observational classification until performance can be reviewed. It is standard procedure for unaligned entries."

Something knotted inside Saulice.

Observational. A word that did not mean guidance or protection. Just surveillance.

Like he was something they were waiting to go wrong.

Not a student. Not a boy.

Just a risk they had not named yet.

"Do not worry," Valos said. His voice dipped as he finally met Saulice's eyes. "If you perform adequately, no one will need to remember how you got here."

He rolled the parchment closed with a flick and held out the scrolls. "Take these to the Masters Halls. North across the campus grounds. Dormitory assignments will be posted by the fourth bell, and daily physical training begins at the fifth. Failure to appear is grounds for dismissal."

Melandra accepted both without thanks.

Valos turned and strode away without another word.

The gate closed behind them, and Saulice stared at the space Valos had occupied. He was unsure whether he felt rejected or erased.

"You handled that well," Drezz murmured as they moved forward. "For what it is worth."

"I didn't say much."

"Exactly."

Melandra marched across the campus, her cloak billowing in the wind like a banner. Saulice and Drezz followed in silence.

The Masters Halls of Brynswick were colder than the climb. Wide, with vaulted ceilings and dark tiles that clicked underfoot. Low-burning lanterns lined the corridor, their glow muted against carved wooden benches. Stone plaques marked each room with codes rather than names.

There were no student titles or decorations. Just utility.

As they neared the final corridor at the end of a narrow hall, a man stepped from a side alcove. His tunic was deep navy silk, gold threads faintly shimmering at the cuffs. A silver badge shaped like a lion fastened his cloak.

His smile came before his words.

"Well. What an unexpected arrival."

Melandra halted, her shoulders stiff before she dipped into a bow. "My lord."

"Sentinel Valcere," he said with soft amusement. "You never travel quietly."

She gave no reply.

The man turned his gaze toward the boys.

Saulice felt the man's presence in a way that filled the hall without raising its voice.

"Lord Winstrom," he said, "Overseer of Brynswick."

Drezz gave a slight nod. Saulice managed a half-step forward.

Winstrom's eyes gleamed. "A fallet in Axbridge. I never thought I would see the day. There is a quiet dignity in your kind that I hope does not dull here."

Drezz did not answer.

Winstrom's gaze shifted.

"And this must be the boy."

Something cold stirred in Saulice's spine.

The man's tone remained pleasant. "No fount. No crest. Survived a bellet, helped kill it even. Rescued from one of the outer villages by a Sentinel. Your name has passed across more than one desk since Hamlen."

Saulice swallowed hard.

Lord Winstrom smiled. "I always pay attention to the unranked pieces moving across the board."

Melandra's voice cut in, low and firm. "They are here to learn, my lord. Not entertain the court or its manipulative schemes."

"I would not dream of it," Winstrom said smoothly. "Though, of course, all students are evaluated equally—by performance, and by potential."

He looked again at Saulice, his voice dropping. "You will find Brynswick keeps its eyes open. Always."

He turned then, his footsteps lingering longer than his words.

-ACT II-

THE WEIGHT OF BECOMING

INTERLUDE

HE WILL COME WILLINGLY

Somewhere far above, fire split the world, and Saulice stood in its wake.

The cave breathed, not with wind or life, but with memory.

Baalo sat unmoving upon a throne of fused basalt and ribbone, hunched yet eternal, like a forgotten monument whose meaning had long faded though its presence endured. The stone beneath him bore the scars of age, cracks filled with soot and forgotten fount runes worn down by silence.

Root-veins dangled from the ceiling like withered cords, brushing the cavern floor with slow, spidery motions. Each time they touched the ground, the dirt recoiled as if remembering who lived here.

No flame burned and no water stirred, yet within the blackness something pulsed.

Baalo's chest rose once, then fell, and again, until faintly it began to beat in rhythm with the world above the stone.

Not a sound but a pull. Like a ripple through blood and ruin, his corrupted fount core shimmered.

Baalo forged his connection with the bellet, observing its final moments.

Heat surged as a memory not his own was gathered. A wound shared from afar. Flesh seared, wings folded, smoke rose. He felt the black bellet, his blade-creature bred from ruin and buried will, had fallen.

Slain by them.

Baalo's eyelids lifted a fraction. The vision confirmed the death. The creature's heart had stopped, severing his connection. And with it, another thread unraveled.

He tasted the bellet's last moment: a boy, burned but standing. A blade through the eye. A scream choked in ash.

Saulice.

The boy had interfered.

He had thrown himself into fire, not for power but to protect the argonaut from the bellet's breath.

And Lazarus had not stirred.

That, more than anything, unsettled Baalo.

He shifted slowly with a sound like stone grinding on stone and rose from his throne. The cave groaned beneath the motion. Small rivulets of dark water, thick and unmoving, trailed from beneath his feet like veins with no heart to reach. All around him the shadows leaned inward, as if afraid he might speak.

But he said nothing.

For a long moment he only listened to the aftershock, to the trembling that had followed Saulice's choice.

His fingers flexed once, joints cracking like dry branches.

"So," he whispered. "He *chooses.*"

The boy had reached for fire with his own hand, and Baalo had felt it.

That was new.

Baalo moved through the cave with the patience of a glacier returning to sea. His shadow, though cast by no light, stretched long across the pitted walls and worn glyphs. The air thinned as he descended into a lower hollow, a chamber sunken and steeped in time where even the roots no longer reached. Here the stone bore the scars of another war, one fought before memory was measured in generations.

Ten broken sigils were carved into the rock face. Worn by centuries, yet still present. Each bore a shape older than scripture. Each belonged to a Titan.

And above them, half-buried in ash, the name burned faint and foul against the stone: *Shaddai.*

Baalo stood before it, still as ruin. His corrupted fount core, still humming with the after-echo of Saulice's defiance against the bellet, tightened within his chest as though recoiling in the presence of the Divine Name.

"I see what You feared," he said, his voice hollow as wind beneath a tomb door. Veartaya had hated Shaddai, the Creator of Myre and the four races that governed its realms. With just a sliver of His power, Baalo could bring Veartaya back from her slumbering exile, and Myre could still be hers. And it would be. Just not yet. And not by Shaddai's oh so righteous hand.

A bitter feeling, like wine, filled Baalo as he stared at the etched stone. "Even now, Shaddai binds His justice to infants, my Lady. But I have a plan."

His hand drifted along the sigils, tracing the fractures with a touch that once could have split mountains. He paused over one, deeper than the others. It was jagged from where he had struck it once, long ago.

Lazarus.

"Shaddai's hammer," he said. "His executioner."

His fingers curled into a fist as he bowed his head in prayerful reverence to his Lady. Veartaya was his liege. Not Shaddai, who every pitiful mortal revered. No… even if she was sealed away from the world, beaten by Lazarus' last Harbinger during the Thousand Year War, Baalo would find and free her. But first, he had to find the *key* to doing so. And he knew just where to start.

"Shaddai shaped him from order and will and called it justice. But justice is a language, my lady, not a law. And I plan to speak it! I just need to find a way to get him to come to me."

Baalo turned slowly, facing the chamber's center where a pit yawned beneath a blackened altar. No fire burned there. Only shadow and silence.

"The Harbinger does not speak with the Titan's voice. Not yet. Time still favors my side."

His memory throbbed with Saulice's lingering echo, the memory of choice and sacrifice.

Baalo's jaw tensed as an idea dawned on him. "The boy acted, without the Titan. Without Shaddai."

He stood in that stillness a while longer as his puzzle grew closer to completion. Then, for the first time in a century, Baalo smiled.

The ache in his corrupted fount core sharpened. It was less pain now, more a signal. He closed his eyes and felt the shape of the others. Not through sight or names, but through impressions. Baalo saw blurred colors of will and weight, proximity and pulse. The Harbinger's light was still marked by fire and defiance while the argonaut woman flickered like a blade half-drawn. The merchant, he was irrelevant.

But one presence was out of place, causing Baalo to tilt his head.

There was a note among the harmonics of his fount, only perceptible to someone timeless and wise, such as him. A frequency he had not felt since the war's final autumn. It was cold and proud, tethered to a place in northern Myre, where frost fell and mountain wind blew through the Jade Forest.

He drew closer to this peculiar presence, discerning who could possess such a fount nature. The creature was young, cloaked in fur and smoke. To Baalo's surprise, he was no human, nor was he another Harbinger.

He was a *fallet*.

Baalo's mouth tightened.

He had not thought of their timid kind in centuries.

The fallet were a generally quiet race even before the war, keepers of land and speakers of stone and storm. When Veartaya rose against

Shaddai so many moons ago, they were the first to hide away. Not because of cowardice, but from refusal. They had sealed themselves away, pulled from the forging world, and broken their ancient vows to Shaddai. Their elders turned against the other three races and realms.

And yet.

Baalo reached deeper into the echo, peeling back the veils of present form. Beneath the soot, beneath the boy's fear, there was a thread. Not of skill or strength, but blood.

A bloodline Baalo remembered. A bloodline that Veartaya had known *quite* well. After all, this fallet's ancestor had been one of Veartaya's fellow disciples, among Shaddai's first students just as She had been.

"You are not just a student. Not just a child. You are the last flicker of a vow unfulfilled."

He straightened, shoulders rolling with sudden energy.

"One Harbinger, and an heir! And the Titan sleeps between them." His lips curled, revealing sharp, stone-gray teeth. "How delightful."

The cave walls thickened as Baalo walked, narrowing around him like the throat of a waiting beast. He descended without torch or echo, yet the path opened before him with grim familiarity. Even sealed, this place had never denied him.

At the bottom of the hollow, the earth widened again, blooming into a low chamber of stone and cinder. Charred vines twisted along the walls. Streaks of old blood, dried and blackened, flaked to dust. They marked the outer rim of a crude circle carved by hoof and claw. Bones jutted from the ash, many still fused to the armor they died wearing.

At the center stood a crooked altar of twisted metal. Once part of a centaur helm, it was now bound with thorn-twine.

Baalo exhaled slowly. His corrupted fount pulsed again, sharp and rhythmic.

He did not kneel.

"Rise," he said.

The silence buckled, steel creaking as the altar shuddered with dark light. From the cracks in the stone came a low tremor, first felt in the ribs, then beneath the feet.

The air changed.

It grew colder, heavier. The scent of sulfur and moss spread like a rot. From the shadows along the edges of the chamber, they came. Shapes with hollow torsos and cracked bone-legs emerged from the shadows. Their limbs were too long, with hooves that floated just above the stone before landing with soft, reverent weight. Their eyes were empty, yet they could see.

Lichtaurs.

Specters of the Thousand Year War. Twisted remnants of centaur warriors who had died with rage in their hearts and were never laid to rest.

Baalo's eyes narrowed. "You remember."

He stepped into the circle, unflinching as one of them emerged before him, horned and taller than a man, shoulders wrapped in chain and old battle cloth.

"You were bound with the Pitch. But your kind has been scattered and your fear forgotten by humanity."

The specter stared back, silent.

Baalo placed a clawed hand on its ruined helm.

"But I have returned. I have found an open wound, and I intend to press it until it *hurts.*"

His corrupted fount glowed faintly in his chest.

"Call the other and draw the stragglers in. Gather beneath the Pitch. When you have finished, send a lone scout into Candur to keep within the shadows of Axbridge. Listen to every whisper leaving the city. I want to know every word spoken about Brynswick."

A second lichtaur emerged behind the first, then a third, pulling itself through solid stone as though the cave had exhaled it.

"There, dwells a boy who possesses the power of Lazarus," Baalo said. "A child of both Titan and flame! I require him shuffling toward us, freely. He must come to the Timfathen."

He turned from them, his voice dropping to a whisper that filled the stone.

"Learn everything about him. If he seeks to wear the mask of an argonaut, then I will watch how well he plays the part."

The lichtaurs bowed, then nodded their heads. Above the earth, where the Timfathen's ruins baked in silence, the ground cracked once.

And the long-settled dust of an ancient war stirred.

CHAPTER 9

THE INTERVIEW

Saulice woke to silence.

It was not the soft quiet of forests or the muted rest of sleeping streets, but a hollow stillness that felt muffled, as though the air itself had been wrapped in cloth. The sensation reminded him of the thick wool blanket draped across him, too clean and too scratchy to be his own. He blinked at the ceiling, a pale arch of stone etched with thin lines that almost looked like script.

His body ached from travel, yet his mind struggled to believe he had truly slept. This was *Brynswick*.

He shifted slowly and sat up. The bed did not creak. Nothing in the room did. The chamber had been built with too much precision for sound to linger.

Near the small desk, Drezz adjusted an ash-colored tunic. His fur, thick and brushed to a faint sheen, caught the first light of morning filtering through the narrow window slit above him. He moved with quiet intention, as though he had already been awake for hours.

Saulice swung his legs over the side of the mattress, his fingers brushing against stone that proved smoother and colder than he expected. "This room's... nice," he muttered.

Drezz did not turn. "Too symmetrical."

Saulice managed a faint smile. "You hate symmetry?"

"I distrust places where even the shadows fall the same."

Unsure how to answer that, Saulice stood instead, stretching until his joints cracked and his grunt broke the morning hush. His gaze swept the chamber: his pack rested near the door, and the twin beds faced one another like mirror images. This was not a cell, yet it carried no sense of home either.

"You sleep?" he asked.

"I rested," Drezz replied, voice even as always.

Saulice dressed without speaking further, groaning as he slipped into another pair of stained garbs. He dreaded the attention they would draw, though his worn clothing would never be the real reason others stared. That burden belonged to the blank leather bracer fastened at his wrist.

A knock sounded at the door, startling him. It was neither sharp nor impatient, but measured and deliberate.

Drezz was already at the handle, opening it without pause.

A girl stood in the corridor clad in the full uniform of *Brynswick*: deep blue fabric trimmed with silver thread, her crest pinned like a blade to her chest. Her dark hair was tied back in a low tail, and her unreadable eyes swept across them with a quiet, assessing glance.

"The name's Rayne. I'm a second-year academ. I'll act as a temporary escort for you both until your Trials," she said. Her words carried no flourish, only fact. "Follow me."

She turned before either of them could answer.

Saulice followed after her, Drezz close at his side. The corridor stretched ahead, its cool grey stone polished to a near-glass sheen that reflected the faint blue light pouring through the windows to their left. Each arch they passed whispered of order and discipline, as if even the walls demanded silence.

Rayne walked without speaking, her steps clipped and sure. She did not ask if they had slept or whether they understood where she was taking them. She made no effort to fill the quiet with courtesy.

And yet, every few moments Saulice noticed her glance back. Never for long, only a flick of her eyes over Drezz or a brief look at the blank bracer on his own wrist. She noticed more than she allowed them to see.

They soon passed a line of students marching in formation, third years perhaps, their polished iron bracers gleaming with fitted fount stones. One boy turned his head and smirked.

"Kennels are on the west wing," he muttered.

Drezz said nothing.

Saulice's fists curled, but before he could speak, Rayne halted. She turned just enough for the boy to see her face. No words, only her gaze.

The boy's smirk vanished.

Without a comment, Rayne resumed walking, and they followed. She did not apologize for the insult, nor did she scold the offender, yet in her silence Saulice sensed a sharper edge than rebuke could have carried.

"She didn't stop it," he whispered.

"She didn't need to," Drezz replied.

They continued into a side hall, where tall wooden doors bore names carved in fine script. At the far end stood a marble statue of a man raising a staff embedded with ten stones toward a rising mountain.

Saulice stared, but Drezz bowed his head. "*Shaddai.*"

Rayne paused beside the figure and turned at last. "You will be tested today. The Cadre will see you, and they will decide what your presence means to this institution. Choose your words carefully. More than that, choose when not to speak."

Saulice nodded, uncertain whether her tone carried advice or warning.

She studied them a breath longer, then added, almost flat, "There are many who do not believe you should be here. Not only students. Staff as well."

Drezz'ss ears twitched, but he kept still.

Her gaze lingered on him. "And yet," she said more softly, "you are."

For the first time that morning, Saulice glimpsed something in Drezz'ss eyes that was not calm. It was fire.

The halls of *Brynswick* stretched on like arteries feeding the heart of some vast and ancient body. Rayne led without hesitation, Saulice matching her pace out of instinct rather than ease, while Drezz glided beside him with a silence that felt heavier than words.

They entered a side corridor paneled in dark wood, the walls lined with polished brass plaques etched with names Saulice did not recognize but suspected he should. He did not linger, for each time he slowed, Rayne was already a step farther ahead.

Their boots struck the stone with sharp rhythm, echoing against the gleaming floor. Somewhere above them, bells tolled once, deliberate and distant. Voices sounded in hushes and clusters, as though conversation itself cost more than most were willing to pay.

Through one tall window Saulice caught sight of a sparring match. Older students fought on the far training fields, their bracers flashing. Stone spikes jutted from the ground, nothing so grand as Melandra's towering pillars, while one boy skimmed them with a burst of wind and another raised a shield of flame.

"Do we learn to do that?" Saulice asked, his voice kept low.

"In time," Rayne answered.

"And if we don't?"

"You'll leave."

Her tone carried no cruelty, but no softness either.

The Annals tower rose ahead, a massive column of stone that dwarfed the nearby buildings. Rayne spoke without slowing. "All academs have access to the Annals. Within lie ancient lore, tactical treatises, elemental fount theory, and even rare fragments of Shaddai's life on Myre. You will not find another collection to equal it."

They passed beneath its looming walls and began to climb the spiral stair within, ascending to an observation hall. Morning light filtered through tall blue-glass windows etched with wear, casting patterns across the floor of the rotunda. From the eastern ledge Saulice glimpsed mountains rising beyond Axbridge's far wall. Trees and mist lingered at their base, and the familiar sight of forest brought him a fragile comfort.

"This place is beautiful," he breathed.

"It is," Drezz agreed. "And dangerous."

Rayne gave no reply. She only opened one last door at the rotunda's end, leading them into a narrower corridor. Portraits of past *Brynswick* Masters lined one wall, while the other bore tall iron-latched doors marked with unfamiliar symbols.

Rayne stopped. "This is where you'll wait. When your name is called, enter. Speak only when spoken to. Offer nothing you cannot defend."

Saulice glanced at Drezz, whose golden eyes stayed fixed on the far door.

"What if I mess this up?" he whispered.

"Performance does not always grant entry," Drezz said with calm steadiness. "But a Harbinger does not need permission to belong."

They pushed open the heavy iron doors and entered a holding room colder than the hall outside. The air seemed weighted, thick from too many anxious breaths exhaled across years of waiting.

Straight-backed chairs lined the wall. Four older academs already occupied them. Two were twins, their identical braids and sharp cheekbones mirrored even in their posture. Both wore deep blue coats with iron bracers gleaming at their wrists. Another student bore silver-trimmed sleeves embroidered with careful precision. The fourth, a girl seated farthest away, crossed her legs and raised her chin as though the others did not matter.

None of them looked at Saulice or Drezz, but the deliberate avoidance felt heavier than scorn.

Drezz sat without hesitation, lowering himself with dignity, his hands folded neatly on his knees. Saulice followed, stiff and uncertain, settling beside him.

There was no instructor, no clock, no welcome. Only one door behind them leading to the hall, and another ahead, waiting.

Saulice shifted. The boy with the embroidered sleeves leaned toward one twin and whispered. Both chuckled, their eyes darting toward Drezz before turning away.

Saulice clenched his jaw. Their silence was worse than insults. They did not consider him an equal, nor even a threat. They did not consider him at all.

He looked at Drezz, who sat motionless, composed as stone.

"You okay?" Saulice whispered.

"I have been waiting a long time for this," Drezz said. "I can wait longer still."

Saulice tried to hold that same stillness, but his heel tapped once against the stone before he caught himself. He fixed his gaze on the far wall where a single iron sconce burned with blue flame. He wondered if it had been lit since morning, or if it ever went out.

Sweat beaded under his collar. The stiffness of his tunic scraped against his skin. His leather bracer dug into his wrist like a brand of failure. No one had asked about it yet, but they would. They all would.

A voice crackled from behind the inner door.

"Gerrin Rouse."

The silver-trimmed boy rose with the swagger of one accustomed to hearing his name called first. Without sparing Saulice or Drezz a glance, he walked through the door as it opened soundlessly. It shut behind him with a click.

Silence settled again. Saulice counted the beats of his heart. Ten. Twenty. Thirty.

The same voice called once more.

"Tylar and Tavin Eames."

The twins stood in perfect unison and vanished behind the door.

Only the girl remained. And them.

Minutes crawled by. The flame flickered but never dimmed.

"Elandra Meyers."

The girl rose with deliberate composure. Her eyes brushed past Saulice as if he were dust in the air, then she entered and was gone.

Saulice exhaled slowly. "What if we're last on purpose?"

"We are," Drezz said.

"Why?"

"Because they do not know how to measure us."

Saulice had no reply. He stared at the sealed door, imagining what waited beyond: robed judges, a circle of fount stones, or perhaps some trial he had not prepared for. The silence pressed heavier than stone.

Then the voice came again.

"Drezz of Fallenan."

Drezz rose as if stepping into a garden rather than a tribunal. He turned back only once, his tone simple, almost tender.

"Remember who you are not."

Then he entered, and the door closed.

Saulice was alone.

For the first time in days, truly alone. No hooves clattered, no shouts from Melandra, no nonsense humming from Oreas. No forest swallowing his steps, no fire-breathing beasts. Only silence, polished walls, and his own breath rattling in his chest.

And somehow this room felt more dangerous than all of it.

The door did not open again for a long time.

When it finally did, the voice summoned him.

"Saulice Sawyer."

His knees twitched, but he pushed himself upright. Cold sweat spread across his back as he stood tall, spine rigid, every step toward the door echoing like a hammer against iron.

The door opened without touch. Light spilled through the crack, blinding in its purity.

He stepped into it.

The chamber resembled a courtroom, rectangular and severe. Black stone walls streaked with veins of silver rose on either side, bare of banners or sigils, radiating cold authority. A single narrow window slit let in a shaft of light that cut across the floor like a blade.

At the far end, three figures sat behind a table. They did not rise. They only watched.

"Saulice Sawyer," said the man at the center. His tone was exact, each syllable honed as though drawn from a script long prepared.

It was Master Valos, the one Melandra had spoken to at the gate.

"Step forward."

Saulice advanced until his boots touched the edge of a dull iron square set into the floor. Close enough to feel their scrutiny. Far enough to know this was no gathering of peers.

To Valos's left sat a gaunt man with clipped black hair and piercing eyes: Cadre Calder. To his right, a woman robed in storm-grey, her gaze measured and patient: Cadre Therin.

Calder leaned forward. "You don't look like the stories."

Saulice kept silent.

"Nothing to say?"

"I don't know the stories, sir."

Calder smiled faintly, unsatisfied. "Exactly."

Valos's fingers interlaced. "You entered Axbridge yesterday under Sentinel Melandra's escort. She has a keen eye for irregularities. You have no recorded history. No fount shard or stone, a bracer without a crest, *and* a core that cannot be measured. I would be remiss if I claimed I didn't have doubts about your admission at this prestigious Academy, do you understand?"

"Yes, sir," Saulice said, nails biting into his palm.

"Do you know why you were brought here?"

He hesitated. Melandra had warned him to reveal nothing. Yet Valos spoke as one who already knew.

"I do."

Therin's voice was calm as she read from a parchment report. "You were born in Hamlen?"

"Yes."

"No noble blood. No inheritance to be identified. And your Trial, let us say, proved inconsistent in identifying your fount affinity."

Valos studied him. "What does that make you, Saulice Sawyer?"

He paused. "I am a Harbinger." The words felt foreign, brittle in his mouth.

The sound struck like flint. Calder stiffened. Therin's brows lifted.

Anger coiled inside him, but beneath it lay something heavier. He had never asked for this. Yet denial had changed nothing in Hamlen, nor on the road. If he kept running, nothing would change at all.

He drew a breath through clenched ribs. "That is what I was told. I don't know why or how. But I cannot deny it anymore."

Valos's eyes sharpened. "You've experienced a rare clarity among peers your age."

Calder scoffed. "We have trained Harbingers from birth, their lines secured, their discipline layered. And now—we must deal with *this*?"

"It is not our decision solely," Therin replied.

"It is now."

Valos's gaze did not move. "This boy helped kill a black bellet. That warrants at least some attention."

Therin leaned forward. "Are you certain?"

"Melandra's report leaves no doubt. A beast with wings and a rune cursed collar. What else could that describe?"

Saulice's hands curled. "I did not kill it. And I was not alone."

"No," Valos said. "But you lived. The creature did not."

The memory surged unbidden—the jaws, the fire, the panic.

"I only did what I could," Saulice said. "I was not trying to be brave. I could not watch her die."

"Survival is not skill," Calder snapped.

"No. But perhaps it is a beginning."

Calder glared. "And you expect us to *hand* you control?"

"No. It is mine to learn. I will learn to fount forge and bear Lazarus's power, whatever it costs."

That stilled the room.

He stepped half a pace forward. "I know what I am. No noble birth. But I have seen what happens when I lose control. I have hurt people. Perhaps worse. I will not let it happen again."

His voice steadied. "I do not want power so others will fear me. I want it so I need not fear myself. I want to mend what is broken. I want control. And I want to prove that the boy who was nothing can be more."

Therin sat back. "There it is."

Calder said nothing.

Valos rose, presence filling the chamber. "You may go."

"That is all?" Saulice asked.

No answer. Only Therin's nod. "Most speak what they think we wish to hear. You spoke what was true. That carries weight."

As he turned, Valos's voice followed, low and unreadable. "Let us see what becomes of you."

The door opened behind him. Saulice walked through, legs trembling, heat rushing to his face. The silence pressed close as the door shut with a final click.

He lingered in the corridor, breath ragged. The word Harbinger throbbed in his chest. It did not feel like power. It felt like a trap. Like something monstrous had been hidden inside him all along.

And the worst part was knowing he had felt it before. In Hamlen, when rage had drowned him. When his hands closed around Will's throat.

"Saulice," a voice said.

He turned. Drezz waited at the end of the hall. Together they descended the library stairs. Afternoon light streaked orange across the floor, unchanged and unyielding, while inside Saulice felt hollowed.

Not broken. But empty.

"I do not understand why I am here," he said at last. "Harbingers are trained from birth. How am I to catch up?"

"We should have died to the bellet," Drezz said. "Yet here we are. You will learn."

They left the Annals Wing. Students passed in clusters, some whispering, some staring. Saulice tugged his sleeve lower over his brand.

Crossing a stone bridge, he glanced down at sparring students below—water against stone, fire against wind. Their forging looked nothing like Melandra's, and nothing like his own.

"What if I do not want this?" he asked.

"What you are is not choice," Drezz said. "What you become is."

At the far side, Rayne waited with folded arms. She gave a curt nod and turned.

"You are assigned to Dormitory Crescent," she said. "Training begins at fifth bell."

Saulice asked, "Even after what they said?"

"If you are here, you train. That is all that matters."

Her eyes lingered a second too long before she walked on.

They followed her beneath carved arches toward the dormitories, where shadows fell thick across the stone streets. Students sparred and studied on benches.

"We are not ready," Saulice murmured.

Drezz stopped at the doorway and looked at him with steady calm. "We must begin somewhere."

The evening bell tolled once, sharp and final. It was time to *train*.

CHAPTER 10

THE SHATTERING

Hail ticked against the dorm window. Saulice sat upright, eyes on the silver blur beyond the glass. His shoulders ached from the night before.

Cadre Pell had made them drag boulders across the training yard with harnesses strapped to their waists. He called it "foundational strength training," but it felt more like punishment dressed in purpose.

Today was the Academy's Trial. They would test his fount core and, after today, his future would be certain.

Drezz stood near the door, brushing his coat. And by coat, Saulice meant his arms, neck, and head. His presence had grown steadying to Saulice, like the hum of a nearby fire.

"You appear troubled," Drezz said, tilting his head. "It is understandable."

"I don't know," Saulice replied. "I feel… ready? But that doesn't make sense."

"It might," Drezz said. "You've earned this moment. Perhaps your spirit knows that."

Saulice stared at his hands, then slowly nodded.

Together, they stepped into the morning haze. Sleet hissed as it struck the cobbled path. The Academy was veiled in a grey light, buildings rising through the mist like ancient statues, tall, elegant, and aloof. Marble columns framed walkways lined with banners bearing the sigil of Brynswick: a golden eye surrounded by ten slanted lines, one for each elemental fount.

Rayne waited near the arch of the dormitory. She leaned against the wall, arms crossed, while another second year kicked at a loose stone with one boot.

"You're up," Rayne said. "About time."

Saulice winced but said nothing.

"Who is the visitor?" Drezz asked.

"Tibbet," he said with a wide smile. "I'm also a second year here. I'll be accompanying Rayne for the day to help answer any questions. For starters, each year of academics has their own set of male and female dorms."

Tibbet gestured toward their dormitory. "This one's for the first years males, Dorm Crescent. Dorm Tiding is for the female first years. Second year academs stay in Northwing and Southshade. You'll probably never step foot there this year unless you get invited or summoned. Which, trust me, *doesn't* happen."

"We've time before the demonstration," Rayne said, striding ahead of them. "Best to eat. You'll need the strength."

The sleet hadn't stopped. They followed the second years past the dueling field's stone rail, then took two sharp turns to the right, arriving at an extensive structure wrapped in ivy and slate. Warmth drifted from its arched doorway, carrying the smell of yeast and spice.

Inside, the cafeteria was cavernous, with high beams and low-set lanterns swaying from chain hooks. Only a few students lingered, seated at wide oak tables scattered like islands across the tiled floor.

Behind the counter stood an older woman with a stern brow and a blunt-cut bob streaked with grey. Her apron was stained, sleeves rolled up to the elbow. She didn't blink as the group approached.

"These two look like river runts," she muttered. "First years?"

Rayne gave a slight nod. "They're with us."

"Hmph." The woman slapped two bowls of steaming spiced grains onto a tray. "Take it while it's hot."

"Thank you, Mrs. Velma," she said, guiding Saulice and Drezz to an empty bench.

Saulice sat with an achy grunt, clutching the bowl with both hands. The warmth helped soothe his nerves, but it didn't stop the whispers. Two boys across the hall were already glancing his way, eyes trailing to his bracer.

He angled his arm, trying to hide his brand.

Drezz was unbothered.

"Eat fast," Tibbet said. "It's best to be arrive early for the Trial."

As soon as their bowls were cleared, Rayne rose without a word, boots already leading them toward their next destination.

The amphitheater rose before Saulice like a monument carved from storm clouds, its white pillars streaked dark from old rains, its great copper dome greened with age.

Inside, torchlight flickered along polished floors. The air smelled of chalk, parchment, and the ghost of old incense. Students sat on benches outside the curtain, some pacing, others whispering under their breath, all of them waiting for their turn to face the Source Stone.

Saulice noted a hand-drawn schedule posted on a wall listing upcoming evaluations, with a note beneath in red ink: Upper-year ACEs held during summer recess. No first-year access permitted.

As soon as he and Drezz sat, his name was called.

He gulped, rising again before stepping through the curtain.

A silence greeted him, vast and complete. The chamber beyond the curtain was circular and enormous, ringed with tiered seating, all empty save for five Cadre seated in judgment behind a long, curved bench. Their robes shimmered faintly beneath the high light of sunbeams piercing through stained glass.

And in the center, glowing like a coiled sun, stood the Source Stone.

It pulsed with shifting light: blues, silvers, reds. The ten colors of the fount blended like oil on water. He had seen nothing so sacred before, apart from an altar.

Saulice's mouth went dry.

"You may approach," said Master Valos.

The cadence of his voice carried, ancient and even. Saulice stepped forward.

"Place your hand on the stone," Valos continued. "Center your breath and do not push. Let the stone resonate with your fount core. Do not worry, nothing dreadful will happen. All fount cores are dormant until awakened, and this is just a way to test your fount affinity."

Calder leaned back in his seat with a bored sigh.

Saulice reached the pedestal and knelt. The warmth of the Source Stone soaked into his hand before he touched it. His fingers hovered over the swirling surface.

Please, he thought, willing himself to calm. *Let this work.*

He pressed his palm down.

A golden pulse flared, and his heart jumped.

Light spiraled beneath his skin. Energy met him, not hostile but uncertain. A humming sound filled the room, low and resonant, as though the stone were awakening, searching for something.

Come on, Saulice begged inwardly. *I have made it this far. I passed the interview, even helped kill a black bellet. Surely, I have earned this.*

The stone flared again, brighter now. Bands of light formed concentric circles that rotated beneath his palm. He gritted his teeth, steadying his breath. The warmth turned sharp, electric.

The Source Stone trembled.

A crack, thin as hair, snaked across its surface.

"No," Saulice whispered, shaking his head. "This cannot be happening. Not now, not like this."

The crack deepened, and the rings of light stuttered, their spin jerking. Another fracture formed, clean and deep, splitting the stone with a jagged sound like a tree being torn apart.

Master Valos jerked out of his seat. "Back away, now!"

But Saulice could not move. The stone felt bound to him, pulling and resisting. It was fighting him.

Please, Shaddai, he prayed, eyes clenched shut. *Please, show me who I am. Just give me something. Anything.*

The crack reached the pedestal base. With a deep groan, the Source Stone split down the center, clean in half.

For a single breath, everything stilled.

Then a blinding streak ripped from the sundered core, searing and jagged, white-blue. It was not fire. It was lightning.

The bolt did not arc. It stabbed, upward and outward. It struck the ceiling with a thunderclap that silenced the room. Smoke exploded from the stone's split, and static coiled through the chamber, lifting dust and hair alike.

Saulice was hurled backward, his limbs flailing. His back struck the floor with a brutal crack, and for a heartbeat, every nerve screamed.

The world swam.

He blinked up at the ceiling, unable to speak, breath caught in his throat. The scent of singed stone filled his nose.

The surrounding chamber buzzed with whispers as residual electricity flickered in faint arcs across the ground. Saulice twitched on the floor, a deep dread spinning in his core. He gnashed his teeth and tried to rise with wobbly elbows, eager to dispel the tension in the atmosphere. He did not want to be feared. Hamlen had already looked at him as a monster, but he was not that.

He only hoped Master Valos and the other Cadre would see it.

Master Valos stood frozen, lips parted. Calder had risen to his feet, hand pressed against his chest as if steadying it.

"I believe we know his affinity," Valos murmured. "Lightning."

"Such power with no control," another Cadre whispered, shaken.

Calder's voice cut through like a blade. "That was not fount forging. More like a detonation!"

"He never even forged," Valos replied, now studying Saulice with unreadable intensity. "The Source Stone responded to him, not him to it."

On the floor, Saulice groaned.

He did not feel powerful. He felt broken.

The warmth that had once stirred in his chest had collapsed into a cold void. His arms trembled and his mouth tasted of copper. Why had it not worked? He had done everything right. Survived Hamlen. Survived the bellet. Helped Melandra. So why now?

He pushed himself to his elbows. The Source Stone still sat cracked and smoking on the pedestal, its once-living light now dull and lifeless. Something sacred had been destroyed, and it was his fault.

Gasps echoed around the perimeter as the chamber doors opened. Assistants in slate uniforms rushed forward, and behind them Tibbet and Rayne arrived, panting from the hallway.

Tibbet stopped short, his eyes wide. "What in the—"

"Clear the floor!" Valos' voice boomed, one hand raised with authority.

An assistant leaned in toward Saulice. "Stand, only if you can. We need to get you to the infirmary."

Saulice did not move. He stared at the stone again, part of him still expecting it to pulse, to flicker, to forgive him.

It didn't.

Rayne approached but kept her distance, her eyes locked on Saulice. Her expression was no longer cold but weighted with caution, as though measuring him anew.

Her gaze flicked once toward Valos, narrowing slightly, before returning to Saulice. It was not mistrust, yet it carried something unsettlingly close.

"It was lightning," she said, her voice low, more to herself than to the others. "He's got lightning."

Rayne took a half step back. Her eyes lingered on the shattered pedestal, then shifted to Saulice, her jaw tightening.

Something in her stance hardened. Rigid, defensive, as if the distance between them had become more than physical.

Tibbet stepped up beside her. "But if he can't control it—"

"Then he's dangerous," Calder snapped. "And unstable. We'll need to convene the Cadre again. I will not have an Academy full of ticking fount bombs."

"Enough," Valos said, his voice ringing through the chamber. "Escort him to the infirmary."

Valos lingered in place as the others moved, his eyes tracking Saulice's every motion. The look was not concern but measurement, as if cataloging something no one else yet understood.

Two stewards moved to Saulice's side and lifted him gently by the arms. His legs buckled, muscles spasming.

He didn't cry. *Not in front of them.* Yet something inside him cracked as the Source Stone had cracked—something quieter, deeper, and unseen.

As they led him toward the exit, he heard Calder mutter, "This is why we don't admit wild cards."

And Saulice, his vision blurred with pain, answered in his mind: *I didn't ask for this.*

The world returned in fragments.

First, the sting of something cool and bitter brushing his cheek. Then the hush of a room too quiet to belong anywhere near a battlefield. Then an earthy scent, spiced and sharp, with old mint and fresh smoke.

Saulice blinked against colored bands of light dancing across the ceiling. Stained glass. An infirmary.

A ragged breath escaped him.

"Well, that's a relief," said a voice from somewhere to his left. "For a moment, I thought I would need to fetch the resurrection bell. And I am supposed to be at lunch."

A bearded man appeared in his view, robes loose, sleeves rolled, hair wild enough to house a nest. One hand held a damp cloth, the other a steaming mug of something that smelled like a burnt forest shoved into a cup.

"I'm Father Laird. I patch students up, but mostly I try to keep them from breaking in the first place. How's your head?"

Saulice tried to speak. His throat felt like scorched linen.

"Good enough," Laird decided, answering for him. "You cracked a Source Stone in half, nearly cooked half the Cadre, and even stumped Calder. Not an awful morning."

Saulice groaned and rolled onto his side, curling his arms around his chest.

"Ah, the guilt cocoon," Laird mused. "Classic response. Don't worry. We all go through it after obliterating a sacred artifact or two."

"I didn't mean to," Saulice rasped. "It just happened."

"Most things worth surviving usually do."

Laird dropped into a creaky chair beside the cot, pulled a lemon-colored blanket from a nearby basket, and tossed it over Saulice's legs like a grandmother dressing a goose.

"You got a name, son?"

"Saulice."

"Well, Saulice," Laird said, slapping his knees, "you're the most talked-about person in Brynswick. Congratulations. You've done what no one's managed in two centuries."

Saulice shut his eyes. "I didn't want this."

"No one does," Laird replied, his voice softening. "At least not the ones worth worrying about."

He leaned forward, resting his elbows on his knees. "You cracked a Source Stone with no fount forging, and no instruction. That is, as you would imagine, quite unusual. But I'm guessing you already knew that."

Saulice's silence was answer enough.

The priest stood and wandered over to a shelf lined with strange trinkets: jars of salve, loose leaves, a tiny iron sculpture of Shaddai, and, oddly enough, a wooden chicken.

"You know," Laird began, selecting a tin and bringing it back, "when I was your age, I once tried to call down rain during a drought using nothing but a prayer, a bell, and a goat. Didn't even use the fount."

"…What happened?"

"The goat got struck by lightning. No rain came. Two-day fire. It was very educational." He grinned. "Still can't grow carrots in that field."

Saulice gave a small, unwilling exhale. It was part cough, part laugh.

Laird opened the tin, dipped two fingers into a pale ointment, and gently smeared it across the burn on Saulice's hand.

He winced, struggling not to yell.

"That wrist is going to be tender for a while," Laird said. "Fount backlash likes to linger. Leaves a scar on the soul before it ever marks the skin."

"I didn't even forge," Saulice whispered. "I just wanted to know my affinity. I thought… maybe I was finally strong enough."

Laird's smile faded. "And instead, you are lying here thinking you broke the world."

"I didn't just fail," Saulice said, his voice trembling. "I broke the Source Stone and damaged the room. What if the lightning had struck someone? What does all this even mean?"

Laird pulled back the cloth and inspected the healing skin. "It means your fount isn't quiet. Lightning rarely is. It listens to no master but One."

He turned Saulice's hand gently in his own. "The Source Stone didn't reject you, Saulice. It couldn't handle you. There is a difference."

"That doesn't make it any better."

"No," Laird said, standing. "But it makes it real."

The priest walked to the window, staring out at the chapel gardens below. "You are not the first with undesired power, and you will not be the last. Most break before they bend. But the ones who learn—who truly learn how to wait and listen? Those are the ones who survive."

Saulice turned his face away, anger bleeding into his voice. "You don't know what's inside me."

"No," Laird said, "but I know what isn't. There is no malice in you. No cruelty. You didn't lash out. You leaked, and that is what untamed power does."

He returned to the bedside, sitting once more.

"Let me ask you something," he said. "When the lightning came… before it cracked the stone. What did you feel?"

Saulice hesitated. "Heat. Pressure. And then… something moving. Not with words. Just… force."

Laird's eyes narrowed. "And did it feel like it came from outside you?"

"No," Saulice breathed. "It came from… inside."

The priest nodded once. "Then you already know who it is."

Saulice's breath caught. *Lazarus.*

Laird did not flinch. "You have heard the name?"

"I have felt the name."

Silence fell, but it was not cold.

Laird reached behind him and retrieved a small carved pendant from the shelf. It bore no fount mark, just a circle with ten lines radiating outward—

The ancient symbol of Shaddai.

"There are things in this world older than the stones," he said, his voice steady now, no humor left. "Older than the Titans. And Shaddai breathed life into both. If Lazarus is your contender, if the Titan of justice stirs against your soul, then you will not tame him with status, ability, or reason."

He placed the pendant on the bedside table.

"Only Shaddai can teach you to master Lazarus. And only if you are willing to be mastered in return."

Saulice stared at the pendant.

Laird stood and stretched again, muttering something about needing tea before his knees stopped working.

"At some point, you will be ready to ask the proper questions," he said. "When that day comes, knock on the chapel door. Don't bring pride or excuses. Honesty is the only currency that leads to real change."

He paused at the door and gave a sly grin. "Also, bring something sweet. I am more helpful with honey bread in my belly."

And with that, he left, his coat flapping. He was already humming something tuneless as he vanished down the hall.

Saulice was alone again. Yet the silence no longer felt empty.

His hands ached and his eyes stung, but somewhere deep inside, a current still flickered—dangerous, wild, and unshaped.

Only Shaddai can teach you to master Lazarus.

He wasn't sure if that was comforting or terrifying. Maybe both.

Reaching out, he touched the pendant from Father Laird.

It was hot.

And growing hotter.

CHAPTER 11

STATUS & SCORN

Saulice sat hunched on the cold bench inside Brynswick's lower rotunda. The last thing he'd shattered was a window in Hamlen after his last Trial. Now he'd broken a Source Stone.

The sleeves of his worn shirt hung past his wrists, his bandaged hand throbbing beneath the cloth Father Laird had wrapped that morning. Saulice tightened the gloves he had found in the bag Dedric had packed for him. They came in handy, covering his Forsaken brand completely.

Students around him buzzed with nervous excitement. One girl twirled the tie on her bracer, and another boy bounced his leg with rhythmic anxiety, muttering names of the fount stones like a chant.

"Ruby. Emerald. Citrine."

Others whispered about the Source Stone incident.

"Someone overloaded the Source."

"There's still a scorch mark on the ceiling."

They didn't know who it had been, not for certain, but Saulice could feel eyes glancing his way all the same. He shifted, stomach churning.

Drezz sat beside him, upright and composed, his hands folded across his lap. The fallet's fur had been combed smoothly, his vest freshly cleaned. His green eyes, sharp and watchful, scanned the hall as though cataloging every face.

"You are trembling," Drezz said softly, without turning.

"I'm not scared," Saulice lied.

"You are afraid you have failed," Drezz replied. "Why lie?"

Saulice said nothing.

The thought had burrowed deep, colder than the bench and heavier than the silence in the amphitheater after the flare. What if the Cadre had already decided? They might not assign him any status at all. What then?

Perhaps they were just waiting to express their gratitude for his attendance. What if they dismissed him, just as Elder Judic had done in Hamlen's learning halls? Maybe Melandra had made a mistake bringing him. Maybe Shaddai had too.

He clenched his jaw, digging his fingernails into the edge of the seat. A crackle of static answered under his skin.

Stop, he told himself. *Do not lose control again. Not here. Not now.*

The rotunda doors opened.

Rayne stepped in first, followed by Tibbet. Rayne's eyes skimmed the crowd without expression, while Tibbet gave a lopsided grin, though even he looked unusually stiff.

"All first-years, follow me," Rayne said. "All first-year academ statuses are being finalized now. You will be called one group at a time."

She turned without waiting, and the students rose like nervous birds startled from a branch. Saulice hesitated before standing. The moment his boots hit the floor, he felt as though everyone could hear it. Their shoes were polished, their backs straight. He still smelled faintly of smoke.

As Saulice fell in line behind Drezz, a sharp voice cut through the low murmurs.

"Hope they're grouping the mutts separately," someone said from behind them.

Saulice turned. A tall boy with curled brown hair leaned against the wall, arms crossed. His bracer gleamed, trimmed in a deep crimson Saulice did not recognize. His eyes raked over Drezz, then over him.

"Didn't realize they let barnyard beasts and walking disasters into Brynswick. What a shame."

Drezz'ss brow twitched. Saulice felt heat flare in his chest but said nothing.

The boy smiled, satisfied, before he pushed off the wall and strolled away with two others. Their laughter trailed like smoke.

Drezz'ss voice came low. "That one is dangerous. He is looking for someone to step over."

Saulice nodded, fists clenched.

The walk through the east corridor was quiet. Fount banners lined the stone walls: citrine, amethyst, onyx, opal, and others, each gleaming with streaks of elemental color. The lapis banner shimmered near the end, threads of water-like light catching the sun.

He did not know what his banner would be. He did not even know if he would get one.

They arrived at an outer antechamber. Two Cadre stood posted by the double doors. Tibbet moved to speak with them while Rayne motioned for the students to sit again.

Saulice lowered himself onto another bench. The air smelled different, like wax, ink, and cool metal. His skin buzzed faintly with the same charged pressure he had felt before the stone cracked.

Rayne stood near the corner with her arms folded. She glanced at him once, only briefly.

Drezz leaned toward him. "Whatever they say," he murmured, "remember that the Source Stone responded to you."

Saulice wished that gave him comfort. But right now, it only made the silence louder.

"First ten academs," Tibbet called. "Come forward."

His name was not among them. But he knew it would be soon.

The rotunda above the Annals offered no comfort. It was only open stone, wind, and sky. Ivy clung to the tall marble columns like restless fingers, and the stone beneath the students' boots pinged with every movement.

A hush had fallen over the crowd, but it wasn't stillness. It was tension stretched tight, like the moment a storm strikes.

Saulice clenched his fists, his neck turning red from lingering gazes. He tried not to look at the other academs, but he could feel them looking at him, whispering not only about scores but about the Source Stone.

Master Valos stepped to the front, standing on an adorned platform, and unrolled a scroll, silencing the muttering chatter. His voice, when it came, was steady as stone.

"These status assignments," he said, "are determined by your performance during your affinity trials and Cadre interviews."

He did not raise his voice. He did not need to.

One by one, names were read. Students stepped forward, received their status, and stepped back, nerves turning to pride or quiet disappointment. Every time someone returned from the line, someone else shifted away from Saulice.

"Drezz of Fallenan."

The fallet marched to the podium and bowed.

"Earth forging. Status: Provisional Academ."

A ripple of murmurs broke out, not because of the status but because of what he was. A fur-haired fallet, fabled and foreign, stood on the stage, and in a city like Axbridge, foreign and furry were not welcoming concepts.

Drezz moved with measured calm, stepping across the field and bowing before Valos. Unlike other students who merely received their status, Drezz was given a bracer. Like Saulice's, his was leather, but there the similarities ended, for his had a stone slot, and Saulice's did not.

"May it serve Shaddai and the greater good," Drezz said, bowing again to Master Valos before descending back to his seat.

Some students didn't meet his eyes as he returned. One boy turned away entirely. Drezz seemed not to notice, or perhaps he did and chose silence to be his shield.

Then Valos adjusted the scroll in his hands, and the murmuring stilled like a breath before a plunge.

"Saulice Sawyer."

A single name turned every head.

Outside, the wind fell dead. The ivy stopped rustling.

Saulice walked forward, his boots too loud against the stone. His shirt, ragged and stained from weeks of travel, hung loosely around his arms. He stepped into the sunlight before the Cadre and stopped.

He thought he saw a figure watching from the balcony above. Tall. Still. Too far to recognize. Yet when he blinked, the space was empty.

Valos's gaze was both curious and wary.

"Affinity," Valos said. "Lightning forging."

The word hung like thunder before the other academs.

Some gasped. Others stepped back without meaning to.

Saulice's ears rang. He wanted to close his eyes, but he could not.

"Status—" Valos paused.

His mouth didn't falter, but his fingers tightened around the scroll.

"Probationary Academ."

The word was not loud, yet it didn't need to be.

A tremor passed through the assembly. Students turned to each other, mouths forming questions they didn't dare speak aloud.

"*Probationary?*" someone whispered.

"Like, temporary?"

"What does that mean?"

"Are they going to kick him out?"

Calder stepped forward, his robe catching in the wind. His eyes expressed boredom, but his voice was sharp and clipped.

"Probationary status is not a curse. It is a safeguard, a signal that something unidentified has gone wrong in the fount core, something that cannot be concretely explained."

"Then perhaps trust is not the goal," Therin said beside him, her tone soft but cutting. "Not all truths arrive in neat sums."

Calder turned to her, heated. "You wish to discuss this again?"

"The Source responded to him," she replied. "With force, yes, but also direction. The lightning struck the ceiling, not the crowd."

Calder scoffed. "He hasn't harmed anyone. Not *yet*."

Valos raised a hand, his authority on the Academy grounds absolute.

"This academ's status is probationary," he said, tone final. "His future will be determined when we reach a conclusion regarding specific elements of his fount core."

"Or lack thereof," Calder muttered.

Saulice's heart was pounding now. He didn't look at the crowd. He didn't want to see their expressions, whether fear, doubt, or pity. He didn't want to know which was worse.

Valos nodded toward him. "You may return."

He turned away.

As he stepped back into the rows of seats, he felt a breath escape that he didn't remember holding. His limbs dragged like lead, his chest hollow.

Probationary.

It echoed louder now, like a verdict.

Behind him, Valos read the next name, but the air had shifted. The weight had moved. Everyone felt it.

Drezz remained calm as ever. "Probationary is not failure. It's still a place in the field. A place here at Brynswick," he said.

"It's not anything," Saulice whispered. "It's not even real."

"Neither is lightning until it strikes."

He spoke the words like an old truth, but they did little to comfort Saulice.

Then something else caught his eye.

Rayne. She hadn't flinched when the word probationary struck like a verdict. She just kept watching.

When the murmurs started, she didn't look away. Now she stood still and measured, seemingly unshaken by anything. Almost curious, as if she was waiting for something.

The boy from earlier, Lucas, strutted to the front when his name was called, a cocky smile meeting any who looked his way. Lucas stopped before Master Valos.

"Affinity: Fire forging. Status: Confirmed Academ."

Lucas boasted an arrogant smirk, his eyes darting to Saulice before he returned to his seat.

A few murmurs rose in response, not at the status but at the name.

House Crawford was an old house, loyalists since the War of Unification. Their crest, a golden stag pierced by a spear, was stitched into the collar of Lucas's uniform, subtle but unmistakable.

It was the first noble house Saulice had learned of in his life, from watching royal processions pass Hamlen's main road. Even his lacking education included the inner workings of the social ladder.

Then, Valos called a girl from House Virellen, whose ancestors once served the throne as royal seers. Her violet sash shimmered faintly with three silver stars, the sigil of her line.

And when a boy from House Astrelle stepped forward, he was tall, aloof, with a bracer already polished. Saulice heard another academ whisper, "That family trains advisors. His sister runs the Council of Scales."

The names were different, but the weight was the same, each carrying power, prestige, and lines so clean they cut.

After each academ's status had been revealed, Master Valos raised a hand for silence.

"Remember, these are not final judgments," he said, his voice firm yet calm. "They are a measure of your present, not your future. At the end of this academic year, those who endure and excel will be granted their fount stones, receiving provisional licenses as argonauts. From that point forward, each of you will compete to rise to the top of Brynswick Academy."

"What you reap today is potential," Cadre Calder added. "Now show us the proof that you belong here."

Saulice recalled Father Laird's warning.

Only Shaddai can teach you to master Lazarus.

The words came back, slow and sure, as if they had waited for silence to return.

The crowd dispersed like smoke. Some students lingered on the practice field, discussing their new statuses, while others darted toward the edge of the commons, eager to relay the news inside the Academy walls.

Saulice stood still. He had received nothing, only a status that shunned him further. Worst of all, it had not come with answers.

Except perhaps it had.

Only Shaddai...

Father Laird's words stirred again like embers refusing to die. Why could he not forget the priest's warning?

The Cadre did not understand. The Source Stone had not given him answers. But Shaddai? Perhaps to Him, Saulice was still someone worth teaching.

Then why do I feel like I am already being pushed out? Saulice thought bitterly. Why does this feel more like exile than calling?

A soft breeze tugged at the hem of his shirt. He still wore the same ragged clothes he had arrived in, no symbol of belonging. Only a bandaged hand and a name half-whispered with fear.

He started walking, not toward the dorms, not toward the mess hall, but forward and away from the voices, away from Calder's sneer, away from the sound of Valos's even, distant tone.

At the edge of the sparring field, he sank down on a low stone bench. The warmth of the sun did not reach here. Trees shaded the alcove, their leaves stirring like quiet thoughts.

Temporary.

He turned the word over again in his mind. It did not mean chosen.

If he failed, he would be out.

A mistake waiting to be caught.

He gripped the edge of the bench. Part of him wanted to tear his gloves off and stare at the brand again, to see if it had faded at all or if it still sat there, dark and unyielding, a mark that had not softened no matter how much he had.

What if they send me home? What if I was never supposed to come?

Melandra had vouched for him. She had believed. But after yesterday and today, would even she be able to stop them?

His chest tightened. He thought of Dedric, of Hamlen's quiet streets and cracked lanterns. The memory of the boy who had stared into the river's glassy surface returned, afraid of what lived beneath his skin.

And he wondered if that boy would recognize who he was becoming.

He buried his face in his hands.

Footsteps clacked on stone, soft and measured.

Saulice did not look until the shadow reached his feet.

It was Rayne. She stood with arms crossed, bracer gleaming faintly in the dappled light. Her face was unreadable.

For a long moment, neither spoke.

"They think probationary means weak. But that status was given to you because they are afraid. Let them be."

He lifted his head.

"Is that supposed to make me feel better?"

"No," she replied. "It is supposed to remind you they are not the ones who decide what it means."

CHAPTER 12

ECHOES AND ERRANDS

Darkness did not end with the dream, it began there. Saulice floated in a void so thick he could not tell whether he was breathing. The air was hot, far too hot, like when heat and pressure pressed against the sky with no escape.

Then came the voice.

"You are not ready."

It echoed from everywhere, even from within him.

"You act like a mewling babe. Without knowing the cost, you reach. You summon what you cannot cage."

The void fractured into flame. He stood now, barefoot and bleeding, his bandages gone, his *Forsaken* brand exposed for all to see. Lightning arced in slow curves around his fingers, untamed and unending.

Panic seized him.

Across from him stood the Titan who had visited his dreams many times over the past weeks, stormlight and memory cloaking him.

It was Lazarus.

Shifting sparks veiled his face, his eyes flickering like twin storms.

"You think your will can bind me?" Lazarus asked, stepping closer. "You cannot even hold yourself together."

Saulice could neither speak nor breathe.

"You carry the seal, boy. Your breath is my leash. But as I said before, even leashes fray."

A tremor shivered through the air, and Saulice collapsed to one knee.

"Leave me alone," he rasped. "I am not your enemy."

Lazarus bent toward him, not cruel but vast.

"Then why do you keep calling on my power?"

The light snapped.

Saulice jolted awake, breath catching in his throat. The dream had been sharper than usual, flashes of fire, thunder, and Lazarus's voice whispering from within bone and smoke. He sat up in his bunk, heart hammering. Morning light filtered through the dormitory window, too high and too bright.

Which meant he was late.

A pang of soreness spread through his ribs as he slid from bed, evidence of the last two evening runs. Both days they had marched around the city's lower battlements at the fifth bell, Cadre Pell leading their training.

He had called it conditioning and driven the first years like pack animals, barking that no fount could be trusted in a body grown soft. Each run had ended with collapsed academs, blistered feet, and Pell's cold reminder that strength was the price of survival.

Scrambling to get ready, Saulice threw on the nearest clean clothes, not bothering to check for holes.

"You were whispering," Drezz said.

"I did not mean to."

"You said that Titan's name again. Lazarus."

Saulice rubbed his bandaged hand, nearly healed now, though it throbbed faintly. "It was not like before. He was… angry."

"He seems always to be angry."

"No," Saulice said, his voice hoarse. "This was different. It felt as though he was afraid."

Drezz rose and padded to the washbasin, pouring a ladle of cold water before handing it over. "You cannot walk both roads for much longer. Either you master the fount, or it masters you."

"I do not even have a fount stone," Saulice muttered.

"You do not need a stone to practice stillness."

Saulice accepted the water but did not drink.

Outside, the first morning bell tolled.

By the time they left the dorm, students were already gathering in columns across the practice fields. Sunlight filtered through clouds above Brynswick's southern towers, gilding the edges of spires and casting long shadows across the lawn.

Drezz walked with his arms clasped behind his back, upright and dignified, while Saulice felt like an old stain dragging through a sea of blue and gold. They stepped out into the mist-hazed light together.

"I thought Tibbet said they were done escorting us," Saulice muttered as they turned the corner toward the plaza.

Drezz made a soft sound, almost a chuckle. "You noticed the way half the school stared at you yesterday, did you not?"

"Hey, you know what?" Saulice said, stopping and noticing something. "Your speech has gotten a lot better. That's great!"

A shy smile spread across Drezz's face. He scratched his neck sheepishly. "I *have* been trying harder to adopt the human dialect."

Ahead, Rayne and Tibbet waited by the garden archway. Rayne stood as still as stone while Tibbet leaned against a pillar, tossing a red apple between his hands.

As Saulice and Drezz approached, Tibbet flicked the apple once more, caught it without looking, and grinned.

"You two ready for your exciting errand day?" he said. "We're headed to the outer market."

"Didn't you say you were finished escorting us?" Saulice asked, crossing his arms.

"I did," Tibbet replied. "And I meant it. Then the Cadre did what they love to, changing their instructions."

Rayne added, "They don't like to let dangerous academs who shatter ancient relics wander unsupervised."

Tibbet grimaced. "Ouch. There is such a thing as *too* soon."

Saulice flushed. "So… what? We're still being watched?"

Rayne did not deny it. "Your arrival at Brynswick with Drezz wasn't through normal channels. You weren't recommended by any of the Great Houses, and the only rumor floating around is that some high ranking argonaut from Furies Fist dropped you off. You're both oddities, and the other academs don't like those. It may suck, but those are the cards you have to play with."

Tibbet took a bite of the apple. "In other words, you two shook the bag a bit more than the Academy likes."

"But I didn't—" Saulice started.

"But you did," Rayne cut in, eyes flicking toward him. "Maybe not with words. But the moment you cracked the Source Stone, you asked. For attention, consequence, and most of all expectation."

Saulice fell silent.

Rayne nodded toward the steps. "Let's go. It's a short walk."

The group crossed the main plaza, weaving through paths of moving students. Most carried books or staff scrolls. Some eyed Saulice's bracer, though he kept his brand covered, unwilling to stop wearing the gloves Dedric had given him. A few pointed at Drezz in passing, then whispered once they thought they were out of earshot.

The architecture shifted as they moved from Brynswick proper into the broader city. Older stone buildings lined the streets, and towering banners waved from rooftops, displaying the royal gold and blue of Candur.

With every step outside the campus walls, Saulice's tension rose. It felt as though unseen eyes burned a hole in his neck, not from Rayne or Tibbet, but from the city itself.

At one point, they passed a group of younger school students, no older than ten, guided through the gates by a robed instructor. One boy stared openly at Saulice's bandaged hand.

"Is that the one?" the boy whispered. "The *Forsaken*?"

Saulice stiffened, checking his gloves. How could they have known? Had word travelled from Hamlen so quickly? Was Corfrick's anger so insatiable that he would poison the rest of Candur with his ignorance?

Rayne twisted her head.

"Mind your tongue," she told the boy, voice cool as glass.

The instructor gave the student a withering glance before ushering the group on.

Drezz moved closer, murmuring, "The younger ones parrot what they hear. What they're told."

"I didn't respond," Saulice muttered.

Rayne offered no answer.

Tibbet whistled low. "Word travels fast. Just hope your reputation doesn't grow faster than you can."

The Axbridge market rolled out beneath the eastern sky, alive with morning business. Crowds pressed shoulder to shoulder as vendors shouted over one another from beneath colorful canvas awnings. Wooden carts overflowed with silver-threaded cloaks, bundles of rare roots, polished bone flutes, and stitched leather scroll-bags..

Saulice kept his hood low. Every few paces he caught mutters or sidelong glances at the blank leather bracer buckled around his wrist and the filthy clothes he had worn for what felt like an eternity.

"They're staring," he muttered.

"Let them," Drezz replied, walking calmly beside him. "Staring is safer than chasing."

Those words gave Saulice little comfort.

Rayne and Tibbet led the way, slipping through knots of people with practiced ease, as though they had done this a hundred times. Which, Saulice supposed, they probably had.

Tibbet paused at a vendor stand of metal combs and pipes. "Azure's Apparatus is just ahead. Don't get distracted by every enchantment booth you pass."

"We won't," Drezz said. Yet his eyes lingered on a stall hung with polished fount fragments embedded in glass. "There is a strange beauty in broken things."

Saulice said nothing.

They passed a girl selling tiny vials of silver powder.

"Shard Dust," she chirped. "For focus or display!"

Drezz frowned. "They sell fragments of failure?"

"Candur wastes nothing," Rayne muttered.

Saulice stiffened. He did not know why the words struck so hard, but they did. Perhaps it hurt because it sounded true, because deep down he feared he might become a display piece himself.

A few more turns brought them to *Azure's Apparatus*, a deep-bellied brick shop with copper pipes running up its sides and steam hissing faintly from vents. A sign hung above the door, shaped like an open palm with each finger tipped in a different stone color.

Inside, the air smelled of oil, metal, and ozone. Tools lined every wall: chisels for tuning fount stones, gloves that resisted fire, reinforced armor, and padded robes laced with fount-tracing thread meant to aid argonauts in their forging.

Behind the counter stood a lean man with thick goggles, turning a tuning fork over in his hand.

"Academy issue?" he asked, squinting at the students.

"Yes," Rayne replied. "We're collecting two base kits. One earthen, one… provisional."

The man's brow ticked upward. "Name?"

"Drezz and Saulice. Put it on the Academy's tab."

A few quick notations and he disappeared through a rear curtain.

While they waited, Tibbet leaned near a cabinet of specially threaded rings. "Used one of these once," he said. "Let me shoot blades of air. Made me feel invincible until I cut my sleeve off."

Saulice almost laughed.

The shopkeeper returned, placing two worn leather packs on the counter. "Standard fare. Compression gloves for Combatives Training, grip chalk for their Fount Principiums, and a bundle of blank slates to record notes. Anything else?"

"Unfortunately, that will be all," Tibbet said.

"Appreciation," Drezz added with a slight bow.

Saulice nudged him, suppressing a grin. "He means thank you."

The clothing shop was quieter, though not by much. Students and citizens moved in and out, clutching tailored robes and house-colored sashes. Most were already mid-fitting. A young woman with chalk on her hands waved them in.

Rayne handed over the parchment with their measurements and school tags. "They'll need two formal tunics and three dailies each. We'll wait outside."

The tailor glanced over both of them before huffing and disappearing behind a beige curtain. She returned a moment later, lips pressed tight.

"I'm sorry, but you're out of luck. We just ran out of uniforms for the academy an hour ago. Most students, as you can imagine, put their orders in long ago."

"So what does that mean?" Rayne asked, her tone edged with irritation.

"We can fit them both, but it will be a week before we can have their uniforms delivered."

Rayne clenched and unclenched her fists before giving a tight nod. "Very well then. I'll have to inform the Cadre, but I understand."

Saulice wondered how often she was told no. She gave him a brief look, then left them to get fitted.

Inside the fitting room, the tailor, a man with a spindle-thin frame and a jeweled monocle, took one look at Saulice's shoulders and sighed. "Standard cut won't do. Too little lean muscle. Training any?"

"Just started," Saulice said. "I'm surviving."

Drezz chuckled.

It took the better part of an hour, and by the end Saulice could have cried from the sore ache in his limbs. The tailor had made him stand in all sorts of poses to ensure proper measurements.

"You look less like a walking storm cloud," Tibbet jested.

Saulice only groaned.

On their way back through the fountain square, a familiar unease crept up Saulice's spine. A man near the edge of the crowd, older and dressed in faded guard armor, stared at him—more precisely at his exposed hand.

"You one of them?" the man asked.

Saulice hesitated. "One of who?"

"The *Forsaken*. You've the brand."

Tibbet stepped forward, placing himself between the man and Saulice.

"Keep walking, pal."

Saulice looked down in a panic, cursing himself. In his rush, he must have forgotten the thin brown gloves Dedric had packed for him, the ones meant to hide what the bracer could not—the brand from his Trial. Without thinking, he slid on the compression gloves from Azure's Apparatus. They fit perfectly, snugger than he was used to but secure.

For all Tibbet's attempts, the man hadn't moved.

"My nephew because of the Trial last spring. He was branded and cast out. Now he's gone! And you're telling me this *runt* gets to wear a bracer?"

Rayne's voice was bitter. "He earned his place."

The man scoffed. "Slim chance of that. *Forsaken* can't fount forge."

Drezz shifted, placing himself slightly in front of Saulice.

But Saulice's body was already humming, the static shimmer crawling across his skin. Anger rose quickly, tightening inside him like a storm about to break. He fought hard to keep it lidded.

Rayne caught it. "Saulice. Breathe."

He exhaled the breath he had been holding, and the tension stopped.

The man finally walked on, but Saulice lingered a moment longer, feeling as though he were back in Hamlen.

The walk back to Brynswick passed without trouble, though silence followed them like a second shadow.

The air had cooled since morning, touched by chimney smoke and damp ivy. Students still milled about the campus lawns, some locked in combat drills, others bent over scrollwork beneath the rotundas. As the academy loomed closer, laughter and routine filled the grounds, but to Saulice they felt distant.

The moment in the square replayed in his mind, the voice of the man echoing with that single word he despised most: *Forsaken.*

He touched the leather bracer strapped across his forearm. Though Rayne had said it made him look like a student, it did not feel like proof. Not when he and Drezz were the only academs without iron bracers.

Drezz walked beside him, quiet but steady, the faintest hum in his throat like a grounding note. Tibbet led loosely through the gates, while Rayne kept glancing over her shoulder more than usual.

None of them spoke until they reached the lower steps of Dorm Crescent.

Then Tibbet stopped and swung around.

"Well," he said, breaking the quiet like a pebble tossed into a still pond, "at least we didn't get chased, cursed, or struck by lightning. And give it a day."

Saulice blinked. "That's your bar for success?"

"Absolutely," Tibbet replied. "You've met this city, right? It's a beast in silk. That we got uniforms, gear, and a not terrible tailor experience? That's a holiday."

Saulice cracked a faint smile. Drezz let out a low, thoughtful chuckle.

Rayne stepped past them, but paused halfway up the steps. "You handled it well."

There was no teasing in her tone, no measured coldness, just a quiet acknowledgment that Saulice didn't know how to react to.

"I know what it feels like," she added, "to have people think you shouldn't be here."

"You?" Saulice asked, genuinely surprised.

She didn't answer right away. Her hand tightened slightly on the strap of her satchel before she turned back toward the steps.

"Don't be late to drill at the fifth bell."

And just like that, she disappeared toward the second-year dorms.

Tibbet raised a brow. "Well. That's practically affection."

Drezz said nothing, though Saulice noticed the corner of his mouth tilt upward.

Inside Dorm Crescent, the halls were quieter than usual, most students already off to lectures or drills. Afternoon light slanted through the upper windows in golden bars.

Their room smelled of new cloth and travel oil. Two clean tunics rested on each bed, courtesy of Tibbet's insistence that they buy at least a couple of outfits to distinguish them from beggars. Drezz set his bag down carefully, straightening the corner of his blanket with ceremonial precision.

Saulice flopped onto his cot without a word.

Outside, the bells marked the second-to-last hour. He groaned, dreading more pushups or sprints.

Light shifted on the dorm windows, casting the room in warm tones. For the first time in weeks, Saulice felt something unfamiliar. It was not safety, but something smaller.

It was possibility.

He looked at Drezz and smirked. "We didn't die."

"Not yet," Drezz agreed. "But we lived a little."

Saulice leaned back and closed his eyes. He was still the boy from Hamlen. Still the *Forsaken*. Still the *Harbinger*. How he would live with both titles, he had no clue.

But for now, he was also just… Saulice.

And that, maybe, was enough.

CHAPTER 13

FIRST IMPRESSIONS
AND QUIET WARS

The cafeteria ceiling stretched higher than any room Saulice had ever seen, a stone-vaulted expanse painted with an elaborate mural of Candurian beasts locked in eternal chase. Gold-tipped chandeliers hung low, casting a warm light on polished floors and long rows of tables carved from dark sycamore.

The brightness did little to ease the tension hanging in the air.

Saulice stepped through the archway beside Drezz, the clamor of students dulling to a hum beneath his unease. Everything about Brynswick's dining hall seemed designed to remind him where he didn't belong: the polished uniforms and the easy laughter, the way some students wore their iron bracers like polished crowns.

Trailing a step behind Drezz as they approached the serving line, he noted how the fallet's height still drew attention, though most students had learned not to gawk for long. A few hushed whispers followed them, and Saulice caught flashes of robes and insignias he didn't yet recognize, noble crests and family banners woven into their sleeves.

One banner gleamed with a golden stag pierced by a spear: House Crawford.

His mouth soured. He had seen that sigil before above the Hamlen barracks when a royal envoy passed through, and even then, it had felt like a warning.

Nearby, another banner showed three silver stars burning against a violet field: House Virellen. The house was of old blood, a name that merchants spoke with reverence, as if it belonged to a vanished pantheon.

The last was harder to miss: a black sun rising over white marble, stitched into the collar of a sharp-faced girl flanked by silent attendants—House Astrelle. He remembered seeing her alone during the fount test, unmoved, as though she had already decided what mattered.

He did not know what the house stood for, but he knew what it boasted. Power and inheritance, status worn like armor rather than earned.

Mrs. Velma greeted them at the front with a smile that barely reached her eyes.

"Morning, boys," she said, sliding two plates of stewed grains and crimson root across the counter. "Eat well. You've got a long day ahead. The Cadre don't go easy on the first years."

"Thank you, ma'am," Drezz replied, as polite as ever. But his eyes lingered past her hand to the other line across the hall.

There, a separate server ladled glossy orange fruit over thick cuts of roasted fowl. Trays gleamed beneath silver cutlery. Nobles in deep blue sashes and gold-threaded cuffs filled the benches at the front of the hall, their laughter loud and careless. A stack of white bread slices sat beside a bowl of cinnamon-coated nuts. A server uncorked a crystal bottle and poured juice into clear glasses with a practiced turn of the wrist.

Drezz glanced back at their tray: plain iron utensils, clumpy grain that looked like glue, root stewed until it bled color into the bowl.

He made no comment, but his ears twitched once, low and sharp.

Saulice didn't notice. He only clutched his tray like a shield and nodded.

"I overheard a few second years speaking of the combative exams. It seems they are our clearest opportunity to prove ourselves. It sounded like they test the upper years near summer's end," Drezz said calmly.

Saulice harrumphed. "So, we're the warm-up act? There to watch us break before the real fighters take the stage? It makes sense, I guess. We are the first years."

They crossed the floor and found a small table near the rear, away from the largest crowds. Saulice sat with his back to the wall, angling his tray so no one could see how little he touched his food.

As silence cloaked their mealtime, a voice rang out behind them.

"Mind if I sit?"

They turned.

A boy with dark curls and a crooked smile stood there, tray in hand. His posture was relaxed, eyes flicking between them like he'd already decided they were worth knowing. He wore the standard uniform, but he had undone his collar and pushed up his sleeves.

"Name's Damian. I've seen you two around. Thought I'd introduce myself at least."

Saulice hesitated, but Drezz gestured to the empty seat. "You are more than welcome to join us."

Damian sat, dropping his tray with a clatter. "Thanks. No offense, but everyone else is whispering or trying hard not to stare. I figured I'd just be direct."

Saulice blinked. "About *what*?"

"You shattered a Source Stone, man," Damian said, as if discussing the weather. "That sort of thing spreads fast."

"It was a unique event," Drezz added.

"Cracked it right in half, didn't he?" Damian grinned, then turned serious as his eyes fell on Saulice's arm. "That being said, the real reason you're getting unwanted attention, and I mean unwanted, based on the look you're giving me, is that few first years walk in with a leather bracer. It's not happened in decades, according to some of the Cadre."

Saulice looked down at his wrist. The leather band, devoid of color or sigil, grew heavy.

Damian leaned back, choosing to change pace. "So, listen. What do you know about the annual combative exams?"

Saulice exchanged a glance with Drezz. "Not much?"

"Expected that," Damian replied with a shrug. "The annual combative exams are a tool meant to encourage growth. Competing against friends… or rivals. That sort of thing."

"Do you speak from experience?" Drezz asked.

Damian chuckled. "Let's say I've had older siblings pass through Brynswick. They left notes. Also, I'm in your Candurian History class. And Fount Principiums, I think. Guess we'll be seeing each other a fair bit."

Saulice let the words settle.

Damian speared a chunk of root with his fork. "Anyway, just figured I'd offer my aid before the vultures circle. This place runs on quiet wars. Better to know who's on your side early."

The rest of their meal passed quickly, Damian leaving before them.

When they reached the learning halls, Saulice's nerves thickened. He double-checked the course list tucked into his satchel and read the etched plaque above the door: *Candurian History.* Drezz gave a slight nod and led the way inside.

The room stretched wide, with tiered seating rising in steps along the walls like a miniature amphitheater. People had already filled most of the seats. Dozens of eyes turned their way at once, tracking Saulice and Drezz like hawks spotting prey. Every stare pierced like a needle.

Before they could sit, a voice cracked across the room.

"Well, look at this. All but two in uniform today."

Saulice froze. He knew that voice.

Cadre Calder stood at the front, arms crossed, a faint smirk tightening his face. "What is your excuse, academs?"

Blood rushed to Saulice's ears. He stepped forward, heart pounding. "Sir, we couldn't buy our uniforms in time—"

"It is Cadre or Master," Calder cut in, his voice booming like a hammer against stone. "And academs hold eye contact when addressing their superiors."

Saulice forced his chin up. His eyes locked on Calder's with a steadiness he barely felt. "Cadre Calder. We arrived later than the other academs and only ordered our uniforms yesterday."

Calder regarded him a moment, then gave a curt nod. "Very well. Take your seats and let us begin."

A few students in the row ahead leaned toward one another, heads bent and voices low.

"That's him… he's the one with the *Forsaken* brand," someone whispered.

A familiar voice snorted behind him. "The mutt flunked the entry trials."

Saulice stiffened but kept his gaze forward as he and Drezz slid into their seats.

The Master strode to the chalkboard. In quick, sweeping strokes, he scrawled *Gregory Calder* across it and circled the word *Master* with crisp emphasis.

"With the matter of titles settled," he said, voice taut with dry courtesy, "let me introduce myself formally. Former Sentinel Gregory Calder of Division Spearhead, Fury's Fist."

He let the words hang like a challenge.

"I've fought many battles, trained more argonauts than most of you have lived years. And you all," he gestured across the room, "are nothing more than children."

A rustle of whispers followed, academs awed by a prior member of the Fist.

Calder's eyes swept the room. "If you pass all four years at this Academy, then… and only then, you will earn the title of argonaut. This is your crucible. Fail, and you will have squandered the opportunity of a lifetime."

He turned back to the chalkboard and began drawing a map in jagged, fast motions. Saulice recognized the curved coastline of Candur as Calder outlined borders and traced the Shattered Pass, the only dirigible path by land out of their realm.

The room buzzed with tension. Candurian History, though barely begun, already felt heavier than any course Saulice had ever endured. Master Calder prowled the front row like a lion, eyes sharp.

"Raise your hand if you can name the five primary battles of the Timfathen."

One hand shot up. Damian.

Calder's eyes locked on him. He nodded.

"There were several, though the Timfathen was originally part of Candur's territory. The Pitch, the Fall of Oxten Valley, the Siege of Ironwell, the Silent Crossings, and the last was…" Damian hesitated, glancing at the ceiling as if trying to catch the memory. "The Blinding of Grannor."

"Correct," Calder said, offering no praise. His voice stayed flat, without warmth. "Most forget the Blinding. It was a grim night. It marked the beginning of a dark practice, the creation of the lichtaurs near the war's end."

A hush fell over the room.

"The Timfathen is now but a no-man's-land surrounding Candur's northern and western borders, a massive grave born of battles long past."

A fair-skinned female academ in the front row raised her hand. "Cadre, will we ever reclaim the Timfathen as a Candurian territory?"

He set the chalk down and turned slowly toward the class, his voice cooling.

"That is not an easy question. During the Thousand Year War, Veartaya's forging did more than scar the Timfathen. It altered it. Her presence seeped into stone, rivers, even roots. Other battlefields have healed in time. This one has not."

He paced, displeasure edging his tone.

"You must understand something. Veartaya hated humanity more than she despised the other four races of Myre. She nearly erased us from existence within that forest, and she left her mark with every strike she made. Repeated exposure to her corrupted fount did not merely devastate the land. It poisoned it."

Calder returned to the board, beginning a diagram of dates. His voice lowered. "No one knows how long such damage takes to fade… or if it ever will."

Saulice shifted in his seat and raised his hand.

Calder didn't look. "Speak, Sawyer."

Saulice hesitated. "Cadre… what are lichtaurs?"

A sharp voice carried from the front row, smooth with disdain. "You going to fight one, *Forsaken*?"

Laughter stirred across the benches.

Saulice turned just in time to see Lucas Crawford leaning back in his seat, a smirk creasing his face. His curled brown hair caught the light, green eyes gleaming with satisfaction.

Drezz spoke before Saulice could. "He'd stand a better chance than you."

Lucas rose slowly, deliberate in every motion. "What was that?"

"Enough," Cadre Calder barked, slamming his cane against the front desk.

Lucas didn't sit.

Calder's eyes narrowed, hard as stone. "I don't care whose house you descend from, Crawford. In this room, your name earns nothing. Discipline does. Speak out of turn again and I'll send you to the stables.

Practice your heroics with horse dung while your classmates study history like proper argonauts in training."

Lucas held Drezz's gaze another second, then dropped into his seat.

Calder turned to Drezz. "And you, fallet. Keep your commentary as measured as your posture. This is a classroom, not a battlefield."

Saulice bit his tongue, forcing himself not to speak. He felt Damian's shoulder nudge his steady and grounding. A silent reminder to breathe.

Drezz inclined his head. "Yes, Cadre. Forgive my outburst."

"And *Sawyer*," Calder said, turning toward him again. "I commend the question. Yet a trip to the Annals could have saved the class some time."

Saulice's jaw tightened, but he nodded.

Damian let out a breath- half scoff, half admiration.

Calder returned to the chalkboard, outlining key dates, war fronts, and the events that shaped the fractured realm of Candur. His hand moved with precision, each stroke of chalk converting blood and conquest into clean lines.

The tension didn't leave. It settled beneath the benches like a storm preparing to return.

Saulice lowered his gaze, then let it drift to the front wall, where Master Calder continued sketching a rough map of Candur. Most students had resumed taking notes. A few whispered behind hands, their earlier amusement already filed away as just another oddity in a school built on unusual things.

Drezz exhaled, slow and measured. But the tightness in his brow remained.

Calder tapped the chalk against the tray with a crisp click.

"Candur's unification under Lector the Lion, the last known Harbinger, marked the end of the Thousand Year War," he said. "He merged five broken territories and forged a single kingdom before falling in the last battle against Veartaya and the Order of Invictus."

He turned back to the board and scrawled the dates across the upper corner.

"Next week's assignment," he continued, "will be a comparative analysis of Candur's alliances during the Thousand Year War. I expect your perspective, not just your memory. Memorization is for parrots."

The second bell rang out, reverberating through the stonework like a heartbeat. Chairs scraped and students stood. Calder gave no parting words, only waved the chalk like a sword while turning back to his notes.

Damian rose with them, stretching his arms in an exaggerated yawn. "First class down. Didn't fall asleep. Proud of myself."

Saulice cracked a faint smile. "You almost did."

"Almost," Damian said, grinning. "But I can sleep through the next one. History is important. Fount theory, though? Wake me up when something explodes."

Drezz gave a slight nod. "The theory explains the explosion."

Damian blinked. "That's why I'm not qualified to teach it."

They moved through the corridor together, the weight of Calder's classroom still clinging to their shoulders like a heavy cloak. Students passed in clusters, some glancing back, others whispering as they walked.

Saulice's gaze flicked to Lucas. The noble boy stood near the archway, arms crossed, still scowling in their direction. But this time, Saulice didn't look away. He had a friend now. Possibly two. And for the first time since entering the Academy, something other than fear pressed on his ribs. For the first time, belonging didn't seem like a distant dream. It felt near.

Drezz blinked, then stood slowly. But this time, he didn't brush off his tunic or lower his gaze. His shoulders stayed tight, jaw clenched.

"He laughed at you," Drezz said, an unusual edge lining his voice. "Mocked you. Mocked what happened back there."

Saulice hesitated. "It's just words—"

"No," Drezz cut in. "Words shape thought. Thought shapes action. And that boy, Lucas? He thinks he's better. Thinks pain is weakness. He's never seen what it means to bleed for someone."

The anger in Drezz's voice wasn't loud, but it was taut, coiled like a bowstring, ready to snap. For the first time since they'd met, Saulice saw the calm behind Drezz's eyes shift. What remained wasn't violence. It was forged.

And that stunned Saulice. Drezz never got angry. Even when ambushed on the road, Drezz remained calm. Not when the black bellet struck. And now, over a classroom insult, he looked ready to snap chalk with his bare hands.

Saulice swallowed a lump in his throat. It was a rare day that someone would grow riled in his defense. His whole life, Saulice had stood alone in rooms like this one, mocked and marked without worth. But now there was Drezz. Strange, serious, wise Drezz, who had burned with fury because someone had tried to shame him.

It didn't matter that Drezz was of a race no one at Brynswick had ever seen. He understood Saulice.

A breath slipped from Saulice's lungs, slow and deep. For the first time since stepping through Brynswick's gates, he wasn't entirely alone.

The bell had scarcely stopped ringing when Cadre Calder's voice cut through the clamor of scraping chairs.

"Sawyer. With me."

Saulice stiffened. Drezz turned toward him, but Calder's stare pinned them both in place.

"Just him," Calder said. "Now."

No explanation followed. Calder pivoted and strode toward the side hall. Saulice hurried to catch up, questions crawling at the back of his throat. None made it past his lips.

They climbed two shallow flights and passed into corridors Saulice had only seen once before, on the day he first arrived at Brynswick with Melandra. The memory came in fragments: polished stone floors, banners from every province lining the walls, his reflection caught in tall windowpanes. Even then, the Masters' Halls had felt colder than the rest of the Academy. Now, walking them alone with Calder, they felt colder still.

The further they went, the less the Academy sounded alive. No chatter from students. No clang of sparring steel. Only the muted hum of wind threading through high arches. Past the outer classrooms. Beyond the quiet grove where second years studied under glass canopies. A left turn, then a right. The deeper they went, the narrower the hall became. Rows of closed doors lined each side, modest offices with small nameplates and sigils carved above their frames. These belonged to Cadres and lesser masters, their thresholds unadorned.

At the far end stood a single larger door, taller and broader than the rest. Silver filigree traced the ten-pointed star of Brynswick across its panels. The surrounding stonework was heavier, deliberate, as if marking where authority deepened. Saulice remembered seeing it before but had never crossed its threshold.

Calder rapped once and entered without waiting for a reply.

The office mirrored the memory that would later etch into Saulice's mind. A tall desk of varnished oak stood beneath the far window. A modest hearth burned low along the inner wall, its light falling across shelves of carefully stacked parchment and bound ledgers. A single bear's pelt softened the stone floor beneath Saulice's boots. The room was not grand, yet every detail spoke of quiet precision and weight.

Behind the desk stood Master Valos. His robes were darker than indigo, so deep they read black in the filtered light, trimmed in silver and marked by the ten-pointed star. The color seemed to draw the firelight inward rather than reflect it.

"Cadre Calder," Valos said evenly. "Leave us."

Calder stepped close instead, leaning toward Valos's ear. His words came low, barely audible, though Saulice caught fragments: Lucas, insult, fallet. Valos's expression did not shift. He nodded once.

"You may go."

Calder bowed once and stepped out, closing the door behind him.

"Saulice Sawyer." Valos's voice was calm, measured. It carried weight without volume. "Do you know why I called you here?"

Saulice hesitated.

"No, Master."

Valos reached into a drawer and withdrew a sealed parchment, already torn open. His gaze flicked across its contents before lifting to Saulice.

"You shattered a Source Stone."

The words struck heavier than Saulice expected. He opened his mouth, but Valos raised a hand to still him.

"Do you have any idea what such an artifact costs? Years of refinement. Hours of forging. Now but a relic on display, broken by ignorance."

"I didn't mean—"

"I know." Valos's tone cut through the protest without harshness. "Which is why you stand here rather than in exile beyond these walls."

He set the parchment down. "That incident confirmed what some already suspected. You are not ordinary. Your condition, your core, is unlike any cadet we have ever seen. Unstable. Untamed. That instability is why you were admitted only on probationary status."

Saulice froze. The word settled heavier than the stone halls themselves.

"You will not be treated as confirmed," Valos continued. "Not yet. Every step you take, every forging you attempt, is measured against whether you can control yourself and your damaged fount core. If you wish to earn your status as a confirmed academ, you must prove more than talent. You must prove discipline."

Saulice clenched his fists at his sides. He did not like the way Valos said condition, as though he were something to be managed rather than taught.

"I know you are a Harbinger," Valos continued. "I know what lies within you. But Brynswick's first loyalty is to Candur. Should the choice arise, the realm will always come before the boy."

Saulice's stomach knotted.

"Then why admit me at all?"

"Because even unstable power can be shaped," Valos said. "Because hope remains, however slim. And because Shaddai almost always works in ways beyond our grasp."

His gaze sharpened.

"But belief does not blind us to reality. And the reality is this: the Great Houses must not be trifled with. Their wealth and influence supply the lifeblood of Candur's cities. Their fleets guard our coasts. Their fount stones feed our forges. Without their support, these halls would not be standing."

Valos stepped closer, voice lowering but hardening.

"Do you think Brynswick can afford to let a first-year academ, an oddity with an unstable core, jeopardize that relationship?"

Saulice swallowed.

"No, Master."

"Good," Valos said. "Then hear me clearly. You are on probationary status. If you wish to rise beyond it, if you want this Academy to view you as one of its own, you must prove you are capable of thinking and acting beyond yourself. You will tread carefully here. You will not provoke Lucas Crawford or any of the other Houses. Do you understand?"

"Yes, Master."

"Good. Now prove it."

Valos studied him for a moment longer, then gestured toward the door. "I do not mean to be harsh, but we have high standards here. Tell no one of this conversation. You are dismissed."

CHAPTER 14

THE RHYTHM OF PAIN

The stave cracked across Saulice's shoulder before he could brace. A white-hot jolt of pain shot down his arm, sharp enough to buckle his stance. He dropped to one knee, breath torn from his chest like a sack ripped open. Grit scraped his palms. His knees burned from the fall.

"Eight-nil," Cadre Pell shouted as Drezz lowered his staff over Saulice.

The words stung more than the strike. Eight-nil. As if the number mattered more than the bruise spreading under his sleeve.

Around them, the noise of other sparring matches faded. The rhythmic beat of staff on staff, the dull thuds of wood against practice armor, all slowed to a lull. A group watched from outside the dueling rings. Loose, but intentional. Whispers flared behind half-lifted palms. It didn't matter, Saulice didn't need to hear them.

He could *feel* them.

Contempt wrapped within curiosity.

The grey and blue Brynswick training uniform clung tight across his shoulders, fitted for mobility but offering little comfort against the stone.

Master Pell's boots struck the stone like hammer blows as he stepped forward. His shadow cut a hard line across the ground, just outside each pair's match ring.

"Again," he said.

No question. Nobody checked for injuries. There was no hesitation.

Saulice rose, teeth clenched as pain stretched across his ribs. Each breath dragged heat into his lungs, but it wasn't the pain that burned deepest.

It was the humiliation. Master Valos' words two days prior etched in his mind, never failing to disrupt his focus. He couldn't stop thinking about his warning.

He hadn't done anything, and already, fingers were being pointed at him. So, the Academy was no different from Hamlen after all.

That wasn't all that bothered him. Saulice had realized a significant detail in his first four days of classes. He was behind, in every topic.

And right now, he was behind again, being beaten with a staff.

But he wasn't angry because he was losing. It was how he was losing, measured like a flawed equation. Every strike wasn't just a blow; it was evidence, a confirmation of what they already believed.

He wasn't falling short. He was proving them right.

Drezz waited, his staff balanced across both arms. Even after half a week of bruises and Brynswick's brutish evening drills, he stood calmly, composed. His fur stuck to his neck, damp with sweat, but his breathing remained even. His eyes gave away nothing.

Something Saulice had learned to respect, and hate.

Nearby, the other students practiced their forms. One group ran high parries in mirrored pairs. Another rehearsed full-body sweeps in coordinated silence. The field echoed with strikes and exhalations, but all of it seemed to drift away from the space around Saulice. Even their drills gave him room to fail.

Cadre Pell paced between students, never still, never absent. He gave no praise, only sharp corrections, his voice cutting like shears. He called out missed blocks or poor balance, but never to Saulice. For him, there were only commands.

Reset. Again. Reset. Again.

The rounds went on and on.

Saulice rolled his shoulder, hiding a wince. He tightened his grip on the staff and readjusted his stance for what felt like the hundredth time. Maybe it was.

Drezz gave a slight nod, barely visible on the other side of the dueling ring.

Not kindness.

Just readiness.

They began again.

Saulice lunged first, a low feint. Drezz caught it without strain. The staff glided across his guard like it belonged there. Saulice twisted his hips and pushed more with urgency than control, sweeping upward.

He connected, a glancing blow striking Drezz's shoulder.

The surrounding ring stirred as a ripple of breath moved through the onlookers, murmurs following in its wake. Nothing rose to a shout, but the subtle change in the air was enough to shift Saulice's pulse.

Drezz stepped back a pace, his stance tightening. It was less training now and more testing, as though he sought to advance past his own barriers.

Then he rushed forward with startling speed. He pivoted with practiced precision, landing a quick jab against Saulice's ribs, clean and fluid, before following with a backward flick that caught Saulice's leg as he twisted away.

Pain shot through Saulice's thigh and forced him to the ground again.

"Eight-one," Pell called, his voice flat.

Saulice's cheeks flushed as he climbed to his feet, moving before Pell could issue the command. He had hit him. He had landed a strike. It did not matter what the score was, nor that the outcome had not changed. What mattered was that it had been real, not a mistake or a fluke, for he had seen a gap and reached for it.

His hands throbbed from gripping the staff too tightly and his knees trembled beneath him, yet something stirred underneath the hurt. It was not victory, and it was not vindication. It was not pride, not yet.

It was possibility.

"Final round," Pell called. "Make it count."

Saulice did not look at the others now, nor glance toward the crowd or search Pell's face for approval. He narrowed his stance, pulled air through clenched teeth, and let the pain settle inside him like a stone. His thoughts quieted until only the rhythm remained.

They circled each other with staves raised. The field blurred at the edges, leaving clarity only in the steps, the spacing, and the stance of his opponent.

Saulice's heart beat hard in his ears, but his grip steadied. Drezz studied him without emotion, his eyes tracking him without pity. There was no smugness, no hesitation, only focus. That made it easier for Saulice, for he did not want mercy. He wanted the moment.

Drezz lunged, thrusting his staff high toward Saulice's shoulder in a classic opener. Saulice saw it clearly, not only the shape of the strike but the intent within it. He batted it aside, let the momentum guide his turn, and stepped into Drezz's guard with a quick feint to the left.

Drezz adjusted instantly, raising his staff to meet him, but Saulice was no longer there. He rolled beneath the block and jabbed upward, striking Drezz's chest with a hard thud, clear and unmistakable.

A gasp lifted from the surrounding students. It was not only noise but release, a breath held too long.

Saulice moved again, his body reacting before his mind could intervene. He turned with the recoil, parried the quick return strike, and stepped inside once more. Drezz's counter came fast, sharp, and close, but Saulice ducked beneath it, letting the blow whistle past as he pivoted low.

Everything outside the moment disappeared. The ring, the students, even the drills across the field all slipped away.

Only the rhythm remained.

He caught movement again, just before it came. Drezz's foot shifted, loading his weight onto his right leg, while a twitch betrayed the tension in his left arm. Saulice struck low, angling toward Drezz's exposed side. The attack did not feel chosen but inevitable, the natural next motion, as instinctive as breath itself.

Yet Drezz was faster. He dropped low, his body folding like a hinge, and swept a leg outward in a quick, controlled arc. Saulice's foot caught on it, too late to pull back and too deep to recover.

The world tilted as his body slammed into the dirt once more, a puff of dust shooting upward while the impact knocked the wind from his lungs.

"Ten-one," Pell said, his voice striking like iron. "Ring is clear."

The silence cracked, and the small crowd loosened. Students returned to drills. Staves resumed their measured clack, boots scuffed the stone, yet something in the ring had shifted.

Saulice lay flat, staring at the wide blue sky. His chest rose and fell like broken wings, the impact leaving his thighs burning and his right shoulder pulsing with pain.

Everything hurt, though none of it seemed urgent.

What mattered more was the moment behind his eyes, the instant when Drezz's weight had shifted and the path for an attack had revealed itself. He had not guessed it, he had read it.

Even if he was too slow, Saulice was no longer blind. He had not been reactive; he had known.

Footsteps approached, heavy and deliberate, until Pell's shadow stretched over his face.

"One can train technique," the Cadre said, his voice pitched to the field rather than the boy beneath him, "but fear teaches itself. Most of you will never learn to fight past it."

His boot landed beside Saulice's hip.

"You didn't hesitate. Noted."

He turned without waiting for a response.

"Instinct without control is still failure," Pell said to the class, "but it is one step closer to success."

He kept walking, voice sharp as a banner snapping in the wind.

"Bruises develop will. They forge it, as we do the fount. If your resolve collapses under fatigue, you will never be more than a liability. Remember that. Class dismissed."

No one laughed. No one clapped. But everyone nearby had heard him. Pell had seen. He had seen Saulice.

Across the far edge of the training field, beyond the rings and sparring posts, Master Valos stood beneath the shade of a cedar awning. His robes stirred faintly in the breeze as he watched with a stillness that suggested calculation. It was the stillness of someone not noting who Saulice was now, but who he might become. Saulice did not notice, but Valos watched him leave.

Drezz appeared without a word, his hand extended. Saulice hesitated for half a breath before taking it. The grip was solid, neither mocking nor soft, but simply steady. Offered without decoration, it was like Drezz himself, present and unreadable.

They walked together toward the shaded bench at the field's edge, leaving behind the broken ring where staff tips clacked and boots scraped the dirt. Saulice sat heavily, knees flaring in protest, and leaned his stave against the wall behind them. His breath came ragged but steadied in the cool shade.

Neither of them spoke for a time. Above, the sky stretched pale and vast, washed in early summer haze. The breeze slipped across the training grounds, lifting the collar of Saulice's tunic and drying sweat along his spine.

Frustration broke first. "I'll never catch up," Saulice muttered, rubbing his shoulder. "Every time I move, you're already three steps ahead."

Drezz kept his eyes forward. "I had training long before this place. My father could not afford me to be unprepared. Where I am from, weakness is not an option."

Saulice glanced at him, catching the faint trace of weight in the words. He nodded once, quietly, though the knot of envy did not vanish.

From somewhere far off, another match was called, another correction barked. The sounds rang clear but felt distant. Saulice's shoulders ached, his ribs throbbed, his spine bent from the inside, yet none of that lingered as strongly as the rhythm. That moment when movement had felt inevitable, when instinct reached forward before thought had time to catch it.

It was imperfect, difficult, but it had felt right. Like a leaf following the wind. Like knowing a step would land before it touched the ground.

He turned the sequence over again in his head: Drezz's weight had shifted, and the opening had been real. That meant he could find it again.

He closed his eyes, not to rest but to seal it in memory. There had been no whisper from the storm inside, no surge of power, no divine interruption. Just him. Just amateur movement trying to close the enormous gap between himself and the other academs.

Drezz sat beside him, arms resting on his knees, staff leaning by his foot. His fur clung damp to his brow, but his expression held no fatigue, only stillness.

"I saw it," Saulice said at last.

Drezz did not turn. "I know."

They let the quiet return, not empty or awkward, but full. Saulice did not need praise, not from Drezz and not even from Pell. What he needed was that moment again, and he would find it. Not for the others. Not to silence the whispers that surrounded him. He needed it for himself, because now he knew it existed.

He wiped his palms on his trousers, the fabric sticking to his skin. Bruises would rise by evening, purple and sharp, and he would feel them when he lay down. Yet somehow he felt lighter, as though something long buried had surfaced.

Across the field, the bells tolled, sharp and clear.

"Fount Principiums next," Drezz said.

Saulice nodded, rising with a suppressed groan. The dust on his sweat-soaked uniform sleeve did not feel like failure anymore. It felt earned.

They walked in silence toward the archway that led to the upper halls. The wind followed behind, tugging gently at Saulice's unkempt blond hair. Staffs clacked in the distance, voices rose and fell, and ahead, the stone corridors stretched wide and waiting.

He had far to go.

CHAPTER 15

THE STILLNESS OF SILENCE

The stone halls of Brynswick stretched long and cold, echoing faintly with the clatter of blades still ringing from the dueling fields behind them. Saulice walked with one hand pressed to his ribs, not to shield the bruise but to remember it, for each throb reminded him he hadn't flinched.

Drezz walked beside him, his steps measured as ever, his silence a rhythm Saulice trusted. They didn't speak. They didn't need to. Both understood what had happened back there on the training grounds, and both knew the match had shifted, even for a breath.

They were late by the time they reached the amphitheater of the Fount Principiums Hall. Other first years had already seated themselves in wide rings around a central stone dais. A mosaic shimmered faintly beneath their feet, sapphire and emerald, ruby and onyx, all colors coalescing toward the center where Cadre Nilus stood, cloaked in grey, a single lapis clasp gleaming near his collar.

He didn't greet them. His eyes, calm and pale as frostweed, followed their entrance with quiet intensity. Saulice met that gaze for one moment, then bowed his head and chose a seat in the farthest corner. Drezz followed without hesitation.

Saulice shifted onto the cushion, searching for a position that wouldn't aggravate the bruise under his ribs. Beside him, Drezz adjusted the leather strap on his satchel, tail flicking once as he took in the room. Damian sat to their right, hands folded, posture near perfect. He caught Saulice's eye and nodded.

His muscles still hummed with fatigue, and sweat clung to the back of his neck. The coolness of the hall brought some relief, though the ache in his shoulder had settled into something heavier, something that would wake him if he turned too sharply in his sleep.

"For the last two weeks," Cadre Nilus said, his words cutting through the hush, "you've studied Candur's past. You've learned to hold a weapon. But you have not yet learned how to wield your own minds."

He paced a slow arc along the platform. "You must learn yourselves, not only your bodies but also the inner instrument, the place where spirit, will, and intention converge. This," he said, "is the fount core."

He stopped beside a long, carved table and drew back the black velvet cloth resting over it. Beneath lay a wooden box inlaid with symbols of all ten fount stones. With care, he opened the lid.

The room fell still.

Inside lay ten small shards, no larger than river pebbles. They shimmered faintly, each one humming with elemental resonance. Without touching them, Saulice could feel their difference. One gave off warmth, another radiated chill, and a third crackled beneath the skin like hidden static. That one stood out from the rest.

"Each of these," Nilus said, lifting a shard between two fingers, "is a fragment of the ten original fount stones, created by Shaddai over a thousand years ago. The first of each element, long before we discovered the stone-filled caves that stretch across all of Myre."

"They are remnants," he continued. "Only echoes now. But even a whisper of the original fount is enough to awaken the core of one who is ready. That will be today's purpose."

The students leaned forward. Even Drezz's stillness shifted slightly in interest.

"Before you draw from the fount," Nilus said, raising the shard until it caught the chamber light, "you must understand what it is, and what it is not. The fount is not a river for those who demand it. It is not a weapon to summon by strength, nor is it mere sorcery as dullards often claim. The fount is a living tether between your soul and the elementary principles of Myre, crafted by Shaddai. It is the breath beneath thought and exists in ambience across all of Myre. Your core produces fount on its own, but argonauts are able to drink of that ambient fount in places where it is richest. First, however, you must awaken your cores."

A girl at the back raised her hand. "Cadre Nilus," she asked, "what about the artifacts from the Thousand Year War? Were those made by Shaddai?"

Nilus turned.

"There are relics from the Age of Rebellion that we do not study," he said heavily. "Tools forged by Veartaya herself, not for aid but for control. After her fall, Myre outlawed their use. You will not learn of them in this classroom."

He paused beside the table again. "Now, there are three foundational steps to fount forging. First, waking the core. This will occupy the coming weeks, if not months. Second, expanding it through ambient mana absorption and then filtering it until it mixes with your native fount nature. The third and last, coursing your fount through a stone itself."

"The last stage will take months, and you'll begin by practicing with a shard," he said, voice sharpening. "But long before then, let us awaken your cores."

He turned back to the shards. "Unlike fount artifacts, which channel power but do not hold it, your core lies dormant until awakened. Even then, you must nurture it, training it like a muscle and expanding it so that your core can hold more, allowing you to learn stronger forging techniques. Your core must be honed like your mind."

"The work is not instant, nor painless. You will not command a stone until you have confronted the truth of the world and the truth of yourselves."

He paced the inner ring, robes brushing softly against the mosaic.

"Force cannot wake the core," he said. "You cannot stir it by shouting. Stillness does not come when you demand it. It comes when you stop demanding anything at all."

He slowed near the front row, letting his words settle.

"What man knows his own self except his own spirit? You must uncover your core like a reflection in still water, revealed only when the wind stills and the ripples fade. Therefore, we begin here, not with stones or sparks, but with silence."

Nilus lowered himself onto the platform, sitting on his own cushion without flourish. His robes folded neatly beneath him as he sat cross-legged, hands resting gently on his knees.

"Close your eyes," he said. "Listen to your breath and nothing more. Do not chase what is not ready to be found. Just explore the silence, and then you will find it, a dull mote waiting to be sparked alight."

Cadre Nilus closed his eyes as his voice faded like mist rising from still water.

The room responded with silence. No one shifted or coughed. Even the fidgeters stilled, drawn into the stillness like leaves pulled toward a settling pond.

Saulice closed his eyes and focused.

At first, there was only black behind his lids. His ribs whispered with each breath, and the heat clung to his skin. He tried to count his breathing, to slow it, to measure it perhaps. But his mind leapt too easily, darting toward Master Valos' scolding, then Drezz's superior combative abilities, then Master Pell's barked orders.

The memory blurred as humiliation churned deep in his gut. Then he sensed something festering, a heat of anger, and underneath even that, something else stirred. But it eluded him.

Focusing on his breath, he tried again. He let the silence fill him and breathed out, stretching it thin.

He made another attempt and something shifted.

It wasn't dramatic, like with light or sound, but the sense of gravity inside him changed. Stillness didn't settle entirely, yet it quieted. As if some deep part of him had stopped resisting. The tension in his limbs softened, the storm behind his thoughts slowed, and then he felt it.

An outline like a dim mote, a blurred shape behind his chest.

His fount core.

It seemed so distant from him, like a faint candle flickering through thick fog. Saulice moved toward it, not by forcing himself but by allowing it. He let go, letting it come closer on its own.

Then something pressed back. A pressure he hadn't felt since the fight against the Black Bellet. That vast presence belonging to Lazarus.

Heat pressed at the base of his spine, and Saulice's lungs grew heavy. He opened his eyes as his breath caught in his throat.

The room hadn't changed and Cadre Nilus hadn't moved. Drezz sat beside him, eyes closed, body still. Around them, students breathed like a tide, slow and steady.

Only Saulice struggled to breathe.

He didn't try again, not right away. It would take time to silence his mind, so that became his focus. Yet the sensation clung to the corners of his chest, like a mist that refused to clear. He remained still, every muscle resisting the urge to move. By the time Lazarus' presence eased, class was over.

Cadre Nilus dismissed the academs with few words, instructing them to continue seeking their fount cores in their free time, even if the process took weeks.

Saulice turned to find Damian slumped forward, chin near his collar. He nudged his arm, and Damian stirred, groaning once before rising with a yawn and muttered curse about "fount philosophy." The three of them, Saulice, Drezz, and Damian, chose not to return indoors.

Instead, they settled beneath an ancient oak outside the west wall. Its bark peeled like parchment, and its branches spread wide, filtering the sun through trembling leaves.

Damian tapped a rhythm on the grass with his fingers.

"So, meditation, huh?"

Drezz opened one eye, unimpressed.

"This is not a jest. Master Nilus instructed us with clear directions. Silence is paramount."

"Right, right. Inner peace. Centering. All that." Damian drew a long breath and shut his eyes again. "I'm centered. I'm peaceful. I'm going back asleep."

Saulice tried to smirk, but his stomach remained tight. The presence from earlier gripped him like a hand at the base of his throat. He looked up. The branches above shifted, casting patterns on the grass that swam with the breeze. For a moment, he wished he were someone else, someone certain, someone in control.

"Begin again," Drezz said softly. "Like Nilus taught."

Saulice exhaled slowly, letting the noise leave and the tension slip from his jaw and shoulders. He tried to let go, but that meant not reliving Alderman Corfrick's gaze in Hamlen. It meant forgetting the black bellet and his unpleasant encounters with the Titan Lazarus. Letting go meant stepping beyond his fears, beyond memory and shame. Still, he tried. He followed Drezz's voice as it drifted toward them like water seeking still ground.

"There is wind. There is sunlight. There is soil beneath you. Focus on nothing else."

Each word sank into him. Each syllable broke the surface tension of his thoughts, as though tossed into a too-loud lake. The noise inside him didn't disappear, but it blurred and softened.

Damian muttered something about having ants in his pants. Saulice let it pass.

He saw flickers instead of the mote-like image from before, just movement, like thin threads of light twisting past the darkness behind his lids. They came and went, like sparks on a hearth not yet stirred.

Then a familiar dim light appeared, like a moon obscured without the sun to light its face. This was his fount core.

Except there was a certain oddity to it. The core was a dim mix of muted white and gold, like the flickering of a lantern carried by someone you loved when you were small and afraid.

"Do you see something?" Drezz asked.

Saulice opened his mouth, then closed it. The mote vanished. He tried to hold it again, scrambling to refocus on the openness, that stillness Master Nilus had spoken of. A silence of attentiveness rather than absence.

He let his limbs fall slack and allowed the weight of his body to belong to the earth. He took another breath in, then reached within himself. The pale orb returned as the core reappeared in his mind's eye, clearer this time. A dim mote in the vast darkness of his inner self, it remained unfixed and unshaped. Just there, waiting.

But something was amiss.

As he drew closer to the core, he noticed something very wrong. The core was damaged, with gold-colored fractures running across from either side. Saulice leaned deeper within himself, just as Nilus had taught, and as the ancient texts whispered between their lines.

He inhaled again, but this time he did not seek out the fount core directly. He breathed, focusing only on rhythm and cadence. In and out, like waves brushing the shore. He let the aches speak and fade, let the noise in his head slow to a murmur.

He counted ten full breaths before anything shifted.

Somehow, the space between it and him shortened. He reached for it, and this time it did not push back as though he approached some wall constructed by Lazarus.

But what he found close up hollowed the air from his lungs.

The core was *unwhole.*

His core floated in shadow, dim and fragile, riddled with large cracks. It was smaller than he expected, with tendrils of gold leaking from the fractures like mist.

A tremor moved through him. It was not fear but confusion.

The more he stared, the worse his fount core appeared. The center was dim and dull, yet the leaking tendrils glowed bright with lively motion. It was still his. He knew that. But his core was damaged somehow.

Something had changed. It was still changing.

Saulice willed himself closer to the core, just slightly, closer to the leaking gold tendrils. Curious, he reached a slow hand forward and dipped just the tip of a finger into the tendril.

The response was instant. He was shot backward, flung away from the fractures. The core faded. Saulice gasped and jerked his eyes open as Lazarus' presence overwhelmed his senses. A jarring revelation struck him without words. He understood completely.

Those gold tendrils did not belong to him. They belonged to Lazarus. Which meant the Titan's fount was bleeding through Saulice's core. He grasped the pendant beneath his shirt, Father Laird's gift, clutching it with a shaking hand.

Shaddai, if You're there, please help me understand.

Silence answered him.

He turned to Drezz, then to Damian. Neither noticed.

Damian hummed a tune beneath his breath, lost in thought. Drezz remained cross-legged, eyes closed, lips slightly parted, tracing whatever presence he had sensed. Saulice could feel it.

He was the one being studied now. Because what Saulice had felt had not come from him. It had come from the Titan's fount, bleeding through his core.

Dread pressed into him as he left his friends behind, muttering some excuse about finding Father Laird.

The thought followed him like a shadow.

What if his core was broken?

Hours had passed since he left Cadre Nilus' lecture, though the weight in his chest had not eased. He had walked the training yard twice, circled the dormitory halls, even sat alone in the chapel with his head bowed and eyes closed, waiting for stillness to come. It never had.

Every time Saulice slowed, the memory returned. And as the echo of Cadre Nilus' lecture rang in his head, how first-year cadets could find their fount cores in absolute silence, Saulice finally saw the pattern. The lightning strike in Hamlen. The fire that had taken his mother. The shards that shattered during every trial. The cracked source stone on his first day here.

Lazarus was the cause behind each event.

The realization didn't bring rage alone. That would come later. What settled heavier, sharper than anger, was understanding. If he didn't face this, if he didn't learn to control it, he wouldn't survive whatever waited for him beyond Brynswick's walls—possibly even within them.

By the time Saulice reached the infirmary doors, his hands trembled. He paused in the shadow of the threshold, forcing his breath to slow, gathering what little steadiness he could.

The scent of dried herbs and candle wax struck him as he stepped inside. Low lanterns burned in recessed alcoves, their light warm and quiet against the stone walls. He had been here before, half-carried after his poor showing when he had cracked the source stone.

The infirmary stretched in ordered silence, divided into several treatment rooms hidden behind curtained archways. Students rested in some, nursing burns, sprains, and the aftermath of failed fount drills. The air smelled faintly of crushed mint and iron.

A young attendant in simple gray robes looked up from arranging bandages near the entrance. Recognition flickered in her eyes, tempered by the cautious distance Saulice had grown used to.

"Are you injured?" she asked.

He shook his head. "I need Father Laird. It's… urgent."

Something in his voice must have carried more weight than he intended, because she didn't question him. Without a word, she slipped into the side hall leading to the deeper rooms. Saulice stood in the quiet that followed, listening to the muffled groans of the wounded and the faint scrape of wind against high windows.

Moments later, Father Laird emerged. His ash-gray robes hung loose, sleeves rolled to the elbow. A wooden emblem of Shaddai swung lightly at his belt, worn smooth from years of prayer and habit. His expression carried no surprise, only a quiet gravity softened by an almost playful curve at the corner of his mouth, as though he had been waiting for this.

"Saulice," he said, voice even. "What trouble finds you this time?"

Saulice hesitated. The words tangled in his throat, heavy as stone. "After Cadre Nilus' lecture… when I tried what he said, to find my core and listen for it, I saw something. There were cracks running through it, leaking." His hands curled unconsciously against his tunic. "I think my core's broken."

Father Laird raised an eyebrow, glancing at Saulice in that knowing way, the same look he had given him after the cracked source stone weeks ago. "You do have a knack for breaking things no one else can," he said quietly, though there was no humor in his eyes.

He motioned toward a curtained arch at the back. "Come on then. Let's see if we can figure out just how broken you are."

The chamber beyond was narrow, lined with shelves of tinctures and folded linens. At its center stood a simple stone table. Father Laird crossed to a low chest in the corner and unlatched its clasp. From within, he withdrew a curious artifact, circular and wide, mounted in a bronze frame that pivoted on a hinge. Its surface resembled a magnifying glass, but etched across the lens were dozens of slender glyphs, glowing faintly in dull silver and white.

"This isn't divine work," Father Laird said as he set the device on the table. "Tinkers in Shallabane built it generations ago. It lets us see beyond the body and into the fount itself. Fewer than a dozen still exist."

The artifact hummed faintly as he lifted it toward Saulice. "Sit," he instructed, tone easy but firm. "Hold still, and whatever you do, child, don't touch it."

Father Laird lowered the Shallabane lens until it hovered just above Saulice's chest. The silver glyphs along its rim brightened and shifted, faint light spilling across the boy's tunic.

"Lie still," Father Laird said. "If you twitch, the reading smears and I have to start over. I hate starting over."

Saulice gripped the table edge. "Will it hurt?"

"Only if you faint," Father Laird replied, peering through the lens. "And if you faint, I am not catching you."

The hum deepened as the artifact's light sank inward. Saulice felt a pull in his chest, strange but not painful, as if something buried inside him leaned toward the lens.

Father Laird's eyes narrowed as he studied the shifting light. He stayed silent longer than Saulice expected.

"You see something," Saulice said.

"I do," Father Laird answered. "Exactly what I expected since the source stone cracked."

Saulice's stomach tightened. "It's bad, isn't it?"

"It is not good," Father Laird admitted. "Your core isn't just dormant. It is fractured. Deep lines running straight through the center."

Saulice's voice dropped. "From Lazarus."

"Yes, fourteen years of holding a Titan's lightning without training will do that. Most Harbingers are trained from birth, taught how to shape their cores, how to widen them slowly so they can carry what they were chosen to bear. You carried it raw. It bled into you unchecked until the cracks you now see formed."

Saulice clenched his hands. "So, I can't fix it?"

"Not quickly," Father Laird said. "And you need to understand something before you awaken. When the time comes for you to draw in ambient fount from air, soil, storms, wherever Shaddai placed it, your core will fill, but it will never stay full. The cracks will always leak. It is like pouring water into a cup with holes in it. You can drink, yes, but you will need to keep pouring far more often than anyone else."

Saulice stared at the ceiling. "Got it. No matter what I do, I will always be behind."

"You will have to work harder," Father Laird corrected. "Always drawing more fount, always steadying yourself. Others will move forward with ease, but you will gain strength through persistence. And if you do not mend those cracks one day, you will never know what it is to be whole."

"And Lazarus?" Saulice asked quietly. "Will he fight me?"

"Highly likely. Titans are not used to sharing space. He may resist, or he may help, but silence will be your only advantage."

"Why silence?"

"Because in silence you find what is truly yours," Father Laird said. "Chaos feeds cracks. Stillness steadies them. Cadre Nilus was right about that much."

The glyphs dimmed. Father Laird lifted the lens aside and set it gently back into its case.

"There is something I can give you," he said, drawing a strip of parchment from his robe. The glyph etched across it gleamed faintly. "A specific prayer. It does not mend the cracks, but it slows the bleeding. When you speak it, your core steadies. It will buy you time."

Saulice took it carefully. "How long does it last?"

"At first, only hours. Later, longer, if you learn to pair it with your own prayers and discipline. But it is only a bandage. The wound remains."

"Can it be fixed?"

"One day it must," Father Laird confirmed. "Or Lazarus' power will tear through you."

The words hung heavy in the room.

Father Laird gestured toward the parchment. "Read it aloud and you'll see for yourself."

Saulice unfolded the strip and swallowed. *Shaddai... steady me. Hold me and my core, for I cannot hold myself.*

The words sank into silence. Something shifted inside him, faint ripples moving outward.

He closed his eyes and felt himself drawn inward. It took a moment before he found the place, but then he saw it. The fractured mote, covered with those leaking tendrils of gold. As the prayer lingered, a gentler glow wrapped the cracks, steadying them. To his surprise, the bleeding really did slow. A soft tingling spread through him, neither painful nor sharp, but pleasant.

When Saulice opened his eyes, Father Laird was studying him. "You did not explode. That is promising."

Saulice exhaled, voice quiet. "I saw it. My core."

"Good," Father Laird said. "Remember that stillness. When it bleeds again, find it. And for once, try not to break anything."

CHAPTER 16

THE THUNDERCLAP

A brittle haze hung in the air as morning settled over Brynswick's eastern field. Dew clung to the grass in soft, glistening webs, and the flagstones beneath the students' boots still held the last breath of the night's chill. Above, the rising sun cast angled light across the lawn, slicing long shadows between columns and hedgerows. Students stood in clusters near the training stones, hushed and alert, every breath tighter than usual.

Saulice lingered slightly apart, hands tucked into the pockets of his uniform. Nearly three weeks had passed since the night he had gone to Father Laird in the infirmary, when he had first seen the cracks lacing his fount core and the lightning bleeding from them like threads of gold. Three weeks of searching the Academy's libraries and listening for whispers in the halls had yielded nothing. No cure, no practice, no method to mend the fractures. Nothing slowed the bleed except for the prayer Father Laird had given him, a tether he clung to more often than he admitted.

The uniforms had arrived the night before.

Drezz had unwrapped his first, folded with military precision inside a waxed linen parcel marked with the Brynswick seal. The coat was deep blue, its silver trim catching light in quiet streaks, and a polished badge shaped like the twin towers of the Academy's crest gleamed from the collar. Saulice's had come second, the same cut and color, though its sharper fit surprised him. The sleeves held structure, the collar carried weight.

They had tried them on immediately.

In the mirror, Saulice looked different, taller perhaps, but also solid. The coat gripped his shoulders with precise tailoring, and the weeks of evening training had begun to mold his frame. Drezz, always upright, now looked carved from intent. Saulice's collar itched faintly, new and stiff against his neck, but the uniform gave him a structure he had never felt before. He focused on the slow rhythm of his breath, ignoring the flickering glances from nearby students.

Cadre Nilus strode across the field with his usual quiet precision, his grey Cadre robes brushing the tops of the grass like a blade. Behind him came two assistants, each bearing the corners of a velvet-lined chest, plain yet humming faintly, the way stones sometimes did before storms.

Saulice knew what this was.

When the box touched the stone dais, conversation ceased. Silence stretched tight like wire.

"You are here," Cadre Nilus said at last, "because forging is no longer a theory for you. Today begins the work of waking your core."

The words did not rise above a murmur, but they cut clean. Nilus knelt and unclasped the lid.

Inside, ten fount shards rested like sleeping stars. Each pulsed with a different light: amber, blue, emerald, red, violet, white, silver, black, pale gold, and ice-clear. Even from several feet away, Saulice felt the hum pouring from the box, muted yet insistent, like distant thunder beneath the skin. His chest prickled with something electric.

"Fount forging does not just occur at your command," Nilus said. He lifted the yellow shard with deliberate care, holding it aloft between his fingers. "It begins with the awakening of your core, and awakening is not granted by force. You must approach it with discipline, and with reverence. Today, you will seek that core. You will find it. And if you are able, you will touch it with this."

He turned the shard slowly, letting the sunlight catch and flare through it. "The shard will not awaken your core for you. It is only proof. When your will touches the shard to the heart of your fount core, if it stirs, you will know."

The citrine shard cast a faint corona of gold light into the morning air, lightning shimmering within like a storm trapped behind glass.

Saulice's gaze drifted to the blue lapis shard. Rayne's affinity was water.

"You will not forge today," Nilus continued, returning the citrine to its velvet cradle. "Not truly. Not yet. You will attempt awakening. If your core, which you have spent weeks seeking in silence, accepts the shard, it will stir. If it does not, you will keep trying."

He looked around the circle, his gaze sweeping over each cadet in turn and lingering a heartbeat longer on Saulice. "Approach this carefully. Your core is yours alone. No one can walk to it for you."

Nilus' eyes moved from face to face, then returned to Saulice. "You," he said, voice neither kind nor cruel. "You will go last."

A flicker passed through the gathered academs as Nilus began calling names.

One by one, they stepped forward. The assistants moved with quiet precision, lifting shards from the chest and placing them into waiting hands as though presenting relics rather than tools. Some approached the circle hesitantly, others carried themselves with sharp-edged confidence, their steps measured and deliberate.

Drezz was called third. He stepped forward without hesitation, neither prideful nor shy, simply present, as though he had been waiting for this moment without seeking it. The assistant placed a green-veined shard into his hands, emerald.

He cradled it against his chest for a breath, then closed his eyes. His shoulders eased as the circle stilled, silence stretching into something heavier than anticipation.

Moments passed.

The soil around his boots shifted faintly. Dust lifted in a slow curl. The shard pulsed once in his hands, light rising through its veins like sap climbing a tree.

The glow faded, and Drezz opened his eyes.

Nilus gave a single nod. "Awakened."

Saulice's hands curled slightly at his sides, not in anger toward Drezz but in something heavier, quieter. He respected Drezz too much to let envy take root, but the ache still cut deep. Drezz had succeeded, and Saulice respected him too much to let envy take root. Yet the ache cut deep. He had trained longer, pushed harder, but each time he reached for stillness, something slipped away at the last moment. What should have been silence turned to distance, an absence that never resolved.

He clenched and unclenched his fists, knowing exactly who was to blame.

More academs stepped forward. Some coaxed faint flickers of light from their shards. A boy's sapphire shard bloomed briefly with frost that melted almost as soon as it formed, while a girl's onyx shard glowed once and dimmed, leaving her smiling in quiet relief.

Then came Lucas.

His name was barely called before he strode into the circle, his presence loud even in silence. He received a crimson shard, a ruby, and grinned wider as he turned toward the others.

"Watch closely," he murmured, his voice just loud enough to carry.

He pressed the shard to his chest, eyes closing in mock solemnity. For a heartbeat, nothing stirred. Then fire bled outward, bright and alive. A ribbon of flame arced into the air and hissed against the wind before vanishing as quickly as it had come.

Gasps rippled through the gathered academs.

Lucas bowed low, lips curved in mock humility. "I will try harder next time."

Nilus offered no reaction. He simply turned and called the next name.

Saulice exhaled through his nose and lowered his gaze. His palms had grown damp, his stomach tightening as the line of students shortened. He already knew what was coming.

Finally, when the chest was nearly empty, Nilus spoke again.

"Saulice Sawyer."

The name did not rise in volume, but it struck like stone against water, rippling through every circle of thought and posture around the field.

Saulice stepped forward, his hands steady only by force of will.

The assistant moved toward the box, then paused, waiting for Nilus.

"Citrine," the Cadre said.

The yellow shard. Lightning.

Saulice's chest tightened, colder than fear. It felt closer to memory— of storms, of fire, of every fractured moment he carried.

The assistant placed the shard into his open hand. Electric warmth bloomed along his fingers at the first touch. The core shimmered with golden light, churning like a storm locked behind glass. It pulsed, not violently but steady, enough to remind him this was real.

He drew in a breath.

You will not command it. You will listen.

Closing his eyes, Saulice pictured stillness. He reached for the oak tree and the light through its branches, the way Drezz had breathed into the earth, the quiet flicker he had felt during earlier meditations. He waited for it to return.

The world inside him opened.

Darkness stretched, not empty but vast. The fractured sphere of his core hovered ahead, webbed with fine cracks, golden lightning seeping through the breaks like molten threads. The shard in his palm glowed faintly, a single point of steady light.

He moved toward the core in his mind's eye. The closer he drew, the stronger the pressure grew.

Something stirred.

A presence vast and coiled pressed against him, neither asleep nor fully awake. Lightning pulsed through the cracks—unyielding, restless, not his own. The air thickened, and a wall rose between him and the core, built not of stone or shadow but will.

Lazarus.

Saulice gritted his teeth and stepped forward, pressing the shard closer. The barrier resisted, silent and immovable. He pushed harder, feeling the pressure mount until the shard trembled in his grip.

A jolt shot through him, sharp and electric. Reflex tore his fingers open.

The shard dropped to the stone at his feet. It struck with a low chime and rolled to a stop. A thin wisp of light flickered up, then faded into nothing.

For a moment, no one moved.

Saulice's chest heaved once, twice, then stilled. He had felt it. The shard had reacted, if only for a breath. Most of all, it had not cracked. That alone made it the smallest success he had known in weeks.

The sound came after.

A slow, deliberate clap.

Lucas.

He stepped from the edge of the circle, bracer gleaming beneath his sleeve, arms crossed like a judge about to pronounce sentence.

"Incredible," he said, voice dripping with mockery. "A flicker. How terrifying."

He took a few steps forward, the crowd parting just enough to let him through. "What's next, Sawyer? Will you sneeze and faint?"

Saulice's hands tightened at his sides, but he said nothing. The urge to answer burned in his chest, yet Master Valos' warning about the Great Houses rang louder than Lucas' taunts. One wrong word, one wrong gesture, and this would follow him far beyond Brynswick's walls.

Lucas waited for the reaction that did not come. The silence turned heavier, more cutting than any retort.

When Saulice finally looked at him, his gaze held no challenge, only quiet resolve.

The smirk faltered. Lucas sneered, louder than he needed to be. "That's what I thought." He turned from Saulice with exaggerated ease, trying to reclaim the moment for the crowd.

Nilus raised one hand, and silence returned to the field.

The tension in the circle broke like a thread pulled too tight.

Lucas scoffed something under his breath and turned away. His performance had ended, and no one applauded.

Drezz stepped close, his voice low enough to pass unnoticed by others. "That was… well said."

"I didn't say anything."

"Exactly my point."

Saulice's chest rose and fell in a slow rhythm, but something in the air had shifted. Nothing about the words had changed, nothing about the moment itself. Yet something inside him had clicked.

Lucas had turned this into something personal, and whether or not Saulice felt ready, he had accepted that challenge.

Nilus returned to the center and addressed the group.

"For the next half hour, break into groups and practice on your own. You will be tested again before the third bell."

The dismissal was quiet but final. Academs scattered, forming small knots of conversation or filing back toward the dormitories. Some glanced toward Saulice as they passed, yet none spoke to him directly.

Still Saulice remained.

He stood beside the shard, the same one that had pulsed in his palm and then gone silent. Its glow had vanished completely. It looked like an ordinary stone now, harmless and inert. He crouched and brushed its edge with his fingers.

It was cool to the touch. No hum. No warmth. Just silence.

But it had not shattered.

That alone should have felt like victory.

Saulice rose abruptly, the motion surprising even him. His hands had curled into fists before he realized they had closed. The weight of the shard lingered in his palm, though its warmth was gone. It was always the same—every time he reached for stillness, the Titan stirred. Never enough to speak aloud, yet always enough to remind him he was not alone.

"You are walking like you lost a war."

The voice came from the edge of the field, calm and dry.

Melandra.

She stood beneath the shadow of a tall hedge, arms crossed and posture relaxed in the way a coiled blade pretends to rest. She wore a uniform without a badge, hair tied back, expression unreadable.

"I didn't see you," Saulice said.

"I am good at not being seen." She stepped into the light, offering a nod to Cadre Pell. He returned it with a narrowed gaze.

"May I have a word with him?" she asked.

Cadre Pell gave a sharp nod, expression carrying questions he knew he would not ask.

"Valos wanted to observe your progress without interference," Melandra whispered as they moved a few steps away from the other academs.

Saulice exhaled slowly. "Then I suppose he got what he wanted."

Her gaze shifted toward the shard at Saulice's feet. "Pick it up."

He hesitated. "It didn't work."

"I did not ask if it worked." Her tone was steady, demanding without rising in volume. She waited, unblinking. After a pause she added, "You are not the only one returning from something broken."

Saulice looked up.

"Furies Fist released your uncle from confinement three days ago."

The words struck like stone against water. For a moment, fount forging vanished from Saulice's thoughts. All that remained was the echo of her words. How long had it been since he had seen Dedric? Five months? Six?

"Is that so?" His throat tightened, yet he forced the words out. "Is he doing well? Was he hurt?"

"Dedric is fine. Those village guards never stood a chance against him, even as out of practice as he was. He has rejoined the Fist," she said. "As part of his sentencing."

Saulice bent slowly and lifted the shard. It lay dull in his palm, heavier somehow than before.

"I haven't given it much thought," he admitted. "To think Dedric was once an Argonaut—that he served with Furies Fist. It is too much to sort out."

He knew the danger of asking questions. Questions like why. He had assumptions, even guesses, about what might happen if he followed that path far enough. Somewhere within that answer, his father's name would echo.

Melandra nodded and placed a hand on his shoulder. It was firm, not delicate. "Do not fret over the past, Saulice. Dwelling on old things will only poison you. I have known Dedric for a long time, and as much as he hates to admit it, he is a soldier at heart."

Saulice sighed, his chest heavier until he shook the thoughts aside. "You are right."

"When will I see him again?"

"In due time. When the Lord Commander of the Fist deems it acceptable. There is much at stake right now, and the Fist needs the wit and might of all its Argonauts."

She turned before he could ask more questions. "Follow me."

They walked in silence past the hedgeline toward the lesser alcoves tucked behind the observation hall. These were not the polished courts of public display. They were older training grounds, forgotten corners, places meant for failure and quiet.

They stopped beneath a collapsed arch where vines had overtaken an old aqueduct. Sunlight threaded through the gaps in broken stone, painting narrow bands of light across the floor.

"Sit," Melandra said.

Saulice lowered himself onto the weathered stone. She crouched across from him, posture balanced and watchful, as though poised between ease and action.

"You have been told to surrender," she said. "You think that means stillness, but it does not."

"I have tried," Saulice replied quietly. "I paid attention, I did not push, but nothing is working."

"Silence is not surrender," Melandra said, her tone patient yet precise. "It is close, but not the same."

Saulice frowned. "Then what am I supposed to do?"

"Try trusting for a change," she answered, placing a closed hand against her chest.

"You have been bracing against Lazarus like a wall," she continued. "But the sealing of a Titan never begins with force, and neither does understanding it. It begins with surrender—not to the Titan, but to Shaddai."

Saulice stared, unsure if he understood. "Shaddai? Why does everyone keep saying that?"

"Shaddai made the Titans long before the Thousand Year War. He named them and still holds authority over them. You are a Harbinger, Saulice. You do not lead the Titan. You carry the name of the One who does." Her voice softened, yet carried weight that stilled the air. "When you have learned surrender, you will begin to understand what was, what is, and what is still to come."

The silence deepened.

"Surrender to Him," she said. "Not as an escape but as a return. When you do that, perhaps Lazarus will be willing to speak with you again."

Saulice lowered his gaze to the shard in his palm. Its glow pulsed faintly, fragile as memory.

He closed his eyes and allowed everything else to fade. He did not imitate breathing patterns he had been shown, nor recite the formulas others whispered. He spoke simply, with the truth he carried.

Darkness spread before him, vast and silent. His fount core hovered in the center of that expanse, a fractured pale mote streaked with golden fissures that leaked fount in restless pulses.

He stepped toward it, the shard glowing faintly in his hand. Each pace forward thickened the air until the space between him and the core felt heavy and suffocating, as though the world itself were pressing him back. Then the wall appeared, unseen yet immovable, built not of stone but of will, the sheer force of something vast and ancient.

Lazarus.

The Titan's presence loomed ahead, unseen but coiled and immense. It had been this way every time: he would draw near, reach for stillness, and be driven back.

Saulice gritted his teeth and gripped the shard tighter. This time, instead of pushing, he prayed.

"Shaddai... steady me. Hold me and my core, for I cannot hold myself. Let me find my beginning."

The words carried outward through the silence. The wall quivered but did not fall. Saulice whispered again, quieter than breath.

If he will not step aside for me, then stop him. Just long enough. Just enough to begin.

A presence older than lightning entered the space. It was neither Saulice nor Lazarus. It was higher. Divine.

The wall trembled, then broke apart like ash scattered by wind. Lazarus' weight recoiled, not in fury but in startled silence. The Titan withdrew, receding into the depths of Saulice's fractured core.

Saulice stepped forward and pressed the shard to the sphere before the Titan could change his mind.

Brilliant light erupted.

The pale glow of the core flared into stunning white, gold lacing every fracture, spilling and knitting together in unison. The cracks still leaked, but Father Laird's prayer steadied them like a fragile bandage, imperfect yet holding. For the first time, the hum of the core was whole enough to endure.

When Saulice opened his eyes, the shard in his palm shone with steady gold light.

Melandra's hand rested on his shoulder, her voice low but certain. "I would wager Lazarus felt that."

"He didn't expect it either," Saulice whispered, still catching his breath.

"No Titan does," she replied. "Not when they are reminded why they were made."

Saulice stared at the light in his hand, not borrowed or stolen. He said a silent thanks to Shaddai.

Melandra rose and stepped back. "Return to the circle and show them."

He nodded and walked from the alcove, the quiet between them carrying more weight than any words.

Crossing the field felt different now. A few students lingered in scattered knots, their voices dropping to whispers as he passed. Cadre Nilus stood at the circle's edge, hands clasped behind his back.

"You are not required to return today," Nilus said.

"I know," Saulice replied. "But I am not finished."

Nilus stepped aside.

The circle was his.

Saulice knelt, grounding himself not in performance but in peace. This time he did not strain for silence; instead, he welcomed it.

Shaddai, he whispered, *steady me. Hold me and my core, for I cannot hold myself.*

The shard answered.

Light bloomed between his fingers, gold mist curling upward in measured spirals. The glow held steady, neither fracturing nor lashing outward as before. Murmurs stirred among the watching students, their surprise a hushed current around the ring.

Nilus' voice came low, focused. "Hold it."

Saulice obeyed. He did not force the light into shape. He simply remained still, and the shard held with him.

Five breaths passed before the glow dimmed on its own, fading gently into quiet release.

Nilus gave a single nod and extended the citrine shard. "Congratulations, academ. You've awakened your core. This shard will be yours for the remainder of the year's studies. You'll need it to detect and absorb ambient fount before you begin expanding your core."

Saulice rose. His knees ached and his hands tingled, but his spirit held steady.

He passed Drezz on the way out with a gaping smile. The fallet answered with a single nod, quiet understanding in his eyes. Lucas said nothing, and Saulice did not look for his response. He no longer needed to.

Whatever came next, however long the road ahead, Saulice knew he would not walk it alone. And the storm within him would no longer rise unwatched.

CHAPTER 17

STRENGTH IN RESTRAINT

A month had passed since Saulice first felt the storm shift inside him.

In that time, everything had changed—not in sudden or dramatic bursts, but in small ways that added up. Drezz's forging had steadied, and Saulice's light no longer sputtered out. Damian had folded into their rhythm as if he had always been there. Most students had stopped whispering whenever Saulice passed. They saw his control, the way his stance held, and they recognized the quiet strength building behind his eyes.

Only Lucas and the circle that orbited him clung to the old script. Their mockery had grown quieter but sharper, thrown like stones from behind taller walls.

"Four coins says you last longer than two minutes this time," Damian said as they crossed the upper courtyard.

Saulice snorted. "Bold of you to assume I will lose."

"I assumed nothing," Damian replied, flashing a grin. "I just bet you will last longer. That is still progress."

"He believes in your odds," Drezz added dryly. "But not your victory. That is the most honest friendship."

They passed under a low arch, where light sliced cleanly between the stone columns. The air carried the scent of parchment and cold iron. The courtyard felt quiet and bright, wrapped in the kind of stillness that made things seem possible.

For the first time in a week, Saulice laughed during their breakfast.

Lucas stepped into their path.

He wasn't alone. Two boys flanked him, thick-shouldered and square-jawed, their bracers already strapped tight. One veered toward Drezz, cutting off his step. Saulice recognized him—Jace Gerisio, another fire forger. Jace shoved Damian in the chest, forcing him to stumble sideways.

Lucas stopped directly in front of Saulice.

"You walk around like you think you've earned something." His voice wasn't raised; it was cold and calculated. "Like you belong here. You think a fount flicker and two mutts trailing behind you makes you an argonaut?"

Drezz tensed. The boy in front of him shifted in response, ready to move.

Saulice stayed still. "Why do you care so much?" His voice was low but clear. "You say I am beneath you. But if that were true, you'd move your lazy eyes to something else."

Lucas's glare narrowed. He jerked Saulice by the collar, lifting him an inch from the ground.

"You are a brand-marked nobody from Hamlen," he seethed. "You think because the shard lit up one time you are on track to be a star pupil? You shouldn't be here. Don't you get it? You're a mistake."

Then his voice dropped.

"And mistakes break."

The punch came without warning. No posture. No pretense.

His fist cracked into Saulice's jaw.

The blow landed flush. Pain exploded just beneath his eye, bright and instant. His vision blurred. His balance faltered, but he stayed upright.

Behind him, Drezz growled—a low, guttural sound Saulice had never heard before—but a forearm caught the fallet across the chest. Damian shouted and drove his shoulder into the other boy's midsection, but it was too late.

Saulice straightened, hands shaking with rage. He knew he couldn't respond. Fighting back would risk his probationary status.

Blood touched the corner of his mouth. His vision swam, then cleared. He met Lucas's eyes.

Lucas shook out his fist, jaw tight, breath coming faster than he meant it to.

Drezz broke free first. He caught the wrist of the boy who had stopped him.

"Touch me again," he said, "and I will snap your fingers."

Damian crashed into Jace a second time, driving his shoulder forward and knocking the boy off balance. He turned toward Lucas, ready to strike.

Saulice bit his tongue so hard that blood welled in his mouth. He couldn't lash out. Master Valos and the Cadre would expel him for striking a member of the Great Houses.

Miraculously finding his restraint, Saulice raised a hand.

"Don't."

Damian stopped, chest heaving. Drezz stepped in beside him, watching. Lucas's friends faltered, confidence cracking.

Saulice wiped the blood from his lip with the back of his hand. "Are you done?"

Lucas said nothing.

"You have been throwing punches at me since the Trials. This one might have landed."

Lucas flinched slightly. He stepped forward again, but this time Saulice didn't blink.

"But if you touch me again before the Combative Exams," Saulice said, calm and firm, "you'd better make it count. Maybe you need a little sabotage beforehand to win your matches. I am sure House Crawford would love to hear that their prodigious heir couldn't win a fair match against a Forsaken."

Lucas hesitated, face flushing. Then he turned without replying.

The silence that followed mattered more than a victory.

He vanished beneath the archway, his friends trailing behind him, scanning for exits instead of allies.

The courtyard went still for a long moment. Those who had been watching, pretending not to, were no longer whispering. They had seen it. Not just the punch, but the restraint. The control. The way Saulice hadn't flinched.

They would remember that.

Drezz stepped closer, inspecting the swelling bruise along Saulice's jaw.

"You are fortunate he didn't strike true," he said. "That punch was clumsy."

Saulice exhaled and let out a short, strained laugh. "Thanks, but I think he meant it to be that way."

Damian shook his head, veins bulging across his temple. "You should have let me break his nose."

"No," Saulice said. "He gave me what I needed."

Damian frowned. "What, a busted lip?"

"A *reason*."

Saulice touched the spot below his eye. It still throbbed, but the pain no longer felt like injury. It felt like clarity.

The Annals were quieter than usual.

Not silent—never silent. There was always the creak of spines and the faint echo of lives reshaped by study. But today carried a different weight, as though the room itself had braced for what was coming.

Saulice entered beneath the tall oak doors, Drezz and Damian just behind him. His lip still stung, the skin already swelling, yet he left it uncovered. Let them see it. Let them draw their own conclusions.

Rayne stood behind the lectern, sorting scrolls with her usual economy of motion. At first she didn't look up, but when she heard their steps, she turned slightly. Her eyes caught the bruise.

She said nothing at first.

"If you bleed on any vellum," she remarked, clipped and dry, "I will ban you for a week."

Damian snorted. Drezz allowed the faintest of smiles before peeling away toward their alcove.

Saulice lingered.

Rayne's gaze never left his face.

"You didn't tell anyone?"

"No need," Saulice said. "They saw it."

"Good."

She reached into her coat and drew out a small tin, setting it on the lectern without meeting his eyes.

"Use that. You bruise too easily. Try not to make it a habit."

Saulice didn't pick it up right away. A trace of irritation edged his voice.

"I didn't start it."

"I never said you did."

Her tone softened—not much, but enough to notice.

He studied her. Not just the words, but the way her posture had shifted when she saw the bruise. Less guarded. Almost reluctant in its concern.

"You're not going to ask what happened?"

"I don't need to." She bound a scroll with quick precision. "Lucas only has one expression when he's planning something. I saw it this morning."

"And you didn't warn me?"

Rayne tilted her head.

"Would it have changed anything?"

Saulice hesitated. "No."

"Then warning you would only have made it worse."

He leaned against the lectern, watching her return to her work.

"You always this careful with people you don't like?"

"Who said I *don't* like you?" She still didn't look directly at him. "I wouldn't waste salve on someone I couldn't stand."

That quieted him.

She paused. Her fingers lingered on the scroll before tying it with silk thread.

"You know, most first years would've gone straight to Valos or Nilus."

"I'm not most first years, if you haven't figured that out already."

"No," she admitted. "You're the one who shattered a Source Stone and came back the next day."

There was no judgment in her tone. Just fact.

"You've been watching me."

"I'm supposed to," she said quickly—too quickly.

For a moment, neither spoke. Dust spiraled between them in a shaft of light. Saulice studied her, not to analyze, but to notice: the pause before she spoke, the way her hand lingered on parchment a beat longer than necessary.

"You're kinder than you let on," he breathed.

Rayne didn't answer immediately. She closed the scroll in her hands with practiced ease, tying it neatly.

"As are you," she said at last. "But stop thinking strength means never needing help."

Saulice blinked.

Rayne returned the scroll to its shelf and reached for another.

"Go," she said over her shoulder. "You're already behind Drezz. He'll take all the best books."

He lingered another second, then picked up the tin. "Rayne."

She didn't turn.

"Thanks."

She nodded once. And though she said nothing more, Saulice spotted a slight curve at the corner of her mouth as he walked away.

He drifted deeper into the second tier of the Annals, where the older texts on fount application and combat theory dwelled. The shelves pressed closer here, the air hushed, the light filtered into long angled bands. He slipped into an alcove near the wall and let the sun stretch across the desk.

He opened his notebook. Then closed it again. Notes would not help today. He didn't need theories or formulas—he needed direction. He had to do more than summon the fount; he had to guide it, shape it with intention instead of fear.

His fingers brushed the citrine shard in his pocket, his constant reminder that the Forsaken brand had been a false label. The stone warmed faintly in his palm, as though pressure stirred beneath the surface, a pulse waiting.

He drew a slow breath, whispering into the stillness.

"Shaddai… please keep him back. Let me try."

The shard warmed again. A shimmer rose from within, no arc, no flare, just a quiet hum. The glow hovered, faint but steady. It did not answer with raw strength but with permission.

The warmth lingered for three breaths, perhaps four, before fading. Yet it had come, and that alone mattered.

Saulice smiled faintly and picked up his pencil. In the corner of his notebook, he wrote a single name.

Lucas.

It wasn't a warning. It wasn't a threat. It was direction.

The light in the Annals had shifted. What had been gold and warm now leaned silver, slanting west through the high windows. Dust caught in the beams, casting delicate shadows across arches and stone. Even the sounds had changed: pages turned slower, footsteps softened, voices melted into whispers.

At a table in the back alcove, the three of them gathered around a mound of books. They spoke little, not for lack of words, but because silence had become its own language. Lucas's blow had drawn blood, but it had also drawn a line.

Damian flipped through a combat manual, mouthing the rhythm of a passage on breath-linked redirection. He pointed at a diagram and slid the book across the table. Saulice studied the sketch, slower this time. The technique wasn't flashy—just a staggered pivot paired with concentrated fount pressure. It redirected force and countered with control.

Useful. Especially for someone like Lucas.

Across the table, Drezz bent over his journal, sketching stances and weight distribution, shaping them into triangles of balance. None of them were studying abstract theory anymore. Every page had become preparation.

"I think I understand the split-circle stance now," Saulice said, half to himself. "It isn't about absorbing the strike. It's about dodging by a half-step and taking the space your opponent gives up."

Damian nodded. "If you respond with a forged strike in time, you punish the gap."

Drezz looked up. "That will take more control than we have right now."

"Maybe," Saulice admitted. "But we'll get there."

His hand brushed the shard in his pocket, then withdrew. No need to test it again. Not yet. One answer was enough for today.

"I won't beat him with strength," Saulice said after a pause. "He's got more control, more reach. If I try to trade hits, I'll lose."

"Then don't trade," Damian replied, flipping to another diagram. "Redirect him. Let him miss. Make him overreach. Then strike his pride."

"His pride is large," Drezz observed. "Easy target."

Saulice chuckled, though the sound soon faded into thought. "He leans forward when he thinks he's winning. That's when I could strike."

Damian leaned back, arms crossed. "He always presses his advantage. Confident opponents unsettle him more than desperate ones."

Saulice turned the page to another illustration. This one showed a figure circling fount through his own frame, a pulse that empowered speed and strength briefly instead of projecting outward. The author called it a circuit reversal.

"I think I can bait him," Saulice said. "Pretend I'm pressing, then let him push back. If I can tire him out, I can save the reversal for the moment he's overconfident and exposed."

Damian narrowed his eyes. "A *circuit* reversal?"

"Yes. I think I could manage it once. Enough to create an opening."

Drezz tapped the corner of his notes. "That will require precision. And endurance. Surging through your own body isn't taught until second year. The stamina alone is punishing."

Damian leaned forward, his tone sharpening. "Look. I won't sugarcoat it. Lucas isn't just one of the best first-years here, Saulice. His father is one of King Emerin's seven generals. His mother? She's a Sentinel in Fury's Fist."

Saulice blinked. "Melandra told me she was a Sentinel once... I never realized what that meant."

Damian's mouth fell open. "A *Sentinel* brought you to Brynswick? Saulice, that's one rank beneath a Paladin. Do you understand? Lord Commander Muir is the only Paladin alive. Sentinels are the ones who stand directly beneath him. They're not just strong forgers; they're the kind who carry campaigns on their backs. That's Lucas's mother. His father is a general. His bloodline is drenched in strength and status, and with their money he can afford the finest trainers in Axbridge. You're not just up against a student, you're up against everything his family represents."

Drezz crossed his arms, his expression unreadable. "That is why he carries himself the way he does. He has always been told he was inevitable."

Saulice's chest tightened. For the first time, the weight of it pressed in: Lucas wasn't just cruel, he was dangerous. Stronger than him in body, in fount, and in lineage. The gap wasn't small. It was a canyon.

"Maybe," Saulice admitted. His voice was quieter now, as if he were confessing it to himself as much as to them. "But it's the only way I'll stand a chance. My forging isn't enough yet. My body isn't enough yet. If I want to face Lucas Crawford, I need to sharpen every weakness until there's nothing left for him to exploit."

He exhaled hard, jaw tight. "I can't answer him with words. Valos made that clear—if I provoke any of the Great Houses, I lose more than my place here. The only way to silence him is in the circle. If I can't beat him there, he'll *never* stop."

The silence that followed wasn't agreement, but acceptance. Drezz and Damian both understood what Saulice was really saying: he was afraid, and he was willing to break himself in training because the alternative was being broken in front of everyone.

Saulice looked between them, his decision hardening. "That's why I'm going to start training twice a day."

Damian groaned. "You… are insane. I envy your conviction, but joining you means neglecting the cafeteria's honey rolls. I don't know if I can make that sacrifice."

Drezz chuckled. "I will join you. It is an excellent opportunity to narrow the gap."

"Fine," Damian muttered. "I won't be the odd man out. But listen. If you want the feint to work, you'll need to sell it. Lucas *must* believe you're at your limit. And you'll still have to master the reversal."

"That's fine," Saulice said. "I don't just want to dodge him. I want him to commit."

Above them, footsteps echoed across the upper tier. None of them looked up.

"I want to start with footwork drills tomorrow," Saulice said. "That has to come first."

"I'll mirror the sequence," Drezz offered. "That way you can see the openings you create."

"I'll spot timing," Damian said. "And fix your pivot. You plant late."

Saulice glanced between them. He didn't voice his thanks, but something in his chest eased. The storm inside wasn't flaring anymore—it was beginning to concentrate.

He leaned back, chair creaking softly. The stained glass above had dimmed, its light fallen to grey. He picked up his pencil again and added notes in the margin.

Lucas. Forward lean. Breaks after second stance. Blind to flank. Forging window: half-breath before reset.

Drezz's tail flicked as he marked another diagram. Damian leaned over his shoulder, pointing at the margins.

The three of them stayed long after the others had left. They weren't studying anymore. They were preparing.

The Annual Combative Exam was coming.

And Saulice no longer wanted to simply survive it.

He wanted to win.

CHAPTER 18

ASHES OF AMBITION

The training grounds stood empty at dawn. Not even the wind stirred. Fog hung low, settling like a second skin across the wide rings and broken stone pillars, unmoving.

Saulice sat at the center of the largest ring, knees drawn, arms slack at his sides. His back ached from sleeping wrong, paired with his first week of double training sessions. But his mind burned hotter than his body could rest.

From the edge of the ring, Drezz watched with folded arms. "You're serious about this?"

Saulice nodded once. "I think I can hold it. Not long. But just enough to test it."

Drezz's ears flattened. "It's not the holding I'm worried about."

Saulice said nothing. He crouched low, palms pressed to the stone. The prayer lingered in his chest, not as words anymore, but as warmth coiled in his ribs, quiet and sacred. He clenched his fists, jaw tight.

The Combative Exam loomed only two weeks ahead. If he could not master the circuit reversal by then, he would lose. And not just to Lucas, but to the whispers, the glances, and all the others still waiting to see him fail.

His lip still carried the faint yellow mark of Lucas's fist. The bruise had almost faded, but the memory had not. He could still see that brutal smile etched on Lucas's face, smug with certainty. That punch had been assurance: Saulice would always take it, always fall silent.

But something had *changed.*

His gaze dropped to the citrine shard at his hip. His body could bear it now. Sometimes even summon it. Not for long, not yet, but the fear was gone. That meant something.

He shifted deeper into the ring, uniform brushing against his knees as he moved. Cold pressed up through scorched stone, seeping into his shins. He had watched older students practice the circuit reversal more times than he could count. No first year was supposed to attempt it. Cadre Nilus had outright warned of the risk when Saulice asked in class. The technique required cores already expanded by weeks of absorbing ambient fount. Students weren't even taught it until their second year.

But Saulice didn't have a year. Not while the Academy whispered. Not while Lucas watched. And not while Lazarus resisted every forging attempt.

Forging with a fractured core felt like stepping into a shared room and finding it already occupied. His fount tangled with lightning that leaked from the Titan, tendrils bleeding through every crack. He had learned to draw only what was his, careful not to touch that power. Yet the moment his focus slipped, the instant his reach grazed a single thread, everything changed.

Just brushing it dragged him deeper, pulled like a weight beneath black water into an ocean of rage. The current there was endless, waves too vast to fight. And beneath the fury lurked something sharper still, grief so hollow it threatened to drown him. He never saw its source, but every time the golden tendrils brushed him, he came away shaking, emptied by sorrow that wasn't his yet lived inside him.

He inhaled slow through his nose, forcing the storm to quiet. Doubts folded in on themselves until one memory remained, sharp enough to cut through noise. The square in Hamlen rose before him, not as a dream but as something carved in blood. Will's hand dragging him behind the cart. Gerald's jeer. Fists hammering into his ribs. His courier pouch torn from him, the red gleam of the stolen ruby shard.

And what did Saulice do? He took it, just like always.

Until he snapped.

His breath stilled at the memory of that feral moment, when hatred had devoured fear and something inside him broke. The truth was, he was exhausted. Not physically. Mentally. Years of being the boy no one defended had hollowed him until nothing remained but the word they branded him with.

Hamlen's *Forsaken*.

But not now.

He exhaled through his teeth, planting his foot firm as he began condensing his fount. He drew only from the whole sections of his core, working around fractures. It slowed him, but he had no choice. Even if it took him twice as long, even if his core leaked and bled while he worked, he would endure.

"Again," he whispered. The bracer on his wrist caught a faint kiss of light, steady and clean.

He stepped back into the stance he had studied in the Annals. Feet wide, breath guided, spine aligned. Melandra's words rose in him—stillness, prayer, quiet focus. His fingers brushed the citrine shard.

Drezz shifted at the edge of the ring. "If you collapse, I'm carrying you to the infirmary."

Saulice gave a thin smile. "Then I'll stand."

He paused, sensing the air tingling, waiting. And for the first time, he wondered if Shaddai could do more than hold Lazarus back. Could He mend the core itself?

He closed his eyes. His voice came low, weighted. "Shaddai. You who breathed life into the Titans, who shaped the first breath from silence. Breathe into me. I don't need to be mighty. Can you mend my core? Can you make me whole?"

There was no reply.

But something moved inside him.

As Saulice prepared the stance again, a familiar throb pulsed near his core. Not the rhythm he'd finally begun to nurture, but another attempt from Lazarus to derail his forging.

He focused, forcing the foreign rhythm from his thoughts as he inspected his core again.

Within himself, where the fractures stretched across the center, the image began shifting. The jagged edges shimmered faintly and from those splintered seams, a single translucent tendril reached outward. It was thin and fragile, quivering like a thread of spider silk in the breeze. And when Saulice realized its purpose, his breath caught.

It was stretching across the fracture, trying to bridge the gap.

Then another appeared.

And another.

Just… reaching across to the other side. But it would take a million of those tendrils to close the fractures. A dozen questions blossomed in his mind, but Saulice was certain of one thing.

It wasn't Lazarus. He felt that clearly now. The tendril was gentle and patient, without chaos or fury.

Maybe, Saulice thought, Shaddai hadn't only helped him forge. Maybe… He'd *been* healing him.

Saulice muttered the prayer Father Laird had given him to slow his core's leaking before trying again. "Shaddai… steady me. Hold me and my core, for I cannot hold myself."

The ring brightened as morning light spilled across polished stone, but Saulice barely noticed. He moved through the first sequence with care, stepping forward, opening his palm, guiding his breath down his spine as Nilus had taught.

The healing would not happen overnight, but it was the beginning.

And beginnings were important.

Saulice reached for the citrine shard. It pulsed steady and bright. He moved slowly, repeating all the steps he'd learned. Step. Reach. Breath down his spine. Hand brushing the shard. And he began condensing the fount in his core, careful once again, not to touch or draw from the yellow tendrils.

Behind him, Drezz's voice picked up, attention focused now. "Five seconds."

Saulice dropped to a crouch, palms against the stone. The motion felt natural.

"Drezz," he said, voice low, "I need you to strike me."

The fallet blinked. "Pardon me?"

"A controlled hit. Something to my chest or shoulder. Just hard enough to give me a chance to a see the circuit reversal in action if I succeed."

"I don't know about this."

"I won't injure you."

"That's not what I'm worried about." Drezz hesitated. "You've done this before?"

"Only visualized," Saulice answered. "The motion. The flow. Just not the full circuit reversal at once."

"And your core?"

"Still fractured," he said, rising. "But something shifted. I need to know if it's enough."

Drezz stepped into the ring with cautious steps, brow furrowed. "You're asking for trouble."

"I'm trying to find out the truth," Saulice said. "If I don't test it now, I'll second-guess my every step in the combat exams."

The fallet sighed. "Fine. For the combatives exam. Just one strike. You'd better control it."

Saulice nodded and moved into a wider stance. Back foot heavy with his right hand low. Left angled across the chest. Core tight and coiled. He whispered the rhythm into himself.

Pulse the fount through his chest and simultaneously through his legs and arms at a quick pace. Then after it reaches the furthest point, he would *reverse* the direction.

Drezz raised a hand, curling his fingers into a measured arc. "On your mark."

Saulice drew a sharp breath, and the shard flared, ready to help guide him. Light crawled along his wrist while his legs tingled with familiar tension.

"Now."

Drezz moved and Saulice began.

He condensed the fount he'd drawn from his core, squeezing it with his will until it was elongated and threadlike. Then, he pushed it through himself like an eel through water. It didn't bend around him; it coursed through him. Heel to spine. Spine to hands. The current obeyed as it branched out into his body.

His body became a conduit, not a container. For one breathless instant, it was working.

Then, just as the fount reached the tips of his fingers and the soles of his feet and he prepared to reverse its course, a violent tremor struck deep in his chest. He froze at once. Feeling it out with growing dread, he realized the strain had split one of his channels. A fork had torn open where none should exist.

The result was immediate.

The entire pathway the fount had traveled began to quake, and the threadlike stream itself fractured under the pressure. Saulice tried to correct the mistake, to redirect or mend it, but the damage had already gone too far. The circuit snapped with ruinous force, flooding his limbs with a searing heat that felt like fire poured into bone.

Light erupted in a concussive peal, raw and unshaped, power without form.

Drezz and Saulice were hurled backward across the ring as if struck by boulders. Drezz collided with a pillar of stone; Saulice skidded across dirt and sand. Heat rippled in every direction, the ground where they had stood left scorched and smoking.

A sharp cry tore from Saulice's throat as sparks flashed across his skin. The burn seemed to sink past muscle into marrow, as though his very body had been poisoned from within. Smoke curled upward from the sleeves of his uniform.

Silence followed.

Then a groan as Drezz moved to sit up, leaning against the stone pillar.

"Drezz!" Saulice scrambled, boots slipping across seared earth. He kneeled beside the fallet, heart hammering. "I- I didn't mean… Please say something."

"I'm alive," Drezz muttered, one eye squinting. "But I *definitely* told you this was a terrible idea."

Saulice exhaled, shaking. "You're sure nothing's broken?"

"My dignity," Drezz groaned. "Maybe a rib."

"I'm sorry."

"I know."

They stayed like that for some time, Drezz slumped against the scorched pillar while Saulice crouched beside him, staring at the tremor in his own hands. His arms stung, his back ached, and beneath it all a deeper fear gnawed at him — his core.

Every possible thought struck at once. What if he had damaged it further? What if his recklessness meant it would take even longer to heal? What if the harm had gone beyond his core and into his body itself?

He forced his breathing slow and turned inward. Casting aside the spiral of worries one by one, he searched for the faint hum he had learned to recognize. It took minutes of quiet effort before at last he glimpsed it.

Relief flooded him.

His core was still intact.

The attempt had failed, yes, but the reversal had not shattered what was already fragile. Warmth ebbed from his chest, leaving him weary yet grateful, though beneath that gratitude something older stirred. Lazarus lingered there in silence, watchful and still. The Titan's presence was neither angry nor hostile, only distant, and that quiet unsettled Saulice more than any rage would have. It left him wondering what, if anything, Lazarus had felt when Saulice brushed against that lightning earlier in the day.

Saulice flexed his burned fingers, then closed them into a fist.

A voice cried out, not Drezz's.

"Someone's down!"

He looked up sharply.

Three students stood near the wall, staring at the scorch mark within the ring. One pointed. Another muttered. A shadow shifted beyond them, watching from a distance. A figure Saulice recognized.

Cadre Pell.

His arms were crossed as he silently watched. Then he turned and disappeared.

Saulice's stomach twisted. "They saw."

Drezz winced. "So what? I'm the one that got blown up."

But Saulice didn't laugh. The failed circuit reversal hadn't just failed; it had drawn attention. He just hoped he didn't hear from Master Valos again because of this incident.

His resolve was no longer private.

An hour later, the infirmary lay quiet, sunlight striping the stone floor. Saulice sat on the edge of a cot with his elbows on his knees, eyes fixed on Drezz's bandaged arm. The fallet's fur was singed, but the healers had assured them the wounds were shallow. No bones had broken, only bruises remained.

"I told you I'd live," Drezz mumbled.

"I know," Saulice murmured. "I still shouldn't have tried it."

"No, you should have," Drezz countered, "just not on a Saturday."

A faint smile tugged Saulice's lips, but it faded quickly.

"I lost control, Drezz. Again."

"You pushed past the line," Drezz said. "You tried to force a second-year forging technique through a fractured core, and you are still breathing. That is not failure."

Saulice didn't answer. He stared at the gauze, guilt pulling at him. He hadn't meant to hurt Drezz. Yet beneath the shame, something else flickered. Quieter. Brighter.

The reversal had almost worked, if only for a moment. He had been so close, more than halfway through the circuit, before it collapsed. Now his core would need half a day to recover, or at least as much as it ever could while leaking.

He stood, rolling his shoulders until his back protested.

"We need to get better," he said. "The other academs won't take it easy on us. They expect to crush us in the combatives exams."

"We're already catching up with the bottom runners of the class," Drezz replied.

Saulice clenched and unclenched his fists, a steady rhythm grounding him. "I know... but we'll need more than that. At least I will."

Drezz tilted his head. "Are you thinking of asking someone?"

Saulice didn't respond, though a name kept circling in his thoughts. Someone who had studied them both closely. Someone who understood the cost of strength. Before he could speak, the door creaked open.

"About time I found you two!"

Damian rushed in with his satchel slung and collar damp with sweat. "Cadre Pell had me running supplies all morning. Then, out of nowhere, some second years mention two first years sparring in the dueling—woah. What happened?"

"Practiced something we weren't supposed to," Drezz muttered.

Damian raised a brow. "Warn me next time before you decide to blow each other up. I'm the fire forger, remember?"

"I didn't explode anything," Saulice said.

"Could've fooled the field," Drezz chuckled weakly.

Silence followed, but it was not uneasy. Just tired and settled. Saulice let it steady him. This wasn't an ending. It was a beginning, and he was eager to see what his core could achieve if he focused on the techniques of a first year instead of reaching too far.

"Everything they said I couldn't do," he whispered. "Everything they think I'll never become. I have to break their mold."

He looked at his fingers, burned but not broken.

"I belong here," he said, louder now. "And I'm going to prove it. I don't care what Lucas thinks, or what Lazarus wants, or what anyone else claims I cannot be."

Drezz lifted his gaze and Damian gave a single, quiet nod.

Saulice turned toward the door. "We'll need to be ready when they expect us to fail."

The next fire would not consume him, nor would he allow it to harm anyone else.

This time, it would *carry* him.

CHAPTER 19

BREATH BETWEEN STRIKES

The training fields smelled of churned earth and sweat. Morning haze clung to the air, thick with spring warmth and the faint iron tang of blood. Saulice stood in the grass, shoulders loose, eyes shadowed with the weight of too many sleepless weeks.

The circuit reversal *still* would not hold.

He had come close, close enough to feel the fount stir awake, rising from his core and slipping across his collarbone with the low hum of distant thunder. But every time he neared the threshold, the flow faltered. The circuit collapsed inward on itself, sputtering into nothing and forcing him to break off before it tore something loose inside him.

Over time, he began to understand why. The problem was not only control, but the core itself. Until he learned how to draw ambient fount into his body and refine it into something of his own, he would never be able to expand his core to the size required for the reversal. And even then, his path would remain harder than the others. Where most first-year academs could pull freely from a single, whole core, Saulice's fractured state left him piecing his strength together from scattered fragments.

Inwardly, it felt like reaching for separate islands adrift in a storm. He had to gather power from each shard of himself and knit it together, while the others drew from one unified sea. Even at his best, he could manage perhaps three-quarters of what they could summon without effort.

Four days.

That was all the time left before the Combatives Exam.

Training twice a day had taken its toll. Saulice, Drezz, and Damian moved like shadows of themselves now. They were bone-weary, feet sore, lungs scraped raw from effort. But they were faster. Stronger. More precise. Endurance had come not as a gift, but as the consequence of pain.

And in that pain, they had crawled every grueling inch toward progress.

Tibbet stood ahead of them, arms crossed, his grey curls matted with sweat. The underarms of his tunic were darkened, and behind him a crooked line of wooden dummies leaned in the grass, their surfaces splintered and scorched from dozens of repeat drills.

Even without answers, the rhythm of training brought clarity. Saulice pressed his hand to the *Forsaken* brand. Not to hide it, but to remind himself of something. Silence was not abandonment. He had learned that lesson easily enough, having to live with Lazarus each day. But Saulice believed silence had a silver lining few discerned. It was a place where strength grew, if one could keep their wits about them.

All he had to do was stay calm and focused. Simple in thought, hard in execution.

Calm while enduring a maelstrom of fists, weaving through barrages of Damian's flame-forged strikes, and dodging Drezz's shifting earth obstacles across the dueling ring's rugged terrain. They had done this for more than a week.

"Before we begin today," Tibbet called, his voice sharper than usual, "I have a question you each need to answer."

The three boys exchanged quick glances, sweat-streaked and silent.

"You've trained harder than any first-years I've seen at Brynswick," Tibbet continued. "Harder than anyone would expect. And it's not just ambition. You train like tomorrow might be your last day in Axbridge. Tell me why."

He pointed at Damian first.

Damian straightened, brushing a leaf from his shoulder with deliberate care. "Because I want to earn it," he said. "All of it. Not through my name or favors, and not using family ties like the members of the Great Houses do. I want the merit, and to know that I stood where I stood because of my own hands."

Tibbet gave one sharp nod. "Good. Stop hesitating before you strike. Footwork drives every good attack, so trust it and commit."

He turned next to Drezz.

The fallet lowered his gaze. His voice, when it came, was quiet but steady. "Because my homeland is fraying," he admitted. "Fallenan will need strength when the storms arrive. They have *already* begun." He lifted his head a fraction, eyes narrowing with quiet resolve. "I intend to be strong enough to change that. To alter their course, if I can. That is my hope."

Tibbet offered no words this time, only a brief glance that carried quiet respect.

Then his eyes settled on Saulice.

He hesitated, his mouth dry. His reasons were simpler than Tibbet likely assumed, yet heavier than anything he wanted to share. Every morning, he woke with the same thought, that Brynswick could send him home before nightfall. That the whispers calling him *Forsaken* would be proven right. That Lucas's taunts were not only cruelty but prophecy.

"I have to grow strong," Saulice said at last, his voice quieter than he expected. "I don't have a choice. I used to think strength meant being feared. Being loud, taking up space. That's what every leader I've ever met has done. I can't name many who gained power and stayed humble. Maybe Melandra. Maybe Dedric. But they're rare."

He glanced briefly at Drezz and Damian, then back to Tibbet.

"You two are confirmed academs," he continued. "Valos won't send you away for mistakes unless they're unforgivable. But I'm different. I have to prove I belong here every day. Prove that my admittance wasn't a mistake, that I'm worth the Academy's resources and the city's funding."

His throat tightened. "And honestly… I'm scared. Not of failing. I'm scared of going back. Back to hiding. Back to cowering every time conflict found me. I don't want to ever live like that again."

A quiet settled over the ring, heavier than any silence they had known during training.

Drezz shifted first, his usually formal tone softer than Saulice had ever heard it. "Then you will not," Drezz said simply. "Not while we stand with you."

Damian nodded, expression serious in a way Saulice rarely saw. "We've got you. The three of us, we'll train together, and we'll stand together. Nobody sends you back alone."

Saulice's chest tightened, not with fear this time, but with something steadier. Something almost like belonging.

Tibbet regarded him for a long moment, unreadable yet faintly approving. "That'll do," Tibbet said at last, and stepped back to ready them for the next round.

He gestured toward the dummy ring. "Partner drills. Five-minute rotations. Damian with me. Saulice with Drezz. Two hours before our first break, starting now. Let's go!"

They moved into position. Saulice shook out his hands and glanced toward Drezz. The fallet had changed since the day they met. His posture had tightened, every movement more contained. Expressions came slower now, more deliberate. His speech had shifted too, adopting Candur's dialect with a looseness far from the stiffness Saulice remembered. Even other academs had begun nodding to him in the halls. Some even asked him questions after class.

A month ago, Drezz had been invisible. But now, when he spoke, people listened.

"You alright?" Drezz asked, lifting his padded staff.

Purple bags lined Saulice's eyes. "I've had worse mornings."

"That is the spirit," Drezz replied, circling him. "At least you haven't exploded again."

Their staves clacked together. Deflect, pivot, feint, retreat. Saulice focused on his footwork, letting muscle memory lead. He moved quicker now. More centered. But Drezz carried a rhythm of his own, natural and steady. Like stone adapting to motion, grounded with an unshakable certainty.

How the fallet kept such balance, Saulice could not fathom. Perhaps it was in their very anatomy.

A half hour blurred as they drilled, swapped partners, and drilled again. Damian caught Saulice with a feint hook before driving a sharp elbow into his ribs. He returned the favor with a low sweep that knocked Damian into the grass. They exchanged grimaces that gave way to grins, then chuckles.

Then the air shifted with expectation. Apprehension curled across the field. Saulice glanced around before wishing he had not.

Rayne had arrived. Rayne had arrived. She didn't announce herself, nor did she need to. One moment Saulice stood recovering between rounds, the next she was demanding he assume different stances, correcting him with sharp whacks on his elbows and knees.

"You're holding back," she said as a matter of fact.

Saulice reset, bitterness threading his tone. "I'm tired."

"Then get stronger faster, and you won't be so tired."

She didn't wait for an argument. Stepping forward, she seized a short staff and rushed at him, drilling him with a precision that bordered on inhumane brutality.

Sweat poured down his face, blurring his vision, clinging beneath his nails. Even with obstructed sight, he endured, though not without taking hits. A *lot* of hits.

Rayne was a powerhouse, even among second-year academs, and she had no reason to take it easy on him. Close-range sparring against her was rigorous; every blow Saulice parried sent vibrations down his arms. She attacked in mixed patterns of quick bursts, low sweeps, and feints that gave way to powerful strikes.

He caught an apologetic frown from Tibbet, now watching alongside Drezz and Damian.

A minute had not passed before Saulice's parries began to slip, his arms and legs taxed beyond what he could bear. Elbow checks came too fast to block, striking his ribs like drums. Her movements weren't flashy; they didn't need to be. They carried a discipline that only hundreds of quiet hours could instill.

Saulice fell once. Then twice.

Again. And again.

Each time, she made him rise.

She moved into position once more, stance set. "Try *again*."

Saulice stepped back, reset his shaking feet, and groaned as he lifted his stave. Every movement burned, and his legs and shoulders felt as though lava coursed through them. He focused his mind on the citrine shard tied at his waist, breathing deep and slow down his spine. He held his breath in his core, just as Nilus had taught. He closed his eyes and emptied his thoughts.

The fount answered, and once again he saw his core. Without hesitation, he repeated Father Laird's prayer. The familiar soft glow settled over the fractured sphere, threading through every crack and fissure, slowing the constant leak of lightning within.

He tightened his grip on the citrine shard, using its steady warmth to guide him. Drawing fount from each broken section of his core was painstaking; every fragment bled energy, forcing him to gather and hold what he could. Some days the fount slipped through his grasp like an eel, fluid and difficult to steer into the circuit he was attempting to form. His focus wavered, and in an instant the fount unraveled, scattering back into the isolated fragments of his core like dispersing smoke.

He exhaled hard, fists trembling. "It's slipping."

Rayne didn't shift. "Again."

He braced and shifted more weight into his heels, digging them into the ground. Letting his arms hang loose, stave extended behind him, he sought absolute stillness before starting the technique's circuit again. His shard pulsed once, eager to help him guide the fount, ironically unaware of how difficult it was for him to pool enough together to forge in the first place.

To his surprise, this time the fount burst upward from his core, fast and unfocused.

It shot up his spine before slowing in his shoulder, but the course quickly fractured. The fount snapped with a sharp sting, then the circuit winked out completely. His left side tingled, feet unsteady.

Saulice knew that if he lost focus, he could injure himself, perhaps even worsen the fractures in his core. Since the incident with Drezz, he had taken extra care, cutting any circuit the moment he sensed it destabilizing.

"Reset." Rayne waited for him to catch his breath, hands on her hips.

He crouched low, muttering into the grass. The words weren't meant for her. They were meant for him.

On his twelfth try, he slowed everything. Drew a square in the dirt with his heel. Set his feet wider. Closed his eyes and tried to see the threads of his core, not broken, but reaching alongside the fractures. If nothing else, reaching.

The warmth came again as he drew the churning fount up his spine. This time it moved steady, lingering. And it held.

But doubt crept in. What if the circuit reversal backfired? What if it broke him in front of everyone?

As though spooked by doubt, the light recoiled, chased away by his poisonous thoughts.

He struck his knee with his fist, frustration boiling beneath his skin. "It's there! I can feel it!"

Rayne stepped closer, her voice low but firm. "Then stop complaining and listen to it!"

A quiet scoff rose from the edge of the field.

Lucas.

He passed by at a lazy stroll, stave slung across one shoulder.

"Why even bother? Everyone already knows how the exams will end. Me at the top, and you at the bottom," he said, voice raised just enough to make sure everyone heard. "I'd start packing my bags now, probationary academ."

Then he left their sight.

Rayne said nothing, but her next strike came harder.

Saulice gritted his teeth and stood again, chuckling at the thought of requesting another training uniform. His was nearly unrecognizable now, stained and darkened by sweat.

His arms throbbed, each thought dragging like a weight behind his eyes. Still, he tried again. This time, he whispered a prayer under his breath. Not long. Not clever. Just the rhythm of his need.

Shaddai… steady me. Hold me and my core, for I cannot hold myself.

He began forging the circuit again, channeling his feeble combined fount as slowly as possible without letting it stutter. It was not wild or sharp, but there was rhythm behind the circuit as he built it.

He moved with it, letting the current follow his breath instead of chasing it. The energy reached his chest, climbed through his arms and legs.

And it held.

With the same slow, deliberate care, just as it reached his fingertips and toes, he halted the fount's circuit and began drawing it back toward his core.

Heat threaded through his limbs as the circuit arrived back at its origin with great friction, pressing against an invisible wall just outside his core. Saulice willed it forward, sweat beading down his face.

And like a dam opening, the circuit rushed into the core. A concussive boom echoed within himself, then he felt it.

Not a burning sensation, but vitality. His muscles tightened then released with unexpected precision. His stance sank lower, more rooted. The ache in his legs faded. His balance steadied beyond anything he had known. His focus grew razor sharp, locked in.

But it would only be for fifteen seconds.

And for fifteen seconds, he wasn't chasing control.

Rayne stepped forward, staff raised. Her stance didn't change, but her eyes did. She had seen the shift.

Her first strike came from the left, a sweeping arc meant to test his guard. He caught it mid-motion, bracing with his forearm. His body moved faster than his mind could follow. Her stave flew back, and Saulice realized he had created the first opening for a counterattack since they had started.

He jolted, pivoting inside her reach before she could reset. Her eyes went wide.

But he felt the flaw, a sloppiness beneath the motion. Speed had come at a cost, and his thoughts dragged, struggling to keep pace.

He didn't strike. He stepped back cleanly, footwork exact, focusing on every movement.

Rayne attacked again, sharper than in any of their previous bouts. A low feint drew his eye, followed by a real lunge toward his shoulder. Saulice twisted, letting the momentum pass cleanly, then countered with a downward sweep. His staff snapped against hers, the sound sharp but contained.

He wasn't overwhelming her. But he was staying with her.

Her tempo quickened. Each strike came faster, more intricate. She spun, redirected, and compressed the space between them with every motion.

At first, he faltered. His body moved, but his mind trailed behind. The rhythm came too fast, too sharp. But he adjusted and caught the beat, matching her breath for breath for the first time.

Each step landed with intent. His limbs moved without strain. The weight of doubt had fallen away, replaced by something steadier. Something earned.

Then time was up.

His legs turned to noodles. Saulice stumbled, the aftershock nearly too much to stand. When he opened his eyes, Rayne was still across from him. She hadn't moved, but she wasn't watching him like a trainer anymore.

Tibbet dismissed them with a single clap and a half-hearted bark about tomorrow's drills. His tone lacked fire, but not intention. Beneath the words lingered something quieter, grudging but real approval.

Drezz and Damian ambled toward the water trough at the field's edge, their posture slumped with the fatigue that only hard-earned effort could bring.

Saulice stayed where he was, kneeling in the grass, breath steady now though his heart still pounded in his ears.

The circuit reversal had worked. Finally.

His fingers tingled from the adrenaline, but for once they did not tremble. No burn from overload, only the ghost of control.

"You almost lost your footing," Rayne said from behind.

Saulice turned slightly, chuckling. She stood just outside the chalk ring, arms crossed, expression calm but open.

"I know," he said. "My mind was playing catchup. It was… very strange."

She stepped closer and nodded. "You corrected it by the end. Barely, but you did."

He looked at the dirt beneath his boots. Scuffed. Flattened. Worn.

For a while, they sat in silence. The kind that doesn't press. The kind that listens.

Then she said, "I've noticed you brace before you strike. Like you're expecting to fall. Like you're still thinking about the last hit before the next one comes."

He didn't answer immediately, but the words sank in. And they weren't wrong.

"Maybe I am," he said at last. "I've had to defend myself for a long time. I don't think I've *ever* won a fair fight."

Rayne didn't smile, but something in her gaze softened, just a fraction.

"I used to think the only people who made it here were the ones who never fell. Powerful people without flaws," he said. "But now I think... maybe it's the ones smart enough to change their perspective."

She looked at him for a long moment, then nodded.

"You're on your way," she said.

From the edge of the field, Drezz called out, "Water or death. Pick one."

Damian added with a groan, "I think we've chosen both."

Rayne stood and offered Saulice her hand. He hesitated, not out of pride, but from the strange weight of it. This wasn't just an offer to stand. It wasn't an order. It was something else.

He took it.

Her grip was steady. She pulled him to his feet in a single motion, no struggle, no strain.

"You're closer than you think," she said, voice lower now. "But you need to stop assuming the next strike will break you. You're made of tougher stuff than you think."

Saulice nodded, breath slow in his chest.

Tibbet stood at the far end of the ring, arms crossed, face unreadable.

"You get one surge like that during the Combatives Exam," he said without looking at them. "Make sure it's the right one."

Then he walked off.

It wasn't praise or dismissal, but the words comforted Saulice.

Drezz and Damian sprawled near the trough, drinking water as if it would resurrect them. Rayne walked ahead of Saulice, her steps easy, her braid catching sunlight like a bronze thread in motion.

He followed more slowly, each step threatening to send him tumbling. His arms and chest were tight, but he made it to the trough.

He was learning to carry his weight, but more than that, he was learning to fight forward.

The Crescent dormitory had finally quieted after lights-out. Muffled voices and evening footfalls faded behind the thick stone walls. A single lantern glowed in the corner of their shared alcove, casting warm gold across the bunks and the worn grey floor.

Saulice sat cross-legged on his blanket, back pressed to the wall, knees drawn. The air in the room had stilled. No one spoke.

Drezz leaned against his cot, legs stretched and crossed at the ankles. Damian hunched near the foot of his bed, deciding to crash in their room for the night. He peeled the dry crust off a slice of bread. Their limbs were sore, their thoughts slower, but none of them were able to sleep.

Saulice opened and closed his hand slowly. He could still feel the echo of the fount's circuit through his body from earlier. Not just the burn or the pressure, but the movement of it—the strange sense that, for one fleeting breath, strength had lived inside him. It wasn't wild; it was contained.

Then, just as fast, it was gone, like a candle's last gasp. But it had been there, and it hadn't lashed out.

Drezz shifted, breaking the quiet. "My shoulder will forgive you. Eventually."

Saulice smirked. "I told you it'd hold when it mattered."

Drezz tilted his head. "I still remember the last time it didn't."

Saulice shrugged. "I don't think I could have done it without Rayne. Her drills forced something into place today."

Damian stretched out a leg and added, "She really didn't go easy on you. My back was howling just watching."

"No," Saulice admitted. "But I think that's why it worked."

He paused, eyes on the shadow flickering across the stone.

"I was sluggish," he continued. "But the flare worked. And it didn't lash out. I didn't lose control, and next time I'll be ready for it."

Damian picked a piece of bread crust from his uniform and tossed it to the floor. "So, when you beat Lucas, what then?"

The quiet that followed was deep and settled.

Saulice leaned his head back against the stone, watching the uneven patterns carved by old chisels.

"I'm not sure. I think maybe I'll just stop and think about how far we've come. Wonder what my uncle would think of me." He rubbed the back of his head.

Drezz nodded slowly. "After the Combatives Exam, I imagine I'll do as I do every day. Hope and dream of peace for my people and my home. Fallenan drifts further from peace."

"I don't want to be strong," Drezz said. "Not for silly scores or accolades. Because when I return, my people will see that strength still exists. That there's a narrow path, a true path they can follow."

Saulice didn't answer, but the words stayed with him.

Damian spoke next. "My family thinks I'll come back early from Brynswick. I'm the weakest forger of seven siblings. Father wants me to serve on some council, thinks I'm wasting my time here." He rested his head against his bunk. "But I'm not building a name they can use. I want to earn something they can't touch."

Another quiet passed between them. The kind that doesn't need to be filled.

Then Saulice said, "I'm not going to just beat Lucas. I want to win. Against him, against the naysayers, and against myself."

Both boys looked at him.

"I want to win," he said again. "But not just because of Lucas. I'm going to win because I've clawed my way forward every step since I got here. I've prayed until my thoughts unraveled, trained until my body gave out, broken more than I thought I could ever rebuild. I want to feel how much I've changed."

He reached toward the citrine shard by his cot. It pulsed once, faint and steady. Outside, the wind shifted. And for the first time since Hamlen, Saulice didn't pray for peace and patience.

He prayed for strength.

CHAPTER 20

WHERE PRESSURE WAITS

The walk to the arena was quiet, though not solemn.

Saulice, Drezz, and Damian moved in step through the Brynswick courtyard, their feet brushing fallen petals from the flowering tree that crowned the stairway.

They had trained hard for this.

Drezz had advanced leaps in the last weeks. Where once he managed little more than a vibration of the ground, he could now tilt earth beneath an opponent's stance with a flick of his foot. His forging had grown stable, sharp, and intentional.

Damian had grumbled through their trips to the Annals, but one afternoon he slumped across a fire affinity codex, claiming he'd only closed his eyes to "see the diagrams better." The next day, he burned through a practice ring with a spiral burst that nearly singed Pell's boot.

Saulice's training had not been gentle. Tibbet's drills left bruises that lingered for days, and Rayne's regimen was unrelenting. Her voice never raised, yet her strikes came fast and without pity. Then, somehow, he had managed to keep his fount stable enough to pull off the circuit reversal technique. But that was not all.

No one knew he had slept less than four hours a night for the last three days, scrounging time to learn another technique, a simple flashbang, in case the circuit reversal failed. No one except Drezz and Damian.

"Alright, boys," Damian said, breaking the silence. He clapped his hands and slung an arm around both their shoulders. "The time has come. The moment of legend. And I, for one, have never slept better in my life. Training is exhausting."

"You napped *plenty* before training started," Drezz replied dryly.

Damian's eyes widened in mock offense. "Would you believe me if I said I have a rare sleep condition?"

"Nope," Saulice said without looking at him.

"What if I told you I'm iron deficient?"

"You're getting warmer."

"Fine," Damian groaned, slumping with exaggerated defeat. "I'm lazy. Blame the city's crafters for making beds so comfortable."

Drezz gave a soft chuckle. "You haven't known comfort until you've slept in a Fallenan tree-bed. They sway with your breath."

Damian stopped mid-step, eyes narrowing. "You've been holding out on me? Such betrayal."

Saulice smiled. The tension around his shoulders eased. He opened his mouth to add something when a shadow fell across the stone ahead.

Master Valos approached from the lower path. His robes were deeper than the standard indigo, so dark they looked black in sunlight, trimmed in silver and marked by the ten-pointed star of Brynswick. He walked without noise.

They stopped without needing to speak.

Valos scanned all three, his gaze lingering briefly on each, then settling on Saulice. "Good morning, boys," he said. His voice was measured, but something hard pressed beneath the civility. "Drezz. Damian. Proceed to the arena. Saulice, come with me."

None of them moved at first.

Then Drezz nodded once and stepped aside. Damian hesitated longer, then clapped Saulice on the shoulder twice. "We'll save you a bench," he said, voice quiet now. "Try not to tick off any more officials on your way back."

Saulice tried to answer, but his voice caught. He watched them leave before following Valos across the courtyard and down the older path that curved beneath the Annals.

He did not ask where they were going. He already knew.

Past the outer classrooms. Beyond the quiet grove where second years studied under glassed canopies. Left, then up two shallow stairs. They entered the Master's Halls. Saulice had been here twice before, once when he first arrived with Melandra, and again during his recent meeting with Master Valos. He hoped the conversation would not be similar this time.

Master Valos' office waited at the very end of the halls, spanning twice as large as any of the Cadres.

A tall desk of varnished oak stood beneath the far window. A single bear's pelt rested beneath Saulice's boots as he stepped inside. A modest hearth glowed beside the inner wall, low and steady. The room was not grand, but quiet and practical.

Valos sat and motioned for Saulice to take the chair opposite. He did not speak at once. Instead, he reached into a drawer and withdrew a single sheet of annotated parchment.

"I debated whether to speak with you before or after your combative exams," he said. "But since this is the second such report, and the name involved is not a small one, I've decided clarity is best."

Saulice frowned. "Report?"

"I warned you last time, Saulice." Master Valos' eyes narrowed. "You were seen in an altercation near the Annals several weeks ago. It was an unsanctioned engagement with another first-year academ. Lucas Crawford."

"He punched *me*!" Saulice explained. "I didn't forge or hit him back. Drezz and Damian were there. They can confirm it. Master Valos, you have to believe me."

"That is not the point," Valos said, irritation creeping into his voice. "You were involved. And that means something when you stand in opposition to a member of a Great House. House Crawford has deep influence in Candur, even at Brynswick. Whether you intended to or not, you've drawn the ire of more than just your Cadre. And that is not the kind of attention this Academy welcomes. I told you to keep your head down, boy."

Saulice did not answer.

Valos set the parchment down with a quiet snap. "You have been given a rare opportunity," he said. "And I am beginning to wonder whether you understand the weight of it."

He leaned back, the fire catching briefly in the silver of his robe trim.

"Today is your last chance to prove your worth, not just to Brynswick, but to Candur herself," he said. "I suggest you give the Academy reason to feel confident in its decision to accept you. Otherwise, the outcome of your matches may not be the only matter decided today."

Saulice gripped his chair with white knuckles, doing his best not to show his simmering frustration. "Is that all, Master?"

Master Valos sorted through a stack of parchments across his desk with a questioning glance, as if contemplating further chastisement.

"You are dismissed."

By the time Saulice reached the arena, Drezz was in the ring with another first-year academ, Feralan Kelm, an agile shadow forger Saulice avoided as much as Lucas.

He took his place on the front bench of the academ's section, the snap of the sapphire banners overhead sharp as a warning. Risers curved like a stone coliseum around the arena's eastern edge, packed with Cadre, students, and highborn officials. The dueling floor shimmered under midmorning light, its wide circles of gravel-covered earth marked with fresh white paint.

Saulice's bracer felt cold against his wrist. Too cold. His hands curled over the edge of the bench, every muscle in his forearm clenched to keep still. His gaze flicked toward the top tier of the arena, where the Great Houses sat cloaked in velvet shade. House Crawford's section gleamed with polished bronze and blue silk.

He stared too long.

The memory of Valos's words replayed, quiet and controlled, but laced with the promise of consequences. He had not done anything wrong in that courtyard, not when Lucas had thrown the first punch. Yet here he sat, punished for proximity while his name weighed heavier than his actions.

Across the pit, Cadre Calder sat in an upper alcove, placed there in Valos's absence, his robe a blade of navy blue trimmed in silver.

Drezz launched from a fount-forged stone column, his legs coiled tight, his copper-tipped staff slicing through the air as he spun. His body twisted once before landing behind Feralan's exposed flank. He crouched then pivoted, one hand slamming flat into the sand while the other whipped the staff in an overhead swing that struck hard beneath the noble's shoulder. And Drezz was not done.

A series of ripples spread across the arena floor, further disabling Feralan from recovering. He stumbled forward, pained and unbalanced. The ground shifted beneath him, subtle but firm, until a sharp incline caught one foot and brought him down.

Saulice did not cheer or smile. He only watched.

The judges leaned forward slightly, though none of them spoke. Feralan rolled to his feet and spun, a streak of forged shadows curling around the tip of his staff.

Then he struck.

The shadow flung from his staff like a whip, striking Drezz clean across the torso. Fabric hissed and smoke lifted from the fresh tear. The crowd inhaled sharply, their surprise hushed and sharp. Drezz's chest rose and fell, but he did not flinch. He adjusted his stance, eyes locked forward.

They circled again.

No movement was wasted. There were no dramatic feints or grapples, only two forms narrowing their tactics, each breath measured. Drezz's heel shifted slightly, and Saulice realized the ring's floor had tightened. The earth beneath him, once loose and pliable, remained compact from his earlier forging. Which meant that if Drezz could not find another way to make use of the earth, he would have to fight head-on.

Saulice's jaw tightened. He could see the moment Drezz noticed it too. The fallet stepped forward with another planned terrain shift, but the floor did not rise to his intended height. The earth slowed mid-movement, like sludge coming to a stop. He was not yet strong enough to move the hardened earth.

Feralan pressed without hesitation.

He swelled the shadows at the tip of his staff, then drove it forward in a horizontal swing. The strike hit Drezz's chest with concussive force, folding him backward onto one knee and blinding him in the same breath.

Drezz tossed his staff to the floor, surrendering the match.

Cadre Pell raised a hand.

"Ring One. Victor: Feralan Kelm."

The sigils across the floor dimmed. The hum of pressure that filled the arena bled away like air escaping a sealed jar.

Drezz did not stay down.

He stood, slow but steady, his shoulder sagging from the final blow. He gave a bow, sharp and perfect, then placed the staff on a rack outside the ring before turning to leave. The wound was fresh, blood darkening the edge of his sleeve, but he walked back toward the benches without a limp.

Saulice exhaled.

He had watched Drezz lose with more control than most would show in victory. It stung, but it did not sour. It confirmed something deeper.

Effort meant nothing to the wrong eyes. Saulice had learned that only moments ago in the presence of Master Valos.

Saulice glanced toward the upper tier again. The Crawford box remained motionless, the figures behind the velvet unmoved by valor or loss. Whether Drezz had won or not did not matter to them. Just as Saulice's defense weeks ago had not mattered to Valos. Just as truth itself seemed lighter than reputation.

Other matches blurred past in flashes of sparks and shouts of victory, but Saulice could not bring himself to focus. He had lost track of who was even fighting in the second ring, his thoughts pulled elsewhere.

The roar of the crowd pressed in like heat, and his hands stayed tight in his lap.

When the announcer called, "Ring Two: Damian Halcroft versus Jace Gerisio," the idle noise of the arena scattered as attention swung back to the floor. The low clang of the bell carried a finality that drew every eye forward.

Saulice blinked, his gaze narrowing on the boy stepping into the ring. Jace. He remembered the broad chest and the gleaming ruby shard at his collar, the cropped hair that hung across his eyes, and the sneer that had not left his face since the courtyard incident. Jace had been there beside Lucas, smirking while he blocked Damian from helping. Another meat shield for a Great House brat who had never been forced to answer for what he did.

Saulice neither leaned forward nor flinched. He only watched.

Drezz said something as Damian passed him, but the words slipped past unheard.

Below, Jace cracked his neck, his bracer gleaming as though polished for the occasion. "Didn't think they'd let a Halcroft in the ring," he said with a mocking tilt of his head.

Damian stopped mid-bow and fired back, "Guess they needed someone to humiliate you."

The judges lifted their hands, and the match began.

Flame erupted across the ring in an arcing strike from Damian. Jace spun his staff to deflect and answered with a swift bolt of fire. Damian did not dodge. He swung his staff overhead like an axe, the motion reckless in appearance but sharp in execution, and the blow split through Jace's flame as though it were brittle wood.

Gasps rippled through the crowd, but Saulice did not join them. He knew the truth. Fire against fire meant this would not be a contest of spectacle but of endurance and skill. The winner would be the one with the deeper fount core or the sharper technique.

He tried to keep his focus on the fight, but Valos's voice kept circling back in his mind—the weight of a seal he had never chosen, the cold way the Cadre looked through him rather than at him. Even when he had broken no rules. Even when he was the one bleeding to prove them wrong.

In the ring, Damian surged forward with a roar, flame twisting up his staff like a climbing vine. Jace sprinted to meet him, striking in rapid succession and pressing him step by step toward the edge. His strength was clear. Damian staggered under the onslaught, defending with every ounce of effort, while the crowd swelled in cheers for the dominant fighter.

Then Saulice's neck prickled, and he turned sharply in his seat. A cold pressure coiled in his gut, not a voice or thought but something deeper. Lazarus had shifted within him. The Titan was braced, coiled tight with a readiness that bordered on hostility, and Saulice felt the echo of it ripple through his chest.

Something had entered the arena.

The sensation was wordless yet heavy, a foreboding presence rooted deep in his bones. His breathing slowed as his eyes swept the stands, searching for what felt out of place. The air itself seemed wrong, unnatural, as though some foreign will had crossed into a space it did not belong. His nails dug into his palms as he clenched his fists.

And then he remembered. The bellet in the forest. The way its eyes had been wrong—too deep, too knowing—as if another will had stared out from within. The same essence lingered here, thick and watchful, hidden among the spectators.

Saulice swallowed hard, sitting straighter as the feeling crawled down his spine like fingers tracing bone. The rings blurred before his eyes, the flames of combat, the crowd's murmur, even the judges' measured gestures. It all seemed to draw away from him like smoke rising from a dying fire.

What was that?

His pulse quickened as he scanned the stands a second time, slower now, expecting to find a pair of eyes fixed on him. Yet no one looked back. Not openly, at least.

"Not yet," he whispered. "Not now."

He still had matches to win.

"Shaddai, remind me that I am not what they say," he breathed, barely audible, pushing past the weight of despair. "Remind me that I am more than what they see. That I am not Forsaken. That I am me."

Grinding his teeth, he pinched himself until his focus snapped back to the ring.

Damian ducked beneath a sweeping arc and retaliated with a cry, forging an extension of fire at the end of his staff. Though worn and struggling, he pressed on with determination, swinging with all his might. The strike landed across Jace's thigh, cutting deep and leaving a smoking wound. Jace cursed as his leg spasmed and his stance faltered.

The crowd murmured again, unsettled.

Damian pressed forward, kicking Jace's staff away, then tossed down his own in fury. Sweat ran down his face as he forged a ball of fire in his palm, growing it larger with every breath until it swelled beyond his hand.

Saulice watched without awe. The strike was precise and controlled, but against another fire forger it would not be decisive. Jace would rise. Boys like him always rose again.

He clenched his fists harder.

Just as Damian began to hurl the flame downward, Jace lunged with a desperate sweep that took Damian's legs out from under him. The flame sputtered and winked out.

But Damian did not stay down. He twisted, planting his hands on the floor and lashing back with a brutal kick that crunched against Jace's nose. Blood spattered the ring as Jace's head snapped back and struck the ground.

Damian forced himself upright, one hand shaking as he forged another flame. It sputtered, but it grew just enough to burn. He leaned forward, holding it inches from Jace's throat, daring him to move.

Jace did not raise his arms. His voice broke as he muttered, "I yield."

"Ring Two. Victor: Damian Halcroft."

Applause came delayed. No cheers followed, only the heavy silence of approval for a brutal victory.

Damian staggered back, extinguishing the flame. Cadre Pell caught him and guided him toward the benches. His legs buckled under him, his torn uniform exposing a chest heaving for air as his body struggled to recover.

Cadre Pell helped him toward the benches. His legs buckled and his torn uniform exposed his chest rising and falling, attempting to feed oxygen deprived muscles.

Tibbet appeared, plopping down with a grunt beside Saulice.

Saulice didn't speak.

He stared at the center of the ring where flame had once drawn a line, where a boy who mocked him now bowed to someone who hadn't.

INTERLUDE

The Timfathen slept above him, but in the hollow where no roots reached, Baalo did not rest. The cave walls pressed close, etched with fractures that glimmered faintly in the dark. Threads of shadow thickened where they fell, curling across the floor like smoke spilling from a dying fire.

He waited.

The silence bent until a ripple passed through the stone. A shape slid into the chamber, horned and hollow-eyed, its hooves drifting an inch above the ground. The Lichtaur, the lone scout he had sent to linger beyond the gates of Axbridge, had returned.

Baalo did not rise from the throne of fused basalt and rib-bone. Instead, he leaned forward, and the air grew taut, as though the cavern itself bowed toward his breath.

The specter knelt without words. Its chest split with a seam of pale light, and whispers spilled into the chamber like smoke carried on a cold wind. They were not its own words but stolen from the lips of men and women who had spoken them in passing. Baalo drank them in.

"The nobles of the city whisper in unrest over a Forsaken boy from Hamlen."

The scattered whispers wove together, and at last their meaning became clear. The name rose again, just as it had in the clearing months ago.

Saulice Sawyer.

Baalo's lips pulled into a thin line. "So, they marked him."

He traced the stone armrest with one claw, feeling the cracks spread like veins beneath his touch. Human hierarchies were fragile things, spun from reputation and rumor. To be Forsaken was to be exiled even among one's peers, a boy branded weak, shamed by trial, and scorned by the Great Houses.

It was perfect.

A tremor passed through Baalo's frame, not from weakness but from delight. At last the pieces aligned. This child, shunned and fragile in the eyes of others, carried within him the storm. Lazarus, hammer of Shaddai, still chained in silence. The Titan who had sealed Veartaya in her prison.

The irony thrilled him.

"They will cast him out without my hand ever touching him. The world itself will wound him for me," Baalo murmured. His Lady's freedom lay not in the strength of nations nor in the will of Titans, but in the breaking of a single boy.

He remembered Hamlen, a forgotten village, and the ash-stained boy curled in the crater. Saulice seemed on the verge of collapse even then. That same boy now walked the halls of Brynswick, draped in borrowed colors yet still branded Forsaken.

An easy catch.

The Lichtaur's chest closed, sealing the whispers away again.

"You have done well," Baalo said, his voice low as wind beneath a crypt door. "Keep close. Watch. Every lash of their contempt will soften him. Every sneer will drive him toward me. And when the moment comes, he will step into the Timfathen of his own accord, carrying Lazarus to my gates. Then I will wield the storm that once sealed my Lady and break her chains forever."

The Lichtaur bowed and dissolved into the cavern wall, leaving Baalo alone with the dark.

He sat unmoving, but his smile lingered, faint and cold.

"Little Harbinger," he whispered, "you are already mine."

CHAPTER 21

CHAINS UNSEEN

Cadre Pell stepped between the rings, his voice carrying without aid. "Ring Two. Saulice Sawyer versus Belan Brakar."

The eastern arena stiffened with attention. Overhead, sapphire banners bearing Brynswick's ten-pointed star cracked in the breeze, casting sharp shadows across risers thick with students, Cadre, and nobles. The Academy's honor hung on those banners, raised each tournament to mark official duels.

Saulice rose at Drezz and Damian's nod, then stopped at the ring's edge. Chin high. Hands tucked beneath his sleeves. The bracer sat snug at his wrist, the citrine shard nestled within. He hadn't forged light yet. He wouldn't unless forced.

A murmur rippled through the crowd. Belan stood taller and broader, among the strongest water forgers of the first year class. His lapis shard gleamed in his bracer. Meanwhile, Saulice held only a probationary status, no title, and stood on the brink of expulsion. All he had was a brand that told the world he was without worth. But it was time to change that.

He stepped into the ring, ready to show them how wrong they were. Ready to prove to Master Valos that he had grown since arriving as the weak, feeble Forsaken boy of Hamlen.

He closed his eyes, muttering Father Laird's prayer to steady his leaking core. *Shaddai… steady me. Hold me and my core, for I cannot hold myself. Let me find my beginning.*

Belan cracked his neck with an amused grin, leaning on his staff. "You sure you want to do this?"

He didn't know. None of them did.

But they would. Soon every eye would see what it had cost Saulice to stand here.

He bowed, slow and deliberate, as Cadre Pell's hand rose.

"Begin."

Belan moved first, fluid and sure. A water forger. He swept his staff low, drawing dampness from the air. A thin coil curved into existence, slender and cold, slithering toward Saulice's ankles.

Saulice didn't retreat. He waited, measuring Belan's stride. Then, seeing Belan's overly wide stance, he moved.

Instead of swinging his staff, he squatted and leapt over the coil, slamming his shoulder into Belan's hip.

Belan folded with a grunt, his balance too low. Stone rang out beneath his fall.

Saulice dropped hard, grinding his knees into the dirt as he tried to keep Belan pinned. A rogue spray of dust blinded him, but his grip stayed tight while his opponent bucked and thrashed.

Don't reach. Don't panic.

Belan was bigger and stronger, and as he began breaking free, Saulice's fingers darted for the citrine shard. He gathered the fount from his core with deliberate precision, coursing it through his chest and limbs before forcing it into his staff. The charge came slower than it would have for Belan, but it would be enough.

But as he pulled the final strand, he nicked one of the fractures and struck Lazarus' fount.

Rather than seizing control, the Titan assailed Saulice with a sharp wave of agony.

Saulice's circuit quivered worse than it had in days. His muscles seized as he cried out, desperate to keep the forging whole beneath the barrage of Lazarus' ancient turmoil.

Then, finally, the fount stabilized. Saulice exhaled.

Just in time, thankfully. Belan was already mid-swing.

Saulice ducked, tilting the copper tip of his staff in front of Belan's face. With a final push of will, the forging circuit completed.

A clean detonation of light filled the ring, soundless.

It was a small flashbang, a simple technique for lightning forgers. He had spent hours each night practicing it as a backup, knowing the circuit reversal might drain him too quickly.

Belan staggered, his water forging disrupted. Droplets scattered mid-flight, catching sunlight like shattered glass.

The bigger academ blinked, and Saulice was there. In a fluid motion, he rose, pivoted, and drove his shoulder into Belan's ribs with all the force he could muster.

This time, Belan didn't catch himself.

He hit the floor hard and slid out of bounds.

Cadre Pell cut the air with his hand.

"Ring Two. Victor: Saulice Sawyer."

The arena erupted.

But Saulice was not finished.

Drezz threw both fists skyward. "Folded Belan like wet parchment!"

Damian smirked. "He distilled Belan's puddle and baptized him in it."

Someone muttered, "Amen."

Drezz cackled. "Should've brought a mop."

Around them, the other dorms turned and pointed, but Drezz didn't stop. He spun once, struck a bow, then collapsed back to the bench, panting.

Saulice didn't join the laughter.

Drezz sprawled across the bench like a prince returned from conquest. Damian tossed in quiet barbs, smiling between remarks.

Around them, murmurs rippled from the other dorms, trailing the wake of Saulice's first match.

He sat motionless.

The heat from the flare lingered in his arms, tingling like an old bruise pressed too soon. Beneath the surface, his fount core pulsed in a fragile rhythm—cracks still stitched with tension, still aching where he had brushed against Lazarus' tendrils of fount.

He flexed his fingers. They obeyed. Worst case, his combative skill would have to be enough.

The next match began. One academ slipped in a burst of water, stumbling before her opponent quickly dispatched her. Cadre Pell named the victor without ceremony. The match ended in a minute.

Another followed, a stone forger outpacing a wind affinity in less than ten seconds. None of it registered for Saulice.

Applause rose and fell. He heard none of it.

The weight of the Academy pressed in. Judgment gleamed in every glance. Not a single Cadre applauded. No glimmer of respect from the nobles of House Crawford. His win had changed nothing. They still saw him as a mistake contained by chance.

In his mind, he walked the ring again. The first charge at Belan's waist. The final burst of light after fighting against Lazarus. It had taken control to hold it—more than they knew. And still it hadn't been enough.

A student passed behind him. Someone muttered a name that wasn't his.

He didn't turn.

Let them forget.

The next time he entered that ring, they wouldn't have that luxury. He would make them remember.

Cadre Pell's voice rose again, clear and measured, echoing across the stone:

"Ring One. Saulice Sawyer versus Toren Fellmere."

Toren bowed. Saulice didn't.

He couldn't fake reverent respect, not while Valos watched with that same measured stillness. As if nothing had changed. As if the first win meant nothing.

"Begin," came Cadre Pell's call.

Stone cracked beneath Saulice as Toren forged quickly, raising a ridge under his feet. He reacted without thinking, jumping aside and landing hard, only for another tremor to follow close at his heel. A sharp jab grazed his cheek, then an elbow raked his ribs. He ducked low, blocking as pain lanced his shin where another ridge of stone caught him. The arena floor shifted again, columns bursting upward like jagged ribs in the sand.

Toren's earth forging was exceptional, especially for a first year.

But Saulice wasn't watching Toren anymore. His eyes kept drifting to Master Valos, seated beside Cadre Calder. There had been no nod of acknowledgment, no flicker of approval. The master of Brynswick wasn't even watching. Saulice's body ached, his ribs throbbed, but the heavier wound was that all his labor, all his pain, still wasn't enough.

Dust stung his eyes as Toren pressed forward. A fist cut past his jaw, followed by another quake rippling through the floor. The rhythm was clear now, almost predictable. Yet clarity didn't make it easier.

The forging was instinct, the footwork steady breath, but none of it felt like a test. He didn't care about Toren. This was punishment for being born with the wrong brand, for daring to blaze too bright, and more than the rest for having the audacity to win against his supposed betters.

His hand closed over the citrine shard at his bracer. He began drawing the fragments of his core together, pooling his fount with painstaking slowness while Toren's attacks continued to hammer him. The strikes were predictable, but relentless.

At last, he felt enough gathered to attempt a forging. He pressed the current into his staff, satisfaction tightening his breath, until the energy shuddered in his grip.

"No," Saulice hissed. He forced the circuit onward, knowing it would be unstable, but refusing to relent.

The forging held, but something was wrong. His staff trembled as the current faltered. He swung with all his frustration, bringing the weapon down in an arc meant to blind Toren, but no flash ignited. Instead, a thin streak of lightning veered wild and struck the far wall.

Toren recoiled, clapping his eyes shut, likely thinking Saulice had repeated the trick he had used against Belan. He didn't realize that Saulice had failed.

Saulice lunged in desperation. His movements turned frantic—an elbow thrown too high, a knee driven weakly into Toren's core, a hook that barely glanced. He no longer counted his strikes or measured the crowd's reaction.

Only silence followed when Toren collapsed.

The judge lifted a hand.

"Ring One. Victor: Saulice Sawyer."

Rayne stood at the edge of the crowd, her eyes narrowed. She didn't look impressed—she looked worried.

Drezz noticed too, watching her with uncharacteristic quiet. Damian's arms stayed folded, and even he had no smile.

Saulice stepped off the ring, sweat cooling along his spine. His ribs throbbed, each breath a reminder of the unstable surge that had nearly broken free.

Rayne moved toward him.

"You forged too hard," she said.

"I'm fine," he snapped.

"You're not."

Her voice carried no accusation, only certainty. "You've trained harder than anyone here. I know that. I've felt it. But something's off."

His jaw locked tight.

"Maybe I'm just tired of everyone acting like I'm about to break."

"That's not what I meant—"

"Then *say* what you mean."

Her brow twitched, but she held her ground.

"You think I haven't seen the way Valos looks at me? Or how House Crawford won't even say my name?"

Rayne stayed silent.

He glanced toward Drezz and Damian. For a heartbeat, he considered telling them about the voice, about the cold that had slid down his spine just before the failed forging.

But he couldn't. Not now.

"I'm fine," he said again, fists pressed tight to his thighs.

Rayne studied him for a moment, then set a water jar on the bench beside him.

"Just don't let whatever's inside you ruin what you've built."

She turned before he could answer. Her braid caught the wind, but she didn't look back.

Saulice sat, heart pounding.

Three matches passed, dust rising in muted clouds as cheers swelled and faded into silence. Saulice's hand drifted to the citrine shard at his wrist, its surface colder than before.

Shaddai, he whispered through gritted teeth. *Stay with me. Steady me.*

The words felt thin, but he forced them out all the same. More matches blurred by, and then his final call came.

Across the ring, Cadre Pell raised a hand.

"Ring Two. Saulice Sawyer versus Lucas Crawford."

Saulice's eyes flicked toward the Cadre's alcove, where Calder sat with a venomous grin. So it would be Lucas after all.

The heat had climbed since midday, shimmering off the stone beyond the dueling rings. Crowds thickened along the risers. Nobles leaned forward. Second years whispered. Even the Cadre in the alcoves fell silent.

A hush rippled across the arena, not silence but anticipation stretched thin. Everyone knew what this was.

A reckoning.

Saulice stepped into the ring. His tunic clung to his back with sweat, and the bruise on his thigh throbbed from Toren's earlier strike. His split lip, gifted by Lucas two weeks before, burned with phantom memory.

This is what you trained for. This is the moment.

Across from him, Lucas rolled his neck and smirked, ruby shard gleaming in his bracer. "I gotta be honest. Didn't think you'd make it this far, Forsaken. If you were anyone else, I would say I'm impressed."

Saulice didn't answer.

The judge raised his hand. Lucas bowed low, mocking.

Saulice braced, offering a final plea before the fight began.

Shaddai, hold the forged light steady.

"Begin."

Lucas moved first. He always did.

A whip of forged fire lashed low and fast, meant to force Saulice into a vertical jump and bait fear. It was designed to provoke instinct.

Saulice saw it forming, felt its heat before it neared him. And somewhere deep inside, a part of him flinched. That part remembered flames consuming his home, the night his mother died.

For four years, fire had meant ruin.

His feet hesitated for a single breath. He remembered the failed Trial, the day a village branded him Forsaken. He felt the web of fear draw tight, its strands commanding retreat.

But the web met resistance.

Anger surfaced, sharp and clear. He thought of Corfrick's scorn. Judic's condemnation as he cut off Saulice's education. Every glance that turned away, every whisper that used his name as insult.

He didn't leap over the flames.

He embraced them, letting the heat wash across his feet.

Lucas narrowed his eyes. He began spinning his staff, and another forged wave of fire followed, wider and brighter. Not a blade, but a screen of flame. Saulice ducked low, hands near the floor, breath even as he narrowly ducked the attack.

He leapt back up and they circled. Lucas held a stance too elegant for endurance. He was quicker and sharper, but his training made for show, not strain.

"Too slow," Saulice baited, just loud enough to carry.

The grin faltered on Lucas's lips. His next strike came harder, a forged blast sweeping toward Saulice's feet, angled to herd him toward the edge of the ring.

Saulice stepped directly into the heat, twisting through it with a cry as flame grazed his shins. Pain stung but did not cripple. The moment seared a truth into him. He could not win through endurance alone. The longer this dragged on, the more it would tilt toward Lucas and his deeper reserves.

He needed precision.

The feint *had* to work.

The duel shifted into a blur of clashing staff and limb. Lucas forged fire along the length of his weapon, swinging with brute momentum. Saulice countered with sharp footwork, slipping inside the arc to strike his opponent's ribs before rolling away from the backlash of flame. The crowd murmured, their voices rising with each exchange.

This wasn't spectacle. It wasn't clean or fast. But Saulice was still standing. For the first time, he was proving that survival was enough to deny Lucas his easy victory. Yet survival alone would not decide this match. He needed to finish it.

Lucas spat toward the ring floor. "Fight me, coward."

"I am," Saulice said.

His fingers brushed the citrine shard at his bracer's edge. He began pooling his fount out of his core but didn't begin building the technique's circuit. Not just yet.

He waited for Lucas to get angry. To overreach during one of his strikes.

Lucas lunged, arm raised in a high arc. Higher than he needed to.

Now.

Saulice stepped forward with precision and a deep breath. He grounded his back foot, twisted at the waist, and coursed the fount into his body, gladly realizing he had just enough in his core to pull off the technique.

His fount circuited through his spine, daring to push it a little faster down his arms, and into his legs and feet. He didn't reverse its course, not yet. The fount coiled outward, reaching and stretching like a compressed storm wound tight behind his ribs. The current built within his chest, stilling the arena in his mind.

He pivoted clean, and the circuit felt solid within him. The circuit reversal would complete in just seconds, just as Lucas's strike fell.

Saulice reversed the fount's course, forcing it back into himself with disciplined speed. It snapped towards his core, cleanly. And as the final tendrils of his fount pooled back together, again, he nicked one of the fractures cleaking Lazarus' fount.

That was when everything went wrong.

It should have snapped clean, the energy settling into his core and granting him the fifteen seconds of empowerment he had trained for. Instead, the light surged out of rhythm, coiling back on itself, layer upon layer, like tempered steel folding without end.

No. I trained for this. I had it right.

But the current refused to obey.

The power ricocheted through him, colliding against his ribs, spine, and arms in chaotic bursts. This was no steady pulse, but a torrent of collisions, each sharper than the last. He tried to reset, to collapse the circuit, to start again, but the current only built faster. And then Lucas' strike was already descending.

A white explosion tore across the ring. Saulice staggered back, blinded as arcs of forged light burst from his palms. They cracked across the circle like living things, jagged bolts clawing outward without order. Dust lifted in waves. One beam split against the barrier wall, carving stone. Another ripped a crater into the earth beside him. He tried to aim them away from Lucas and the stands, jerking his hands from anything living, but the arcs did not heed him.

The crowd gasped as the air shuddered. Saulice fought to contain the storm, his body trembling, every vein lit with violent current. He was no longer forging. The light was forging itself.

High in the stands, Master Valos rose.

At the arena's edge, Saulice glimpsed Rayne. She had stepped back from the railing, her fingers locked white around the stone. Her eyes did not flinch. For a heartbeat she looked not shocked but still, as if she had seen this before and recognized it.

Then the rogue circuit sputtered and died, leaving only scorched stone and silence.

Lucas advanced with forged fire curling around his staff like a massive serpent preparing to strike. The crowd leaned forward, but no one moved. No one intervened.

"You think you belong here, Forsaken?" Lucas growled, refusing to use Saulice's last name. "Look at you. You're a freak."

A burst of flame struck Saulice's side, searing through cloth and biting into skin. He crumpled to one knee, gasping. Another blast followed, driving him backward. His chest locked tight, unable to release breath. Lucas's boot slammed into his ribs with a sharp snap that echoed across the arena. Saulice choked as the world tilted.

"You think you're helping anyone?" Lucas's staff cracked against his shoulder, flame cutting flesh. Saulice pitched forward, barely aware of stone beneath him. Another strike landed against his spine, and his scream split the ring. His citrine shard cracked, and his words died in his throat.

He collapsed, his body spasming as blood filled his mouth.

"You think you're special?" Lucas shouted, punctuating the words with another blow.

Shouts erupted for the match to be called. It should have ended already. Saulice glimpsed Cadre Pell's face—hopeful, pleading, silently urging him to rise. But he couldn't.

Lucas dragged him upright by the collar, Saulice's legs dangling uselessly. "You're a weight," Lucas hissed. "And I'm done carrying you."

Saulice's hand curled. A last surge of defiance spurred him. He swung, not clean or powerful, but fueled by spite. His fist connected. The crack rang sharp. Lucas staggered half a step, stunned.

A gasp rippled across the arena. One of the Cadre cursed under their breath. Across the far ring, Pell shifted, a single step forward, his gaze narrowing.

Saulice coughed, chest shuddering. "I didn't get this far because of you," he rasped.

Lucas's fury ignited. He hurled Saulice down, skull striking stone. Saulice drifted, unmoored, his core aching with absence. His shard lay cold and dim, useless. Lazarus stirred, watching as always—silent, unhelpful.

"Lucas! Stand down! The match is over!" Pell's voice cut across the silence.

But Lucas didn't stop. Fire coiled bright around his arm. He raised his staff for a final strike.

And the sky cracked.

A figure descended from the Cadre's perch like a thunderhead given shape. Stone erupted beneath his landing, heat rippling outward in concentric waves. Lucas flew back, tumbling until he collapsed in a scorched heap.

Calder stood in the ring's center, tall, robed in grey-black linen. Twin bracers gleamed, forged steel set with rubies. Dust curled to ash at his feet. The crowd froze, bent beneath his presence.

"You disgrace the ring," Calder said, voice heavy with displeasure. "Such arrogance dishonors the Academy. You shame your lineage."

Lucas clawed upright, chest heaving. His bracer still glimmered faintly. "I didn't—"

"You were seen." Calder did not raise a hand. The evidence stood clear: the ruptured stone, the scorched circle, the blood staining Saulice's uniform, and the silence of hundreds.

"The mark of what you've done is already written," Calder continued. "Not in fount. In memory. And I will not allow it to stand unchallenged."

He stepped forward, flames folding inward at his heels. "You forget yourself, Crawford. You think power entitles you to cruelty. You think a bloodline grants you license. You were given fire." Another step. "You wielded it like vengeance." Another. "You thought no one would stop you."

Behind him, Tibbet knelt at Saulice's side, pressing cloth to his bloodied mouth. The boy stirred faintly.

Calder's voice dropped, final and immovable. "Return to your bench. You will be dealt with soon enough."

Lucas turned without protest, shoulders slumped. No bow, no words. He walked away as the arena held its breath.

They watched Saulice lifted by Tibbet and a healer, burned and battered but breathing. His boots dragged grooves through the dust, yet his fingers still clenched weakly.

Drezz gripped the wooden rail at Crescent's edge, claws digging into the grain. He didn't blink. His breath came slow and deep, like thunder waiting.

Drezz gripped the wooden rail at Crescent's edge, claws digging into the grain. He didn't blink. His breath came slow and deep, like thunder waiting. "They let it go too far," he muttered.

Damian stood beside him, jaw locked. "They didn't think Lucas would… snap like that."

Drezz's ears flicked. "He didn't snap."

He turned to Rayne.

Her voice was steady, but her hands stayed clenched behind her back, knuckles white. "He chose it."

Damian's head tilted, disbelief in his eyes. "Chose it? You mean he meant to—"

"Yes," Rayne said, sharper than before. Then lower: "You saw it. Every strike was deliberate. He wanted Saulice broken, not beaten."

Silence lingered until Drezz finally spoke. "You trained him for this."

Rayne gave a small nod. "He was ready. The stance, the rhythm—he had it. He held the circuit in drills. Four times, clean. The feint, the push, the pull. We ran it all."

Damian's mouth twisted. "And he still couldn't finish it."

Rayne flinched but didn't deny it. "It was working," she whispered. "Until now." Her eyes never left the scorched ring. "He should've won."

Drezz's tone fell quiet. "That wasn't just nerves."

Rayne finally glanced at him, her jaw tight. "I know."

Drezz waited, but she only shook her head once before whispering again. "That light… it wasn't his."

CHAPTER 22

CONTROL'S QUIET OFFER

The infirmary ceiling blurred in and out of focus. Crossbeams, dusty rafters, and strips of sunlit haze drifted between shelves lined with vials and poultices. The scent of mint balm and myrrh clung to the air, bitter and unrelenting.

Saulice lay on his back, ribs bound tight, arm wrapped in bandages to the elbow. A slow, steady throb pulsed from his chest to his temple, echoing without end.

Across the room, Tibbet leaned against a corner chair, arms crossed and face set in stone.

At the basin, Laird sighed as he wrung a blood-soaked cloth into the water, muttering about reckless boys and overbearing Cadre.

Saulice winced when the salve touched raw skin. His words scraped from cracked lips. "Feels like I lost a fight to the sun."

"Not quite," Laird said, dabbing again. "Lucas is a fire forger. This here"—he tapped the bandages—"is what pride and power do to a ribcage."

"I didn't lose to power," Saulice murmured.

"No?" Laird leaned in. "Then what did you lose to?"

He hesitated before whispering, "Myself."

Laird nodded as though he had expected it. "A good start. Better than blaming the ring, or your opponent, or Shaddai, for that matter."

He reached for a strip of gauze and wound it carefully around Saulice's arm.

Tibbet remained by the door, silent as a shadow.

"I did everything right," Saulice said. "Every drill and stance. I trained for weeks." His voice twisted. "I prayed. I surrendered. And still I lost. And Master Valos will not care that I've shed blood. He'll expel me—just another pest who dared to stand against one of the Great Houses."

"Did you truly surrender, Saulice?" Laird asked, his tone gentle. "Perhaps you lost because something inside you is not finished shifting."

Saulice's jaw clenched as fear rose in his throat.

"Lucas was right," he whispered. "He knew what would happen if I tried to stand up to him."

A somber breeze moved through the room.

"I'm sorry," Tibbet said, rubbing his hands together. "I thought you'd win. Even if you lost, you did well for a first year. If it was anyone but Crawford, this would be different."

Saulice growled and tried to sit. Laird pressed lightly on his chest, easing him back down.

His bloodshot eyes narrowed. Bandages wrapped nearly his whole body. "Look at me, Tibbet. Does it look like I did well? If I had managed the circuit reversal, I would have won."

"You almost won."

"Almost will not keep me here."

"Would you just take a compliment?" Tibbet shouted. "That's what this is about, isn't it? You don't care what the Cadre think. You're just afraid they were right. Always so insecure."

Saulice turned away.

Tibbet stepped closer, boots thudding against the stone. "You're not weak, Saulice. You're just bleeding in places others can't see. Most of the other academs were born with shields. You weren't."

A stillness passed through him. "What if I'm tired of bleeding?"

"Enough," Laird said, glaring at them both.

The room fell quiet. He finished the final wrap and tied it off with a steady hand. "No internal damage. Just surface burns across the shoulder. The pain will linger, but in a few weeks, you'll be good as new."

He rose and wiped his palms on a linen cloth, then turned to Tibbet. "You'll stay until his replacement arrives?"

Tibbet nodded.

Laird placed a firm hand on Saulice's foot, kind and steady. "I do hope to see you again in the future, but whether I do or not, it has been my honor to help you on your way. May Shaddai keep you for all your days."

He turned toward the door.

Saulice watched him leave, the faint scent of ink and myrrh trailing behind like a veil. For a moment, he envied how someone could simply step through a door and be gone. Free and decided, not having to wait for a life changing verdict.

Tibbet sank into the corner chair, arms folded tight.

For a long time, neither spoke. Then the bed creaked as Saulice forced himself upright with a grunt and limped to the cold hearth. He knelt and did not ask for strength this time, only for the will not to give up.

A breeze stirred the ashes, but no voice answered. Only the corridor whispered through the open shutter, carrying distant cheers for matches that no longer mattered.

Saulice returned to the cot and stared at the ceiling. It was only a matter of time before the Cadre came to expel him. If only Lazarus had not interfered.

The infirmary door creaked. Tibbet was already on his feet before the hinges settled.

Rayne entered, shadowed in the silver-blue of Brynswick's dress uniform. Her braid hung damp with sweat from the heat of the arena. She gave a single nod.

"Master Valos sent me to take over."

Tibbet offered no protest. He crossed to the door, gave Saulice a final look—more respect than comfort—and disappeared down the stairwell. The click of the latch left the room quiet.

Rayne waited a moment before taking the chair at Saulice's side.

"You breathing?"

"Barely."

Silence lingered, not awkward but heavy with weariness.

She leaned back, boots crossed at the ankle. "You were holding the match in the beginning."

He gave no reply.

"You had him," she continued. "Not just in footwork. You were reading him, Saulice."

Still nothing.

Her eyes stayed on him. "What happened wasn't your fault."

"Then whose was it?"

A pause.

"I don't think it was his either."

Saulice swallowed. "You were there. In the drills. In the dark. You saw me hold it. I felt the circuit reversal hold. So why did it break?"

Rayne's face remained still, her voice slower now. "Some things inside us wait until the moment we need them most. Then they show their teeth."

Saulice exhaled. "So that's it? I train harder, grow stronger, and something else still decides whether I fail?"

"No. You decide whether it breaks you."

Heat edged his tone, the thought brushing too close to the truth about Lazarus. He knew she could not know, yet her words struck like she did. And he was not ready to tell her. If he was dismissed, there would be no point.

"It already did," he muttered. "And I'm tired of fighting."

"I saw it," she said at last. "Not the fount. The change. Something else was in the ring with you, and no one could name it."

Fear tightened his throat. Did she know?

"I don't know what it is," she added carefully, "and I won't ask."

"You should," Saulice whispered. "Anyone else would. If you knew the truth, you'd be gone before the words left my mouth."

Rayne shook her head. "Then don't tell me. Let me stay without needing answers."

Relief flickered, but her measured tone and eyes that avoided his made him pause. She wasn't lying. But she wasn't telling the whole truth either.

"I know what it did," she said. "And what it almost took from you."

Saulice looked down at his bandaged hands. "It took everything I was trying to become." He forced his gaze up to meet hers. "I'm sorry for snapping earlier."

He drew a breath before admitting what weighed most. "Master Valos summoned me this morning. Someone reported the incident with Lucas, claiming I struck him first. He warned me it could spark conflict with House Crawford. He told me Brynswick had gambled on me, and that I wasn't honoring that trust. Rayne… he said if I didn't perform today, my probationary status would be terminated."

Her hands clenched until her knuckles went white. "That's absurd. The gall of it."

A long silence passed.

Then Saulice asked quietly, "If you knew something inside me could burn this whole place down, would you still sit beside me?"

Rayne didn't flinch. "I trained with you. I watched you bleed for control. I saw how hard you worked not to give in. So yes, I would stay."

He stared at her.

"I'm falling apart," he whispered. "This half-control, waiting for something to snap. I have to master it…" His voice thinned. "…or it will end me."

Her gaze held steady. "What is it?"

"I wish I could say. But I can't."

After a moment, she reached forward and rested her hand over his, just for a breath.

"You stayed during the matches," he said, surprised.

She gave no smile, no nod, only the words: "Of course I did."

She hesitated, then added, "Everyone else left after your match. They cheered, then moved on like it was nothing. But I couldn't. I couldn't watch you walk out of that ring alone."

"Why?"

Her eyes shifted as if searching for the right shape to her thoughts. "You're the only first year who trains like the world might end if you fail. I thought I might see what you were fighting for if I watched."

Saulice blinked.

She looked up once more. "And I stayed because someone had to make sure that kind of resolve didn't burn itself out."

Then she rose and left.

The infirmary hushed again, absent of soft boots and clinking vials. A quiet creak was the only sound, as the rafters settled with the coming of evening.

Saulice closed his eyes, breath shallow in his chest, stomach knotted with anxiety. There was nothing he could do now but wait. It maddened him to feel so powerless after all his work.

He had thought Rayne's visit would be the last before Master Valos came to deliver the verdict. But the door creaked again, and a face appeared that he had never expected to see.

These steps were measured and deliberate, a cold presence entering before the man himself.

Lord Winstrom.

The name carried weight, not merely noble but sovereign. He was not just a patron of Brynswick; he was Axbridge itself. Guards bowed at his passing, the Senate deferred, and every corridor bent around his silence.

Saulice stiffened as the man came into view.

Winstrom wore deep navy robes trimmed with a silver collar, a crescent pin glittering at his chest. Black leather gloves covered his hands, smooth and creaseless, while his uncovered gaze cut sharp as a blade.

"You've had an eventful afternoon," Winstrom said, his voice dark and smooth as ink.

Saulice tried to sit straighter and failed.

"I trust I'm not disturbing your recovery?"

"No, my Lord," Saulice answered, voice raw. "I didn't know you watched the matches."

"I don't," Winstrom replied, gliding toward the cot with practiced grace. "Not directly. But I make it my business to remain well-informed. The city is my charge… even the Academy within it."

He stopped at the foot of the bed and folded his hands behind his back. "What happens in Brynswick reflects on me. And what happened in your last match reflected loudly."

Saulice lowered his gaze.

"You fought with precision," Winstrom continued, "until the moment you did not."

The words struck sharper than judgment, not cruel but utterly true.

"I trained for it," Saulice said quickly. "I was ready."

Winstrom stepped forward, his boots making no sound on the stone. "And yet something inside you was not. Already some whisper that your days here are finished. Others say your skill surpassed every other first year. Tell me, Saulice—what do you believe?"

The cot seemed smaller beneath him. Saulice's throat tightened. His mind leapt to Master Valos and the expulsion he feared, to the faces of Drezz, Damian, Tibbet, even Rayne. Would he be able to say goodbye to any of them?

Winstrom's presence filled the space without effort. He neither loomed nor raised his voice, yet he remained the tallest man in the room because no silence dared shrink him. He drew a chair to the bedside and sat, every movement deliberate, almost ceremonial.

"There are some," he said, "who claim your loss was weakness, that you cracked under pressure. I do not believe that."

Saulice blinked. "You don't?"

"No," Winstrom answered, studying him with a gaze too precise to feel human. "Weakness runs when fire spreads. It shatters silence. What you displayed was not weakness. It was something far older."

A beat passed.

"You carry something the Academy cannot account for."

Saulice's hands tightened beneath the covers. "You mean my fount."

"I mean the being disrupting it."

Silence pressed close around them.

Winstrom's tone remained calm, deliberate. "I know more than you realize, Saulice. I know about the cracked Source Stone and what happened in Hamlen. I know of the black bellet you survived, the ire you have drawn from House Crawford, and, most importantly, the nature of the forging you performed today."

He leaned back slightly, eyes never leaving Saulice. "I have seen it once before."

Saulice's breath caught. "Where?"

"In the old records," Winstrom said. "The sealed ones, written before this age of bracers and status. And besides…" His gaze sharpened. "There is another like you at Brynswick. Their future is assured. Yours is not. That is why we must discuss something that may yet serve you."

He folded his hands across one knee.

"Before the Cadre. Before Brynswick. There were Harbingers— the first wielders of the divine Titans, chosen to bear their lives beside them in a fractured world."

Saulice felt the blood chill in his veins.

"They were raw, untrained. Their burden immense. And when the Titans resisted, as they sometimes did, the Harbingers turned to a device."

He let the word settle slowly, as though naming it carried its own weight.

"The Pitch."

The air seemed to tighten. Saulice leaned forward, drawn despite himself.

"It was not born of the Academy," Winstrom continued. "Nor forged by human hands. The first circle of Fury's Fist devised it in the earliest days. A weapon of necessity, not of ambition. It bound Titans when nothing else could—a seal, yes, but more than that, a yoke."

He rose from the chair and paced toward the shelves. The lantern light stretched his shadow across the wall, long and cold.

"It does not teach. It does not tame. It only compels."

Saulice swallowed hard, dread and curiosity churning in equal measure. "And does this device still exist?"

Winstrom did not turn. "Some believe it was destroyed. Others whisper it was hidden. But I am certain—buried deep beneath the Timfathen's inner valley, beneath the stones once used to crown kings before the Thousand Year War."

Now he looked back, his eyes cold and clear.

"That is why I tell you, Saulice. Not the Cadre. Not Valos. Unlike them, you do not have the luxury of time. If you truly wish to secure your place here, you must act."

The words pressed into him like iron. His bandaged arm felt heavier, as though the very choice threatened to crush him.

Winstrom stepped closer. "If you go, if you find it, Master Valos will have no power to cast you out. Consider how many faces would be silenced—nobles, academs, even Cadre Calder, who already expects you to fail."

Saulice stared at his hands, trembling faintly above the linen. "And if I don't go?"

Winstrom's voice dropped, soft enough to scrape. "Then I would not count days here. I would count seconds. And when your forging breaks again, there will be no one left to repair the damage."

He let the silence carry its weight, sharp as any threat.

Winstrom turned toward the door. His gloved hand settled on the iron handle, deliberate and unhurried.

"If you take this path, no one else can know."

The words lingered, heavy as stone.

He paused, still facing the door. "Mastery," he said, his voice low and measured, "is seldom granted. It is claimed by those bold enough to seize it."

The latch clicked beneath his hand, and then he stepped into the corridor.

The room seemed to exhale as the door shut behind him, yet the air remained colder than before.

Saulice lay frozen on the cot, pulse racing, the echo of Winstrom's words burning in his ears. His bandages felt tighter, the infirmary smaller, as though the choice had already begun to close around him.

CHAPTER 23

BENEATH THE WALL, BEYOND THE GATE

The window above Saulice's bed stretched a long line of moonlight across the stone floor. He had been watching it for hours, tracking how it crept slowly from the foot of his trunk to the edge of Drezz's cot.

He had not moved. Not once. But his thoughts refused to rest.

Winstrom's message coiled through his mind like mist. *You must take action.* Saulice closed his eyes. The words remained.

After he'd been aided back to dorm Crescent by one of Father Laird's assistants at the infirmary, Drezz shared with him that Master Valos had sought him out in the infirmary. Saulice hadn't left his bunk, chest bundled with anxiety, waiting for a knock at the door.

Would he come tonight to tell him? Would he wait until tomorrow? Saulice could not bear it. It wasn't fair.

He saw Lucas's grin after the match. Rayne's silence. Tibbet's quiet concern. Drezz standing at the ring's edge, frozen, while the flare tore free from Saulice's grasp.

He knew what would happen if he stayed.

Even if Valos didn't expel him, even if by some fragile mercy he remained at Brynswick, the next failure might not end with a singed wall. If the blast had landed seconds earlier, or at the wrong angle, Lucas wouldn't have walked away.

And Saulice would've become exactly what they feared.

But with the Pitch, he wouldn't have to fear the fount slipping again. He wouldn't have to wrestle Lazarus for control. No more tremors in his spine, no more gasps in the dark.

There would be no more risk of hurting anyone.

He would hold the current steady, bend it without splintering. Forge cleanly, cleanly enough to silence every doubter, every whisper.

They would see—Brynswick, Lucas, Alderman Corfrick, the entire House of Crawford.

He wasn't an insect to be stepped over. He was the storm they had mistaken for a crack in the floor.

After two hours had passed, Saulice could take it no longer. His heart drummed in his ears, stuck between two difficult decisions.

Lord Winstrom's words echoed in his mind again. *Mastery is rarely granted freely. But it is always claimed by those bold enough to reach for it.*

Saulice eased back his blanket and swung his legs off the bed. The floor was cold beneath his feet. He moved without lighting a torch. The moon gave just enough light for him to see.

He slowly packed his bag, careful not to move too quickly, lest he open the cut across his chest. He also couldn't afford to wake Drezz. If the fallet knew what he was planning, Saulice knew he'd only try to stop him.

With quiet precision, he began packing. A few coins. Dried fruit from the cafeteria. A balm tin tucked in the lining of his coat. He had wrapped his old dagger inside a spare tunic. His fingers brushed the cracked citrine shard he'd earned in his Fount Principium class, lightless and dull after his duel against Lucas.

He pulled on his bracer last. It still looked blank, still unfinished, still wrong. But it held what little control he had left.

He crept across the room, avoiding the floorboard near Drezz's bed that always gave the faintest groan. The doorknob turned beneath his palm with a sound quieter than breath.

He pulled it open—and stopped short.

Drezz sat just outside, arms crossed, tail twitching behind him.

"Going somewhere?" Drezz asked, tired but awake.

"This doesn't concern you, Drezz." Saulice adjusted the pack on his shoulder with a groan. "I don't need permission."

Drezz gave a slow shrug. "You were staring at the ceiling for hours. Thought I wouldn't catch on that something was up?"

"It's none of your business."

"Well, it is now."

They stared at one another in the dim corridor.

Saulice shifted his pack higher. "I'm leaving."

"Okay," Drezz replied.

"There isn't another option."

The fallet sighed. "I know."

Saulice lowered his gaze. "It's not safe with me here. Not until I can stop Lazarus."

"It won't be any safer out of these walls. That's why I packed beforehand."

He looked up. "Drezz…"

The fallet raised a brow. "If you don't need permission, then neither do I."

"You don't get it. The Timfathen isn't just dangerous. It's crawling with Lichtaurs. This Pitch Winstrom told me about, it might not even exist."

"And you're still going," Drezz said, watching him.

"I don't have a choice," Saulice said. "I can't stay either way. Master Valos will come at any second and tell me to leave. This way, at least, I'll know I did everything I could."

"I arrived with you, and I'll leave with you, Saulice. We are not blood, but we are brothers."

Saulice couldn't respond as his frustration bled away.

They stood in silence.

Then Drezz turned toward the stairs. "Let's move. If Tibbet finds our beds empty at dawn, we're finished."

Saulice followed without saying another word.

Damian would wonder where they'd gone off to, but their companion hadn't come back since the Cadre summoned him after the match for questioning. Valos, maybe. Or Cadre Pell. Someone had pulled him into a debrief, and he hadn't even returned to the dorm yet.

There was no time to explain. No time to say goodbye.

As they slowly crept out, the hallways were silent. There were no voices or patrols. Only the creak of floorboards beneath soft boots, the occasional pain-filled grunt from Saulice, and the slow exhale of stone cooling from the day's heat.

They slipped past the final stairwell and into the shadows beyond.

Whatever waited in the Timfathen, they would face it together.

The doors of Dorm Crescent eased shut behind them with a soft clunk.

Saulice kept his steps light as they crossed the courtyard. The lanterns lining the outer walk had burned low, most extinguished altogether. The moon did the rest. Statues of past Brynswick Masters stood in long shadows, their carved gazes judging every inch of the path.

He tugged his cloak tighter.

Drezz kept pace beside him, tail low, eyes scanning the walk ahead. "You sure about this?"

"No," Saulice said. "Not at all."

They cut across the grass near the southern lawn, where the trees thinned and the stable path curved into view. The wind picked up, cool and damp with the scent of moss and hay.

That's when he saw her.

A lone figure sat at the base of a dry fountain just beyond the courtyard arch.

Rayne.

She didn't move when they approached. She didn't speak.

Her arms were folded across her knees. Her pack rested beside her like it had been there for hours. The tilt of her head said she had heard them coming long ago.

Saulice slowed. "You're awake."

"No," she said. "I'm sleepwalking. Can't you tell?"

He winced. "Did someone see us?"

Rayne stood and grabbed her pack. "No one's been out since curfew."

Drezz glanced between them. "You're coming?"

"Yes," Rayne said. "Obviously."

Saulice narrowed his eyes at her. "No. Absolutely not. How did you even know?"

Rayne looked at him for a long moment.

"I know you. When you set your mind to something, it's impossible to stop you. Besides," she said, "I heard a few words between you and Lord Winstrom. After seeing him entering the infirmary, I couldn't help but wonder why he'd make a trip there of all places."

The words carried something heavier than sarcasm. Rayne slung her pack over one shoulder and stepped toward the stable road.

"You eavesdropped?!" Saulice felt his blood turn hot.

"You're dang right I did. City officials don't just approach first year academs, Saulice. It doesn't matter; I could see it before then. You had that glint in your eyes, that crazed look from someone who would do whatever it takes to achieve their goal."

Silence filled the space between them. Saulice's anger crumpled.

"So, it just goes to show that you were planning to disappear alone after what happened in the ring." Her eyes bored into him. "Which means you're even more reckless than I thought."

Saulice looked between them. The night was too still to carry more lies.

"This doesn't concern either of you," he said. "I must do this… because of what's inside me. What I've been hiding since Hamlen. If I get expelled, I'll be putting everyone around me in danger until the day I croak."

Rayne's expression flickered, but she said nothing.

Saulice met her eyes. His voice came low and clear. "I'm a Harbinger. There's no point in trying to hide it anymore. That Titan, Lazarus, he's out of control. And my fount core is damaged from years of neglected training."

The air between them stretched thin.

Rayne didn't blink.

"I know," she whispered.

Saulice froze. "You… knew?"

"Since your first day at Brynswick." Her tone stayed quiet. "Master Valos told me. Not everything, but just enough. Enough to know you weren't normal. That you carried something old and dangerous."

"So, he sent you to watch me?"

"He did."

Saulice swallowed. "Why you?"

"Because I know how to follow orders without being seen. And because Valos doesn't trust anyone else with something like this."

"And you just went along with it?"

Rayne's voice didn't rise, but it hardened. "I didn't have a choice. Not then."

A beat passed.

Drezz stepped slightly aside, letting the space between them settle. Saulice could feel the blood behind his eyes now, hot with shame, confusion, and something else.

"So, all that training," Saulice said, his fists clenching, "everything you did to help me was just part of some assignment?"

"At first, it was," Rayne said, hands up in surrender. Her gaze held steady. "But you were relentless. You fought for control. Poured yourself into training with a focus most academs never touch. And even when it tried to consume you... you didn't let it. That's when I stopped following orders."

Her words trembled. Not from fear. From strain. Saulice caught it—the way her knuckles whitened, and her breath misted in the cool morning air.

Saulice didn't know what to say. His breath came unsteadily. Because someone had seen all of him. And stayed.

Drezz looked his way. "Are we arguing or catching up?"

Rayne slung her pack and started toward the Academy's gate. "Neither. We're moving."

The Academy's southern wall loomed ahead, cloaked in silence and ivy. Beyond it lay the open hillside. Beyond that, the royal stables nestled against the tree line, low and quiet like a sleeping beast.

But first, they had to pass the gate.

Two guards stood at their post, spears planted, half-shadowed in the lamplight. Their cloaks stirred in the breeze. One leaned against a stone column. The other paced in brief intervals.

Rayne crouched beside a trimmed hedge just short of the gate's line of sight. Saulice and Drezz flanked her, pressed low in the wet grass.

"We wait for the pass," she whispered. "When the pacing guard reaches the outer post, we cut across the hall's shadow."

Drezz nodded. Saulice adjusted the strap of his pack.

The midnight bell tolled deep in the Academy's heart.

The pacing guard turned.

Rayne moved.

They slipped low to the ground, silent over the gravel path, hugging the curve of the marble hall that edged the courtyard. The lamplight thinned as they passed the final colonnade. The sound of breathing, tight and measured, filled Saulice's ears louder than the wind.

When they reached the wall, Saulice knew climbing it was going to hurt.

Rayne produced a coil of rope.

"You've done this before?" Saulice asked, leaning against it while catching his strained breath.

"Enough times to stop asking questions."

She looped the hook over the top edge of the inner ledge, gave it a hard tug, then climbed. Drezz followed. Saulice came last, groaning as the cold stone bit through his clothes and scraped the fresh bandages across his upper torso.

They slipped into the brush beyond the outer wall, leaving the Academy behind for good, or for whatever came next.

Silence reigned as the city slept.

Lanterns along the Axbridge outer lanes flickered low, their flames pinched by the wind. The sky above had begun its slow fade into grey. Not even the market crows had stirred yet. The muddy roads were slick, and the alley behind the Traveler's Post smelled of wet hay, horse sweat, and old beer.

Rayne pointed to the stable door. "This is it."

Drezz checked the latch. "Not locked. They're not expecting thieves."

"They're not expecting academs to ride out before dawn either," Rayne replied.

Saulice stood back, eyeing the sagging beams and the horses inside. "Are we sure about this?"

"Not really," Drezz said. He pushed the door open anyway.

Inside the inn's stable was a mess of loosely stacked hay, old saddles, and horses that shifted with lazy confusion. A few snorted. One flung its head and stomped once. None sounded the alarm.

Rayne moved first, selecting a tall mare with a white blaze and calm eyes. "She's fast, but she'll keep steady even if we're pressed."

Drezz circled until he found a short-legged dun gelding with a sour expression. "He looks stubborn. I respect that."

Saulice, meanwhile, stayed near the door.

Rayne turned. "Pick one."

"I don't know how to ride," Saulice admitted. "I've never even saddled one before."

Drezz grinned faintly. "This is going to be fun. You're going to have to learn in a hurry."

Rayne tossed him a bridle. "Just find one that doesn't bite."

Eventually Saulice settled on a brown gelding that stared blankly at him. It looked bored enough not to bolt. With Rayne's help, he looped the reins correctly. Drezz showed him where to tighten the girth without cutting off the horse's breath.

The moment Saulice swung into the saddle, he nearly slid off the other side.

Rayne caught his shoulder.

"Easy," she said. "Use your legs. Sit deep."

"I don't think I have a deep," Saulice muttered as he fought to sit straight. Every movement from the horse jolted him with a dizzying spasm of pain. After a few minutes, the pain lessened to a tolerable throb.

Drezz patted his own mount. "You'll figure it out. Just don't fall. Or die."

"That's the spirit," Rayne said.

They led the horses through narrow back lanes. Skirts of mist curled around their boots. The city remained asleep, but not blind.

The gate to Axbridge's eastern pass rose a dozen paces high, heavy with blackwood beams and iron bolts. Two guards kept vigil beneath its lanterns. One stood firm at his post, spear in hand. The other leaned against the wall, arms crossed and eyes half-lidded but not unaware.

Rayne pulled them into the shadows behind a garden wall just short of the open street.

"We can't bluff past them," Drezz whispered. "Not with weapons and saddles."

Rayne scanned the wall. "No patrols on the inner tier. If we reach the right flank, there's a blind spot near the merchant tunnel."

"The culvert?" Saulice asked.

She nodded. "Opens into the drainage trough beyond the wall. They use it when carts jam the gate."

"It's locked," Drezz said.

Rayne showed a thin key in her palm. "Not anymore."

They waited. When the standing guard turned to pace the opposite post, Rayne moved first. Drezz followed. Saulice came last, ducking into the alley and hugging the stone as tightly as he could. The horses moved softly under their reins, hooves muffled in the grass and grime.

They reached the grated archway. It was half buried in moss and mud. The iron gate was rusted but still intact.

Rayne crouched low, worked the key in silence, and pulled the latch open with a breathless wince.

The tunnel was narrow. Wet. It reeked of mildew and stagnant rainwater. They led the horses in a single file, crouching beneath the arched ceiling. Water splashed against Saulice's boots. The air pressed heavier with each step.

After a few dozen paces, the wall curved and opened into the fields.

They emerged beneath the outer tree line, the gate hidden in the tangle of stone and brush.

The road ahead lay empty.

Only then did they climb back into the saddles. Saulice gave a grunt and nearly slipped, forcing Drezz to catch his reins again.

"Still feels like this horse wants to throw me," he muttered.

"He probably does," Rayne said. "Try not to give him a reason."

The wind shifted.

"Let's think," Rayne said. "There are only two valleys in the Timfathen. The one in the south saw very little combat during the war. I'd wager the other valley is the one we need to look for."

"Where is the other one?" Saulice asked.

Rayne answered by steering her horse north. Saulice and Drezz followed.

And with the first hoofbeats striking the frost-laced trail, the city of Axbridge disappeared behind them.

The road narrowed as they rode, rimmed by thorny hedges and frostbitten ferns. Light had not yet broken over the hills, but the sky had begun to pale. Their breaths became visible now, curling faintly from their lips as they rode in silence.

Saulice gripped the reins tighter, focused on adjusting his body to the horse's gait so that each step didn't set off new waves of pain. The leather bit into his palms.

The bracer on his forearm felt heavier than it had in days.

They were doing this. Just the three of them.

No Cadre, no instructors, no guards at the gate. Just three students fleeing into the wild in search of something half-legend, half-threat.

And still, it was the only path that felt true.

They reached the first bend in the road. The last of the Academy's towers fell from sight behind a frost-covered slope.

Drezz rode ahead, adjusting the strap on his satchel. Rayne followed close, watching both flanks.

Saulice rode last.

The wind rose.

He did not look back.

-ACT III-

WHERE POWER KNEELS

CHAPTER 24

WHERE REALMS ONCE KNELT

A pale fog stretched over the edge of the Timfathen valley, low and clinging, as though the land itself was exhaling something it had never meant to keep.

The trees of Candur, bright and thick with spring, had faded behind them. Now the world smelled of ash, rot, and frostbitten soil.

The three riders camped at the edge of it all, just beyond where grass thinned into dead soil and pale stone.

Saulice sat cross-legged on a patch of moss, his chest aching with soreness. A pot of water warmed beside him, but the fire beneath it barely cracked. Kindling here was scarce, and everything they'd found thus far was damp. Nothing near the Timfathen seemed willing to burn.

Drezz stood several paces off, facing east. He wasn't praying, not exactly. But he had his palms open toward the light, shoulders still.

"In Fallenan," he said without turning, "we burn the dead. Ash returns to ash. We speak their names and scatter them to the wind. We don't leave them like this."

Rayne glanced up from where she was binding a leather strap around her shin. "The Timfathen doesn't care what we would do. It remembers its own."

Drezz lowered his hands, then headed towards a nearby ridge to scan the area. A somber note tinged his voice. "That is a sad problem."

The birds were gone. Since they crossed the northern ridge from Candur's border, not one had sung. No wind had moved the tall grass. Even the horses had grown quieter. Their breaths came harder here, as if they were carrying more than weight.

Mist curled between gnarled trees like cautious fingers, clinging to the horses' backs like frost. The silence almost felt watchful.

Saulice rubbed his hands together, then reached for the citrine shard. He hadn't tried to channel since the match. He hadn't dared. Not while knowing it could potentially break further or simply disintegrate if he forged again. He didn't know if he'd ever be able to use it again. When he held it in his palm, the light flickered at the edges, a twitch of gold, but nothing more.

And when he stilled his mind and looked within, his fount core appeared. A dim mote of light within his heart of hearts.

That's where he caught a glimpse.

It was weak, the fractured lines slightly wider after his fight against Lucas. Saulice felt that the little progress he'd made, the little tendrils reaching together in reparation, were now too far apart to come back together.

To fount forge again, he would need help.

He said a silent prayer to Shaddai.

You who formed me in my mother's womb. Please make whole what has been broken.

His thoughts were interrupted by the crunch of gravel. He opened his eyes to find Rayne standing to scan the fog line. A faint shimmer traced along her boots, like heat rising from the pavement but thicker. The mist curled toward her, drawn close.

Not noticing, Saulice looked up. "You think it's in there?"

She didn't answer at first. "Winstrom said it was in the inner valley, didn't he? So, it's got to be in there somewhere."

Drezz returned from the ridge with filled canteens and a bundle of bark-wrapped roots. "There's no birds. No fresh game. Just cracked bone in the mud, half buried armor, and tattered banners too old to discern."

They sat quietly after that.

Saulice flicked a spider from his boot. Even the insects here moved slower.

"I used to think the stories were exaggerated," he said. "Dead rising. A valley that would never heal."

"They weren't," Drezz said.

"Most stories fade if they're wrong," Rayne added. "Fewer so because others want them to."

The pot on the fire hissed. Steam lifted, giving no warmth.

Saulice looked down at his bracer again. If the Pitch couldn't fix his predicament, or even if it worked too well, then what?

Drezz checked the horses. "There are records. Argonauts of old marked the place where the last battle happened. Built a monument with a slab taller than three men. It wasn't just a marker. It was a symbol, signifying the end of Veartaya's conquest. If it's still there, it could point us to what we're looking for."

Rayne stood and shouldered her pack. "Then we find the monument."

Fog reached for them like a wafting breath as they packed the camp.

And somewhere within it, something watched.

They didn't say goodbye to the clearing. They just left.

Shapes loomed beneath the mist. Twisted piles of metal. Broken hilts. Shattered helms. Once, Saulice saw the curve of a shield, half-sunken into the dirt. Its emblem was unrecognizable, scratched raw by time. Further on, a banner pole jutted from the ground like a snapped bone. No cloth remained. Only frayed thread and a jagged crest of rust.

The ground swelled in uneven mounds, as though the land remembered where bodies had fallen. In some places, the earth had collapsed inward, revealing layers of armor and bone bleached to grey.

They reached a series of ancient trenches, sunken and overgrown with dead vines. They dismounted and led their horses between mounds of crumbling dirt and bent stakes. Some still held the remains of old ropes.

"It's like walking through the ribs of a grave," Drezz said.

A hollow clang echoed ahead. The horses shifted. Saulice froze.

"What was that?"

"Probably the wind," Drezz said.

"There is no wind," Rayne replied.

They moved deeper. The basin's full depth became clearer as the fog thinned. Surrounded by broken stones and scorched earth, the air pressed harder. Their boots sank into brittle patches where blood had once soaked the ground.

Saulice crouched by a slab of rusted iron. It looked like armor once, but now it barely held shape. He touched it. It was warm.

"Rayne," he called.

She pressed her fingers to it and pulled back quickly.

"It's humming."

Drezz stood tense on a small ridge. "Something happened here. Maybe a final push during one of the five battles?"

Saulice scanned the basin. "The monument might be close."

"Look there."

A stone outcrop rose from the center of a narrow valley way off in the distance. It was flat-faced with the top half missing. Vines avoided it, and fog peeled away from it.

They marched toward it, curious. Up close, the stone towered over them. Scratches marred its face. Inlaid metal had long since blackened and peeled.

Saulice stepped forward. He didn't recognize the symbols, but something cold moved beneath his ribs. Not Lazarus, but the same presence he'd felt before his match against Lucas. His citrine shard pulsed faintly, emitting a brief flicker.

"It feels like it's holding something," he whispered.

"Or remembering something," Rayne said.

"I don't think this was meant for the living," Drezz added, stepping away from the structure. "I think we should continue on."

Saulice touched the stone. It didn't respond. It only waited.

The fog shifted behind them.

He turned, but nothing was there. But the stillness felt crowded now, as though something unseen had drawn near.

"I thought it would feel more. It sounds silly, but I thought it would call to me somehow."

They moved on, searching further within the valley. Drezz found a series of small colored stones arranged in a broken half-circle, cracked and buried around an empty stone jutting from the ground. Markers of something once sacred.

"This is familiar." Drezz rubbed his chin, speculating. "These were once part of a monument built by the four races. It was meant to serve as a reminder that the four nations together were stronger together than alone."

Drezz crouched beside the lowest stone and ran his fingers through the dust. His brow furrowed with memory.

"There's a song," he mumbled. "From Fallenan. It is taught to the young before their name day. It's meant to hold us steady when the old fears of war rise again."

He didn't look at them as he spoke. He didn't need to.

"Most of it is older than our speech. But I remember the words we use now."

He closed his eyes and sang—

"Sleep, stone of morning.

Breathe, flame of peace.

When shadow climbs the tallest pine,

Still, You do not cease.

Hold, heart of silence.

Wait, light of grace.
Though fear may walk the woodland paths,
You do not leave this place."

The song rose gently, each line slower than the last, until it faded into the stillness like a breath returning to the soil.

No one spoke when he finished. Even the mist seemed quieter.

Saulice stared at the broken ring of stones. The cold remained like a blanket drawn over a wound.

Rayne's voice came softly. "That was for them?"

Drezz nodded. "And for us."

Saulice knelt and uncovered a faint carving—four roots spreading from a single tree.

"If the Pitch was used anywhere, it was here."

Rayne nodded. "Then we're close."

Drezz glanced toward the north rim. His ears perked. "But not alone."

The fog shifted again.

Something was watching.

Three shapes moved through the haze at the far edge of the basin, dozens of feet away. The only sound that reached them was of something large brushing through scorched brush and loose stone.

They looked like centaurs… but wrong.

Their bodies stretched too thin. Black fur hung in patches. Limbs moved stiffly, like bone without sinew. The largest carried a long spear strapped across its back, rusted and pitted. Saulice caught a glimpse of its face, white and hollow, without eyes.

Lichtaurs.

The trio dropped low. Rayne held a fist up behind her, signaling stillness. Saulice barely breathed.

The Lichtaurs passed within forty feet. One paused, nostrils flaring. Its head tilted toward the monument.

Rayne's hand moved to her dagger.

Don't, Saulice thought. *Please don't.*

But the creature only sniffed, then moved on. The others followed, gliding across the dead earth.

When the last one vanished, no one moved. Saulice's legs ached from crouching, but he didn't dare stand.

Rayne exhaled, slow and tight. "They're patrolling. They weren't hunting. Not yet."

Drezz stood cautiously. "What are they looking for?"

Rayne looked back toward the ridge. "Whatever lives near this monument, it's not us."

The fog closed in again, quiet but no longer still.

The fire cracked low beneath the hollowed limbs of a dead tree, just outside the boundary of the Timfathen. Mist slipped between the roots like a patient breath. Saulice sat near the edge of the light, arms folded over his knees. The warmth barely touched him.

He shifted slightly, staring at the brittle flame as it flickered. Then he glanced toward Rayne, who sat across from him beside Drezz, her head bowed over a half-laced boot. She hadn't spoken since they circled the basin.

Saulice rested his chin on his knees, watching the fire shrink like a breath drawn too tight. The silence between the three of them wasn't empty. It pressed in like fog, thick with unspoken things. Since the monument, they had barely spoken more than a dozen words.

He wanted to believe it meant nothing. That they were just tired and cold.

But he detected something else lingering behind Rayne's stillness. It wasn't doubt or anger, but something quiet and wounded.

Saulice shifted on the cold dirt. His voice came low. "Back in the courtyard, you said you followed me because you overheard Winstrom."

Rayne looked up, brows knit. "I did."

"Was that all?"

She tilted her head. "I wasn't. Until I got your note."

Her hand went to her coat pocket. "Not exactly."

She drew out a folded scrap of parchment, its edges smudged with charcoal. "This was on my bunk the night you left. Said you needed me. That no one else could come."

"What?" Saulice reached for the note, heart suddenly cold.

He stared at it, heart tight. The handwriting was close. Almost his. But the words were too formal, like someone copying the shape of his voice without knowing him.

"Rayne. I didn't write this," he said.

"I know," Rayne answered, steady. "I knew the moment I read it."

The fire popped once. Across from them, Drezz stirred, tail flicking. "So, you followed anyway?"

"I followed because it meant someone else knew," Rayne said. Her voice stayed quiet, sharp in the stillness. "Knew what you were planning. Knew where to find me."

"Someone wanted you out here," Saulice murmured.

Rayne folded the paper again, slower this time. "Not just me. All of us."

"Together," Drezz said darkly. "They wanted all three of us in one place."

The wind didn't move. Even the mist seemed to hold still.

Rayne stared at the fire, her voice barely above a whisper. "I believed it anyway. Not the words, but the warning behind them."

Saulice closed his eyes. It wasn't about the letter or the lie. It was about the truth beneath it. Someone out there knew. Knew about Lazarus. Knew what it would take to control the Titan's power.

Rayne's gaze lifted toward him. "You didn't bring us here. Not really."

"But I made it easier for them…" Saulice said.

Drezz tossed a twig into the fire. "So, someone's been watching us. Someone who knew what it would take to pull us out here. We keep our eyes open, and don't let our guard down. We'll be alright."

The words settled hard in the air.

No one spoke again for a long time.

The fire had shrunk to a low coil. Drezz muttered something about patrol shifts and tucked himself tighter into his blanket. Rayne stayed seated, her back straight against the tree until she finally slid to her side and closed her eyes.

Saulice remained upright. His bracer pressed against his ribs. The earth beneath him was too cold to sleep. But his body was worn, and his mind was numb.

Just as he began to drift, something scraped.

He opened his eyes. Mist coiled at his knees.

The fire had died.

"Rayne," he whispered, rising quickly.

She was already crouched, blade half-drawn. Drezz stood nearby, gripping a torn bridle. His face was pale.

"Where are the horses?" Saulice asked.

"They're gone," Drezz whispered. "The lines must have snapped while we slept."

Muffled hooves clopped on stone, slow and distant. More than Saulice could count.

"Then what's that sound?"

Rayne yanked Saulice to his feet. "Weapons out. Now!"

He scrambled for his belt. The dagger came loose in his shaking grip. Drezz had nothing but his claws. Rayne readied her bow, then lowered it, realizing too late it wouldn't matter.

Shapes emerged in the fog.

Twisted. Four-limbed. Wrong.

First came the silhouettes. Then the eyes.

Blue rings, faint at first, then flaring into ghoulish blue as they surrounded them.

Lichtaurs. And there were over a dozen.

Saulice's mouth went dry. Sulfur burned in his throat. Beneath the panic was something deeper, familiar.

The fog parted.

One stepped forward, larger and horned. Bone exposed beneath rotted flesh. His voice rasped, jagged with decay.

"This is the one," he said, pointing at Saulice. "The vessel."

Rayne stepped in front of him. "You don't want him. Take me instead."

The lichtaur ignored her. "Do away with the rest as you please. The Harbinger comes back to the cave."

Then they rushed forward.

Drezz lunged, but one tackled him mid-step. Saulice reached for him, but something grabbed his shoulder and yanked him back.

Rayne gripped his sleeve. "Don't let go!"

"I won't!"

But they came from behind.

Hands wrapped around Saulice's chest. Rayne's fingers slipped. She tried to step forward.

"He's not who you want," she shouted. "You'll get nothing from him."

They didn't listen.

They pulled her next. Her fingers tore away from his.

Then came a low voice, too close for comfort. Rotting breath brushed against his cheek.

"The seal… won't save you."

A blow struck his neck, the lichtaur's hand cold and crushing.

As the world spun sideways, he reached blindly with his hands. And just before the dark claimed him, he heard:

"You were always meant to kneel."

When he came to, stone scraped against his back.

The air was thick and wet, the bitter stench of sulfur permeating his garments. Saulice blinked in the dark, limbs stiff as the pain settled behind his eyes.

When he rolled, his hand brushed a skull. He recoiled, stomach twisting. Without warning, he vomited. Unable to do anything else, he crouched in silence, trembling.

Hooves shifted beyond the bars.

A shape leaned into view, its blue eyes flaring.

"You won't last long," it whispered.

Saulice forced his voice out. His chest was still tight from his wounds, but his throat was wound with fear. "Where are the others?"

"Praying. Bleeding. Still hoping maybe." The lichtaur smiled. "You'll stop hoping soon enough."

Then it vanished, leaving him alone.

His fingers found his bracer. The shard was dull, but there. He remembered Melandra's words.

The fount isn't commanded. It's invited.

"Shaddai," he whispered. "I need to know You still see me."

No sound answered him. But a sudden warmth filled the space. A flicker jolted through the shard, gone as fast as it came.

His chest tightened.

Why now?

As he thought about his matches, he realized something. A mistake that he'd blindly made. In the arena, he hadn't asked for power. He had demanded it, believing it was his to begin with.

"It was never about control, was it, Shaddai?" His voice cracked as he spoke. "It was about trust."

No answer came. Only the same unmoving dark.

His jaw tightened. "I know you're there too, Lazarus. You've always heard me. Every time I bled. Every time I begged you not to take over. Why stay silent?"

Still nothing.

"You ache," he said, standing in the cell, voice rising. "I get it. That's all I've done since I could walk. And still, you say nothing. You sit in there, buried inside my ribs, and let me drown."

The walls did not echo back.

"Say something. Anything. I am so done *waiting* for you!"

He slammed his knuckles into the stone. Once. Twice. A third time, until his hand burned and blood rose.

"I did not run from this," he said through gritted teeth. "I faced it. Trained for it. I have fought harder than anyone should have to."

His chest heaved.

"You do not get to ignore me."

He pressed his palm against his ribs, fingers trembling. "You do not get to disappear."

He lowered himself to the floor, breathing shallow. Fury still pulsed beneath his skin, but the silence swallowed it whole.

"I am still here," he whispered.

And this time, he meant it as a warning.

INTERLUDE

EVERYTHING LEFT BEHIND

The sun hung high over the southern rim of the Timfathen, its light filtered through dry willow branches that stirred only slightly in the still heat.

Dust clung to Dedric's boots as he stepped into the hollowed village, every stride kicking up a powdering of earth that hovered midair before settling back like ash.

He wore the Fists' uniform now, its black and red lines bleeding together, but it felt more like mourning garb. He'd been sent weeks ago to investigate the quiet places. The disappearances began as rumors, just missed festivals and silent farms.

A yellow ribbon clung to a fence slat. It flared briefly as he passed. A small cottage nearby had its door ajar. Dedric stepped inside, a hand near his blade.

The air was thick. A table sat with bread left half-cut. Flies buzzed over a bowl of decaying fruit in the windowsill. A chair lay overturned and scratches marred the floor by the hearth. A painted toy soldier sat by the wall.

Dedric knelt. The soldier was warm from the sun but untouched for days.

There were no bodies. No signs of flight. No blood. Just erasure. They were gone.

He exited slowly and crossed to the barn. The doors were open, left as though someone meant to return. Dust hung in the beams. Tools lay dropped and a rusted scythe leaned by the stairs. The air smelled of sweat and something metallic.

Four gouges marked the support beam near the far wall.

Dedric approached. The marks were deliberate, low and angled, left by something upright. He placed his gloved hand on the grooves. These were marks he'd seen before, a long time ago.

It was the work of lichtaurs, remnants of centaurs and people, corrupted by Veartaya's dark fount forging during the Thousand Year War. But lichtaurs weren't organized beings, not since humanity had won and survived.

Yet here, under the fall sun, a village had vanished.

He turned slowly. Nothing moved, but he placed a hand on his blade and left the barn.

Footprints curved around the grain silo toward the well, baked into the dirt. He followed them, each step pressing into a story the village could no longer tell.

Later, he rode along a ridge sloping east, where the wheat grew thin and the Timfathen trees reached upward like bones. The path had shifted. A hedgerow had collapsed. The river had carved a new channel.

The land itself had changed.

He dismounted near a crumbling stone pillar that once bore the Candur crest. Moss and mist covered it now. He crouched beside it.

"This was the boundary line," he muttered. "So why has the mist moved?"

The air was hot and silent. No birdsong. No wind.

Down the hill, a sliver of canvas fluttered beyond a wilted grove.

Dedric moved carefully. A hidden campsite came into view, its cold firepit surrounded by three bedrolls and a small cooking tin.

This was no accident. The layout was disciplined, cautious travelers who were prepared for danger.

He knelt by the fire. Ash crumbled under his fingers. It had burned for days. The footprints that remained were booted and small. These were youth.

A slashed satchel rested under a flattened cloak.

As he picked it up, his hands trembled.

The bag was old and scuffed. But the stitching along the edge was familiar. He had chosen it himself in Hamlen, gifting it to Saulice years ago. The boy had held it like it was all that mattered.

Now it lay torn.

He opened it. A few food scraps tumbled out, followed by a cracked compass. A final jostle released a frayed ribbon of blue cloth.

And at the bottom, the dagger.

The black hilt bore the lion's head of the Fist. One of only two dozen in the realm. It had been given to Dedric when he became an argonaut decades ago, a gift from his brother. Benedict, Saulice's father, was long dead; his memory carried only in steel and blood. Dedric kept the dagger as a reminder and a promise to keep Saulice safe, no matter what.

Dedric had packed it for the boy as a means of defense.

He closed his fist around it. It was too light. Too cold.

Saulice would never have left it unless forced.

He rose, breath quickening. Around the camp, hoofprints circled, at least a dozen sets.

So many hooves could only mean one possibility.

The Lichtaurs had taken them. Had taken Saulice.

It looked like they had surrounded the camp while the fire still burned.

Dedric cursed, shoved the dagger into his belt, and ran for his horse.

This was no longer an investigation. It was a rescue.

He mounted and wheeled the stallion back toward the village with a sharp crack of the reins. Toward Melandra and the Fist. Toward the only people who might believe him.

The dagger pressed against his side.
It had been given to protect Saulice.
Now it became Dedric's promise.
He would find his nephew.
Or die trying.

CHAPTER 25

THE WEEPING TITAN

The fourth mark on the wall was fading.

It wasn't from wear but from the dampness that worsened each day. The air in the cell had grown heavier, as if the stone itself had begun to sweat.

Saulice traced the notch with the edge of a pebble, pressing hard until the groove deepened again. He didn't know if it had been nine days or twelve. The cracks in his sanity didn't keep calendars.

But his core had changed, and that much he could feel. The fractures in his core had turned translucent, slowly disappearing. The raw ache that flared whenever he touched the shard had also dulled.

Still, the shard remained cracked and uncertain.

Some mornings, it flickered, warm in his bracer, the citrine catching like fire behind fogged glass. Other times, it stayed cold, dull as bone. Saulice never knew which version he would wake to. Even when it pulsed, when he knew the fount was rising, it never held for long.

This morning, it had flickered, just once.

He now sat in the center of the cell, legs folded beneath him, back straight despite the cold. His fingers hovered near the bracer, as they had many times before. He didn't pray this time. Instead, he focused on his breath. Three counts in. Hold. Four out.

It was the way Drezz had taught him, and the way Shaddai had shown him in silence.

A pulse stirred, warm, steady, and hopeful.

He reached toward it and felt it stop.

There was no violence or explosion. Only stillness, as if a massive hand inside him had pressed the storm down and whispered that it was not yet time.

Saulice lowered his arm as the warmth drained from his body.

He opened his eyes, his heart tight with something between grief and confusion. The walls of the cell hadn't changed. The skull in the corner still waited, silent and grim.

He stared at the bracer and touched the crack in the shard with the edge of his thumb.

"Why?" he murmured.

"I called on Shaddai, and He answered," he continued.

His voice cracked.

"But you've never helped me."

He wasn't shouting. He didn't have the strength. His voice stayed low, filled with betrayal that had no target and trust that had leaked away.

"You were supposed to serve justice," Saulice seethed. "Isn't that what history claims? That you won't stop until justice is done?"

He curled his fingers slowly.

"So why do you stay silent now, when the one trying to destroy everything you fought for is returning?"

His gaze dropped to the stone floor, lips trembling.

"If you and Shaddai serve the same purpose, then why is He helping me and you're trying to destroy me?"

He didn't expect a reply, but the ache in his core twisted.

It wasn't pain, but disappointment.

Was surrender not enough? Had it ever been?

Footsteps approached. They were soft and wet, dragging like hooves through ash and rot.

Saulice stood slowly. His legs ached from the cold, but he remained steady. He didn't flinch when the shadow appeared on the far side of the cell door.

It was the same lichtaur that had been watching him for days. Smaller than the horned leader that had taken him, but no less deformed. Its body sagged where rot had thinned it. A bony frame protruded from sagging flesh, and a skull peeked through flaps of torn skin. Two blue eyes flared like lantern wicks.

It smiled.

"You should be honored," it whispered. "Master is coming. He will tear your storm from its cradle."

Saulice's jaw tightened.

"I'm not a cradle," he replied.

The lichtaur chuckled, a sound like bone grinding in a socket.

"You're a vessel. Already cracked."

Its hooves scraped the stone once as it backed into the dark.

"We'll see how long you last. Master can be very persuasive," it called, disappearing once more, never far from his cell.

Saulice stood alone again.

He didn't remember falling asleep, and when he opened his eyes, the cell was darker. The shard had dulled again, reflecting nothing but the iron bars.

He couldn't stop thinking. His thoughts kept circling back to Lazarus.

With so much time in silence, he kept returning to the Titan's interruptions, how they had scattered through his life like sparks without warning, always breaking something just before it could heal.

He leaned against the wall, arms draped over his knees.

"I don't know what you want from me," he said aloud. "I've tried being brave. I've tried being angry. I stopped pretending I was in control."

The words tasted like metal. He waited for the echo to fade.

"Answer me, Lazarus."

He slammed a fist through the ancient skull like it was parchment. "I need to know why. If Shaddai can answer me in this pit, so can you!"

There was silence.

Then, a breath that was deeper than silence.

It wasn't a sound exactly, but a presence. Something in the air exhaled once, long and slow.

The shard flickered, then turned black, and it was gone.

Saulice stiffened. That was new. Images surged into his mind. They weren't memories, but impressions.

Ash poured from the sky, split open. Women and children screaming. The gates of a city collapsed inward while thousands shouted a name Saulice didn't recognize, but Lazarus clearly did.

Grief crashed into Saulice's chest, heavy and unbearable, laced with betrayal. He staggered forward and caught himself on the floor.

The visions did not stop.

Chains wrapped something. Fire consumed it. A hand reached from the heavens and was slapped away. Then darkness returned, accompanied by silence.

Saulice gasped. He fell to his knees, sweating down his spine.

"That's not an answer," he muttered.

But part of him recognized it was.

Lazarus wasn't just resisting. He was grieving. And the Titan was angry.

Not at Saulice, but at something older. Something unresolved that should have already been put to rest.

"You've carried this longer than I've been alive," Saulice said. "If I'm supposed to carry you now, I need to know how."

There was no response.

"You know I'm not your enemy," Saulice added. "I never was."

He pressed his fingers to the shard.

The images surged again. A city appeared in his mind, wreathed in golden towers, its gates shattered by black lightning. Smoke curled like torn silk through the streets. Rubble glowed with residual energy, veins of thunder etched into stone.

The images quickened.

A man stood atop a ruined wall. He was older, his eyes lined with wear, armor dented and scorched. His hands trembled, but his stance remained steady. His bracer pulsed with the color of a storm veiled in glass.

Saulice had never seen him, but he felt him.

Lector.

The name pulsed like a drumbeat beneath the silence. Beside Lector, no, within him, another presence loomed. Massive and furious. Iconically wordless. It was Lazarus. And they were one, yet not.

The scene shifted once more.

Pain jolted through Saulice's temple, but he had to see.

Lector screamed in defiance as black tendrils rose from a chasm. A silhouette emerged, wings bleeding with shadow and claws sparking with sickly arcs. Baalo's master— Veartaya.

She was more void than flesh, her presence rippling like a curse beneath moonlight. Her eyes cracked the air itself, filled with power older than grief.

Lector rushed forward, and lightning coiled beneath his ribs, pleading to be released. But then Lector turned away. He opened his hands and the fount swelled inside him, vast enough to make Saulice's own storm feel like a spark.

Then Saulice understood.

Lector was not preparing for battle. He was preparing to *die*.

Saulice clenched his jaw, pushing past the rising pain. This might be his only chance to understand the Titan.

Lazarus roared with grief.

Light exploded into a corona of lightning that split the ground and clawed at the heavens.

Chains wrapped Veartaya, sealed by divine will.

Lector fell, his body lifeless.

The vision broke.

Then reformed.

Lazarus stood, colossal and free. No longer within Lector. No longer tethered. Tears fell from the Titan's face, grieving the loss of a friend.

He dropped to one knee beside the body of his Harbinger. The Titan bowed, with tears streaming down his large face.

The clouds rolled, but there was no thunder. And Lazarus remained there, unmoving, as Veartaya was defeated at the cost of someone dear to him.

Then the cell's darkness returned, and Saulice scrambled back, collapsing against the wall of his cell.

"That's… a lot," he said.

So that's what it was.

"I'm not Lector," he muttered.

The bracer flexed faintly, as if responding to thought.

A whisper followed, barely audible.

He said goodbye… without me.

The words tore through Saulice.

Lazarus had been left behind. The Titan had been used and feared, then abandoned.

Saulice said nothing, choosing to *allow* the silence. He let it hurt, and after a long time, he looked at the shard. The crack no longer looked like failure. It looked like a scar.

"I don't want to use you," he said. "Not like others have in the past."

He breathed deeply. "I want to understand you."

The warmth that stirred wasn't bright or strong, but it was there. He tried forging again, carefully; the cell filling with his reverence. The fount rose through his core, coiling, only for a breath.

But it stayed and for a moment, it felt like a bridge was being built towards trust. Then the silence ended.

Footsteps echoed, calm and seemingly human-shaped.

A figure appeared, cloaked in black robes that drifted like smoke. His face was nearly handsome until one looked too long. His eyes were black, rimmed in silver veins, while his skin was cracked with lines like mud.

Saulice stepped back. His breath caught. It wasn't the face that alarmed him. It was the feeling.

The same sick pull he had felt when the black bellet locked eyes with him. The same one he had felt at the Twin Spires.

Saulice breathed, rising to his feet. "You were watching us through the black bellet."

The figure stepped inside. The cell door creaked open without touching.

"I watch all things worth watching," the figure said.

Saulice's voice caught. "Who are you?"

"I am merely a servant," he said, smiling without warmth. "A faithful steward. I am Baalo."

The name landed like a warning. The air shifted, becoming thicker and colder. Even the walls seemed to recoil.

Saulice remembered the name from one of Cadre Calder's lessons. Saulice shrank within the cell. If this figure was who he claimed to be, then he was in severe trouble.

Baalo wasn't just some servant. He had been Veartaya's second in command during the Thousand Year War.

"I've followed you since Hamlen," Baalo said. "Since the storm touched you."

He stepped forward.

"You've carried the Titan longer than most untrained children. It is impressive. Yet, you still think you are Lazarus' master."

Saulice said nothing. The storm in his chest compressed.

"The Source Stone cracking wasn't you. It was him," Baalo added.

Saulice's jaw tightened. "Then why hasn't he broken free?"

"Because he's still grieving," Baalo said, his voice hardening. "Even Titans weep when they're abandoned. I would know. I was there when his last host died... so honorably."

Saulice felt something stir in his core. A sense of recognition.

"You're not afraid of him anymore," Baalo said. "That's good."

"I'm not afraid of you either," Saulice lied.

Baalo's eyes narrowed. "You will be."

He stepped back.

"The Pitch is almost ready. All that remains is your decision."

He smiled with pointed teeth before turning to leave. "I believe you'll choose to willingly obey."

But something deeper stirred in Saulice. He thought of Drezz, of Rayne, of Dedric. He remembered the prayers that had gone unanswered yet had never been unwelcome.

"I won't," he whispered. The words tasted like iron and ash, but they steadied him.

Then the truth struck like ice. The Pitch could only work through a Titan. Which meant Baalo didn't have one.

He needed Lazarus. He needed Saulice.

The realization hollowed his chest, leaving only the cold certainty that Baalo didn't plan to break him. He planned to use him.

CHAPTER 26

PARTING WATERS

The river took Rayne before she could scream.

Cold hit her like a wall of stone. The current spun her sideways and dragged her under. Water filled her ears and pressed against her lungs. Every breath became a losing battle against panic.

She kicked hard. Her boots skimmed unseen rocks until she broke the surface with a gasp that barely cut through the river's roar.

Where was Drezz?

She turned, squinting through the mist and moonlight. The river had become a living thing, writhing and thrashing, hiding what she sought most.

"Drezz!" she cried. Her voice tore against the air and vanished beneath the crashing current.

There. Just ahead.

A dark shape struggled against the pull. Too small and too far away.

Her arms ached as she fought upstream, the cold chewing through muscle and will. She could not reveal it. Not here. Not like this.

Then his hand slipped under and did not rise.

Something inside her broke.

No more hiding, she thought.

Her fingers found the lapis stone in her bracer, hidden beneath her soaked cloak's sleeves. It was smooth and cold, familiar. The one thing she had sworn never to reveal.

Her lips parted around a shallow breath.

Forgive me, Master Valos.

She forged the fount within her core, coiling it in parallel layers. Then she channeled it deeper within herself, a place no ordinary argonaut could reach. To Malaya, the weeping Titan, sealed inside her.

Her world changed.

Cold fount flooded her veins like the river had turned inward. Her blood filled with terrible momentum. Her eyes snapped open, glowing an unnatural, brilliant blue. The power was not quiet. It roared beneath her skin.

She pushed toward the riverbank, planted her boots in the mud, and raised her arm in a sharp, deliberate arc. Water rose in answer. It towered above her, defying weight and reason.

There, Drezz surfaced, gasping with wide eyes.

Rayne drew a breath and swept her hand across the river in one smooth, commanding motion.

The waters split.

The river hissed and groaned as it parted. A clean path carved through chaos. Slick stones gleamed in the moonlight.

"Move, Drezz!" Her voice carried like a current, breaking through the river's rage.

Drezz stumbled forward, choking, coughing. His limbs thrashed until he found footing on the exposed riverbed. He collapsed onto the bank, hands clutching the earth. His lungs dragged in air like a man pulled from death.

Rayne lowered her arm, shoulders trembling. The river closed behind him with a final, thunderous crash. Water sprayed outward. Droplets hung in the moonlight before falling like soft rain.

She stood over him, breathing hard. Her hands still glowed faintly as the last echoes of the fount retreated.

Drezz turned, wide-eyed. His voice was raw.

"Your eyes… they—"

Rayne met his gaze. The glow in her irises lingered like embers beneath ice.

She swallowed.

"I'm the other Harbinger, Drezz. It's me."

The words hung between them like a drawn blade.

Drezz sat up slowly, fur matted with water.

"You…" He shook his head. "But how? Since when?"

"Since I was a baby. Long before we met," Rayne said softly. She tucked the stone beneath her cloak. Though the glow faded, the truth remained undeniable. "Master Valos knew. Others too. They ordered me to watch Saulice, to see if…" She turned from the river. "It doesn't matter. Now you know."

Drezz pulled in a shaky breath. "You saved me," he whispered. "Shaddai above. Thank you."

Rayne offered a faint, tired smile. "We don't have a lot of time. Saulice is still out there, Drezz. Alone."

Drezz pushed himself up, each movement heavy. As the river settled behind them, something clearer settled in him.

"We'll need help," he said, voice steadying. "I have contacts in Grimwode. A clan of centaurs that fight more than talk."

Rayne's eyes sharpened.

"Then that's where we go."

Drezz wiped his face. His trembling gave way to resolve.

Rayne lingered at the river's edge. Her gaze remained on the water, now calm and indifferent.

Her thoughts were not on her power.

They were with a boy lost in the heart of the Timfathen.

Hold on, Saulice, she thought. *We're coming.*

The land changed as the river turned.

The dark woods of the Timfathen thinned to scattered groves. The emerald hills of Grimwode opened before them like a long-forgotten promise. Mist clung to the lower slopes, but above, the sky brightened. Cold silver edged toward dawn. Northward, the magnificent ring of mountains loomed against the horizon, jagged silhouettes guarding Fallenan.

Rayne and Drezz walked in silence along the northern banks of the Archaic River. Here, the water flowed gently. It whispered over smooth stones as if reluctant to recall the chaos downstream.

Drezz led the way. His pace stayed steady despite exhaustion. His eyes scanned the landscape with quiet vigilance.

Rayne noticed his glance drifting toward the hills and sparse woods.

"You've been here before?" she asked.

He nodded. "My falne brought me when I was young. Before the borders closed and our old alliances faded." His voice hardened. "It was before a lot changed."

Rayne said nothing. Her fingers brushed the stone beneath her cloak. The river still hummed faintly in her blood. She could feel the pulse of the fount core she had unleashed. Her hands trembled, but not from cold.

She would not use her powers again. Not unless there was no choice.

The terrain rose. The path narrowed. Then, beyond the next rise, they saw them.

A patrol of centaurs stood silhouetted against a ridge. Six figures, massive and broad shouldered. Their equine bodies bore dark steel and weathered leather. Spears tipped with blackened iron glinted in the light. Bows hung across their backs, quivers bristling with arrows longer than Rayne's forearm.

Rayne's hand hovered near her stone before she stopped herself. Her breath slowed.

"Easy," Drezz said, lifting a paw. His posture shifted into the old sign of respect.

The centaurs moved as one. They circled the pair in a silent, practiced arc. The leader, taller than the others, wore his mane braided with silver beads. His eyes were hard and clear.

Drezz straightened, drawing a long breath. His voice rang out.

"Centaurs!" He straightened into a regal posture. "I am Drezz Dulce'n, son of Monarch Farthum of Fallenan. Grimwode stands at the edge of great peril. The dead walk again beyond the Archaic, within the Timfathen. Lichtaurs gather, led by something more than old curses. And worse yet, someone of great importance has been taken."

He paused.

"A Harbinger."

The air thinned as the patrol stiffened. Hooves shifted. Leather creaked.

Drezz pressed forward.

"If that power falls into the wrong hands…" His voice sharpened. "You know what it will mean. Every realm across Myre will be at risk. The Harbinger must be recovered."

The centaur leader's expression darkened, and unease rippled through the patrol.

Finally, he spoke. His voice was low thunder.

"You bring grim warnings. And who walks at your side, Falleni son? A water-forged sentinel from one of Candur's tall towers?"

Drezz glanced at Rayne.

"She is with me. She is no soldier beneath a banner. Only a friend."

The centaur studied him. Then, with a flick of his tail, turned.

"Come. Our clan lord must hear of this. You will tell him."

The patrol closed ranks and turned north toward the hidden settlement in Grimwode's woods.

Rayne walked beside Drezz. Her thoughts raced faster than her feet. She still felt the river's thrum within her. The power she had denied now refused silence.

The centaur camp lay hidden beneath a canopy of ancient redwoods, their trunks wide as towers and their crowns lost above the mist. The air smelled of damp earth and old fires. Between the trees, Rayne glimpsed smoke trails and the faint orange glow of watch fires.

This was not a village. It was a fortress grown from the forest itself.

Centaurs moved along the paths, their armor battered but functional. Weapons stayed close at hand. Their dark eyes tracked Rayne and Drezz with the judgment of battle-seasoned sentinels.

Rayne adjusted her cloak. Despite its weight, she felt exposed.

"They don't trust me," she muttered.

"They don't trust anyone," Drezz replied. "But you carry a Titan beneath your skin. Centaurs are spiritually attuned creatures. They can smell it on you."

At the camp's center, a wide clearing opened among the roots of a redwood older than kingdoms. Stone pillars ringed the space, their surfaces worn by age and war. In the center stood their leader.

He was larger than the others, his equine body muscled and scarred. His bronze skin gleamed in the morning light. A mantle of dark wolf pelts hung across his back. An iron gorget, carved with ancient sigils, covered his chest. His eyes were deep as caverns, cold as mountain stone.

Drezz stepped forward and knelt, fist to frost-bitten ground.

"Lord Athekk," he said, voice low.

Rayne remained standing, but bowed her head in a warrior's gesture.

Athekk studied her. Then he returned his gaze to Drezz.

"The Falleni son returns to Grimwode," he rumbled. "And brings a Harbinger to my fire."

Rayne's heart clenched.

So they knew.

Athekk stepped closer. His hooves cracked against the frozen ground.

"You've crossed borders in dark times. Speak plain."

Drezz rose. His voice stayed steady.

"We have no army. Only a mission. Lichtaurs gather near the Timfathen, led by something stronger than themselves. We were attacked." He let the weight fall. "They captured our friend, a Harbinger. We were thrown in the Archaic River, but we survived."

Silence fell. The fires flickered lower. Eyes narrowed. Fingers twitched near weapons.

Athekk's jaw tensed.

"You understand the weight of these words?"

"I do. If that power is turned," Drezz said, "no kingdom, no mountain, no sea will be able to stop what will ensue."

Athekk's eyes darkened.

"What would you wish of us?"

"Help us recover him. Before it is too late for him, and for the rest of Myre."

The clan lord said nothing.

Fires crackled over the silence. Dawn crept over the mountain ring, casting light into mist.

Then Lord Athekk nodded. The motion was slow, heavy with decision.

"We will march," he said. His voice held the weight of stone. "But our aid carries a price."

Rayne stiffened.

"What price?"

Lord Athekk turned to her, his stare unblinking.

"When this is over," he said, "we will call for you. You will return to Grimwode and hear our demand. An eye for an eye."

Her pulse pounded. She knew this was the Harbinger debt, even if its shape remained hidden.

She looked at Drezz. He offered no answers.

Rayne stepped forward.

"I swear it."

The clan lord nodded.

"So be it."

He turned to his warriors, his voice rising like a battle horn.

"Arm them. Gather half our force and prepare to march before the sun is full!"

His declaration rippled through the camp. Centaurs moved with speed and precision. Orders passed quickly, and supplies were gathered.

Rayne exhaled. The tension in her shoulders eased. But a deeper chill lingered.

She was not sure if it came from the promise or from what waited beyond it.

Drezz watched the preparations, eyes narrowed.

"This matter is of grave importance to them," he said. "A Harbinger's capture is more than tragedy. It is an omen."

Rayne studied him. His jaw was tight. The exhaustion in his eyes still lingered.

"You knew they'd demand something."

He gave a small, bitter smile.

"Centaur debts are never written lightly. Or forgiven quickly. But they keep their word."

A young centaur broke ranks and approached. His armor was simple, and his mane unadorned. But his steps held purpose.

He offered them supplies without comment, a roll of dark fabric and a set of leather harnesses.

"For the march," he said, voice gruff. His eyes darted toward Rayne.

Rayne unrolled the bundle. A reinforced cuirass waited inside, oiled leather lined with metal studs. Not ceremonial. This was forged for war.

She strapped it on, adjusting the weight. It felt heavier than Brynswick gear, but such was necessary.

Drezz donned a fitted breastplate and slung a small round shield to his back. He accepted a pair of hooked blades with a nod.

Rayne touched her bracer. Her fingers brushed the stone hidden beneath. Her fount still coiled within her, prepared for anything.

"Rayne," Drezz said.

She looked up.

"You sure about this?"

He meant the promise, not the mission.

She drew a breath.

"No. But I'll stand by it."

For the first time since the river, Drezz smiled. "Then let's go get our friend back."

The horns of Grimwode sounded, low and deep. The ground seemed to shake beneath them.

Centaurs formed ranks. Spears lifted. Bows strung. Athekk mounted a rise. His skin shone bronze in the rising light. He raised his great spear high.

And Clan Athekk of Grimwode marched, five hundred centaurs strong.

CHAPTER 27

POWER WITHOUT PEACE

The cell had grown smaller.

Or perhaps his mind had stretched too far inside it, pressing against stone and shadow, trying to find space where none remained. Saulice sat against the icy wall, legs drawn up, eyes unfocused.

He barely noticed the chill anymore. It had settled into him days ago, a constant presence like the ache of an old wound.

Baalo had visited him many times, almost every day, with attempts to coax him to use the Pitch, to put an end to Lazarus' tyranny and to grasp real power. He told Saulice twisted stories from the Thousand Year War, opposite of the textbooks in Brynswick's Annals. As each day passed, Saulice had less and less to argue against it.

It mattered little. Baalo's honeyed words might provoke thought, but they were not tangible.

The visions Lazarus had imparted were. They hadn't faded one bit. Saulice still saw the cliff, each rock jutting like angled pikes. Still saw Lazarus, colossal and broken, lightning-chained against a sky that refused to weep. The great Titan bowing over Lector's body, wracked with grief Saulice couldn't fully realize.

Grief was an old acquaintance, laced deep within his innermost self. Nothing of his bloodline remained except for his uncle Dedric.

He had never known his father, and his mother had been claimed by flames. Flames Saulice could have snuffed out or prevented if he had been properly trained as Harbinger children were supposed to be.

He told himself that Dedric had good intentions, that he had only tried to protect Saulice from what the world would try to turn him into. But the whispered assurances fell flat.

Even worse, the broken image of Lazarus from his vision wouldn't leave him. Rather, it seemed more real than the surrounding cell.

Why show me that? Saulice wondered, hands shaking in anger. *What am I supposed to do with your grief? I have my own friends to grieve. They're probably dead because of you!*

His mind drifted further from the Titan, toward faces he'd never see again.

Rayne. Drezz.

Could they be alive? It seemed impossible.

Saulice pressed the heels of his palms against his temples and forced himself to breathe. His chest convulsed instead, every inhale snagging as if his ribs had become a cage too narrow to hold him. Moisture blurred his vision before he even realized he was crying. It gathered and fell, silent at first, then with a trembling sound that reminded him of water striking stone. The sound mocked him, steady and unrelenting.

He should never have brought them here. He could have waited until the dormitories slept and slipped out alone. He could have spared them this ruin, spared them from the screams that still echoed inside his skull. He should have taken the danger on himself.

The thought lodged like a shard in his chest. Oreas's face rose unbidden—creased brow, half-laughed grin, the strange warmth that always carried hidden sorrow. Saulice could almost see that grin collapse, replaced by a silence heavier than shouting. He imagined Oreas's voice in the darkness.

You lost her.

She was just a girl… and you lost her.

It should have been you.

His fists tightened against his temples as if he could crush the words back into silence. The pressure only sharpened the ache behind his eyes. He trembled in place, holding the breath he could not steady, until his body betrayed him and the sob broke free. It escaped as a low moan, thin and raw, too human to hide.

In an instant, the fight left him, leaving only the husk of that same scared boy, cowering in the corner of Hamlen's market square while being bullied.

Accused.

Slandered.

Struck by Will and his friends.

The weight beneath his ribs turned bitter and cold. He folded forward onto the stone as his stomach burned with hunger. His knees scraped against grit, and Saulice curled up as if being smaller made him safer. The cell's silence felt endless. No warmth of lightning stirred within his chest. No flicker of water or earth to remind him of Rayne or Drezz. Their absence became its own presence, filling every corner of him with the certainty that he was alone.

His empty belly growled. He had not been given food since the day Baalo arrived. How long ago had it been? Saulice's mind swam, no longer certain of anything. Anything except that he must escape Baalo's clever speech.

He stayed there, shaking, until even the tears thinned. All that remained was a hollow throb and a single thought that frightened him more than pain. If Rayne and Drezz were gone, if this was all that waited ahead, what reason was there to rise again?

His body slackened. His hands slipped from his head to the stone, palms open. Breath slowed until it barely moved his chest. A whisper came, low and insistent, though he could not tell if it was memory or something darker.

Why live at all?

The words lingered, unanswered, as cold water dripped in the distance.

Above the storm of regret, a memory rose, unbidden and sharp. Melandra's voice, low and calm beside the campfire on the road to Brynswick. The firelight had caught the edges of her sharp features as she stared into the flames, her hands steady even as Saulice's shook.

"True strength, Saulice," she had said, "isn't found in clenched fists. It's found in open hands."

He remembered staring at her then, bitter and angry. *Open hands fold,* he had wanted to say. But he hadn't. He had simply nodded and pretended to understand.

Now, the memory felt like a condemnation.

He had opened his hands. He had surrendered. And here he was sweaty, alone, and chained.

The shard on his wrist pulsed the dimmest light it ever had, like a heartbeat stretched thin.

He closed his eyes and drifted toward the vision that haunted him the most.

The cliffs rose before him once more, jagged and black against a sky splintered by silent lightning. The air was thick with the scent of scorched ozone, and the ground itself seemed to pulse with the weight of a storm barely held back.

Lazarus knelt at the edge of that broken precipice, his body a living storm of lightning threading through translucent, monumental limbs. Chains of light coiled around his wrists and ankles, rooted deep into the stone beneath him.

And yet… he did not roar.

He bowed his head.

The wind howled through the empty spaces between the cliffs, but above it all came a single word, low and thunderous, a whisper made from storms and centuries of sorrow.

"Why?"

That word echoed through the hollow places of Saulice's heart, and for a terrible moment, he didn't know if the Titan spoke to him… or to a ghost long gone.

His eyes snapped open.

The cold had seeped deeper now, into marrow and thought. But the worst thing about it wasn't the cold.

It was silence.

The question that had been at the edge of his mind since the Combative Exams returned, sharper than ever. It had first come when his circuit reversal had failed against Lucas, and his shard had cracked.

Is surrender really enough?

His voice cracked the stillness of the cell.

"Maybe… Baalo's right."

And deep within, Lazarus' presence stirred, warning him.

The cell door creaked.

There were no footsteps this time, nor a shadow crossing the light. Just the long, grating sound of rusted iron being pulled open by hands trying to draw him in.

Saulice's head snapped up, prepared as he could be for another of Baalo's hospitable visits.

Baalo stood in the threshold as if he had been there for a while. Cloaked in robes darker than the corners of the cell, his presence seemed to absorb the faint torchlight, not reflect it. He folded his hands loosely in front of him, his expression almost gentle.

"Still here sobbing and weeping," Baalo said. "Tsk. Tsk. You're a stubborn one, I'll give you that. But you fight no one but yourself. You will willingly use the Pitch, Saulice Sawyer."

Saulice backed against the wall, jaw tight. "You think this is me fighting?"

Baalo smiled faintly and stepped inside, the cell door drifting closed behind him without a touch. "This is your unraveling, as you fold to your fears. That is what comes before true surrender. Not that poor excuse for divine alignment they teach you about at that blasted Academy."

His eyes dropped to the bracer on Saulice's wrist as he stepped deeper into the cell. His throat tightened as his raspy voice rose. "How many times have you called on him now? And how many times has he left you to drown? Give it up, foolish boy!"

Saulice said nothing, but his hand curled involuntarily toward the cracked shard.

Baalo crouched low, his voice dropping until it felt like the stone walls themselves carried it. "Tell me, if Lazarus cared, why does he answer you with silence?!"

He seethed, wildness entering his eyes as though he'd begin foaming at the mouth at any second. "Why does he wait while you fray, string by string? Eventually, you will tear."

Saulice swallowed against the lump in his throat. "You'd never understand."

Baalo tilted his head. "Wouldn't I? I've known the Titans longer than you've drawn breath. I've seen what they are, judges wrapped in the skin of Shaddai, blind to the suffering of those beneath them, just like their Creator. They see only failure."

His smile widened, and this time, it chilled. "That is what Lazarus sees in you."

The words struck harder than they should have.

"That's the truth of surrender," Baalo continued. "It's a chain, not a freedom. And you were never intended to live in chains. Your father tried to seal with that same light you've been seeking after so pathetically hard," Baalo jeered. "Tried to embody all those quaint traits. Love. Sacrifice. Peace. And what did it earn him? Madness and silence. Loss. My way needs no divine permission. Only will!"

He stood again, slow and deliberate, every movement precise.

"All you must do is say the word. We can break those chains here and now," he said, voice smooth as flowing water. "The Pitch is no myth. It is not a curse, but a gift Veartaya made. Power… true power, that can be yours alone. With it, you could seal Lazarus's will forever. You'd never fear losing control again. Never fear him breaking free and tearing you apart from the inside. You could stop him from doing what he's done to you, to anyone else. Why, that's honorable, isn't it?"

Saulice shook his head, the memory of Melandra's words rising faintly in his mind.

Open hands…

Baalo's voice cut through like a blade. "You could be great, Saulice! The fount would answer you, no prayers needed. No divine permission. No more waiting silence."

Saulice bit his lip, refusing to respond to his bait. Yet Baalo's words promised more than hope.

Baalo stepped closer, his voice dropping to a whisper, coiled tight with dangerous promise.

"The greatest truth is that surrender is weakness," he said. "It is control that yields power."

Saulice squeezed his eyes shut. When he opened them again, Baalo was already fading into the shadows. His voice trailed behind like a lingering thought.

He saw it then, burning through the shadows behind his eyes. A world where he never failed the Trial. Where Dedric was more than a blacksmith. Where Will bowed to him, and he was never labeled a Forsaken.

He stood again on the Gauntlet dais, unbranded and unshaken. The ruby shard flared beneath his touch, whole and radiant, brighter than should be possible of a shard. The crowd erupted in cheers. Even elder Judic covered his mouth, overcome with awe. Alderman Corfrick lowered his gaze, as if in reverence.

Dedric stepped forward with pride. He placed both hands on Saulice's shoulders and whispered, "You've now surpassed even me!"

Rayne stood at his side, her face calm and reverent. She did not look like someone following a commander. She looked like someone standing beside a king.

And Lucas? Lucas knelt, as did all the great houses of every city in Candur.

The Forsaken brand was gone. In its place, a golden circlet ringed Saulice's wrist, marked with ten radiant lines. Not one element, but *all* of them. Fire, storm, ice, light, shadow, water, poison, and even the rarest fount affinity—time. They shimmered with a harmony no bracer had ever held. The Pitch sang to his core. It wasn't a curse but a crown.

The image hovered just above his palms, almost solid. If he reached, he could take the Pitch into himself, bind it with his will, and never be abandoned again.

He reached.

Just barely.

And the fount recoiled.

Then, without warning, the world shifted.

Stone walls dissolved into open sky, and Saulice stood once more on the jagged cliffs. The same storm-wracked precipice returned, sharp and silent, scorched into the memory of his soul.

Before him, Lazarus knelt.

The Titan's massive frame flickered faintly. Translucent limbs strained against chains of living lightning. The sky above churned without sound, heavy with thunder that refused to fall.

The chains groaned as Lazarus lifted his head. His storm-forged eyes glowed dimly through the gloom.

His voice broke the silence, low and ragged. It carried sorrow deeper than oceans.

"Child, I abandoned the world long ago."

Saulice took a cautious step forward. "But why?"

Lazarus' gaze floated to the ground. "Because the world... abandoned me."

Lightning danced weakly along the chains. The storm within him barely pulsed now, like a failing heart.

"But Baalo…" The Titan's voice cracked, mouth trembling with unseen pain. "He is not your friend. He is not here to free you."

A cold wind cut across the cliffs, slicing through the silence like glass.

"He will rip me from you," Lazarus said, his voice breaking like thunder beneath stone. "And in doing so, he will destroy us both. You, your life. And me, whatever remains of who Shaddai created me to be."

The wind swelled, and the storm above them twisted tighter, drawn into a silent spiral.

"He will wear my power," the Titan warned. "And use it for evils the world no longer remembers how to name."

Saulice could not breathe.

Then the vision shattered. Lightning tore across the sky, jagged and blinding. The cliffs crumbled. The storm screamed once more.

And the prison cell snapped back around him.

Saulice dropped to his knees. His breath came shallow, his limbs trembling with what he had seen, forgetting his hunger entirely.

And in the darkness that followed, Baalo's voice returned. Soft. Patient. Inescapable.

"Decide soon, Saulice. Storms do not wait for the will of men. They choose the strongest shore… and *break* it."

CHAPTER 28

FIGURES IN THE FOG

The ground of the Timfathen shuddered beneath the march of hooves.

Mist curled low across the cracked earth, thick as smoke, wrapping around gnarled roots and broken stone. Overhead, dim beams of the crescent moon pierced the fog, offering just enough light for them to watch their steps.

At the head of the column rode Lord Athekk, a towering figure even among his kin. His bronze skin gleamed faintly under the shifting light, his battered armor marked by long, jagged scars from clan wars long past. He held his great spear loosely across his shoulders, his gaze scanning the mists ahead with the practiced wariness of a commander who knew death was close but purposed to beat it.

Drezz walked near the front ranks, his posture upright despite the exhaustion creeping into his limbs. Rayne strode at his side, her cloak pulled tight against the damp air, her eyes sharp and forward, every motion composed and measured.

They had not spoken since the march began. There was little left to say.

"The mist lies heavier here than it should," Lord Athekk muttered, his voice carrying just enough to reach them. His dark gaze swept across the forest edges. "They are near."

Rayne did not flinch at the words. She had spent too long in the cursed grounds of the Timfathen to doubt it. Still, she kept her eyes moving. Her fingers brushed occasionally against the lapis stone hidden beneath her bracer. The fount within her core swelled, ready to be forged.

"They have never gathered like this without purpose," Athekk said grimly. "And not of their own will. Something calls them. What that is, I do not know."

Rayne let her breath slip out slowly, a cold mist against the colder air. If not their own will, then whose? Who could be leading the lichtaurs?

But she buried the question. Dwelling on it would bring no answers and no victory. Her focus had to remain on the mission, on rescuing Saulice.

Her fingers tightened briefly against the stone. Would he understand why she had hidden her identity? Why she had revealed herself? She had tried not to think about how he would react, what he would say when they found him. She wasn't afraid of his anger. She was afraid that he would be disappointed.

And yet, none of that showed on her face. Every step remained precise. Her gaze was unwavering. Composure was her shield now, and she would not lower it until the moment demanded it.

Lord Athekk raised his spear suddenly, signaling a halt. His deep voice rumbled low over the ranks.

"Form lines. Keep tight. The mist is moving."

It was true. The fog ahead curled strangely, as if with intent, moving against the natural flow. A slow tension rippled through the centaur ranks. Hooves stamped restlessly. Weapons creaked in leather bindings.

Rayne pulled her cloak back over her shoulders and flexed her fingers, the cold air biting against her skin. She glanced at Drezz, who simply nodded once. The quiet strength in his eyes steadied her more than words ever could.

"If they come," Drezz muttered under his breath, "stay behind me."

Rayne gave him a sharp look, the faintest smirk curling her lips. "That's not how this works, Falleni son."

Drezz's mouth twitched humorously. "Earth strikes harder than water."

Lord Athekk's voice rose again, sharp and commanding. "Prepare yourselves. Danger is near."

The mists ahead thickened, swirling into strange patterns, warning signs of the darkness moving just beyond their sight. And somewhere beneath the earth, Rayne swore she felt the faintest tremor, as if something vast had stirred, waiting.

She pushed the thought aside and focused on the ground ahead. Whatever came, she would meet it head-on and would not break.

The forest grew quieter the deeper they pressed into the heart of the Timfathen.

The air itself felt wrong here. It wasn't merely the mist or the cold. It was a kind of absence, an unnatural stillness pressing against their ears and settling in their bones.

Even the centaurs had fallen silent. Their hooves landed softer now, as if instinct warned them that every sound might awaken something better left sleeping.

Lord Athekk raised a fist, and the column came to a halt. His eyes scanned the gnarled landscape ahead, filled with twisted roots, splintered stone, and soil that looked blackened, scarred by old corruption.

"This is where the trail ends." He spun around to face his troops. His voice rose with authority. "Spread ranks, horizontal formation! Half-step forward march!"

The earth rumbled as half a thousand sets of hooves moved in unison, inching forward one step at a time. Rayne stepped forward beside Drezz as they pressed into the thick fog, eyes narrowing at the strange patterns etched into the earth. At first, she thought they were just deep gouges in the soil. But they weren't. There was a strange order to them. Circular symbols overlapped, burned into the ground by something unnatural.

Drezz crouched low, his paw running carefully along one mark. He drew back with a sharp hiss.

"It's warm," he muttered. "Still fresh."

"Lord Athekk," she called after a dozen paces in, her voice low but firm. "What do you make of this?"

Athekk halted their advance and approached slowly, his bronze features drawn tight with grim recognition. His gaze swept the corrupted ground, then lifted toward the mist-thick trees ahead.

"They have never gathered before with purpose," he said at last, voice heavy with certainty. "And they do not mark their paths."

The meaning hung clear.

This wasn't a mindless gathering of lichtaurs. This was a hunting ground. A trap.

Before the thought could settle, the fog shifted ahead with shape. Shadowed forms stalked at its edges, their movements eerily synchronized.

"Blaze formation!" Athekk ushered his forces into correct array with a series of signals.

"Move faster, dolts!" he bellowed.

His centaurs formed tight defensive lines in an instant. Shield walls rose in the first rank with a deliberate break in the center while spears pressed through the wall from the second. Bows were drawn at the ready within the third rank, and a heavily armed cavalry unit prepared to punch through the center gap, waiting in the formation's rear.

Rayne's hand went instinctively to her fount stone, but she hesitated. The mist pressed close, thickening like a wall around them. And then she saw them.

Eyes. Pale and empty, scattered through the darkness like dying stars.

It wasn't an attack yet. It was a warning.

The lichtaurs were watching. They were waiting.

Her heart pounded in her ears. Drezz stood firm at her side, his hand resting calmly on the hilt of his hooked blades.

"We're not alone," he breathed, voice as steady as his stance.

Rayne forced her own breathing to steady. Her composure stood like a wall between her fear and the creeping darkness.

For now, it was a standoff. But the air tasted like violence, and Rayne knew it wouldn't last long.

The mist moved first.

It didn't break or thin. It surged. Mist rolled over the centaur lines like a living thing, blotting out the meager light. The fabric of her glove darkened slightly, as if kissed by dew.

Rayne's hand went to her bracer. Her fingers brushed the stone hidden beneath. She hadn't drawn on it yet, not until she had no other choice.

Eyes appeared all around them then, dotting the surrounding hills.

Hundreds of them, pale and lifeless, materializing in the mist like blue-lit embers half buried in ash. In the distance, claws raked the earth. Low guttural snarls spread throughout the landscape, accompanied by the heavy breathing of creatures far beyond expiration.

"Hold the line!" Lord Athekk's voice rang out like a war horn. "Do not advance!"

But the mist swallowed his words. Because it was then that the lichtaurs charged.

They came in a storm of bone and rot, blackened forms with sinew pulled tight over their skeletal frames. Their eyes glowed faintly in the dark. Their mouths split open in silent screams. Where once they were mere beasts corrupted by old magic, now they moved with purpose. Their formation was unnervingly precise.

Rayne and Drezz fought side by side. Their movements were sharp and economical. She ducked low under the first sweeping strike of a lichtaur's poisoned blade, coming up with a clean cut across its exposed ribs. Between strikes, she forged mist into spiral cones, condensing the fog until it was liquified. The action taxed her fount core, but she struck a balance, forging a single spear of water between every three swings of her blade.

Even though she was a second year academ, her fount core was not much larger than a first year's. If she forged any quicker, her fount core would drain rapidly. And while she could use Malaya's—her Titan's fount, she knew better than to start a fight with her best card.

Beside her, Drezz fought with brutal efficiency, his hooked blades finding weak points and tearing through them while he managed to forge small rises in the terrain that tripped up the lichtaurs. While only a first year academ at Brynswick, he was cunning enough to press any advantage he could.

But no matter how many they cut down, more lichtaurs pressed forward.

Then the mist parted, for a worse presence had come upon them.

A horned lichtaur stepped through the haze, its towering form unmistakable. Heavy, ridged horns curved back over its head. It was the same creature that had dragged Saulice away into the night. Its eyes weren't lifeless like the others. They flickered faintly with a cold, alien intelligence.

Rayne froze.

The beast seemed to recognize her too.

It moved toward them, stiff and slow, while the other lichtaurs veered away, giving it space.

Rayne's heart pounded. She stepped in front of Drezz. Her fingers curled tight around her bracer, brushing the lapis lotted within it.

The creature lunged.

Rayne moved to intercept, but it was faster than anything that size should be. Its horn swept toward her, and she felt the sickening rush of air as it passed inches from her face.

A maelstrom of arrows rained down just in front of Rayne and Drezz, courtesy of the centaur archers within the third rank.

Then Lord Athekk sped through the mist like a thunderclap, flanked by five riders of the fourth rank cavalry. Arrows drove into the horned lichtaur's flank, forcing it back as Lord Athekk dared the beast to test them further. It snarled and retreated into the fog, disappearing as suddenly as it had come.

The lichtaurs rushed forward in a second wave, frenzied by the horned lichtaur's appearance.

Earth shook as the centaurs held their ground. Arrows arced overhead in dark volleys, their tips glowing faintly in the fog. Where they struck, lichtaurs howled, their corrupted bodies writhing before collapsing in broken heaps.

Even still, other lichtaurs leapt over their fallen comrades. Like a hammer striking an anvil, they collided with the defenders. And the shield wall held.

Spears jutted in and out of the wall, skewering any lichtaurs that grew too close to overwhelming the centaur ranks. Chaos reigned across the front lines, summed up by blurred steel and rust, sprays of blood, and expiring screams as both the dead and undead fell.

Rayne pressed forward, cutting low beneath a sweeping claw. Her blade found the hollow between a creature's ribs. She wrenched it free, and the withered lichtaur crumpled. Another came at her from the side, faster than she expected. Before she could turn, Drezz lunged in. His hooked blades caught the creature's throat and tore it wide.

"Watch your flank!" Drezz barked, his voice sharp through his ragged breathing.

Rayne allowed herself a brief nod. "Stay alive, and I'll thank you later."

But there was no time for banter. The mist thickened again, and the horned lichtaur reappeared through it like a nightmare refusing to be driven back. It roared this time, charging straight for Lord Athekk.

The centaur lines faltered for a breath. Rayne could feel the doubt creeping through the ranks.

Then Lord Athekk roared back, louder than the beast. His spear rose high. His warriors rallied at his side, their charge breaking through the press of corrupted bodies like a battering ram.

Rayne stood frozen for a breath. Her pulse still hammered in her ears.

And for the first time since entering this cursed place, she hoped they weren't too late.

CHAPTER 29

RESOUNDING THUNDER

Saulice scrawled his ninth gouge into the cell wall, hands shaking. The tallied marks had been pocked and cratered, as wide as his fist. Saulice stopped counting. At first, he had marked days. Then strikes.

Now he just measured the sounds. Bone crunching against stone. Blood striking the wall with a wet smack. Breathless grunts that filled the narrow cell like prayers no one would ever hear.

He resharpened the splintered bone from the cell's previous tenant, then grated it across the stone. Saulice drove it forward again, cleaving to what little fire he had left in him. His strikes were weak with hunger, but he could no longer take Baalo's visits. The lichtaur liege's temptations were growing stronger, and Saulice had nearly succumbed more than once.

Crack.

Again.

Snap.

His shoulders howled in protest, arms long past aching. As much as he grieved, as much as he no longer desired to live, his blood stilled with every visit from Baalo. There was a dark twinkling in those eyes that told Saulice he would achieve great power if he did as the lichtaur liege said.

But there would be a cost. A cost that Baalo had purposely not specified.

The back wall, damp with cold and laced with veins of old mortar, flaked apart near the base as he repeated the motions. He struck then sharpened, sharpened and struck. Each stroke of bone sent tiny fragments of dust into the air, stinging his eyes and catching in his throat. He did not care. If he stopped now, he would never leave the cell.

Sweat slicked the sides of his face despite the frigid cave air. His knees were raw. The rag he used as a bandage had fallen hours ago. He could not remember the last time he had eaten. The only thing that kept his body moving, fingers cracked and bleeding, knuckles swollen, was the voice that never left him.

Baalo's whisper: *"The Pitch waits. The chains are ready. All that's missing is your choice."*

He clenched his jaw. He had already made his choice. Even if his body failed him, even if Lazarus abandoned him again to the dark, he would carve his way out through the stone with his own hands if he had to.

Even if his friends were dead.

He slammed the bone forward again. This time, a larger chunk came loose. Light from a torch two cells down bled through, weak and smeared. Saulice gasped, laughing softly. It was a broken sound, like something scraped from the inside of his chest.

He braced himself and drove the bone once more into the wall, wrenching away another slab of mortar. The gap was now shoulder-width, just barely. He dropped the bone and pushed his hands against the frame, gritting his teeth. His arms trembled from the strain, but he forced one through, then the other. Cold bit into his skin where stone scraped flesh.

"Come on," he whispered. "Just a little more."

He pressed his shoulder through the narrow hole. Jagged stone tore through the sleeve of his tunic, biting into his right bicep. He grunted, twisting. His ribs caught, then slipped through. Halfway.

The stone snagged again. His left was stuck. He wrenched harder.

Then sound erupted.

Distant shouts and cries. Clashing steel, and hooves pounding across stone.

Sounds of battle.

Muffled through the stone corridors, but unmistakable, there was fighting above.

His heart surged. Someone was here. Someone was close enough for the noise to reach this far down. Which meant—

"They're coming," Saulice spat, coughing. Hope blossomed in his chest, easing his fatigue. "You won't win."

Footsteps echoed behind him. Slow. Weighed. Calculated. He knew the weight they carried. The temptations Baalo would bring. He had to hurry.

He froze.

Not now.

He pushed harder. His shoulder screamed as he tried to force himself through, blood smearing across the jagged edge. Still stuck. Still straining.

Then a hand seized the back of his tunic and yanked.

He screamed as Baalo pulled his body backward through the hole, scraping his ribs against the frame before he crashed to the ground on his back. Light flared above him, then dimmed.

The first thing he saw was teeth.

Yellow and crooked, a smile curled at him like a cat watching a mouse.

"Trying to slither out like a worm!" Baalo growled, kneeling beside him. "After all I've offered. All you've been given."

Saulice gasped, blinking away the tears. Rot wafted from the lichtaur-liege's cloak, heavy and coppery. His black eyes gleamed with unnatural hunger.

"Let me go," Saulice rasped.

"You were offered a gift," Baalo snarled. "A chance to stand with us. And you choose dirt and broken stone? You disgrace what you could become."

A heavy backhand slammed across Saulice's face, cold and hard. His head snapped to the side. Metal rang in his ears. He tasted copper.

"They're coming," Saulice whispered again, voice hoarse. "You're out of time."

Baalo leaned close, his voice a venomous hiss. "I already have what I need. The chains are in place. The Pitch stirs. And your Titan," he paused, gaze narrowing, "will be reduced to memory."

Saulice felt himself being dragged again. His feet scraped stone, blood marking a trail behind him.

The fighting. It had to mean someone was near. Someone was pushing through.

Drezz.

Rayne.

Dedric.

Shaddai.

Someone.

But the further they moved, the quieter it became. Saulice's heart sank. The clash of metal faded into echo as they delved deeper underground. They were going beyond the place where light reached, where even his fear dulled from sheer exhaustion.

He tried kicking Baalo's legs again, twisting like before, but the lichtaur liege was ready this time. Another blow met Saulice's temple. The world spun.

Stone stairs scraped beneath him. He was being pulled downward, each step jarring his spine.

Still, Saulice tried to gather himself. He refused to go limp.

"Shaddai… please…" he whispered.

There was no answer.

Just the hiss of air in the deep dark, and the indistinct sound of a door opening ahead.

Then Baalo stopped.

The grip on his collar loosened, and Saulice's body slumped to the floor. He blinked hard, vision swimming.

He pushed himself up on an elbow and turned.

They had entered a massive room. Stone walls were hewn, smooth and black, the ceiling lost in shadows. The ground shimmered faintly beneath his gaze, carved with a circular design.

A raised platform sat at the far end.

Upon it, a black obelisk stood six feet tall, polished smooth. Its surface was darker than the void, carved with thousands of ancient runes, each line pulsing faintly with a sickly purple hue.

The Pitch.

It wasn't a myth or some forgotten relic.

Saulice could tell with a single glance that it was a prison, waiting to wrap around anything that touched it.

Lazarus stirred within Saulice with a ripple of dread.

He felt it in his chest, as if the air had been sucked from the room. As if someone had taken the sky and crushed it into a weapon.

Baalo's voice cut through the stillness.

"This is your last chance."

He dragged Saulice across the platform.

"Touch it! Let power become yours. Shaddai has already turned His face, and your Titan grieves a past long dead. But the Pitch will give you control you couldn't dream of."

Saulice stayed still on the ground, face bleeding, his body half-broken, but his gaze locked on the thing before him.

If I just held it… just once… maybe I could steady everything. Maybe I wouldn't lose control again. But another thought pierced through the dark:

If the cost of power was peace, was it worth it?

Something was coming. He did not know what. Only that it would begin here.

Saulice's blood stuck to the floor in smears, on his chin, his palms, the right shoulder of his tunic. But he didn't bother wiping it away, too focused on trying to stop the stench of the room from burying itself in his lungs. The air here seemed older than smell. Older than the stone. It crackled with a pressure that had no wind or temperature.

The Pitch pulsed faintly in the center of the pedestal. Lightless and rune-bound, it seemed to breathe a shimmerless power that drowned everything else out.

The surface appeared carved from a starless night sky. Smooth, perfect, unyielding. Ancient glyphs slithered across it in looping patterns that formed no language Saulice knew, yet some part of him understood the danger. Every line felt like a door nailed shut from the inside.

A memory flickered, and he remembered a voice from the Academy. Cadre Pell.

"Some tools were never meant to be wielded. Only buried."

He swallowed, throat raw.

Baalo moved as if he had waited for this moment a thousand years. Slow and sure, like a priest approaching an altar.

But Saulice knew he was no priest. At least not one of Shaddai's.

"The Pitch," he said reverently, "forged by Veartaya herself before the war turned. A cage for the Titans. Not through power, but through consent. A Harbinger must place the seal. Only then can the binding occur."

Saulice stared at the pillar. "You're lying."

Baalo smiled. "I'm breathing. That's worse, isn't it?"

He turned slightly, robes whispered across the carved floor as he gestured to a small pedestal nearby. Resting on it was a dagger, plain and long, its blade the color of soot, the hilt wrapped in dark cracked leather.

"Your blood is required," he hissed. "A Harbinger's blood to open the Titan's seal. And you will receive power…" He held the blade toward Saulice. "Power that will never betray you."

Saulice couldn't move. If he touched that blade, touched that pillar, somehow he knew there would be no turning back. He peered into the lichtaur liege's eyes and saw that dark twinkling. There was more to the workings of the Pitch than Baalo had let on.

Baalo's voice lowered, smooth as frost. "I know what he's done to you. You've begged for his help repeatedly, and all he gives you is suffering. Saulice, dear boy. Why defend him?"

"I'm not," Saulice said, almost too softly to hear. "Not anymore."

Baalo tilted his head.

"I'm trying to understand him," Saulice whispered, low enough so Baalo wouldn't hear.

He stood slowly, knees aching, chest pounding. Every step toward the pedestal felt heavier, like the room itself resisted his motion. The glyphs on the floor thrummed faintly beneath his boots. The Pitch's shadow stretched toward him like it knew he would come.

He reached for the dagger and the hilt fit his hand as if it belonged there.

Lazarus stirred faintly within as though breathing over Saulice's shoulder. The kind that might precede words. Or grief. Or surrender.

"If you do this," Lazarus whispered within, *"I will not stop it."*

Saulice's chest froze.

"I will not harm you. But I will not fight anymore. I cannot." The voice that followed was threadbare, hollow. *"There's nothing left to fight for."*

The words carved straight through Saulice's ribs.

He staggered back from the Pitch, overcome by the Titan's anguish. Lazarus' voice was without fury. All it possessed was the emptiness of something once majestic, now reduced to ash. A hopeless pit in his gut, the same one Saulice had succumbed to during his childhood.

And yet—

The Pitch pulled at the marrow of his bones. It promised power without prayer. Control without cost. And still, something deeper whispered.

You do not need it.

Saulice stepped forward again, voice a fiery whisper. "If you have nothing left to fight for… then fight for the ones who can't fight for themselves," he said. "Fight for what's right."

Lazarus did not speak.

"Shaddai didn't forge you to be a monument to sorrow. He made you to bring justice," Saulice pressed. "You were created to protect the weak. To cast down the wicked. To carry the will of paradise where no one else could."

Still no answer.

But something shifted.

A low rumble echoed in his soul.

Then the world flipped.

Not literally, but in that way visions do. Saulice's breath caught as the stone floor beneath him bled away into sky.

The jagged cliff appeared.

Jagged stone outcrop beneath a sky soaked in stormlight. Chains of living lightning stretched taut between heaven and earth. The Titan knelt on one knee, bowed low, a mountain of grief wrapped in power.

Saulice was there, standing closer to the Titan than ever before.

The wind howled, and the clouds churned.

Lazarus looked up. His eyes were dim, two hollow spheres of quiet mourning. He was vast, yes. Monumental… but still. Not because he lacked power.

Lazarus had forgotten his purpose.

The chains snapped tight again with a low groan, pinning him further down.

Saulice stood at the edge of the cliff, close enough to see the cracks lining the Titan's arms. They glowed faintly, like glass etched by lightning long ago.

"You were forged by Shaddai," Saulice said, breathless. "Not to mourn, but to rise."

Lazarus looked up at him, and something flickered in his gaze.

"I failed," the Titan muttered. His voice caught on the last word, as if admittance broke something further inside him. "Lector left me. My brethren abandoned me. My name itself became a curse on children's lips."

He closed his eyes.

"I am justice that was twisted. Memory without purpose."

Lazarus opened his eyes again.

Saulice stepped closer. The wind lashed against his skin like salt and fire. "You've forgotten who you are. Let me remind you. You are the storm that bound Veartaya. The light that locked the lake of fire. You are the hand of Shaddai that shatters darkness."

The chains trembled.

Saulice didn't know why he said what he did. His mind only recalled that still, small boy, cowering in an attic while a hungry fire engulfed his home. Took his mother. He still recalled that despair. No one should have to carry that weight. Human or Titan.

"You are not vengeance," Saulice said, voice rising. "You are justice. And justice never stays silent when the innocent suffer. You have shown a poor example in your last decades, but you can't change the past. But your future is still undecided."

The Titan's eyes widened. His chains flickered dim and bright, waging a war no one else could see.

Saulice took a step closer. And reached with an open hand to the being who had caused the fire that took his home. The being responsible for the lightning strike in Hamlen. Responsible for his certain-to-come expulsion from Brynswick.

And for the first time he could recall, he could not weave a single thread of hostility to Lazarus. His own message echoed:

You can't change the past. But your future is still undecided.

Saulice grounded his jaw, and not knowing what would happen, laid a hand atop the Titan's shoulder. "Lazarus, you must help me defy Baalo!"

The Titan's gaze lifted to meet Saulice's. His eyes were brighter, possessing a clarity Saulice had never before seen. Lazarus gave a small nod. And a bolt of gold lightning flared across the sky.

The wind went still. The chains groaned and stretched, then cracked.

Lazarus stood. Resolve lit his eyes—no longer dim, but alive with something Saulice saw seldom—conviction.

The Titan lifted his head; gaze scanning the distant horizon.

"Prepare yourself," he said.

His arms spread wide, and the damaged chains exploded into light. The cliff vanished.

The chamber returned, but Saulice's bones still hummed with that presence.

Lazarus was no longer sleeping. No longer silent and lost.

Saulice opened his eyes.

His hand hovered over the dagger.

Baalo leaned forward slightly, watching with reverence, ignorant of the vision Saulice had just had. "Yes," he murmured. "That's it. Place the seal."

Saulice looked at the blade in his hand, the conduit. The executioner's tool.

His pulse pounded in his ears, and beneath it all, Lazarus' presence hummed steady and silent, waiting to act.

Saulice took a shaky breath and whispered just loud enough for Baalo to hear, "So this is what you wanted."

Baalo smiled.

Saulice turned the blade over, angling the edge toward the base of his palm.

And slid it across.

A sharp gasp escaped his lips as the dagger ripped flesh. Blood welled instantly, spilling down his stinging wrist and dripping to the floor.

But so was his resolve.

He clenched his jaw and stepped toward the Pitch, bloody blade in hand.

Baalo's eyes gleamed. "Let the blood bind. Let the stone listen."

Saulice raised the dagger toward the base of the Pitch, slowly and carefully, as if ready to insert the blade into the groove waiting at the bottom of the pillar.

His hand hovered inches above it.

Baalo leaned forward, breath held.

Then Saulice's expression shifted. He met Baalo's eyes and whispered, "You were right about one thing."

Baalo's grin faltered. "What?"

"I've always been stubborn."

And with a flick of his wrist, Saulice hurled the dagger across the chamber.

It clattered against the far wall, blood flicking across the stone.

Before Baalo could move, Saulice stepped in and slammed his uninjured hand, open and firm, against the base of the Pitch. He pushed every strand of fount circulating in his core and condensed it.

"Lazarus!"

The name cracked like lightning.

It wasn't a command, but a call.

And Lazarus answered with power.

Foreign fount rushed into Saulice's core like a dam rupturing. Hot and brilliant, Saulice noted for the first time, it was the same color as the cracks veining his core. Saulice's body shook as the fount welled beyond what his meager fractured core could hold. Feeling Lazarus guiding him, he circuited the fount up his torso, into the arm pressed against the Pitch. Saulice wasn't doing it. No. This was unlike any time he had forged in the past.

There was no resistance, just pressure. But he was used to pressure. Saulice was guided by something larger than him, sharper than instinct.

This was unlike any kind of forging he had ever done before. This was raw power, pointed in a single direction, unlike the lessons Cadre Nilus taught.

The fount roared through his fingertips, and a concussive bang echoed as Lazarus' power split the runes covering the Pitch.

The ancient artifact cracked.

Baalo fell to his knees with a wounded growl. "No!"

But it was too late.

The runes unraveled, lines of ancient magic splitting like seams in rotted cloth.

A groan echoed from the depths of the pillar. Deep and wounded, like the cry of something ancient being torn from its slumber.

A second crack spread upward.

Then a third.

Lazarus's voice rose. *"Run."*

The floor shook.

Stone dust fell from the ceiling in thin sheets. A high-pitched whine emanated from the center of the Pitch, growing louder as fractures raced across its surface.

Baalo lunged forward to intercept him, but the ground between them erupted, sending shards of stone skyward.

Saulice kept moving. The world came apart behind him.

Stone screamed. The floor heaved once, then again, like a beast waking beneath the mountain. The carved runes along the walls unraveled in flickers of dying magic, their light pulsing erratic and wild, no longer controlled. No longer bound.

Saulice did not look back.

He ran.

Or stumbled, really. Half-blind from pain, his breath ragged, warm blood from his palm dripped a trail behind him. The chamber collapsed in pulses. The corrupted fount—the dark, whatever twisted forging Baalo had bound to the Pitch—was unraveling. And the cave was collapsing with it.

But Saulice wasn't worried. Lazarus was with him now. Every step that should have been a crawl, every gasp that should have been his last, pushed him forward.

For the first time ever, he and Lazarus had shared their will. They had escaped. Mostly.

The corridor twisted in his vision. The floor cracked beneath his boots, and a rush of heat blew through the tunnel like breath from a ruptured forge. Saulice staggered to one side, his shoulder colliding with the stone wall. His knees nearly gave out.

He caught himself as the hunger returned, sapping his strength.

He pressed onward, half-hunched, blinking through dust and blood. Far behind him, Baalo uttered a guttural cry like an unearthly roar, something too twisted to sound human.

Then came silence.

And after it, laughter, quiet at first, but cold and certain, with a promise buried beneath each note.

The echo chased him into the dark.

The next bend in the tunnel opened suddenly into a junction. One Saulice did not recognize. The left path bled darkness and twisted downward. The right carried a current of fresh air; the left was stale.

He turned right.

His lungs burned. His wound throbbed with every heartbeat. He did not know how long he could keep going.

But something in him refused to fall.

"Lazarus," he gasped between strides, the name ragged on his breath. "A little help here."

Nothing came.

"After everything I just did… don't you dare go quiet on me again."

Still, there were no words. But the silence did not feel like abandonment. It felt like awe.

Like Lazarus was still trying to comprehend what Saulice had done.

He had called a Titan back from despair. Had reminded justice why it still mattered.

Another corridor loomed ahead, its floor slick with moss. The air trembled faintly. Saulice reached the corner and half-collapsed against it, chest heaving. His legs buckled. He slid down the wall to his knees. His limbs trembled, shouting that they could go no farther.

His head dropped. Blood dripped from his palm, thick and slow now, smearing across his knee. The wound ached in rhythm with his heartbeat.

The silence returned, and this time, it was heavier.

A voice stirred at last, clear and unbroken.

"You chose pain over power," Lazarus said softly. *"I do not understand you."*

Saulice let out a half-laugh, half-sob. "Yea. That makes two of us."

The Titan did not speak again immediately, but Saulice felt the shift. Something being built that hadn't in a long time.

Trust.

"I'm still learning," Saulice murmured.

"As am I," Lazarus replied.

Multiple footsteps echoed beyond the next corner.

He braced himself. Too weak to run again. But unwilling to cower.

Then a voice rang out, sharp and familiar.

"Hold on! I see someone!"

The light of a torch flared and Saulice sighed with relief.

Drezz barreled around the corner, bow in hand, quiver bouncing against his back, fur matted with soot and sweat. He froze, pulling back an arrow before realizing who he was seeing. "Saulice!"

Rayne followed fast behind, a short sword drawn in one hand, a torch in the other. The flickering fire caught Saulice's bloodied silhouette against the stone wall.

"You're alive," she whispered, voice fraying.

He tried to answer. Throat too tight, he just nodded.

Rayne dropped beside him, clasping his shoulders tight. Her eyes filled the silence with their own message. Drezz scanned the corridor behind them, bow half-drawn, still ready.

"You're bleeding out," she said, already pulling a strip of cloth from her belt.

"The Pitch is gone," Saulice rasped.

"What?"

He looked at her, eyes glassy but bright. "I broke it. Lazarus… he helped."

Rayne froze. Her hands slowed as she wrapped his palm. "He helped?"

"He remembered."

She didn't answer, but her grip tightened around his wrist.

Drezz exhaled. His posture eased slightly. "We have to get out of here. This entire cave system is shifting. I think Baalo triggered something."

Rayne nodded. "The way we came is open. Lord Athekk's clan breached the northern side."

"Can you walk?" Drezz asked.

Saulice gritted his teeth and forced himself upright. His legs shook. His breath wavered. But he stood. "I can now."

Together, they vanished down the last passage, the remnants of the ancient cave trembling in their wake.

And far behind them, in the dark heart of the crumbled ritual chamber, a single jagged fragment of obsidian still pulsed once.

CHAPTER 30

POWER WITHOUT PAYMENT

The air beyond the cave reeked of scorched stone and sulfur. Echoes of battle cracked faintly across the hills behind them, clashing steel, cries of the wounded, and the steady rhythm of hooves pounding through the mud.

Saulice limped forward, bloodied and sore, one arm braced over Rayne's shoulder, the other over Drezz. His wounded palm throbbed, the cloth bandage soaked and stiff. The fount within him had quieted but not vanished.

Lazarus stood now like a watchtower, peering out with renewed purpose. The Titan no longer raged, no longer drifted in grief.

Drezz walked ahead, bow in hand, his eyes sharp despite the dried blood caked across his cheek. He glanced often toward Rayne, not Saulice, and something about the way he moved was careful and alert, a touch too distant. It spoke of some shift, but Saulice lacked the strength to question it.

Rayne remained silent. She walked with measured steps, her blade sheathed, but the tension in her arms remained. She glanced at Saulice more than once, at his face, his trembling hands, and the scorched skin visible on his shoulder.

He was no longer the boy she remembered from the infirmary, the one who had collapsed under the weight of a cracked source stone. He had changed, and that unsettled her more than she wanted to admit.

Ahead, a red shimmer appeared on the ridge. Two riders crested the slope, their armor catching the pale morning light through the mist. Their horses bore black-plated barding. Their cloaks snapped in the breeze, and Saulice's breath caught.

Help had arrived, and not just any.

Furies Fist.

A male argonaut dismounted first. His armor was old and battle-worn, but still regal. The red trim along the plates matched the cloak at his back, and his helm bore the lion head insignia of Candur's ancient vanguard.

When he removed his helm, tears welled in Saulice's eyes. "Dedric!"

He limped forward and wrapped the man in a massive hug.

Dedric smiled and squeezed his nephew with a quivering lip. His face had aged, eyes sunken with fatigue, and the tightness in his jaw had not been there in Hamlen. He had trained hard since his return to the Fist.

The other rider lifted her face plate, revealing a familiar guardian. Melandra gazed knowingly, then smiled at Saulice and his companions. Her black armor was crisp and clean where it had not yet been bloodied. Crimson accents glinted along her gauntlets. Her horse bore a scar across its flank, its armor already marked from battle that very morning.

Dedric stepped forward slowly, scanning the others before returning to Saulice. His voice came low. "I wasn't expecting to find you upright."

From his cloak, Dedric withdrew a blade—the same dagger Saulice had once carried in Hamlen. The hilt bore the old insignia of the Watch.

"I found this outside an abandoned camp two days ago," Dedric said, his voice heavier than Saulice remembered. "Thought I might never see it again. When I found it…" His jaw shifted. "Let's just say I feared the worst."

Dedric's voice hardened. "I never meant for you to carry this alone," Dedric said. "The brand. The silence. All of it. When I first left the Fist, I thought I was just abandoning a post. Now I see I was answering something higher. I thought I was protecting you, but I made your life more miserable."

His voice caught. With grief in his eyes, he bowed. "Forgive me."

Saulice felt the weight of his words. Had Dedric brought him to Axbridge earlier, his life could have been immensely different. He glanced up at the dark sky above, knowing Shaddai was watching.

And Saulice felt no anger or resentment toward Dedric.

"Lord Commander Muir summoned me after I was carted off in chains," Dedric said. "He showed me a letter written by the previous Lord Commander. Turns out old Boreau knew I'd vanished the moment your father disappeared after the city of Mortare was destroyed. He knew the whole time, and he never condemned me for it."

Saulice looked down at the dagger, then sheathed it at his side. He touched the hilt gently. The match was perfect.

Melandra stepped closer, unreadable. "You look like the cave tried to eat you."

"It almost did," Saulice said. "Imagine its shock when I broke the Pitch."

Rayne turned sharply toward him. Her expression flickered.

Dedric exhaled. "Then we'll need you whole. Lord Athekk's line is collapsing. The centaurs are backed to the creek and cut off on both sides."

Drezz, still watching the field, muttered, "There's over six hundred lichtaurs. And that's just the ones we can see."

"We make for the heart," Melandra said. "We break through, or we fall."

Dedric swung into the saddle and paused. "Saulice. If you lose control… if that storm turns on us, I'll be the one to stop it."

Saulice didn't flinch. "Then I'll give you no reason to."

Rayne steadied him as he stepped forward. Her voice came quiet, edged with hesitation. "I remember what you looked like in the infirmary. Pale and shaking. You couldn't sit up on your own."

He looked at her.

"You've changed," she said. "But just… don't forget who you were."

He did not know how to answer. Instead, he held her gaze longer than he meant to.

Then the wind shifted, and the scent of blood rose from the valley. A centaur's scream broke through the fog.

Dedric growled, "They're breaking."

Melandra snapped her reins. "We move now."

They turned. Drezz stepped beside Saulice without a word, bow drawn. Rayne unsheathed her sword, jaw set firm.

This time, Saulice did not run from war. He walked into it, his fount quiet, his prayers sharper than his strength.

Let justice rise, Shaddai. Not vengeance.

His hands no longer trembled.

The moment they crested the ridge, the battlefield opened before them like a wound.

Smoke drifted from broken trees along the edges. The hills sloped down into a muddy basin clogged with bodies. Three hundred centaurs fought in tight knots, their once-unified line cracked into chaos. Lichtaurs swarmed between the ruptures with the hunger of a plague, moving not like soldiers but like ruin. Hooves churned through mud and flesh alike. The soil steamed red.

Drezz rushed forward and loosed an arrow as they descended, his mount bounding over the twisted ground. Beside him, Saulice clung to Dedric's back, pain shooting through his body with every trot of the horse. His ribs flared hot beneath torn cloth. His palm had soaked through its bandage again. His vision blurred, but he managed to keep putting one foot in front of the other.

Dedric and Melandra led the way, cutting down lichtaurs with brutal precision. Melandra's blade moved through armor like water. Dedric's greatsword rose in sweeping arcs, each strike clearing space as they waded toward the centaur ranks.

They veered toward the creek, a shallow channel clogged with corpses and churned red water. What remained of Lord Athekk's line had fallen back to the far bank. On top of a rise, the centaurs held their ranks, but they were losing. Arrows flew in bursts from their third rank, pinning a dozen lichtaurs at a time.

But the lichtaurs pressed forward without tire.

A shriek tore through the air behind them.

Saulice turned, and a lichtaur hurled itself from a broken ledge, slamming into Drezz mid-gallop and knocking him from his horse. The fallet tumbled backward with a sickening crunch, landing hard in a tangle of reeds by the ruddy water while his injured mount fled.

"No!" Saulice cried.

Rayne sprinted into the reeds with blade drawn, carving a path. Saulice lowered himself from Dedric's mount, boots sliding through the mud. The ground was slick with blood and moss. When he reached Drezz, the fallet was groaning, barely conscious.

Blood streaked his side as one arm hung useless.

Drezz gasped. "See. I told you I could take a hit."

Saulice tore a strip from his shirt and pressed it to the wound. "Save your breath. I'm not letting you die here," he said tightly. "Not after everything we've been through. I won't let you leave me in this hellhole."

Rayne knelt beside him, eyes scanning the field. "We'll carry him."

"Don't," Drezz murmured. "I can walk."

Rayne didn't answer. She crouched under his arm and hauled upward. "You can survive."

They lifted him together. Drezz hissed in pain but stayed upright.

Farther up the slope, a voice rang out, deep and raw, commanding.

"Hold the crest! Anchor the line!"

Lord Athekk crashed through the fog, his horned helm split and his silver-washed pike already raised. Blood streaked his chest, and a second sword hung sheathed across his back.

He turned toward Melandra and Dedric. "Our ranks now number fewer than three hundred. Maybe two. If we lose the ridge, we all die. Any plans posed by these lichtaur liege will be unchecked."

Melandra's sword dripped. She didn't hesitate. "Then we hold the ridge."

Athekk's gaze fell on Saulice. Though bloodied, Saulice stood tall and steady.

"This is the Harbinger?"

Melandra nodded once, voice edged with pride. "The Harbinger of Justice."

Athekk stared at him a moment, eyes like daggers, before pointing toward the slope. "Then he fights with us."

They regrouped at the fork where the creek cut through the battlefield. High ground turned to mire, a natural chokepoint drowning in blood. The remaining centaurs reformed their ranks in a battered crescent shape across the hilltop, a bloody shield wall at the front, dull spears poking through from a second rank. They were holding, barely.

Athekk cut down a line of approaching lichtaurs and slammed his pike into the ground while another wave of arrows soared through the air.

"Hold here!" he bellowed. "They come again!"

And they did.

Lichtaurs surged through the fog like a curse let loose. Horned and half-dead, bodies fused with rusted steel, eyes glowing with unnatural light. There were more of them than before. Too many.

Melandra returned to Dedric's flank. Rayne stood beside Saulice. Drezz crouched behind a hastily built barricade, an arrow notched between two shaking fingers.

Lightning danced faintly along Saulice's wrist.

He looked out at the creek, the slope, soldiers from the rear ranks filling holes in the front when lichtaurs cut down another shield bearer. They were slowly losing.

Rayne whispered, "We stand here, or we fall."

"I know," Saulice replied.

He glanced at his cracked citrine shard, now lifeless, and launched it into an oncoming wave of lichtaurs. He would have to get a new one from Cadre Nilus if they made it back. Lazarus' power would have to be enough.

As the lichtaurs began breaking down the centaur ranks, Dedric and Melandra stepped forward with angry shouts.

Dedric touched his diamond stone within his bracer, then launched forward, forging a spiral of air around him that battered any opponent unfortunate enough to get too close. His wind-enhanced greatsword made quick work of the eastern front.

Melandra forged the cracked ground of the hill's front side, creating an earthen pit lined with spears across the centaur ranks, forcing the lichtaurs to either leap toward the defenses or fall to death.

Rayne condensed fog, forging fewer spears than Melandra, but her blasts struck with equal fervor.

Drezz altered Melandra's pit, adding a smooth slope on the approaching side, causing lichtaurs to slide into the trap before realizing they had lost their footing.

This was no longer survival.

This was the stand.

The first lichtaur broke the line just before sunrise, after the pit filled with corpses.

A string of lichtaurs struck the right flank, shattering a centaur's shield and tossing the warrior into the creek. Another followed, horns low, claws outstretched, splitting into the shield wall. More spilled behind them, moving in eerie silence, bone and steel grinding in rhythm.

Three dozen centaurs fell before the shield wall was restored, and Lord Athekk's forces were exhausted.

Saulice stood behind the forward line, his bracer warm on his wrist, the pulse of Lazarus's fount beneath his skin. The Titan watched closely, coiled and prepared.

Another part of the front line broke, and a lichtaur veered toward Rayne.

Without thinking, Saulice lifted his hand. Lazarus' fount surged through his core, roaring through his body at the speed of light. A crack of lightning split the fog, striking the creature's shoulder. It spun, stumbled, and fell into the creek.

Silence followed, but Saulice felt his friends' eyes on him. He sensed their pride. Glancing down at his hand, his eyes struggled to unsee what he had done.

Rayne turned, her eyes finding his. Wide with recognition.

Drezz exhaled, half-crouched behind a barricade on the left flank, boosting their morale. The shimmer still danced across Saulice's wrist, faint and flickering. But with the shimmer came a sharp pang inside him.

Melandra, mid-strike, paused. She didn't look at the light, but at Saulice.

He lowered his hand. The light faded, but the warmth lingered, nestled in the grooves of his palm like heat from a banked fire.

The storm had heard him and answered.

He stepped forward, placing himself between the stream and the defenders behind him. His heart pounded with certainty. The fount had not broken free with dysfunction or frayed. It had responded.

And Saulice was still standing.

Rayne stood beside him. "That wasn't like before."

"No," Saulice said.

"You didn't lose control."

He didn't answer. She could already see it in the way the light moved beneath his skin.

Behind them, Athekk bellowed again. The right flank buckled. The centaur lord's shoulder bled, yet he held his ground, driving back a half dozen lichtaurs with a single strike.

The centaurs now numbered fewer than a hundred, and Saulice was beginning to worry they would not leave the Timfathen.

"We hold this hill," Athekk roared, "until there is no one left to hold it!"

His stallion stamped the torn earth, hooves flinging mud behind him as he repositioned at the crest. Melandra regrouped with Dedric, streaked with blood as they launched forward to back up the centaur clan lord.

"The next wave hits in under two minutes," Melandra growled.

"We're too few," Dedric said. "If they breach the ridge—"

"They won't."

Suddenly, the battlefield quieted as the lichtaurs halted their advance. The space between assaults stretched long and terrible.

Across the field, a large rank of lichtaurs gathered, more than they had seen since the start of the battle. Their shoulders hunched, weapons raised, eyes glowing with hunger. But for some reason, they didn't charge.

They watched as if waiting for something.

CHAPTER 31

THE STORM THAT STOOD

Dawn had not yet broken, but the Timfathen sky glowed thin and gray, like a wound trying to scab. Below it, the creek gurgled with unnatural stillness, bodies and splintered shields choking its current. The air hung damp and acrid, thick with ozone and the copper tang of blood.

Centaurs braced along the ridge above, shields interlocked in two battered ranks where four had once stood. Their hooves churned the mud, holding ground with grit alone. Beyond the fractured barricade, lichtaurs gathered in the mist, horned silhouettes swaying like reeds before the tide. There seemed to be no end to the corrupt beings.

Saulice stumbled toward the center barricade, chest heaving as each breath raked fire along his bruised ribs. Lightning flickered faintly in the veins of his forearms, a whisper of power already burning him from within. His cracked bracer hummed against his wrist, pulsing with Lazarus' restless stir.

Then silence rolled across the valley.

Through the thinning fog, a figure emerged, tall and armored in pale bone, horns curving blade-sharp from his brow. Tattered crimson cloth hung from his frame in strips, each step marked by the soft clatter of vertebrae along his mantle. Orbs burned black where his eyes should have been, rimmed with silver veins. His skin cracked with lines like dried mud, every fissure pulsing faintly with hostile light. Mud parted under his weight as though the earth itself yielded to him.

Baalo.

Every motion carried intent. He advanced with calm precision, each step heavy enough to shake the barricade's timbers. He moved like a conqueror who already owned the field.

A tremor rippled through Saulice's chest. He tensed as Lazarus' presence sharpened into warning.

Baalo's arm swept outward in a single violent motion. Bone-plated armor along his forearm glowed with a pale hue, then shifted with a grinding scrape. His strike split across the battlefield, far beyond his reach. The swing struck the earth beneath their front lines, the force ripping through centaurs in an eruption of mud and splintered pikes. The creatures screamed as they were flung aside, their formation broken cleanly down the middle.

Saulice gulped, never having seen such power before. This was beyond fount forging, a power twisted.

"You," Baalo said, eyes focused on Saulice. His voice was soft but sharp, brittle like fractured glass. "You ruined everything."

Saulice staggered against the barricade, ears ringing, vision swimming. The world tilted as the centaur line that had protected them collapsed into two fractured arcs, divided by the fresh chasm Baalo's strike had carved through their center.

Rayne cried out somewhere near Saulice's left, the sound sharp with panic. Drezz shouted back from the opposite flank across the chasm, his voice distant in the chaos.

Saulice's stomach clenched. They were cut off. Alone.

Baalo's voice crossed the broken line, raw and furious. "You dare shatter the Pitch, Veartaya's gift to Invictus, and still raise your hand against me?" His eyes burned hotter, fixed on Saulice. "You are more a fool than I thought, boy."

The ground shook beneath Saulice's feet. A tide of lichtaurs surged through the opening Baalo had carved, silent and merciless. Horns lowered, claws raised, they poured into the gap like floodwater breaching a dam.

Three vaulted the barricade directly in front of Saulice, axes raised high, rusted steel catching the thin morning light.

Water rose to meet them.

It erupted from the creek in a spiraling column, striking the lichtaurs mid-air and slamming them into the mud with bone-snapping force. The column twisted downward into mirrored arcs, scattering fragments of rusted steel into the churned earth. Steam hissed where the water struck the land's bloodied soil, and their side of the battlefield trembled with the silence that followed.

Saulice stared, stunned with shock as his breath stalled in his chest.

Rayne stood in the muck just beyond the barricade, lapis stone clutched in one hand, the water around her circling like ribbons of living glass. The blue light that poured from her palm traced her movements in mirrored arcs, catching along her shoulders and hair.

"Rayne?" Saulice's voice cracked with disbelief, raw and unguarded.

"I wanted to tell you," she said, her voice low and steady. "But I was afraid."

A dozen questions surged in Saulice's mind, but he swallowed them. This was no time for explanations.

Another wave of lichtaurs charged. Rayne glanced at Saulice, eyes locking with his in unspoken agreement. If she were the other Harbinger, then so be it. He wasn't confident he could match her pace, but he tightened his grip on the barricade and lifted his hand anyhow.

The lightning that answered was not his own but surged into his core from the leaking fractures of gold, a torrent forced into him rather than drawn out. His core filled beyond its limits, leaking power as quickly as it received it, every fissure searing with light. It was no forging technique, no controlled cycling as Melandra had taught;

this was raw will, Lazarus' and his together, straining to hold against collapse.

The sensation cut through him in waves, each pulse scouring his nerves. He felt it pour through every fracture, sparking across his ribs and spine, racing to his fingertips as if searching for escape. Somewhere in the cracks, he sensed Lazarus' presence: steady and resolute, sharing this burden rather than commanding it.

So this was the power of a Titan.

Questions clawed at him. Why Rayne had hidden her power, what it meant that they fought side by side as Harbingers, and whether he could even survive this storm coursing through him—but none of that mattered now. Not with Baalo towering over them.

Rayne planted her feet, hands sweeping in a precise spiral before slamming upward. Water erupted at her call, tearing free from the creek and rain-slicked earth. It spun into a massive cone above her head, wide as a siege ram, churning with a roar that drowned the battlefield.

Saulice dragged deep, forcing Lazarus' lightning through the cracks of his core. It burned him from within, searing nerves and bone until his arm trembled violently. Golden arcs crawled up his wrist and forked across his fingertips, wild and alive.

The world narrowed to two colors.

Gold and blue.

Rayne's tide met Saulice's storm as he thrust his hand into the rising cone. Lightning exploded with a boom at his touch, racing along every droplet until the entire construct shimmered with gold fire. The cone became a living spear of flashing light.

"Now!" Rayne shouted.

They hurled it together.

The spinning torrent smashed into Baalo's chest with a deafening crack. Lightning rode the water's weight, punching through his corrupted armor in a flash of white-gold. The impact drove him back a step, and he staggered. His gauntleted claws gouged trenches through the mire. Steam hissed off him in curling sheets as the blast ripped away, leaving charred furrows across his pale armor.

Baalo laughed, raw and jagged, like rust grinding stone. Steam hissed from his scorched chest as he straightened, claws flexing.

"Is that it?" he rasped. "Two broken vessels pretending at divinity. Lazarus chose poorly. Malaya worse." His grin split wider, feral and mocking. "Come then, Harbingers. Show me the might of your god, Shaddai."

His hand lashed out, seizing a fallen lichtaur by the throat. In one violent pull, he drained its life. Flesh collapsed to ash in his grip. Another followed, and another. Each corpse withered into husks as the cracks across Baalo's chest sealed in gruesome, snapping jerks of bone and sinew.

Mud trembled under his steps as he advanced toward Saulice.

The ridge had come apart like wet parchment. Centaur ranks were scattered across the slope, some retreating uphill toward the far barricade where they had first formed, others driven downhill toward the creek where bodies choked the current. Archers at the high barricade loosed what few arrows remained, but most had dropped their bows for pikes or been pulled into the melee below.

Baalo moved through the chaos with measured steps, bone armor cracked from the lightning strike yet mending with each breath he stole from the dead. Silver veins pulsed faintly beneath his blackened skin, light crawling along the fissures like sickly worms squirming beneath ice.

Dedric surged into the gap Baalo had carved, greatsword raised high. His diamond shard glowed faintly within his bracer, light spiraling around his wrists as he traced an arc with both hands. Wind gathered in tight spirals, wrapping the length of his blade until it hummed with an invisible current. He swung in a wide sweep, the forged air carrying the strike farther than steel alone could reach.

Melandra followed low and fast. Her emerald stone flared as she pressed her palm to the churned mud. The ground answered. A jagged wall of stone erupted behind Baalo, closing his escape and forcing him toward Dedric's swing. She rose into a pivot, her second hand tracing a sharp gesture that fractured the earth beneath his footing, sending shards upward into his legs.

Baalo met them without hesitation. His bone blade clashed against Dedric's wind-forged greatsword in a spray of sparks, the shock reverberating down Dedric's arms to his shoulders. Melandra's upward spike cracked against Baalo's shin, splintering, but Veartaya's zealot shifted with impossible precision, driving a backhand toward her face. She ducked low and rolled, her blade cutting across his flank. Black ichor struck her armor and hissed.

"Press him!" Dedric roared, circling wide. "Keep him between us!"

Above them, Drezz anchored himself at the far barricade with the remaining centaur archers. His hands trembled from exhaustion, yet every arrow he loosed found its mark. Between volleys, he pressed his shard briefly into the churned earth, forcing moisture through the soil until the slope gleamed slick beneath the charging lichtaurs' hooves. Their momentum faltered as they slipped, claws scrabbling for purchase, and the centaurs below seized the moment to reset their shields and brace for impact.

"More incoming on the right flank!" Drezz shouted across the slope, already nocking another arrow.

Down by the creek, Saulice braced himself against a shattered barricade. Lightning flickered faintly through the cracks of his bracer and skin, spilling from Lazarus' fount rather than his own reserves. Rayne stood beside him, lapis stone clenched tight, mirrored water threading upward from the creek in protective arcs. Together they held a shrinking line of battered centaurs, pikes lowered against the swarm pressing downhill.

Another wave of lichtaurs vaulted toward the water's edge. Rayne thrust her hand forward; a wall of spiraling water crashed upward, catching the first wave mid-leap and hurling them back against the slick slope. Saulice followed with lightning, threading it into her current; gold crackled along blue ribbons, fusing the strike into a single wave that split bone and claw alike.

Baalo's laughter cut through the din above. "How many of you must I bury before Furies Fist learns silence? Humans are not capable of ruling. Bow to me and live!"

Dedric gritted his teeth and lunged with another wind-forged strike, the air whistling sharp around his blade. Baalo caught it with the flat of his bone sword, sparks flashing. Melandra slammed her palm to the ground, forcing a chasm open at Baalo's back. The lichtaur liege shifted his weight effortlessly, planting his foot on the rising edge of the stone and using it to launch himself upward, bone blade crashing down toward Dedric's shoulder.

Dedric barely raised his guard in time. The impact drove him to one knee, armor shrieking under the force.

"Hold him!" Melandra shouted, her emerald stone flaring again as she raised a jagged wall of stone between Baalo and the centaurs scrambling downhill. "Saulice, hold the creek!"

Saulice barely heard her. His fractured core pulsed with lightning that was not his own, Lazarus' presence steady but unbearably heavy inside him. Each surge scraped deeper into the cracks, pain threading through his ribs and spine until every breath felt raw. He could sense it, the damage growing with every strike he drew from Lazarus, each pull fraying something vital inside him.

He gritted his teeth and forced the current outward anyway. The others didn't need to know. Rayne was locked in focus beside him, Drezz was already bleeding and spent. If they saw how much each strike cost him, they might falter, and he couldn't risk that.

So he said nothing. He swallowed the fear, locked it behind clenched teeth, and pushed harder. Lightning gathered along his arm again, wild and unsteady. Every pulse told him the damage was getting worse. But stopping wasn't an option.

He chose silence. And kept fighting.

Another wave hit the creek barricade. Centaurs lowered their shields, hooves braced deep in mud. Rayne's water lashed forward in mirrored whips; Drezz's arrows arced down from above, pelting the lichtaurs that slipped through the lower line. Saulice's lightning burst outward, catching the fallen midstream and finishing what Drezz had begun.

For a heartbeat, the ridge held.

Then Baalo's voice cut across both fronts, low and brimming with contempt.

"You think this is all I am?" He drove his heel to the ground. The earth quaked, cracks spidering in all directions. Silver light flared along his veins as he seized another lichtaur and stripped life from its body. Another followed. Then another. Each husk collapsed to ash as his bone armor sealed with sickening snaps and groans.

"Enough," Baalo growled. "I am done waiting. The Pitch is not all Veartaya gifted me with."

The air buckled around him as bone plates along his arms flared outward and locked into place, each fissure in his blackened skin blazing silver. The corpses at his feet convulsed, then collapsed inward, husks imploding as raw fount spilled from them in threads of dark light.

Melandra felt it first, a faint tug pulling at the edges of her near-empty core. "Dedric—" she warned.

The ground beneath Baalo cracked open as his life-drain surged outward. Lichtaurs nearest him convulsed, their eyes hollowing to black as the energy was ripped from them. The drain did not stop with the dead. It swept wide, invisible but suffocating, crawling over centaur lines both uphill and downhill.

Rayne staggered at the creek barricade, water faltering around her arms as the drain leached strength from her muscles. Saulice gasped as lightning sputtered along his skin, not pulled outward but dragged toward Baalo as though gravity itself had turned against him. The fractures in his core screamed with every pulse, light leaking from cracks along his ribs and forearms.

Centaurs fell where they stood. Some collapsed to their knees, hooves skidding in the mud; others toppled backward altogether, weapons slipping from lifeless fingers. Blood streaked from nostrils and eyes as the drain tightened.

Dedric roared and lunged, wind spiraling around his blade in a cutting arc. Baalo caught the strike with one hand. Bone met steel, sparks flared. He twisted sharply, wrenching Dedric's sword wide, and slammed a knee into his chest. The impact hurled Dedric across the mud and into a shattered pike wall. He didn't get up.

Melandra planted both hands on the ground. Her emerald stone flared as a jagged spire of rock erupted between Baalo and Dedric, buying precious seconds. She pivoted, slamming her palm down again; the ground buckled, opening a narrow trench that swallowed two charging lichtaurs whole.

Baalo did not even glance at them. His eyes fixed solely on Saulice.

"You destroyed Veartaya's gift," Baalo hissed, voice shaking with restrained fury. "And for what? To crawl behind barricades and continue begging for borrowed power?" His voice rose, sharp and ragged. "I could have given it to you! And you spat in the face of generosity."

The drain intensified.

Saulice dropped to one knee, breath tearing in shallow gasps. Lightning flared and died across his forearms. Every pulse of Lazarus' fount felt like fire across broken glass. He clutched his chest, knuckles white, unable to contain the leak. He said his prayer again, but relief did not come.

Above, Drezz loosed arrow after arrow from the high barricade, just out of range of Baalo's life drain. His aim never wavered, but his arms trembled violently with each pull. Centaurs beside him struggled to stand; one collapsed mid-draw, bow clattering into the mud.

Rayne's water ribbons thinned, faltering with each passing second. She grit her teeth and forced them back into form, eyes locking on Saulice through the haze.

"Stay with me!" Her voice was raw.

Saulice barely heard her, his vision doubling as black crept in at the edges.

Baalo stepped through the fractured stone wall Melandra had raised. Black veins glowed silver as he closed the distance, bone blade forming in his grasp. The ground around him smoked with spent corpses, their husks crumbling to ash in the sucking wind of his power.

The battlefield narrowed to sound and pain. Screams blurred into the crackle of lightning that no longer belonged to Saulice. His ribs throbbed with every breath, fractures in his core splintering ever wider as Lazarus' fount leaked in wild arcs through his limbs. He could barely hold it, barely stay upright.

Rayne's water ribbons had thinned to wisps beside him. Drezz's arrows still whistled from the ridge above, but slower now, strained and desperate. Dedric struggled to rise from the shattered pike wall, blood streaking his jaw. Centaurs lay strewn in heaps across the muddy creek, husks collapsing inward as Baalo's drain consumed the last remnants of their strength.

Baalo moved toward him through the haze, a bone blade forming along his arm like a living growth. Each step pressed deeper into the sodden ground, sending ripples through the bloodied water. His voice carried low at first, trembling with barely contained fervor.

"You defiled my Master's creation," he hissed, words thick with fury. "Her holy instrument… and now you crawl, clinging to borrowed scraps of power." His voice rose. "You spit on everything she bled to give, and for that, I will unmake you!"

Saulice's knees buckled. Lightning flickered weakly down his arms, a ghost of the storm he had unleashed minutes ago. Every instinct screamed to rise, to fight, but his body refused.

Baalo raised the blade.

Saulice's breath caught, a hollow stillness washing over him. There were no prayers left, no techniques to summon, no borrowed strength to reach for. Only the faint echo of Lazarus in the cracks of his mind, steady but silent, with him to the bitter end.

He closed his eyes.

If this was where it ended, he thought, let it be quick. At least Rayne would live a moment longer. At least Drezz might escape the ridge. At least someone would carry their memory.

The air tightened, pressure closing in around him as the blade fell.

Melandra watched as Baalo's blade descended toward Saulice. The boy knelt in the mud, head bowed, too drained even to raise his arms. Lightning sputtered along the cracks of his skin, a dying storm without wind to carry it.

Her chest tightened. She saw his father in him. Long ago, she had been just like the boy, running with Dedric and Benedict as young academs. Now his son knelt helpless in the mud, Dedric's last living family, the only remnant of what they had both lost. To watch him die would be to fail them both.

Dedric was too far, and Rayne's water ribbons had faltered, thinning to mist. Drezz's arrows broke harmlessly against Baalo's advancing guard. No one else could reach him.

Her emerald stone flared as she pushed off the churned earth, legs driving her forward to do something unthinkable. She did not ask Shaddai for strength. She simply trusted He would meet her in the act.

The world narrowed to the space between Saulice and the blade.

Baalo's black eyes turned, rimmed in silver, feral in their zeal. He brought his bone weapon down in a killing arc. Melandra leapt, sword raised, intercepting the strike with all the strength left in her arms. Steel screamed against bone; sparks flew in the haze of mud and blood.

The force drove her backward, knees buckling, but she held long enough to shove Saulice aside. The next blow came instantly. There was no time to parry, no space to brace. The blade tore through her chest.

Time fractured.

The battlefield noise faded to nothing. There were no screams, no steel clashing atop the ridge, only the steady rush of blood in her ears. Melandra's eyes found Saulice's, and in him she saw another boy: Benedict, years ago, standing shoulder to shoulder with Dedric in their Academy blues, brave in ways that broke her heart.

Her voice trembled as she spoke.

"True strength… isn't found in clenched fists, Saulice. It's in the hands willing to open, even when they're afraid."

Her fingers, shaking, rose to his cheek. Warmth barely lingered in her touch.

"You have his eyes," she whispered, tears brimming. "Your father… you're so much like him."

The light in her gaze faltered, then fled. And with it, something inside Saulice cracked, sharp and soundless.

Then the world crashed back, filled by Dedric's raw scream that tore at his throat while he forced himself upright through the drain's pull. His skin had gone pale, veins blackened, sweat pouring down his face as he staggered forward. His sword dragged through the mud, lifted by nothing but fury and grief.

CHAPTER 32

WOEFUL WATERS

Lazarus' light faded from his core, leaving only the haze of mist and blood that drowned the ridge in shadow. The lightning that had once burned through every vein ebbed to a dull ache, retreating into the cracks of his core. Pain replaced it, and a weight he could not name settled in his chest, heavier than the mud clinging to his knees.

Melandra's body lay sprawled before him, her emerald stone dim, her hand still outstretched where it had brushed his cheek. For a long moment, Saulice only stared, unable to breathe or blink. Her words hung suspended in the air as if time itself refused to let them fall.

His chest heaved. A broken gasp escaped his lips as his vision blurred. Tears cut clean tracks through the blood and grime along his face. The boy who had endured Hamlen's scorn, who had faced the Pitch and survived, broke beneath the weight of this moment.

He clenched his fists in the mud. Only something solid could steady his flaring anger. His breath came ragged, teeth bared against the ache in his ribs. Why her? Why any of them?

A voice stirred in the cracks. Quiet, steady.

I am still here, Lazarus said.

The presence was faint and restrained, but Saulice loosened his fists. He opened his hands, letting blood mix with rainwater between his trembling fingers.

The roar of the battlefield returned in his ears.

Baalo's voice rose above the chaos, sharper and viler than before. "How many more will you sacrifice? Admit your weakness! Beg for their freedom, child. Come now! Beg for me to have mercy on your friends."

He didn't respond.

The life drain intensified a second time.

Rayne buckled with a cry at the creek barricade, water ribbons collapsing into the mud. Drezz's arrows fell silent on the high ridge as his bow slipped from his trembling hands while the drain's influence reached even him. Dedric, veins blackened as sweat poured down his face, staggered mid-step, but finally made it to his destination. He dropped to one knee beside Melandra's body and gasped for air.

Baalo was close enough to cut him down, but he didn't so much as twitch toward him. His gaze burned past the dying man as if he weren't even there, fixed wholly on Saulice. The others were obstacles, nothing more. Saulice had shattered the Pitch. That was all that mattered.

Saulice felt it too, his core leaking power faster than he could gather it. Each crack screamed with light, every fracture widening until he thought he might tear apart entirely. He whispered into the storm of pain:

"Shaddai… steady me. Hold me and my core, for I cannot hold myself."

No answer came. The prayer had never been meant for a soul being hollowed from the inside out. The only reply was the sucking wind of Baalo's drain and the weight of silence where Melandra's voice had been.

Saulice lifted his head. Baalo loomed over him, blade raised, black eyes rimmed in silver zeal. Around them, his friends were dying.

He looked at Melandra's body. At her open hands and the final tears she shed.

In that instant, he understood.

True strength was not in clenched fists. It was in open hands, willing to give, willing to offer, willing to let go. And Saulice had a choice to make.

He rose, slow and unsteady. His chest burned, and his core splintered. But his eyes, tear-streaked and hollow, no longer held fear.

"I won't beg," he said. His voice trembled, but it carried. "Not for mercy or power. You're not worthy, Baalo."

He opened his hands to the storm, and the world fell away.

Baalo froze mid-step, bone blade raised high. For a heartbeat, the lichtaur liege only stared, face twisted with rage and disbelief.

"You dare," Baalo hissed, voice shaking. "Then watch them die for your pride."

And Saulice, unflinching with eyes closed, vanished to a place where only Lazarus would find him.

Saulice opened his eyes and saw mist rolling across a clearing, curling through blackened trunks and spilling toward a cliff ahead. The trees bore scars of lightning, their branches twisting upward as though pleading for a storm that never came.

He stood barefoot at the clearing's edge. Blood and mud streaked his body, yet neither belonged to this place. This was Lazarus' soul laid bare, a place he'd visited before. But never had it felt so cumbersome.

Lazarus stood at the cliff's brink. The Titan's form was immense, cut and scarred with golden fissures. His shoulders bore the weight of centuries; his frame hummed with quiet thunder. Where once chains had coiled around his limbs, binding him in his own grief, now there were none. Only faint grooves in the stone where they had been, lingering reminders of a prison never cast from iron.

"I know what you're about to do." Lazarus' voice rumbled low, rolling across the mist. "You're going to abandon me. Just like Lector did."

Saulice stepped forward, voice raw. "Lazarus, I'm not abandoning you."

"Then why do I feel the end?"

"Because they're dying." Saulice's voice broke as images surged behind his eyes: Rayne's collapsing ribbons of water, Dedric staggering pale and hollow, Drezz falling to one knee, and Melandra's body crumpling in the mud. "They gave everything to save me. To give me this chance."

He stopped a few paces behind the Titan, staring into the mist. The Forsaken brand on his hand itched, drawing his attention.

"I have always hated the name," Saulice whispered, inspecting the old mark. "Forsaken… Ever since I was nine. Since Hamlen spat on me with its expectations. The world turned its back on me too, Lazarus. But I'll carry it and every sneer, every curse, if it means saving them. The only ones who ever stood by me. Against the rest of the world."

Lazarus turned slowly, molten eyes locking on him.

"Do you know what I saw in Mortare? The city I destroyed before I was sealed?" the Titan asked, thunder whispering at the edges of his words. "I was told the city had fallen to Invictus spies. That every man, woman, and child was a weapon waiting to strike. Humans I trusted fed me lies, and I believed them." His voice grew heavy, raw with memory. "I rained judgment on the innocent, killing thousands. And when the fires cleared, a lone man stood against me, broken and bloodied, carrying, of all things, a baby in his arms."

Saulice's breath caught.

"That man sealed me," Lazarus continued. "He begged me to stop, for the child he carried. I realized a long time ago that child was you."

The Titan's gaze faltered, the light in them flickering. "And I have hated ever since. Loathed those who lied and cheated. Detested those who failed. I've even scorned myself."

Saulice's throat tightened. "You've carried that hate as long as I've carried being Forsaken. Longer, actually."

"I have."

"Lazarus… I can't watch everyone else die." His voice cracked, ragged and small. "Not for my sake. Not Dedric. Rayne. Drezz."

The mist stilled. For the first time in an age, Lazarus' molten eyes shifted clear as the storm within him quieted.

"What you are about to bear," Lazarus said, voice low and solemn, "only a few have, and their cores were five times the size of yours. For what it's worth, I must show respect for the actions you have taken. You are a fierce mortal."

The Titan of justice turned to Saulice. His towering frame loomed like a mountain at the clearing's edge, yet his gaze no longer carried rage.

"Prepare yourself," he said. "And… thank you."

The vision shattered, though Saulice realized it had never truly left him. The cliff and the battlefield overlapped; the mist of Lazarus' soul still clung to his senses even as screams and steel crashed around him. Every breath he took on the ridge carried both realities: pine-scented mist and the copper reek of blood.

The clearing lay in ruins. Shattered pikes jutted from churned mud like broken ribs. Corpses of lichtaurs sprawled in grotesque heaps, their limbs twisted at unnatural angles. Barely two dozen centaurs still stood at the top of the hill, shields splintered, blood streaking their muzzles as they backed further from the life drain. Another dozen lay scattered behind them, unmoving. The rest had fallen, either to Baalo's drain or beneath the endless claws of his creatures. Lord Athekk himself knelt near the barricade, breathing hard, his once-bright pike buried point-down in the mud to keep him upright.

Rayne clutched her head where she knelt, streams of crimson running from her nostrils and ears. Drezz's bow hung loosely in his hand; blood trickled from his eyes, soaking into the furs around his neck. Even Dedric, gaunt and hollow-eyed beside Melandra's body, had blood streaking from his nose, each gasp ragged, his veins dark with exhaustion and the toll of Baalo's life drain.

And still Baalo fed upon them.

Black tendrils crawled outward from the evil disciple's chest, coiling into every living body around him. With every heartbeat, they pulsed, stealing another fragment of life.

Saulice forced himself upright.

Every muscle trembled as he rose from the mud, yet power flooded through him, raw and unrestrained, coursing through every fracture of his shattered core. Lightning threaded along his limbs, veins of white-gold climbing his arms, spreading across his chest, bleeding light from his throat and eyes.

It was volcanic and uncontrolled. A storm unbound.

The surrounding air shimmered with heat and static; pine needles lifted from the churned ground and hovered, weightless, in the electric haze. The mud hissed where lightning touched, steam rising in soft curls around his feet. His open hands hung steady at his sides, the calm at the center of the storm.

Baalo's head snapped toward him, black eyes rimmed in silver, wild with hate and zeal. His grin split bloodied lips as he advanced through the carnage.

"You still stand?" His voice was low, jagged. "Look around you, boy. The dead litter this ridge because of you. Their blood calls out your name."

His words sharpened, each one laced with venom. "You think yourself chosen? You think that Titan's light can stop what's coming?"

Saulice didn't answer.

Above the ridge, the sky darkened beyond the veil of mist and blood. Storm clouds converged from every horizon, roiling and twisting together as if drawn by some unseen hand. The wind turned heavy with the scent of ozone and iron; pine needles rattled across shields and shattered barricades as the air thickened. The darkness pressed low, the whole of Timfathen narrowing into the space above Saulice's open hands.

Baalo roared and surged forward, bone blade raised high. The drain widened, and two more centaurs collapsed, their lifeblood drawn into the black veins crawling up his arms.

Rayne and Drezz buckled fully to the mud, blood expanding beneath their struggling faces. Dedric slumped over Melandra's body, unable even to lift his head.

Saulice thrust his hands outward.

Lightning *erupted* in a wave of storm.

Golden-white arcs poured from every fracture in his body, jagged and wild, converging high overhead in a spiraling vortex.

The sound was not thunder. It was stone breaking and mountains splitting, the full unleashed power of one of Shaddai's Titans.

Baalo charged into it. He met the storm head-on, his bone blade swinging in a desperate, final arc even as molten light burned through his armor.

The vortex collapsed downward in a single strike.

It struck Baalo full in the chest at the same heartbeat his blade tore across Saulice's ribs.

Agony seared them both.

Baalo was hurled backward half a hundred yards, bone armor cracking apart in molten shards. He smashed through a wall of splintered pikes and skidded across the mud, carving a deep trench through the corpses of his own lichtaurs. The drain faltered, the black veins recoiling like severed cords.

The battlefield gasped as air rushed back into a hundred starving lungs.

Saulice staggered at the strike's center, a hot gush spilling down his side where Baalo's blade had cut deep. Lightning still crawled faintly across his skin, but each arc sputtered and dimmed. His core burned like molten glass, fracturing with every heartbeat. He felt each break, every splinter wailing against his ribs.

Baalo rose slowly from the mud, smoke curling from the shattered plates along his chest. His breath came ragged, but his cracked grin refused to fade.

"You think this changes anything?" His voice trembled, half fury, half awe. "Veartaya will rise, with or without you."

His gaze swept over Saulice, blood-soaked and swaying, and his grin deepened. "You're finished, boy. You only have minutes left. Enjoy them while you can."

He stepped backward into the mist, the last traces of the drain curling inward, black tendrils coiling like serpents around his frame as his form began to dissolve into shadow.

A low chuckle echoed across the ridge, growing sharper, crueler.

"Your father would tell you the same… if he remembered your name." Baalo's grin widened, jagged teeth flashing through the fog. "Here's a secret. Benedict never died. But he doesn't remember you and he never will. Not the fire, not the seal… nor the Forsaken son who carried his history to the grave."

The words cut deeper than the wound in his side. Saulice's breath caught, chest tightening as the cracks in his core spread like spiderwebs across glass.

And then Baalo was gone, swallowed by the mist and the shattered forest beyond, his laughter lingering like a scar across the silence he left behind.

Saulice swayed. Lightning still flickered faintly across his arms and neck, the glow within him guttering. Blood soaked his tunic, dripping steadily into the churned mud beneath his boots. His knees weakened, every heartbeat forcing another rush of warmth down his side.

His core flared hotter, burning as if the molten glass within him had begun to spill. The white-gold light that had always anchored him sputtered. Hairline fractures raced outward, jagged and unstoppable.

One step forward became a stagger. His legs folded, dropping him to the mud. Blood pressed between his fingers where they clutched his side. The pain in his body was sharp and immediate, but the greater agony was inside: that slow, tearing unravel of what had once been whole.

Inwardly, he saw it.

The core at his center, once bright and laced with golden threads of Lazarus' fount, now hovered in a vast blackness. Light flickered along jagged seams, spilling out into the dark before vanishing. Each tremor in his body sent new cracks spiderwebbing across its surface. Every thud of his heart was a hammer blow.

A shudder rippled through him. His arms weakened, falling limp to his sides. The sound of the battlefield dulled, as though he were sinking beneath deep water. His chest rose shallow, then stalled, forcing him to gasp just to keep breath in his lungs. His legs twitched in the mud, a final, instinctive resistance to stillness.

Cold crept inward from his fingertips, replacing the heat in his veins. His head dropped forward, chin to chest. Fear had long since faded, and regret no longer held a place in him. What remained was the weight of what he had chosen.

His core, the well of every prayer, every forging, every fight, trembled once.

It split again.

Then it gave way.

The sphere shattered, and his life's light spilled into the void.

The clearing was silent.

Pine trees, blackened and twisted by centuries of lightning, stood like grieving sentinels around the cliff's edge. Mist curled low across scorched stone, carrying the faint echo of distant storms.

Lazarus stood alone.

Saulice was gone. He hadn't vanished yet, but his presence was rapidly ebbing from the realm of the living, beyond the Titan's reach with each second. Where the boy's core had once flickered in this place, there was absence now.

Lazarus closed his eyes. In the silence, fragments of their last words lingered.

I hate that name. Forsaken.

But I'll carry it, every curse and sneer, if it means saving them.

The Titan's chest tightened. For centuries he had mistaken sacrifice for betrayal. He'd seen every fallen Harbinger as another chain, another abandonment. He had clung to his grief, convinced no mortal could hold him without leaving him in the end.

But this boy had not dropped him.

Saulice had sacrificed everything.

The mist thickened. Lightning trembled faintly along Lazarus' frame, thick and heavy.

"I thought you were leaving me," he whispered to no one. "But you were staying. Even now, at the end… you stayed."

A light stirred at the center of the clearing.

Soft at first but then searing.

The mist split, pine silhouettes bowing as radiance poured between them. It was old and pure, a preeminence. A presence that needed no name, yet one Lazarus knew before he turned to face it.

Shaddai.

The name left him voiceless.

The Titan collapsed to his knees. Lightning bled from him in jagged arcs, snapping across the scorched ground as sobs tore free, raw and shaking, dredged from grief buried for centuries. His hands pressed to the earth as his brow touched the dirt. The storm that was his body bowed low.

A thousand years since he had felt this light. A thousand years since Shaddai ascended, leaving the Titans to uphold balance in Myre as He returned to His heavenly realm. Not in abandonment, but in trust. He had left them purposefully.

And now, that light had returned.

Lazarus trembled. Every wound, every exile, every whispered prayer he had cast into the silence came rushing back in a single breath. The Father of the ten Titans stood before him, a radiant light not even he could face.

For the first time since his forging, Lazarus felt small, for he remembered then that he was not just a Titan, but a son of Shaddai.

The Light spoke. One word.

"Rise."

The word reverberated through the clearing, steady and unshaken. In its echo came another, deeper truth.

"Greater love has no one than this," Shaddai said, calm and resounding, "that he lay down his life for his friends."

Lazarus could not lift his head. "I forgot why You made me," he choked. "I twisted justice into wrath. I thought hatred would keep me strong. But this boy…" His chest convulsed with another sob. "He gave me back what I had lost."

"You see now."

"I do." His voice shook. "Forgive me. For forgetting."

"What will you do?"

"I will give him half of me," Lazarus whispered. "Bind what is broken. Let him live, and if his core breaks again, we both will fall."

"Then do it," Shaddai said. His voice deepened, final and irrevocable. "And be what you were always meant to be."

A breath trembled through the clearing.

"*Justice.*"

Lazarus rose, trembling, and turned toward the abyss.

The light of Shaddai remained behind him, steady and still, as he stepped toward the darkness where Saulice's presence flickered and fled. Agony and peace warred within him, lightning bleeding from his frame in long golden tendrils, each one tugging at the core of who he was.

He reached outward, plunging into the void where Saulice's core hung shattered, its fragments adrift like pale glass in black water. There, on the brink of silence, he gathered what lingered of the boy and drew him back.

For the first time in an age, Lazarus *reached* for his Harbinger.

CHAPTER 33

NOTE GONE AFTER ALL

Saulice drifted beyond a horizon of black water that emitted a strange glow.

He floated in silence, his mind quiet, his limbs unbound. The pull toward the light carried no urgency, only a strange invitation to rest. He thought of how tired he was, how each battle had stripped away a little more of him. Here there was no strain, no ache. His friends would continue without him. He could let go.

The glow widened until it filled his vision, its warmth brushing against the black water. The edge was near, so near that his next movement might carry him across it.

Then something caught him.

The pull halted with a jolt, as though a hand had seized the tattered pieces of his soul. The current reversed, drawing him away from the light. The motion was slow at first, almost gentle, but it gathered strength until it became an unrelenting force.

Heat surged through him, a fire that burned every fragment of his being. The pieces of himself that had scattered in death slammed together, fusing with pain enough to wrench thought from him. Shards locked in place, edges sealing. With each moment, the light grew more distant, and he realized that crossing into it would have meant leaving everything behind forever.

The black water split apart toward a familiar clearing.

He drifted upward, pulled from the black expanse toward it. Shapes took the form of charred pines, scorched earth, and Lazarus bowed low in the center, lightning bleeding faintly from his frame. The sight rooted Saulice in place. Lazarus, the Titan of Justice, breaker of armies, bent in reverence to someone unseen. The air thickened around him, heavy with a presence that pressed into bone and thought alike.

Then the light came, bright and commanding.

His knees buckled. He dropped to the earth, pressing his hands to the ground as his head bowed low. Terror seized him from the disorienting awe of facing something… someone Divine. The truth struck as his gaze lifted toward the light above Lazarus' bowed form. There was only One who could bring a Titan to its knees.

And Saulice knew the name.

Shaddai regarded him, radiance folding over the clearing like a living mantle. When he spoke, the sound pierced Saulice's very being.

"Live."

The word drove into the marrow of his soul. Strength poured into him and tore through him at once, a heat that seared along every frayed edge of his spirit. Fragments of himself, scattered and drifting moments ago, began to pull together under a force that would not yield.

The clearing dimmed. The light swelled, then fractured, its brilliance breaking into a thousand threads that wrapped him in their grasp. His breath surged back as though he had been drowning, chest heaving against the pull of the unseen current.

The world around him dissolved. Mist and pines gave way to darkness, and in that darkness the drag became a plunge, a sensation of falling into something that was waiting for him.

And then—impact.

The world rocked.

For a heartbeat, Saulice believed the battle still raged as Baalo's drain clawed at his soul. The smell of mud and charred flesh clung to memory so strongly it felt present, as if closing his eyes would drag him back into the chaos he had barely escaped.

Air returned instead, warm and still, laced with the dry sweetness of hay and the faint tang of old iron. No screams filled the air. The only sound came from the slow creak of wooden wheels beneath him, jostling over uneven ground.

Awareness crept in with that quiet.

He was alive.

Memory answered in jagged fragments: Melandra's sacrifice, Rayne's collapsing ribbons of water, Baalo's laughter retreating into mist. Somehow, against all odds, they had survived.

Yet beyond the battle's ruin, another image clung to him: a blinding light, sharp and pure, flashing through the darkness as he departed from the land of the living. It had burned too bright to look upon, yet it steadied him as the world fell away. He didn't understand it, but the memory lingered with warmth.

A voice stirred in that silence, deep and familiar.

You are safe.

Saulice's breath caught. His voice emerged hoarse and cracking. "Lazarus?"

I am here.

The Titan's presence filled him, quieter than ever. Where wrath and storm had once surged, only steady strength remained, a calm Saulice had never known from him. The absence of anger startled him more than the words themselves.

"What happened?" His throat ached with the question.

The answer came slow, almost reverent. *Your core shattered. Without intervention, you would have passed beyond this world. To hold you together, I made a decision. I gave you half of what I am to rebuild your core.*

Shock dulled his senses. "Half of you?"

Half of my storm, half of my life. I parted with it so yours might continue. A pause followed, heavy yet unashamed. *You carried me in ways no Harbinger before you ever has. We are no longer divided, not entirely.*

Saulice's fingers curled weakly against the pallet, the weight of that confession heavier than pain, heavier than grief. Though Saulice's chest still trembled with shallow breaths, beneath that soreness, a new quiet thrummed at his center.

He looked inward.

Where fragments once floated, a whole sphere now hovered. Light pulsed softly across its surface, two halves bound together. One side shone white, calm and steady. The other burned gold, threaded with lightning that hummed like a distant storm. The seam where they met glimmered faintly, neither color overpowering the other, as though boy and Titan now shared the same breath.

Awe rooted him in place. The storm inside him felt different, not wild but anchored. He touched it gently, and gratitude swelled when he felt it accept his touch. Lazarus' essence breathed within the gold, his patience bleeding into the white. There were no erratic tendrils of Lazarus' fount plunging him into an ocean of grief and despair. The silence was in fact so complete that it startled him.

For the first time since Hamlen, Saulice felt whole. Their lives no longer ran parallel but were braided, inseparable. Lazarus had given half of himself to mend what was broken.

And Saulice would never forget it.

"Why?" The word scraped out like a child's plea. "Why would you do that for me?"

Because you stayed, Lazarus said. *No Harbinger before you has done so. Lector, and the others, saw me as a weapon to wield or a burden to cast away. Even in your fear, you treated me as something more. You listened when I raged. You spoke to me when silence was easier. When every other soul would have closed their hands and clung to power, you opened yours and trusted me.*

The words sank deep, unmaking what Saulice thought he knew about himself. Tears rose without permission, raw and silent. Gratitude filled the hollow spaces where anger had once lived.

A quiet lingered after, thicker than silence. Saulice sensed something unspoken in Lazarus' tone, a hesitation, as though there was more he might say but the Titan withheld.

"What else happened?" Saulice asked.

Your core was rebuilt, Lazarus answered. *But not only by me. You saw Him, did you not?*

"I did," he replied, his mind still grappling with the fact Shaddai had told him to live.

Silence followed as he clenched and unclenched his hands. Saulice closed his eyes, tears slipping free, no longer from fear but from awe at the gift he had been given. Not only was he alive. He was changed.

A rustle near the wagon's canvas drew Saulice from the quiet. Footsteps approached, steady but soft. The curtain shifted aside, and Rayne stepped into view.

Her hair was loosely braided, strands falling free around her face. A bandage crossed beneath her collarbone where something sharp had cut her during the last charge. Though her sword rested across her knees, her posture held none of the tension it once had. There was a softness in her eyes, and the tension that usually kept her shoulders taut finally had eased.

"You are awake," she spoke low.

"How long?" Saulice's voice cracked as the question escaped.

"Three weeks."

The words stunned him. Memory told him the battle had been moments ago. Yet the world outside this wagon was already moving on.

Rayne lowered herself onto a crate beside him, careful of the jostling boards beneath her feet. "Lord Athekk sent riders to Grimwode as soon as Baalo fled. They returned with aid, and we were carried there. The healers kept us until two days ago." Her eyes lingered on him. "We left when they were certain you would live."

A shiver crawled along Saulice's spine. "We won?"

"Yes," Rayne said softly. "But not without cost."

Melandra's name hovered unspoken. Dedric's silence since the ridge spoke loud enough.

Saulice turned his face away, throat tightening. "I thought… none of us would leave that ridge."

"You were close," she murmured. Rayne reached for his hand and closed her fingers around his. "But you held on."

The contact stilled him. Silence existed between them, fragile yet alive. The wagon wheels clattered over loose stone, carrying them toward some distant horizon neither of them understood.

After a while, Saulice found his voice again. "You are a Harbinger." The words were filled with quiet wonder.

Rayne nodded. "Malaya has been with my family for three generations. My father, Oreas, never pursued fount forging. He chose the life of a merchant instead." Her fingers brushed the lapis stone in her bracer as she spoke. "But Malaya remained with us."

"You fought like you had always known," Saulice murmured, still marveling at the memory of her water swelling across the lichtaurs.

"I have always known." A faint sadness touched her tone. "But there was already too much on your shoulders. I saw how hard you were working to control your own power. Twice-a-day training, sometimes more. Hours at the Anaals. I didn't want to load more weight on you than you already carried."

"Would it have eased me? Or broken me further?"

Her thumb traced the hilt of her sword. "I wondered the same thing every day."

The wagon jolted suddenly, sending a ripple through the wooden frame. A muffled whicker came from the horses up front. Saulice gripped the edge of the pallet and groaned through the ache in his ribs.

When the wagon settled into a steadier rhythm, Saulice's thoughts drifted beyond the canvas walls. Hoofbeats kept pace beside them, slow and deliberate, joined by the faint creak of armor and the low murmur of a voice he knew too well. It was Dedric. His silence felt heavy with something quiet. Loss, and sorrow too great for words.

Saulice wanted to speak Melandra's name but could not shape the word. Gratitude warred with grief in equal measure. She had given everything for him. For all of them.

Lazarus stirred faintly within. The Titan's voice was low and steady. *Her choice was hers. Do not let it be in vain by marinating in sorrow. Do not do as I have done.*

The curtain lifted again as Drezz climbed into the wagon. His fur was matted and streaked with dried blood, the sling at his shoulder stiff with old bandages. He settled cross-legged near the pallet, eyes scanning Saulice as though to make certain he was real.

"You're awake!" Drezz said. Relief edged the words.

Saulice met his gaze. "You made it."

"Barely." A flicker of a grin tugged at Drezz's mouth, faint and fleeting. "You look worse than me."

"That is saying something," Saulice murmured.

For a brief heartbeat, the corner of Drezz's mouth lifted again. The moment faded quickly, quiet returning heavier than before.

Saulice's fingers curled weakly against the blanket. "What happened to Baalo?"

Drezz's grin vanished. "He fled into the mist after your strike. We were in no shape to chase him. No one was."

Saulice hesitated, throat dry. "The centaurs… how many survived?"

The wagon creaked as Rayne turned her head slightly from the driver's bench, listening but silent.

"Less than two dozen," Drezz said at last. The words landed like stone. "Out of the five hundred we arrived with."

Saulice stared at the worn boards beneath him, unable to speak. Images of the ridge returned unbidden: shields splintering, horns breaking, bodies sinking into the creek. It felt less like memory and more like a nightmare.

"They fought to the last," Rayne said quietly. "Lord Athekk sent his strongest surviving riders back to Grimwode after Baalo fled. They brought help. Without them, none of us would have left the Timfathen alive. And I owe them a promise."

Wind pressed softly against the canvas walls, carrying the faint scent of pine and distant smoke. They were alive, but the cost had been high. Too high.

Hoofbeats sounded close to the wagon's side. Drezz reached for the small wooden shutter set into the canvas wall and slid it open on its narrow rail. Cool air rushed in.

"You've been out for a long time," Dedric said from the saddle, his tone low and rough. His armor bore dents and claw marks, and fresh scars scored the left side of his face in a series of three jagged lines crossing from temple to jaw. His eyes were shadowed but steady as they met Saulice's.

"I spoke with Rayne and Drezz while you were unconscious," Dedric began. His voice was quiet. "They told me about the note Rayne was given the night you fled Brynswick. Forged to look like it was from you."

Saulice frowned faintly, his mind recalling the night they'd been attacked.

Rayne kept her eyes ahead on the winding road. "I told him what we realized by the fire in the Timfathen. Someone planted it to lure us out, to get all of us together in one place."

Drezz crossed his arms, leaning back against the wall. "Whoever did it knew about Lazarus and gave us a trail to follow. We walked straight into Baalo's trap."

Dedric's expression hardened, but his tone stayed even. "I don't know who it was. Not yet. But someone close to Brynswick wanted you gone, Saulice. All of this was planned to happen."

He glanced away briefly, voice low. "And Melandra paid for it. She died because someone inside Brynswick handed Baalo exactly what he wanted."

Drezz's eyes shifted toward Saulice, then Rayne. "But doesn't that mean Invictus still has eyes in Axbridge? That this isn't over?"

"Baalo's influence is deeper than we imagined," Dedric murmured. His scarred face softened as he studied Saulice. "But for now… I just want you to rest. We all need to rest."

No one spoke. The sound of hooves and wheels filled the quiet. The wagon rolled onward.

By late afternoon, the trees they'd been passing for hours began to thin. Through a break in the ridge, rooftops rose pale against the fading sky. Axbridge stood in the distance, obscure yet undeniable, its spires bathed in copper light, gold and blue banners snapping faintly in the wind. Smoke curled upward in slender threads, carrying the scent of hearth and forge across the valley.

Relief swelled in Saulice's chest, warm and steady. They had survived. Against all odds, and all the shadows that had hunted them, they were going home.

For the first time in months, the thought of Axbridge did not bring unease. The Academy's stone halls, once strange and cold, now felt like the closest thing to belonging he had ever known. He thought of Miss Velma in the cafeteria, her sweet smile and warm bread rolls, the way she always slipped him an extra portion when she thought no one was looking. He thought of Cadre Nilus and his quiet patience, firm yet kind, during first-year fount-forging lessons, urging him to steady his breathing and trust the rhythm of his own core, however damaged it had been.

Even Lucas came to mind. Their duel that had once felt impossible was now a distant echo, a battle dwarfed by what they had faced in the Timfathen. Saulice could almost laugh at the memory, in quiet recognition of how far he had come.

The city's glow spilled across the horizon as the wagon creaked forward, and gratitude washed through him in waves. Acknowledgment to Rayne and Drezz beside him. For Dedric's steadiness. For Lazarus, whose quiet presence hummed like a heartbeat within. For Shaddai, whose light he did not fully understand, yet somehow believed was still guiding them.

Saulice rested his hand on the blank bracer at his wrist.

He was not who he had been when he left these gates. And when he crossed them again, the boy who had carried only shame would not be the one returning.

CHAPTER 34

WE REMEMBER

The wagon creaked beneath Saulice as it passed through the main gates of Brynswick Academy. The spoked wheels dragged across gravel worn smooth by countless student boots, their slow rhythm echoing off pale stone walls. Vines curled lazily along the archway, half-green and half-brown with late season.

The sight struck him harder than he expected.

The walls loomed overhead as they always had, tall, noble, unchanged. No scorch marks marred the gates. No signs of battle scarred the stones. For all that had happened in the Timfathen, the storms, the death, the endless clawing fight for survival, Brynswick remained untouched.

That was the problem. Everything still looked the same.

Saulice shifted under his blanket. His shoulder burned where the bracer had split weeks earlier, a dull ache radiating down to his ribs. Every bump in the road sent pain knifing through him, but he bit it back and stared upward.

Above the central archway, a sapphire banner rippled faintly in the breeze. A white ten-pointed star gleamed at its center, clean and unfrayed. The sight stirred something in him he could not quite name, memory and longing, reverence and ache. Brynswick's colors had never looked brighter, yet their meaning had changed.

The Academy was as it had always been.

He was not.

Rayne rode ahead on horseback, her reins held in one hand, the other resting near the hilt of her sword. Drezz limped beside her, a sling looped tight at his shoulder. The wound had been cleaned and bound again that morning, but the linen still spotted faintly with blood. Dedric rode behind them, silent, posture rigid as ever, his scar catching stray sunlight when he turned his head.

None of them spoke.

Even the campus itself felt quiet. Class hours, Saulice guessed. Only a few first-years lingered between halls, their faces unfamiliar. They paused in doorways or under colonnades, whispering as the wagon rolled past. Some stared openly; others glanced away, uncertain. One boy pointed toward Rayne's sword before a girl tugged him back, her expression wary.

They were being seen but not welcomed.

Inside the wagon, Saulice leaned forward slightly, peering past the curtain toward the familiar sprawl of training yards and dormitory arches. It looked exactly as it had the day he first arrived, polished stone, measured symmetry, banners snapping in the breeze.

But it was not the same.

The training fields were empty where there should have been sparring pairs and shouting Cadres. Windows that usually stood open were shuttered, though the day was warm. Even the air smelled different, heavy with polish and stillness rather than sweat and fire.

"Strange seeing it so quiet," Drezz murmured beside the cart. His voice was hoarse from days of travel.

"Feels wrong," Rayne added without looking back.

Dedric's voice carried from the rear, low and flat. "Wrong, but safer."

Unscarred by war. Unmarked by the Pitch.

And yet, within Saulice, nothing was untouched.

He caught himself remembering his first day here, trembling in those same archways, carrying nothing but shame and a broken bracer. Brynswick had been foreign then, colder than Hamlen's stones. He had wondered if he would ever belong.

Now he realized the halls had not changed. He had.

The boy who arrived Forsaken was not the boy returning.

The wagon turned into the main courtyard, wheels grinding over a stone groove carved by centuries of use. The familiar echo startled Saulice; he had dreamed of it in the Timfathen, though he had not known why. He drew the blanket closer around his shoulders from the weight of memory pressing in.

Overhead, sunlight angled through the high arches, painting long bands across the flagstones. The white star on the nearest banner flared briefly as wind caught it. For a heartbeat, Saulice could almost imagine it was light, a beacon, steady and guiding.

Rayne slowed her horse at the wagon's side. Drezz dragged his pace to match hers, tail flicking absently behind him.

"Never thought I'd miss this place," Drezz muttered.

Rayne gave a tired half-smile. "Guess that means it's home."

Dedric tightened his grip on the reins, eyes fixed ahead.

They had survived. Against odds that should have killed them all, they had returned.

Wind rustled through the ivy trailing the stone, the only welcome they received. Saulice glanced around, but no voices called out, no music or applause rose from the halls. Only silence met them, expectant and unchanged. And strangely, Saulice found he did not need more than that.

For the first time since Hamlen, the silence felt like peace.

The wagon rolled to a slow halt in the courtyard. The last clatter of wheels faded into Brynswick's stillness, broken only by the faint wind tugging at the sapphire banners overhead.

Master Nilus waited near the steps of the Masters Halls. His robes hung loose on his frame, stained with ink along the sleeves. His beard was uneven, as though sleep had been a stranger for days. He watched them, his eyes lingering on Dedric's Fury's Fist emblem stitched along his sleeve.

"Lord Commander Muir said you were supposed to return days ago," Nilus said quietly.

Dedric dismounted without flourish. "We ran into complications."

Before Nilus could answer, another voice cut across the courtyard.

"Do not suppose anyone's planning to explain why I nearly got trampled by a horse with more armor than sense?"

The words came half-laughing, half-exasperated.

Oreas stepped from behind a supply cart, an apple in one hand and a lopsided satchel slung across his shoulder. His shirt hung untucked, boots dusty, a familiar grin playing at the corners of his mouth.

Rayne froze in the saddle. "Oreas?"

"Last I checked," he said, biting into the apple. "Though I've been told I look worse after a week on the road." He gave a shrug. "Was halfway to Eastmere when I heard things were turning sideways here. Something about students missing, Cadre screaming at each other behind closed doors. Figured I had better swing back and see which of you was still breathing."

He walked up to Rayne's stirrup and extended one arm. "Come here, girl."

Rayne hesitated only a moment before sliding down to meet him. Oreas wrapped her in a one-armed hug that smelled of dust and peppered bread.

"Still scowling," he said as he let her go. "That's a good sign."

He turned next to Drezz, eyeing the fresh sling and faint limp. "And you… walking like you fell off a roof into a confession booth."

Drezz tried, and failed, to keep a laugh from slipping out.

Finally, Oreas looked toward the wagon. His grin softened. "And you," he said, squinting. "You've got that look."

Saulice blinked, exhausted. "What look?"

"The 'I may or may not have exploded a sacred artifact and insulted a council member' look."

A small, tired smile broke across Saulice's face despite himself.

"Do not worry," Oreas added. "You are still the same scrappy kid. Just taller now."

For a moment, Oreas lingered there, studying Saulice with an expression that carried more weight than his jokes. He opened his mouth, then closed it again, rubbing at the back of his neck.

"I'll give you space," he said finally. "Looks like you have heavier things to talk through than a merchant with bad knees and too many opinions." He turned, lifting a hand in farewell as he walked toward the courtyard's edge. "But if you ever need a ride out of this place, I charge double for soul-searching types. And I do not take payment in trauma."

With a wink over his shoulder, he was gone, whistling something off-key.

The quiet that followed felt lighter somehow.

Footsteps scuffed the flagstones near the wagon's wheel. From the far side, a familiar figure stepped into view, hair shorter than Saulice remembered, uniform wrinkled, eyes rimmed in red.

"Damian," Drezz breathed.

Damian did not speak at first. He simply crossed the courtyard in three long strides and pulled Drezz into a brief, firm clasp.

"You are alive," Damian whispered.

"Mostly," Drezz muttered against his shoulder.

Damian released him, then turned to Saulice. No words passed between them; none were needed. He only gripped Saulice's arm, held it a heartbeat, then let go.

Rayne watched quietly from a step back, a faint smile ghosting her features. The four of them had been scattered and broken, remade into something stronger. They stood together in silence while the wind tugged at Brynswick's banners overhead.

Nilus cleared his throat, then ushered them up the stairs. "Come. There is much to speak of."

Dedric adjusted the strap across his shoulder and started toward the hall.

Rayne climbed down first, then helped Saulice swing his legs over the side. He staggered on the landing, one hand catching the frame. Drezz stepped forward to brace him, but it was Rayne's shoulder he leaned on as they began the climb. He hated the weakness, but not the contact. Not after the beating he'd taken, being half dead and all.

Two shallow flights. Past the quiet grove. Into the narrow corridors where tile clicked underfoot and silence pressed close. No student voices. No clashing drills. Only the low hum of lanterns burning between plaques etched with numbers instead of names.

At the end of the hall stood a single tall door, engraved with the ten-pointed star.

Dedric pushed it open.

Inside, the fire burned low behind the wide desk and bear's pelt. Shelves lined the far wall, ordered and still. The light from the left-side windows angled across the tiles in gray slats.

Cadre Calder stood beside the hearth, one arm wrapped in a stiff sling. Master Nilus waited near the desk. Elmes leaned against the far column, his expression unreadable.

Calder looked up and froze.

He took them in with a single glance. Bandaged and bruised, fresh scars covered them all. Dirt was still ground into the folds of their uniforms. Saulice could feel the heat of his own wound permeating down his side.

"What happened?" Calder said, eyes narrowing at the academs. "Where have you been?!"

Dedric stepped forward with practiced bearing and struck a formal salute.

"Sir," he said, his posture stiff but weary. "We have come from the Timfathen. These academs were led to believe an artifact existed there that would aid Saulice in his abilities as a Harbinger. I requested aid from Furies Fist to pursue them after discovering an abandoned camp on Candur's northern border. We were forced to engage alongside a large supportive force from Clan Athekk's centaurs."

Calder's voice dropped. "Engage *what*?"

Dedric hesitated.

"And where is Melandra?" Calder continued.

The salute faltered.

"She is gone," Dedric said quietly.

Calder flinched, then his hand lifted slowly, pressing over his chest.

"She was one of our best," he said as though remembering his time in Furies Fist. "A fast thinker, and an argonaut that will be missed by many. I am sorry, Dedric."

No one spoke.

"It was Baalo," Dedric added after a beat, his knuckles tight. "He struck her down."

Calder's eyes flicked upward. "Baalo? Impossible."

"*No*... he is very much alive," Saulice replied. "I was held captive by him for nearly two weeks, and he knew who I was."

Rayne shifted beside him while Drezz chose to stare at the tiles. The fire cracked once behind them.

"That is not all," Saulice continued. "He said my father sealed Lazarus inside me. That Benedict may still be alive."

Elmes straightened slightly but said nothing. Nilus's jaw clenched.

"Is there anything else?" Cadre Calder asked, eyes twitching as they tried to process the statements.

The air grew hot as Saulice looked to Dedric, unsure how to share what had happened next.

"Saulice sacrificed himself... to save the rest of us. We were doomed," Dedric added, his eyes hardening.

Calder faltered a step. "What do you mean, sacrificed?"

"I died," Saulice said, throat closing. "Lazarus gave up half of himself to restore me. To rebuild my core. He could have kept fighting. But he chose to save me."

The silence that followed was not denial. It was belief, struggling to settle in.

"You are telling the truth," Calder said finally. "I see it in your eyes."

Then, quieter, "I see it in all of you."

He moved toward the desk and rested his good hand against the carved edge.

"I can no longer call you probationary," he said. "Not after this. Saulice Sawyer, as of this moment, you are a confirmed academ in full standing, viewed with all due respect."

Saulice's throat tightened. He blinked hard.

Calder nodded slowly. "And I owe you an apology. For what you have suffered in these halls. For the slander and the silence. For what Valos, Winstrom, and Cadre like myself allowed to fester because of a brand none of us understood."

Then Dedric stepped forward again. "With respect, sir... why are we speaking to you? Where is Master Valos?"

Calder's jaw tightened.

"Three days ago, documents were discovered that contained evidence of redirected funds from the Academy into his own coffers. When we confronted him, Valos attempted to flee through the north wall tower."

His good hand dropped to his side, flexing slightly.

"He injured three staff during the escape. One may still lose her eye."

Saulice noticed the stiffness in Calder's gait now. The wound was real.

"He escaped," Calder said. "And I have since been promoted to the acting Master of Brynswick."

He paused. "Lord Winstrom is also gone, his manor abandoned. We believe he fled a week or so ago, just before Valos."

Nilus looked down. Elmes's gaze had not shifted.

Calder exhaled. "The king will want answers. But until we know what rises from what we lost…"

He looked to Saulice, then to Rayne and Drezz.

"You three are dismissed."

Saulice hesitated, but Calder's gaze was steady.

"I would punish you for leaving the Academy, but… it would be fruitless in spite of what you've just endured. Go and rest. You have earned it."

Rayne nodded once. Drezz touched his fist lightly to his chest in silent respect. Saulice gave a short bow before turning.

They stepped toward the door.

As they crossed the threshold, Calder turned to Dedric.

"Stay. There is more I need to hear."

The chamber doors closed behind them.

Nothing about the courtyard had changed.

Stone tiles still stretched beneath the arches, worn smooth from centuries of passage. The basin at its center remained dry, circled by brittle leaves that rustled faintly in the wind. Overhead, banners bearing Brynswick's seal drifted in the pale light, untouched by war, unmoved by memory.

Saulice stepped out first, careful as his boots met the lower stairs. A dull ache still bloomed under the wrap along his ribs, but he no longer moved like someone half-broken. Rayne moved beside him without needing to speak, and Drezz followed with slower steps, one hand grazing the stone railing for balance.

At the far edge of the courtyard, someone stood waiting.

Damian's arms were crossed. His uniform looked hastily pulled on, and his face held the weight of too many sleepless nights. He just waited, as if the act of standing there might be enough to bring them home again.

Without hesitation, Drezz made the approach.

There was no ceremony in the way he stepped forward. He simply crossed the space between them and pulled Damian into a one-armed clasp. A breath passed between them, unspoken and needed. It lingered, then passed.

Afterward, Damian turned to Saulice.

His hand reached out in silence, and Saulice took it. Their grip held for a heartbeat, steady and wordless, before parting once more.

Rayne had already settled on the bench beneath the ivy-wrapped pillar. She sat still, posture eased but alert, as if unsure whether they were truly back. Saulice eased down beside her, inhaling slowly, letting the last few days settle into his chest like cooled ash. Drezz took the spot on her opposite side, tail curling around his boots. Damian remained nearby, leaning against the stone post with arms folded and his eyes watching everything.

Drezz tilted his head back with a groan. "Just a normal week at Brynswick, right?"

Rayne rolled her eyes.

A labored laugh escaped Saulice's throat. "There is no such thing."

Beneath the upper arches, a few students lingered in clusters, whispering behind stone columns. They watched from a distance, unsure whether to approach or look away. None came closer.

A shadow passed slowly across the courtyard, cast by the rising edge of the spire. Its shape slid over stone and banner alike, folding across Saulice's boots and onto the bench where they sat.

Nothing pressed on him now.

He simply basked in the strange stillness of returning to a place where he had found himself.

Across from them, the basin remained empty, as though waiting for a new season to begin.

He exhaled again, slower this time, and turned his hand over in his lap. The Forsaken brand on his skin caught the sunlight.

It now held a different weight. He had lived in its shadow for a time, even shed blood beneath the judgments it sometimes incurred. But he realized then that it had never truly defined him.

It had been a test meant for him.

His *crucible.*

And he had won.

REFERENCE GLOSSARY

Places & Locations

Myre — The vast continent where the story unfolds, a land shaped by Shaddai's creation and scarred by the ancient Thousand Year War. Its realms, ruins, and battlefields still bear the echoes of Titans and disciples.

Axbridge — A bustling city north of the Twin Peaks, known for its markets, strategic trade routes, and the presence of Brynswick Academy. Gold and blue royal banners of Candur line its streets, signaling loyalty to King Emerin.

Brynswick Academy — Candur's premier military academy for training fount forgers into disciplined argonauts. Its cadets wear blue and silver uniforms marked with a ten-pointed star, and its halls are steeped in centuries of military tradition and political intrigue.

Masters Halls — The chamber where Brynswick's leaders gather, its walls layered with banners, maps, and history. Decisions made here often ripple across Candur's future.

Candur — A strong kingdom ruled by King Emerin. Candur's power rests in its disciplined military, noble Houses, and long history of defending the continent's central heartlands against ancient threats.

Fallenan — Homeland of the fallet race, a land of snowbound forests and mountain strongholds. Once a proud nation of wisdom and restraint, it now teeters on the brink of civil war.

Hamlen — A quiet farming village at Candur's southern edge, known more for its markets than for defense. It is here that Saulice failed his Trial, was branded Forsaken, and began his life as an outcast.

Mortare — Once a thriving city, reduced to ash when Lazarus was deceived into rampaging under Invictus influence. Its fall is etched into memory as proof of both Titan power and the cost of betrayal.

Timfathen — A cursed battlefield smothered in mist, haunted by lichtaurs and dripping with old blood. It is here that Baalo set his ambush, ending in fire, loss, and Saulice's greatest trial.

Grimwode — A fortified city where healers and scholars gather. Saulice and his companions find refuge here after the horrors of Timfathen.

Sloan Hill — A grassy rise overlooking Hamlen, known to locals as a place of graves. Saulice's mother is buried here, and it becomes a quiet anchor to his grief and memory.

Eastmere — A small town mentioned by Oreas, lying on one of the outer trade routes of Candur.

Shallabane — A frontier region referenced in future assignments. Known for its rough terrain and distant outposts.

Characters

Saulice Sawyer – Protagonist of the tale. A Forsaken orphan from Hamlen, burdened with the Titan Lazarus sealed within him. His path from rejection to becoming a confirmed academ at Brynswick is marked by doubt, resilience, and divine purpose.

Rayne – Harbinger of Malaya and daughter of Oreas. A strong water forger whose kindness and discipline temper Saulice's reckless streak. She becomes both ally and steadying presence throughout his journey.

Drezz – A fallet of Fallenan blood, loyal and fierce, with a heart bonded closely to Saulice and Damian. His wisdom and heritage carry the weight of ancient vows yet unfulfilled.

Dedric Sawyer – Veteran Sentinel of Fury's Fist and Saulice's uncle. Scarred by decades of war, he is both mentor and father-figure, steadying Saulice with blunt honesty and unyielding strength.

Damian Halcroft– Drezz's closest friend, their reunion at Brynswick rekindling trust and healing. His loyalty to Drezz and his growing trust in Saulice tie him to their shared battles.

Benedict Sawyer – Saulice's father, once a revered Sentinel of Fury's Fist. In desperation, he sealed Lazarus into his infant son, losing his memory in the process. Later revealed to still live, Benedict embodies both guilt and sacrifice.

Melandra – A courageous Argonaut of Fury's Fist. She fought alongside Saulice and Dedric in Timfathen and gave her life to protect her comrades.

Lord Athekk – Centaur commander of Clan Athekk, who led his warriors into Timfathen with dignity. His death became another scar on Saulice's conscience.

Oreas – Rayne's father, a traveling merchant whose humor masks deeper burdens. His return to Brynswick provides comfort and humanity in a world weighed down by war.

Master Nilus – One of Brynswick's weary masters, often found ink-stained in his robes. Represents the quiet weight of leadership amid betrayal.

Cadre Calder – Wounded yet resolute, he rose to Acting Master after Valos's disgrace. Calder confirms Saulice's status as a full academ, recognizing his worth through trial and fire.

Cadre Elmes – A quiet observer in Brynswick's leadership circles. His silence masks careful thought.

Lord Commander Muir – A commanding presence within Candur's military, deeply tied to Dedric and Fury's Fist. Represents the unbroken backbone of Candur's order.

Boreau – The former Lord Commander, remembered in Dedric's stories and decisions.

Judic – The stern elder who oversaw Saulice's Affinity Trial in Hamlen. His judgment marked Saulice as Forsaken.

King Emerin – Monarch of Candur, his gold and blue banners binding his people to one throne.

Monarch Farthum – Ruler of Fallenan and father of Drezz.

Lucas Crawford – Noble-born academ of a Great House with powerful ties, rival to Saulice. His arrogance masks the dangerous pressure of his family's expectations.

Belan Brakar – A fellow student at Brynswick, remembered chiefly as Saulice's duel opponent.

Toren Fellmere – Another student duel opponent, testing Saulice's growing strength.

Baalo – Veartaya's second-in-command, a master manipulator who broke free from his seal. He orchestrates the ambush at Timfathen and slays Melandra, becoming Saulice's great enemy.

Veartaya – Once a disciple of Shaddai, now the betrayer. She enslaved Titans in the Thousand Year War and seeks revival through Baalo's schemes.

Lector – A former Harbinger of Lazarus, whose bond with the Titan ended in tragedy. His death remains an echo within Lazarus's grief.

Master Valos – A Brynswick Master corrupted by greed. He fled after betraying his colleagues, leaving behind wounds both literal and political.

Lord Winstrom – A lord of a Great House who abandoned his manor, his cowardice staining his title.

Factions & Orders

Fury's Fist – Candur's elite vanguard, comprised of its strongest Sentinels. Known for valor and sacrifice, their presence commands respect in every city and battlefield.

Order of Invictus – A shadowy cult loyal to Veartaya and Baalo. Their agents infiltrate kingdoms, sow corruption, and twist truth to bring about their master's return.

Clan Athekk – A noble centaur clan allied with Dedric and Saulice during the final battle within the Timfathen, remembered for their courage and sacrifice.

Great Houses – The noble families of Candur. Their wealth and power shape Brynswick's politics as much as skill or merit.

Brown Clad – Extremist rebels in Fallenan, clothed in rough brown garb. Their uprising threatens Drezz's homeland and heritage.

Titans & Divine

Shaddai – The Divine Creator of Myre, source of the fount stones and the Ten Titans. He appears directly to Lazarus, and then later to Saulice, guiding him toward restraint, sacrifice, and truth.

The Ten Titans – Shaddai's champions, created to resist Veartaya. Each embodies one element and nature of the Divine:

- **Lazarus** – Lightning, justice; sealed inside Saulice.
- **Malaya** – Water, mercy.
- **Eldon** – Light, hope.
- **Kragneer** – Earth, strength; once manipulated into betrayal.
- **Umbre** – Poison, corruption.
- **Sepitus** – Shadow, secrecy.
- **Malis** – Fire, fury.
- **Dominis** – Ice, resolve.
- **Mortas** – Air, freedom.
- **Mulmohr** – Time, inevitability.

Magic & Spiritual Terms

Fount Forging – The art of channeling elemental energy through one's spiritual core, using deliberate gestures and trained control.

Argonaut – a fount forger who has graduated Brynswick and will serve the realm using their fount forging abilities.

Fount Core – The heart of every forger, where energy is stored, refined, and released. It may awaken, expand through training, or break under strain. Saulice's fractured core defines much of his struggle.

Fount Stones – The ten divine stones left by Shaddai, each tied to a Titan and element: Citrine (Lightning), Emerald (Earth), Ruby (Fire), Onyx (Shadow), Lapis (Water), Amethyst (Poison), Opal (Air), Diamond (Time), Carnelian (Light), Sapphire (Ice).

Shard – A fragment of a fount stone, used in Affinity Trials and early training.

Ambient Fount – The natural current of energy flowing throughout Myre, which forgers absorb to expand their cores.

Circuit Reversal – A rare technique involving reversing the fount's flow. Saulice attempts it with dangerous consequences.

Core Awakening – The first step of a forger's journey, stirring dormant energy within the core.

Core Expansion – The process of absorbing ambient fount to deepen the core's capacity.

Divine Alignment – Attuning the heart to Shaddai's virtues of sacrifice, love, peace, restraint, and selflessness. Essential for the sacred act of Titan sealing.

Sealing a Titan – A divine act of binding a Titan into a mortal vessel, achieved only through perfect alignment and immense cost.

The Pitch – A forbidden tool created by Veartaya, used to enslave Titans through corruption and domination.

Source Stone – The primal essence of the fount stones, fractured during Saulice's path.

Races & Creatures

Fallet – A furred and wise race from Fallenan. Though often seen as passive, they defend their homeland with fierce resolve when threatened. Drezz carries their legacy.

Centaurs – Clan-based warriors of strength and loyalty. Their alliances with men are rare but deeply honored.

Lichtaurs – Twisted abominations, the corrupted remains of centaurs and men, bound to Baalo's will.

Bellet – Another lesser-known race of Myre, referenced in old accounts.

Symbols, Colors & Items

Ten-pointed Star – The emblem of Brynswick, symbolizing order, unity, and aspiration.

Brynswick Uniform – Blue with silver trim, marked by a badge on the collar. Worn with pride by confirmed cadets.

Candur's Royal Colors – Gold and blue, representing the authority and legacy of King Emerin's line.

Sapphire Banner – A banner flown over Brynswick, displaying a white star against sapphire cloth.

Bracer – A forging tool strapped to the arm, worn by all citizens of Candur as evidence of social heirarchy. Saulice's bracer is leather and blank without a slot for a fount stone, marking his trials.

Dedric's Dagger – A weapon with a lion-head hilt, bearing the insignia of The Watch. Passed from uncle to nephew, it becomes a symbol of heritage and hidden vows.

Key Concepts & Themes

Harbinger – A mortal chosen to carry a Titan within. Saulice bears Lazarus, Rayne bears Malaya. The role is both burden and destiny.

Forsaken – Title for children who fail their Affinity Trial, branded as unworthy. Saulice carries this stigma into Brynswick.

Forsaken Brand – The mark given to Forsaken children, transformed through Saulice's journey from rejection into resilience.

Affinity Trial – Ceremony where children test their bond with a shard. For Saulice, the trial brought only failure and rejection.

Confirmed Academ – A full cadet at Brynswick. Saulice earns this status after surviving Timfathen.

Provisional Academ – Lower statuses within Brynswick, reflecting unsteady or untested students.

Probationary Academ – Lowest status within Brynswick, reflecting an academ who is viewed by the Cadre as highly dangerous or unpredictable.

Second-year Duels/Exams – Trials of skill and control, pitting cadets against one another in combat before their masters.

Thousand Year War – An ancient war where Veartaya betrayed Shaddai and enslaved Titans, leaving Myre scarred. The final battle of which was fought more than a century before the story begins.

Anaals – The written records preserved at Brynswick, holding accounts of wars, Titans, and the Divine.

STAY CONNECTED

Want to stay connected and get early access to future
books, behind-the-scenes lore, and exclusive content?
Join my newsletter and follow me across my media:

https://linktr.ee/TheAaronCovington

You'll be the first to know when the next
chapter of Saulice's story is ready.

AUTHOR'S NOTE

Writing Forsaken Fate began as an act of survival. In 2019, I was deployed as a Military Policeman, and the darkness I lived in back then left its mark. I wrote to keep breathing. I wrote to stay whole. But somewhere along the way, this story became something more than a lifeline. It became a mirror.

Through Saulice's journey, I began to see my own. The questions I asked as a child. The ache of feeling unwanted. That quiet, flickering hope that maybe God still had a purpose for me. In a world shaped by Titans and fount forging, I poured my memories into every stone and shadow. Memories of fear. Of fractured identity. Of being too much in one room and not enough in the next.

Saulice's story was never meant to be clean or easy. It is a story of shame and struggle. A story of silence. A story about the slow, stubborn discovery that you are not the names they gave you. That being branded "Forsaken" does not mean you must live like you are.

This book is not just a fantasy. It is a prayer in disguise. A cry for justice that does not rise through vengeance, but through mercy. And for me, that mercy has always had a name. Jesus.

The world of Forsaken Fate may be fiction, but the ache it answers and the hope it reaches for are real.

To every reader who has ever felt abandoned, unseen, or forgotten, I see you. This story is for you. May you find in these pages not just wonder, but healing and peace. Not just a Harbinger, but a reminder that your identity was never defined by what was taken from you.

It was defined by what has been given.

Thank you for reading.

Aaron Covington

ACKNOWLEDGEMENTS

This journey has been long, and at times, unbearably wearisome. There are more faces deserving of thanks than I could possibly recall. But among them, those heroes of creativity, endurance, and prayer, I will remember three. You may notice, if you continue reading my work, that I am drawn to this number.

First, I thank God. Not out of habit or formality, but because I cannot imagine claiming the glory for something that was never mine to begin with. I know the fate of Herod Agrippa. I do not want it. This story was not what I intended when I began. Somewhere along the way, the Lord rewrote it, reshaped it, and handed it back with gentler hands than mine. If there is power in these pages, it is not from me. It is from Him. And I pray it reaches the heart of every teenager who has ever felt unseen.

Second, to my wife, Alexis. You stood when I sat. You believed when I doubted. You reminded me this book was worth finishing even when I could no longer see the end. I remember the nights I gave up entirely. You never did. And that is something I will never forget.

Third, to my mother. You are not a reader of fantasy, and yet you listened to every chapter as though it were Scripture. I have laughed quietly and fondly—at your awe over moments I barely wrote, but your love gave them life. I would not trade those memories for anything.

To Corey, Staley, Christian, and so many others: thank you. Your encouragement pushed me farther than you know.

This mountain has been climbed. But more mountains await. And by that, I mean more books. Many more.

LEAVE A REVIEW

If this story moved you, if you saw yourself in Saulice, or found hope where there once was silence, I'd be deeply grateful if you'd leave a review on Amazon, Goodreads, or anywhere else of your choosing.

Reviews help stories like this reach the hearts they were meant for.

Even just a few words can make a difference.

Thank you for walking this journey with me.